Middle Falls

POPULATION 39065

Home of Artie's Famous Burger Basket

The Tumultuous Lives of Karl Strong
by Shawn Inmon
Copyright 2023 © Shawn Inmon
All rights reserved

No part of this book may be reproduced or retransmitted in any form or by any means without written permission from the publisher, with the exception of brief quotations in a review. This book is a work of fiction. Any resemblance to events or people, living or dead is purely coincidental.

**Dedication
For Marta
My friend**

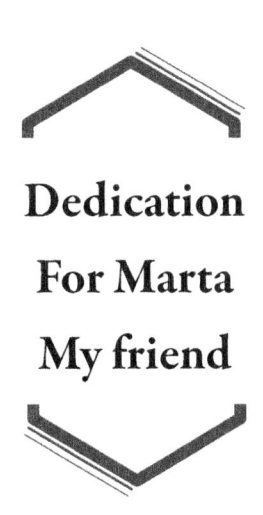

Chapter One

Bright sunlight streamed through the window as Karl Strong walked into the kitchen. It was empty, but that wasn't unusual. He woke up to an empty house every school day. It was his birthday, but there was nothing to commemorate that fact. He thought it was possible that he might go the whole day without having it recognized.

When his mother was alive, she did all the special mom things. Blueberry pancakes with the blueberries arranged like a smile. Chocolate milk for breakfast. And always, a small present that she had found room in the budget for. It was like their own tiny birthday celebration every year.

That had come to a stop when she had died four years earlier. Now, he woke to an empty house and came home from school or football practice to the same.

Karl's father, Finley, had not handled his wife's death well. Since she had been gone, he had checked out in every way he could while still continuing to live and breathe. He was up and out to work at the box factory before Karl woke up and most days he stopped off at the Do-Si-Do for a few beers that typically stretched into *too many* beers.

At first, Karl had worried that his dad might kill someone one night or get arrested for drunk driving coming home from the bar blind drunk. He learned that at a minimum, he didn't have to worry about the DUI arrest when old Chief Deakins had pounded on his door after midnight one Tuesday night.

Finley had fallen asleep behind the wheel right in the middle of Main Street in Middle Falls. Deakins had pulled him out of his truck, poured him into the back of his prowler, and driven him home. He handed Karl the keys, telling him to make sure his dad didn't go back out that night.

The benefits of living in a small town, where everyone probably knew why you had turned yourself into a drunk.

This was Karl's eighteenth birthday, but try as he might, he couldn't see any reason to get excited about it. The things that excited him were still almost eight months away—graduation and getting out of Middle Falls.

He had plans, but he had to finish the preliminaries, like graduating with good grades and getting at least a partial scholarship to college. He knew he couldn't expect any help from Finley when it came to paying for school. Any extra money they ever had went to the Do-Si-Do. Twice in the last year, their power had been turned off for a few days while they waited for the next paycheck to get it back on.

He grabbed a box of Cheerios from the cupboard above the stove, then reached for a bowl. That cupboard was empty, which, after a glance at the sink, piled high with dishes, was not surprising. He briefly considered tackling the dish situation, but, just as he had every other day that week, decided against it.

Karl sighed, found a cereal bowl that wasn't too caked with food, and ran some water into it. He took a few swipes with a dish rag, then wrinkled his nose. As he held the rag toward his face, he gagged slightly. It had gone over and had moved into the realm of a science experiment.

He tossed the rag into the sink and looked at the bowl. Not perfect, but passable for an eighteen-year-old boy.

When he opened the fridge and saw there was no milk, he knew he was beat.

He hurried back to his room and saw that he had almost a dollar's worth of change. He decided to stop at Smith's and grab a package of Ho-Hos and a pint of milk.

"Happy birthday to me," he muttered as he walked out to the dirt driveway. His dad's old truck was gone, of course, but his '69 Ford Falcon was sitting off to the side. It wasn't much, but it beat the humiliation of being a senior and having to ride the bus.

It was already a warm morning and when he slid inside, the unpleasant smell of cat urine hit him. Finley had bought the car years earlier before giving it to Karl and told him that the smell came with the car—that the guy he had bought it from had driven around with his cat in the back.

Karl tried to tell himself that he was used to the smell and that it didn't bother him, but that was a lie. He had cleaned and scrubbed and scrubbed and cleaned, but sunshine and heat brought the ghost of that smell out no matter what.

He glanced at his watch and saw that if he stopped at Smith and Son's, he would probably be late for school. As a senior, though, he didn't mind a few tardy reports on his record. He was the starting running back for Middle Falls and the Homecoming game was coming up. He knew the school wouldn't do anything to risk having to sit him out.

He dashed into Smith's, grabbed some Hostess cupcakes instead of the Ho-Hos, pulled a pint of milk from the refrigerated case and hurried to the register to pay. When the cashier rang up the sale, he fished the coins out of his pocket and saw that he was five cents short.

The cashier, a middle-aged woman who had manned the cash register at Smith and Son's for twenty years raised her eyebrows. There was no give in her, and she would rather restock his items than give them to him for a nickel less.

Karl glanced down and saw a small container that said, "Need a penny? Take One. Got an extra penny? Leave one."

He tipped it up, slid the five pennies into his hand, and put it with his other money. After flashing his lopsided grin at the woman to no discernible impact, Karl shrugged, let the smile slip from his face, and headed toward the Falcon. He ripped open the package and had an entire cupcake stuffed in his mouth before he got inside.

When he turned the engine over, *Call Me* by Blondie was playing on KMFR. He pulled into the Middle Falls High parking lot as the song finished.

He opened the car door just as the bell rang for first period. "Not bad," he said to himself, draining the last of the milk and tossing the carton onto the passenger side floor.

The halls were empty, but Karl bobbed and weaved as he jogged, eluding imaginary tacklers left and right. He skidded to a stop at the door to his English class, took a breath to compose himself, and opened the door as quietly as possible.

"Mr. Strong," Mr. Polk said. "How nice of you to make it."

That elicited no reaction from any of the students already sitting at their desks in a Monday morning haze. No one even bothered to turn and look.

Karl slipped into his seat and found that by virtue of his last name starting with *S*, he was able to answer when Polk called his name.

Immediately after that bit of luck, Karl fell into the same near-slumber that the rest of the class was in. As the minutes passed, he would have been hard-pressed to remember any of what was discussed that day.

It wasn't that Karl was a bad student because he really wasn't. His mom had died at the end of his eighth-grade year, and the devastation from her death had carried over to his freshman year. For the next year, he didn't give a damn about anything, including whether he did his homework or got decent grades. At the end of that year, Mr. Harvey, the new guidance counselor, had button-holed him in the hall.

When they sat down in Mr. Harvey's cramped office, the counselor had told him that if he didn't pull his grades up, he wouldn't be able to get into college, even if he got a full-ride athletic scholarship. That was Karl's dream—to be able to get out of Middle Falls and be anywhere else—so that reached through the haze of his grief.

He had recommitted to doing the work and studying for tests and he had done well enough that he had been in the National Honor Society his junior year. Now, with his grade point average at 3.35, he knew he could coast a little his senior year.

When the bell rang, he stood and realized that he hadn't even stopped at his locker to get his books. That was okay, though, because he had wood shop next. He had taken as many P.E. and shop classes as he could this semester, the better to keep that GPA up.

Karl stuck his hands in his pockets and whistled a little as he headed down the hall toward the woodshop.

"Hey, stranger," a girl's voice said from behind. "You ignoring me?"

Karl turned and saw Lisa Hanson. "How could I ever ignore the prettiest girl in school?"

Lisa's head didn't seem to be turned by the compliment. "Who are you taking to Homecoming?"

"Nobody yet. Why? Are you applying for the job?"

Lisa shook her head. "You know better. I'm going with Mike, of course. You know, Mike? The guy you've been friends with since kindergarten?"

Karl grinned a slightly sheepish smile and said, "Never hurts to check."

"So you don't have a date for Homecoming."

"I don't think I'm going," Karl said, which was the truth.

"I think you should ask Anna."

"Anna? Which Anna?"

"Anna Masterson, silly," Lisa said this as though it was the only possible answer, even though there were three girls named Anna in the senior class alone.

"Isn't she going with Kenny? They've been going together for a long time."

"Not anymore."

"Since when?"

"Since yesterday. Don't you pay attention?"

"Not to that sort of stuff. So they broke up and now you want me to ask her to Homecoming."

"Your grasp of the obvious is keen. So, you going to?"

Karl thought. Anna was pretty enough. He didn't really care about Homecoming, but maybe it would be okay to go. "Tell you what. If I run into her, I'll ask her. Now I've got to go to class."

Lisa grabbed his arm to hold him in place. She had surprising strength for a girl so small. Over her shoulder, she said, "Anna, come here. Karl wants to ask you something."

Karl gave Lisa a blistering look that had absolutely zero effect on her.

Anna Masterson, all wide-eyed innocence said, "Oh, really? What, Karl?"

Karl drew a deep breath and knew that he had been expertly trapped without ever feeling the steel close on his ankle.

"Umm, I don't have a date for Homecoming. I know it's kind of last minute, but do you want to go with me?"

"I'd love to," Anna said. She handed him a slip of notebook paper that already had her address written on it, encircled by small hearts. "Pick me up at 7:00?"

Karl Strong had a date for homecoming, whether he liked it or not.

Chapter Two

The Middle Falls football team was surprisingly good in 1981. The Bulldogs hadn't had a winning record in six seasons, but going into Homecoming, they were 5-1 and tied for first place. If they won their last three games, they would go to the divisional playoffs for the first time in almost a decade.

Karl was a part of that. In a big school, he would have likely been an afterthought, a bench warmer. He was a little too tall and a little too skinny to be a classic, bowl-em-over high school running back. He wasn't the fastest guy on the team, but he did have a good burst when he saw an opening and had a good sense of balance. He was tough to bring down.

Most of the way through the season, he showed up at the top of the league rushing leaders that were printed every week in the *Middle Falls Gazette*.

Two days before the Homecoming game, Coach Bulski was slow coming out of the locker room and had assigned David Shield, the assistant coach, to warm up the team. It was apparent that Shield had missed his original calling of being a Marine Drill Sergeant as he led the team through burpees, jumping jacks, and finally, leg lifts.

When Coach Bulski led the team through leg lifts, he would typically have the boys lift their heels off the ground for fifteen or twenty seconds. It helped them build a strong core.

Coach Shield expected a lot more.

"Heels up!" he said, with a shrill blast from his whistle. "Hold 'em there until I tell you to drop 'em. Davidson! Not that high! No more than six inches off the ground. If you touch the ground before I release you, we'll all run two laps around the track. You've got to learn to focus, to concentrate. To block out pain. Keep your mind on your assignments, no matter what. Right now, that assignment is keeping your damned heels six inches off the ground."

The players were in good shape, but holding their legs up for this long was pushing them. The lighter skill position players like Karl were straining, but the bigger boys, like the offensive and defensive linemen, were grunting with effort.

Shield blew his whistle. "Good job. Now, let's take those two laps just to show what we're made of. Don't worry, I'll run them with you." He looked at Karl. "Strong, if I beat you, you'd better hang your head in shame. An old man beating a young buck like you."

Karl knew that anything he said would be wrong, but even so, he couldn't keep the small grin off his face.

"Smirk at me, will you, Strong? I appreciate the motivation. Let's go!"

One more sharp blast on the whistle and Shield took off for the track. He was the gym teacher and was only in his late twenties himself, but even so, Karl had passed him by the first turn and then loped comfortably ahead of him for the rest of the half-mile run.

By the time Karl crossed the finish line, Coach Bulski had made it out of the locker room. Karl looked at him and thought that he looked a little more peaked than he usually did.

If that was the case, he did his best to disguise it. He blew his whistle three times as the final stragglers crossed the line. That, again, was the linemen. They all bent over, hands on knees and struggled for breath. They knew better than to lie on their backs, though. That would only result in more laps.

"Two more days to the big game," Bulski said. "I've got some scouting reports on these guys and a few new plays I want to install before we play them. Let's head to the practice field."

Karl had regained his breath and jogged along a fence line as they made their way there.

This fence was where middle-aged men would gather and watch the practices, commenting on every aspect. They were almost exclusively former players themselves, come to share their experience and wisdom with each other. No one ever really listened to what the others were saying, and everyone was okay with that. It was about expressing yourself, not actually seeking input.

As Karl ran past, he heard one of the men—like all the men leaning against the fence, he was dressed in jeans and an old work shirt—say, "Look at the damned kids. Two laps and they're winded. When I played, we started every practice off with a mile run and if Coach didn't like our attitude, we did another one just for fun." The man took a long swig from an Olympia Beer can, then belched.

Karl looked at the man, who was big and beefy with a heavy paunch and three days' growth, and smirked. That grin had gotten Karl into more trouble than almost anything else. It wasn't really his fault, though. No matter how he tried to smile, it came off as a smirk. The man saw him looking and shook his head. "No respect from these kids, either. In my day, if we didn't pay the proper respect, we'd be picking ourselves up off the floor."

"Have to be able to catch me first," Karl said, loud enough that the man could hear. He kept running and was soon out of hearing range of the man. A moment later, he had forgotten him entirely.

The new plays that Coach Bulski put into the playbook weren't too tricky. It wasn't like he was changing the whole offense, he had just added a few more sweeps and a running back screen, which was good news for Karl. The more the ball came his way, the more he liked it.

When practice was over, Bulski called the boys into a semi-circle.

"Listen up. I want you to hear this from me. I got a little bit of bad news from the docs. It's nothing serious, but I'm going to have to step down as coach for a while. We're lucky we've got Coach Shield here. He's been with you from the start, and he's a good man. You won't miss a beat."

Karl risked a glance at his teammates around him. No one groaned or complained that Shield was going to be their coach full time. That wouldn't do any good. He saw it in their eyes, though. There would be a lot more calisthenics and running in their immediate future.

When Karl turned back to look at Coach Bulski, he could kind of see it now. It wasn't just an overall lack of energy. He looked a little gray, and he seemed to be moving a little slower, like maybe he had a bad backache.

"I'm not going to make a big speech here, boys, because this is only temporary. I think I'll be back in time to coach you in the divisionals and the state final."

Danny Jenkins, the starting quarterback, led a cheer for Bulski, but to Karl's ears, it rang a little hollow, as if everyone wasn't really sure what they were cheering.

On the way to the locker room, Karl found Bulski and reached out a hand. "Just wanted to say thanks, Coach. Thanks for giving me a chance. Thanks for making me the starter."

"You earned it, son, but this isn't a big deal. I'll be back before you know it."

Karl nodded and turned to run toward the showers. Before he got a dozen steps, Bulski called him back. "Almost forgot. I called Coach Andrews at Oregon State. We went to school together. I told him about you, and that I thought you were still growing into your frame. I think he'll give you a real serious look for a full ride."

Karl's face lit up. He ran back and pumped Bulski's hand again. "Thanks, Coach! That's so great of you to do that for me."

Bulski waved that off. "Like I said, you did the work. You deserve it."

Karl grinned and ran toward the showers. Whatever vigor had been lost to a ninety-minute practice was restored by the thought of playing for Oregon State. It wasn't that he loved the Beavers so much as he relished the opportunity to get out of town.

Bulski watched him run, an old man in the sunset of his life, watching a young man charge into his future. He smiled, shook his head a little, and walked slowly toward the locker room.

⟨ ⟩

THE SUN WAS STARTING to set behind him as Karl drove the Falcon into the small neighborhood known as Crampton Village. Years earlier, some wit had painted *Crapped-on Village* on the sign at the edge of the neighborhood and it had stood ever since. Like the smell of cat urine in his car, Karl tried to tell himself that he didn't care, that it didn't bother him. But like that stink that wouldn't leave, the effect of living in Crampton Village wore on him as well.

They had lived in a better neighborhood when his mom was alive. In fact, they had owned their own house, or had at least owned it along with the bank.

Karl turned down Tyler Street and was surprised to see his father's truck parked in the driveway. He checked his watch and saw that it was only 5:45. That meant that his dad had come straight home after work.

There had been no real homework that he couldn't handle in study hall the next day, so Karl didn't have any books to take in. He pushed in through the front door and saw his dad sitting in his old recliner—the one that had been left behind by the previous tenants because they didn't want to haul it away. He didn't have his feet up because that part of the chair didn't work so well anymore. Importantly, Karl noticed the lack of a beer in his hand.

He had developed the skill that many children of alcoholics did—the ability to instantly read a room when he walked in. Tonight, the vibe was mellow, so he relaxed a little. It wasn't that Finley had ever been violent with him, but when he hit a certain number of beers, he could get belligerent. The challenge was, the exact number of beers had never been established.

"Hey, Dad," Karl said, plopping on the couch. He glanced at the TV, where the CBS Evening News with Dan Rather was on.

Finley nodded in Karl's direction, then said, "I can't get used to this guy. He doesn't look like he belongs behind that desk. I miss Walter Cronkite."

This was not a subject that Karl had any interest in, so he just nodded.

"Picked up a pizza from Shakey's on the way home. It's in the kitchen."

"What's the occasion?"

Karl hadn't really meant it as a jab, but he could see that Finley took it that way.

"I know it's your birthday." He looked a little defensive. "I know I forget things, but I remembered that."

Neither Karl nor Finley said a word about how different things were with his mother not there. They never mentioned her name. It was as if a dome of delicate glass had formed between the two of them over the years and a single mention of her name would shatter it.

"Thanks! I'm pretty hungry. I'll grab some."

Karl hurried into the kitchen and saw that Finley had done the dishes. "Thanks for doing the dishes, Dad. I was going to do them tonight."

"Sure you were," Finley said from the other room, but there was no sting in his words.

Karl took a plate out of the dish rack and rubbed it against his shirt to finish drying it off. He slapped three pieces of pepperoni pizza on the plate and headed back to the living room. As he opened his mouth to ask his dad if he wanted to watch the Mariners game that would be on in a few minutes, he saw that his dad was standing at the door, keys in hand.

Karl managed to stop himself from saying anything about the game. Instead, he raised a slice of pizza as a toast, and said, "Thanks for the pizza, Dad. It's really cool."

Finley waved and disappeared out the door. To Karl's ears, it sounded like his dad backed out of the driveway in a hurry, making his escape.

Karl flipped through the channels, but there was nothing but news and a stupid gameshow on, so he turned it to the channel where the Seattle Mariner game would be on and sat down to eat his pizza alone.

Chapter Three

Karl Strong swiveled his hips and made a would-be tackler whiff at empty air. He sped toward the sideline and turned upfield. A lane opened and he saw the promised land of the endzone in front of him. He high-stepped it down the sideline past the thirty yard line, the twenty, and the ten.

He raised the ball in a somewhat preliminary celebration, when, out of nowhere, the strong safety of the Carpentersville Wildcats slammed into him at a full sprint.

Karl was knocked off his feet, the air whooshed out of his lungs, and he fumbled the ball, but it didn't matter too much, as it fell out of bounds.

What did matter to Karl was that it felt like he'd been run over by a truck. The safety, wearing the red number forty-five, stood over Karl and grinned through his mouthguard.

"Didn't see me comin' did ya? That's why they call me Freight Train."

He was quickly pushed aside by Karl's teammates rushing to see if he needed help. Mike Tomkins, who was indeed taking Lisa Hanson to Homecoming, was the first to reach a hand out.

"You okay? That dude is *fast*."

"Fast, and he hits hard," Karl agreed. He accepted Mike's hand and let himself be pulled to his feet.

Coach Shield ran down the sidelines as Karl got to his feet. "You okay, Strong?" He looked in Karl's eyes and made a quick judgment.

"You got your bell rung. It's good for you. Rub a little dirt on it and we'll get you back in there."

Karl took one wobbly step and Shield reached out and caught him. "Just a stinger, son." Over his shoulder, he said, "Miles, get in there for Strong."

Karl walked to the sideline under his own power and sat on the bench as the backup running back, Miles Wilson, scored on an easy two-yard run. That put the Bulldogs ahead by a score of 21-7. It was late in the fourth quarter and that essentially put the game out of reach.

The Wildcats tried to do a complicated return on the kickoff, but ended up fumbling a lateral, and the Bulldogs fell on it.

Don Johnson—who took a lot of flak for not being *that* Don Johnson—did three kneel downs and the game was over.

The Bulldogs were 6-1 and had won in front of their Homecoming crowd.

Karl looked hopefully up into the stands, but his father was nowhere to be seen. He would have been a little surprised if he had been. He couldn't remember him ever putting in an appearance at a game.

He lined up with his teammates and shook hands with the Wildcats. When he came to number 45, he was surprised to see he wasn't very big. In fact, he barely came to Karl's shoulder.

"I know," he announced with a gap-toothed grin. "I'm taller when I'm leaning over somebody I knocked on their ass. Good game."

"Good game," Karl said and headed for the showers.

After showering, he stood at his locker, getting his street clothes on.

Don Johnson approached him, holding a pen up and moving it left and right in front of his eyes as though testing for a concussion.

Karl slapped it away. "I'm fine."

"Good thing. We'll need you next week against Summerton." He leaned in and quietly said, "Miles is okay, but he ain't you." He straightened up and in a normal voice, said, "A bunch of us are going to Artie's to celebrate. Wanna come?"

"I can't. I told my dad I'd come home after the game and tell him all about it."

There was a better than even-money chance that everyone knew that Finley would be closing down the Do-Si-Do again that night, but the quarterback didn't press him.

Johnson gave him a mock salute and said, "That was a hell of a run until that guy blindsided you. See you tomorrow at the dance, then."

"I guess I'll be there."

"You're taking Anna, aren't you?"

Karl had to stop and think. "Yeah, I'm sure I am."

"You really did get your bell rung, didn't you?"

"Nah, not really. It's just weird. Lisa told me to ask her, and I did, but then I haven't talked to her since."

"She doesn't want to scare you off," Johnson said, raising his eyebrows and making his face a mask of fright.

"See you tomorrow," Karl said and pushed out into the cool early October air. The parking lot was still mostly full. There were pockets of people—some of whom had returned to Middle Falls for the game—here and there.

As he passed one small group, a man said, "Hey, good game twenty-two."

Karl waved, climbed in the Falcon, and drove home. As expected, the house was dark.

He didn't feel like watching TV, but he drew a bath that drained the hot water heater and climbed gingerly in. He lay in steaming hot water up to his nose until it went cold.

When he went to bed, his father still wasn't home.

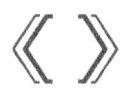

WHEN KARL HAD BEEN boxed into taking Anna to Homecoming, he hadn't had any time to think about what he would wear. In fact, he hadn't had a chance to think about anything, which was almost certainly Lisa's intention.

Now, it was almost time to leave, and Karl poked through his closet, which was mostly a collection of jeans and T-shirts, with a few sweaters thrown in that he never wore.

Homecoming wasn't a formal. No one would be wearing tuxes, and most people wouldn't even wear a suit or tie, but Karl knew that his AC/DC *Highway to Hell* T-shirt wasn't going to cut it. He held up a green sweater and looked at it doubtfully. He couldn't see himself wearing something so uncool.

He slapped the hangers from one side of his closet to the other, but no dress shirt and slacks magically appeared.

Karl had the house to himself again, as his dad had been gone since he woke up. That was a little unusual on the weekend, but not unheard of. It was always possible he'd been offered an extra shift at the box factory. Time and a half was too good to pass up.

Karl went into his father's bedroom. It was dark and depressing in there, but not too messy. It was likely that Finley never spent enough time there to make it too much of a pigsty.

The unmade bed took up most of the room, but there was a scarred three-drawer dresser against the wall. Karl turned sideways, scooted between the dresser and the bed and opened the closet.

The selection there wasn't too much better than it had been in his own closet, but there were a few things that looked better than anything he had. He picked out a burnt-orange shirt and held it up in the pale light that shone around the closed curtain.

Stiff and almost new, it was a western shirt, with pearl buttons that ran down the front.

It couldn't have been farther from the suddenly *New Wave* eighties that had taken hold of the rest of the country. There were no *Flock of Seagulls* haircuts or Adam Ant fan clubs in Middle Falls, though. It wasn't that change *never* came to Middle Falls. It was just that it was like water slowly wearing away stone—new trends took a while.

The slacks hanging in the closet were more dubious. Finley wasn't much bigger than Karl, but he didn't have the leanness of youth. Karl held up a pair of somewhat-worn gray slacks and tried to imagine where his dad might have donned them.

He decided they must have come from *the before*. The time when there was light and laughter and the occasional Saturday night date night for his parents.

He slipped them on, but there were a few problems. The waist was a few inches too big, though that might have been solved with a belt cinched all the way up. The real problem was that even to Karl's untrained eye, the slacks and the shirt didn't look like they went together or even like they were manufactured on the same planet.

Karl smoothed out the slacks, hung them on the hanger and slipped them back into the closet. He took the shirt and tossed it on his bed. One last look through his closet told him that he was out of options. He picked out his newest pair of jeans, the ones he had gotten just before school started. They would have to do.

He showered and shaved, though the second part of that process was not really required. It did take off the half-dozen stray hairs that tended to accumulate on his chin. He ran his hands through his hair, which was long and curly. He grinned at himself. He liked being a jock and having long hair. It made people wonder about him.

He got dressed in his jeans and the orange shirt. When he opened his drawer, there was nothing but white athletic socks. Even Karl knew that wouldn't work. He hurried back into his dad's room and took a pair of dark socks from the top drawer.

He checked himself in the mirror and thought he looked at least passable.

The phone rang, which made Karl jump in the quiet house. His stomach knotted a little. Phone calls at home rarely equaled good news. He considered letting it ring, but curiosity got the better of him.

"Thanks for calling Artie's. Can I take your order?"

There was no hesitation on the other end of the line.

"You're hilarious, Karl."

"Lisa?"

"Don't sound so surprised. You are listed in the phone book, you know. What kind of a name is Finley, anyway?"

"It's Irish. Dad always said it meant *fair-haired* and *courageous*, but I think he's full of crap. Now, why are you calling me when I'm getting ready for the big date you trapped me into?"

"Sometimes, boys need to be pointed in the right direction. I'm calling to see if you got Anna a corsage for tonight."

That stopped Karl cold. "No. Don't tell me I was supposed to."

"Yes," Anna said, her voice was calm and patient. "You were supposed to."

Karl glanced at the clock on the table, which showed it was after 6:00. "Well, I'm kinda screwed then, because the florist is closed." He almost added, "And I don't have any money because I blew my monthly entertainment budget on the tickets," but he didn't.

"I figured that was the case. Luckily for you, my mom worked at the florist shop for years. I'll have her throw something cute together out of the flowers in our yard. Just leave early enough that you can stop by my place. Remember where I live?"

"Yep." He wanted to hang up, but instead said, "Thanks, Lisa."

"Anna's a nice girl and a friend."

"I could have guessed that or you wouldn't have been running interference for her."

"Maybe you should leave right now. Are you dressed?"

"As good as it's going to get."

There was something of a sigh at the end of the line, as though maybe she had picked a project that was too big, even for her considerable abilities. "See you here."

"On my way."

Karl stepped out and saw that the long and glorious Indian summer of September had disappeared and autumn had arrived in Middle Falls. A strong breeze blew in from the east and it carried a swirl of colorful leaves with it.

Karl wished for a sports coat to fend off the wind and rain, but he knew he was lucky to find the shirt that he had—a nice jacket was out of the question. He opened the car door, hoping against hope that the smell of the cat pee would be gone. It was not to be. Even though the temperature had dropped into the low fifties, the smell remained. Now it smelled more like cold cat urine, which was not any kind of improvement.

He threw the door open and sprinted for the door of his house. Inside he hurried back into his bedroom and grabbed a mostly empty bottle of *Musk by Jovan* that he'd gotten for Christmas the year before. He spun the top off and inhaled deeply. First, he splashed a little on his face, then ran back to the car. He sprinkled a few drops here, there, and everywhere. He knew that if his dad was there, he would say the car smelled like a French whorehouse. And if his mom were still alive, she would pointedly ask how Finley knew what a French whorehouse smelled like.

In any case, he thought an overdose of cologne was preferable to the more organic smell of cat urine.

He felt like he was running a little behind, so he pushed the Falcon as fast he dared through the rain-slicked streets of Middle Falls. He pulled up in front of the Hanson house and hurried up to the door. Lisa opened it before he got there.

She looked him over, sucked in her breath and nodded as if to say, *Not great, but it will do.* "Come on in. Mom's finishing up the corsage."

When Karl stepped into the living room, he felt like he'd stepped into another kind of life. There was a fire in the fireplace. Something smelled good on the stove. Mr. Hanson was smoking a pipe and watching the news, ignoring everything that was happening around him.

Karl knew this was a life that was forever denied him unless he was somehow able to create it for himself in some unknown future.

"A little more warning next time would be good," Mrs. Hanson said from the dining room table around the corner.

"Sorry, Mrs. Hanson."

"Not you, Karl. I was speaking to Lisa. She knows."

If Lisa was bothered, she didn't show it.

Karl looked at her. She was in a modest but very pretty butter-yellow dress. Her hair was up, and he felt a little stab of envy toward Mike, who would have her on his arm when they walked into the dance that night.

Mrs. Hanson came around the corner. She held out a small white corsage that looked professionally done. It was tightly wrapped with green florist's tape and had a pin with a green head stuck through. She handed it to Karl.

"Thank you. I really do appreciate it. I didn't know I was supposed to have one or I would have ordered it."

A fleeting look of pity flashed across her face. That look said, *You don't know about these things because you don't have anyone to teach you anymore.* That look was much more painful than if she had slapped him across the face. "Really. It's no bother. Lisa tells me you're taking Anna Masterson."

"Yes, ma'am." He glanced at Lisa, who was conspicuously looking elsewhere.

"How nice. She's a lovely young girl. I'm sure you'll have a good time."

Lisa raised her eyebrows at Karl and said, "You better scoot, boyo, or you'll be late picking her up."

"Right." Karl turned toward the door and when he opened it, Mike was standing there, dressed in a suit, corsage in hand. They did an awkward tango with Karl trying to get out and Mike trying to get in.

When they had finally accomplished that maneuver, Mike waved at Karl and said, "See you there!"

From behind Mike, Lisa had one last parting bit of wisdom. "Don't make me look bad now!"

Karl opened the door to the Falcon. Being out in the open air and then coming back in, he realized that he had gone overboard with the cologne. He reached across the passenger seat and rolled down the window. Rain started to blow in. That wouldn't do. Couldn't have Anna sit on a wet seat. He rolled the window back up, shrugged, and hoped she wouldn't notice.

He pulled the slip of paper out of his pocket and drove to her house. He had never been there, but it was in the same neighborhood he had lived in before they'd moved to Crampton Village.

He pulled up to the curb in front of the neat, single-story house and picked up the corsage. If he'd had a coat pocket, he would have stuck it inside, but instead he just carried it, trying not to stick himself with the pin.

Karl was going to have a night that would change his life forever.

Chapter Four

Karl knocked on the door and it swung open immediately. In the movies, it was the grumpy father who answered the door while the girl waited in her bedroom, keeping her date cooling his heels while he survived an unpleasant few minutes trying to make conversation with the parents.

Anna did not play any games. She stood just inside the door, wearing a knee-length, pale green dress, a broad smile on her face. If she was feeling depressed about her recent breakup, she was doing her best not to show it.

Karl really looked at Anna for the first time. He realized that though they had gone to school together for more than a decade, he couldn't remember ever speaking to her, outside of that one short conversation in the hall. It wasn't that he didn't like her, it was more that they seemed to perpetually run in different circles.

To tell the truth, Karl didn't have any close friends. His elementary school best friend, Tim, had moved away during eighth grade, the same year his mother had died. Since then, he'd been friendly with plenty of people, but didn't have anyone he would have dreamed of sharing his inner secrets with.

Anna was pretty in the classic small-town, young woman way that would slide easily into her pretty twenties, and pretty middle age. Not gorgeous. Not a knockout, but the kind of girl that a young man would be happy to be seen with.

He searched his mind for what he knew about her. He seemed to remember that she was a member of the science club, and that she had appeared in the Junior Play that year. Karl hadn't attended, but he remembered hearing others talk about it.

"Hi, Anna," Karl said uncertainly, holding the corsage out because he had no idea what else to do. It was his one move in this situation, and he used it immediately.

Anna stepped away from the door and Karl glanced around the living room. Unlike Lisa's house, there was no parent instantly on hand.

"You're supposed to pin it on me, silly."

That was a new conundrum. His corsage-pinning skills were non-existent. Anna made it easy by stepping close to him, lifting her chin a little, and pulling the fabric below her collarbone away from her skin.

As Karl stepped close, he realized she smelled very nice. The scent of a soft, girl's soap, so different from the Lava that was always in the Strong bathroom. There was also a hint of a flowery scent that seemed to float to his nostrils on its own.

Karl swallowed and opened his eyes wide, as though he was about to do some fine work.

His hands shook slightly as he tried to pin the corsage onto the dress without actually touching her. He managed, but he could feel her warmth emanating against his fingers. He finished and grinned, happy to have jumped over that hurdle without committing any faux pas.

Just then, Mrs. Masterson came from the back of the house. "Oh, I didn't hear anyone come in." She smiled at Karl and said, "I'm Candace Masterson."

"Nice to meet you, ma'am. Karl Strong." He glanced around as though Mr. Masterson might appear suddenly and need to be introduced as well.

Mrs. Masterson noticed, and said, "My husband passed away last year."

"Oh, I'm sorry. I didn't know."

"Of course you didn't. I wanted you to know why he isn't here." She looked at Anna with obvious affection and a glint of tears. "He would have loved seeing his girl, all grown up and going to a dance with such a handsome escort."

Karl had no idea what to say to that, but Anna rescued him by saying, "Last chance for pictures, Mom."

"Of course." Mrs. Masterson hurried to the coffee table and picked up a small Kodak Instamatic. She looked around the living room as though seeing it for the first time. "Why don't you two stand over here." She gestured to a picture window that had burgundy curtains pulled across.

Anna and Karl moved to the appointed spot and stood rather uncomfortably next to each other.

"Oh, no. Pretend like you know each other."

Anna laughed a little, though Karl recognized the truth of the situation—that they really didn't know each other at all. Anna glanced up at Karl, who was eight inches taller than her, and smiled a little shyly. She took a step toward him, and their arms touched.

Karl felt the warmth of her again and it was not at all unpleasant. The classic Karl smirk showed up just as the flash went off. The moment of awkward attempted intimacy was captured for posterity.

Anna hugged and kissed her mom, then picked up a white shawl that was draped over a chair and put it on.

"You look really good," Karl said, and he meant it.

Anna blushed prettily but didn't say anything.

Karl opened the door, offered a small wave at Mrs. Masterson, who again seemed to be near tears, and escaped into the October evening. After opening the passenger door for Anna, he ran around to the driver's door.

It had stopped raining, though there were still puddles everywhere.

"You look really nice too," Anna said as Karl slid in beside her.

The confusing smell of cat pee and cologne seemed stronger than ever.

"Sorry about the smell," Karl said, putting the key in the ignition.

"Oh, I didn't notice anything," Anna said. An obvious lie, because anyone with a nose couldn't avoid the overwhelming smell, but a sweet lie.

"You played really good last night. I thought you were going to score another touchdown at the end of the game."

"That makes two of us. That kid on the other side was fast, though."

"Didn't matter. We won. Are we going to the playoffs this year?"

"I think so. Unless we fall completely apart."

Anna slid a little closer to Karl, so their shoulders were almost touching. "I know you won't let that happen."

Karl looked at her with an uncertain smile. "I hope so."

They drove the short distance to the school and pulled into the Middle Falls High parking lot.

"I think we timed it just right," Anna said. "Lots of people are here, but it's not too crowded yet."

Karl jumped out and opened the door for Anna, who swung her legs out and he noticed she was wearing panty hose and shoes with a heel. He definitely felt underdressed, but Anna didn't seem to mind, so he decided not to worry about it.

Inside, there was a table set up outside the multipurpose room. Karl handed the girl behind the table the tickets. She stamped their hands with a red X and they went inside.

It would be nice to say that the multipurpose room, which was where they ate lunch every day, had been magically transformed into a fantasy wonderland.

It was still just their lunchroom, though, with some colorful streamers running from the ceiling to the walls, and the rectangular tables had been stored away in favor of smaller round ones. Each table was decorated with confetti and a small vase with a carnation in it. There was a long piece of red butcher paper with the words "Middle Falls Homecoming, 1981," written in black paint.

"Looks good," Karl said.

"Thanks. I was on the decorating committee." She looked at Karl and an odd expression came over her face. "I should confess something. I put Lisa up to getting you to ask me out."

"Yeah, I kind of figured that out."

"Not too subtle, huh?"

"It was nice, though. If you hadn't done it, I'd have been sitting alone at home right now, watching Portland Wrestling."

"I love watching that!" Anna said, her eyes lighting up.

"No. You don't."

She took half a step back and fixed him with a stern look. "Sure do. Jimmy *Superfly* Snuka? He's the best."

"I can never figure out if he's a good guy or a bad guy. It seems like he changes from week to week."

"Do you think it's all fake?"

"Probably, but I don't like to think about that. It takes the fun out of it."

The two of them had found their first piece of common ground. Combined with Anna's unnecessary confession that she had manipulated herself into the date, everything suddenly felt more comfortable.

"There's Lisa and Mike," Anna said. "Wanna sit with them?"

Karl leaned over and whispered, "Matchmaker, matchmaker, make me a match," in Anna's ear.

She looked a little embarrassed for a moment, then poked Karl in the ribs and said, "I *knew* there was a theater geek under all that jock attitude."

"I don't know what you mean," Karl said innocently. He thought of telling her that *Fiddler on the Roof* had been his mom's favorite movie and that she watched it every time it came on television, but he decided not to.

Just as they sat at the table with Lisa and Mike, the band started to play. There was an alcove at one end of the room where the school plays and choir concerts were presented.

Tonight, that stage had been taken over by *Rite of Spring*, a band brought to Middle Falls all the way from Portland, Oregon.

It was possible that the band needed to improve their ability to read a room, as they kicked off their first set with a cover of the B-52's *Rock Lobster*. It was an infectious dance song, but it was also a little too far on the *New Wave* spectrum for Middle Falls. The band sounded good, but the dance floor remained empty.

"Feel free to dance any time," the shaggy-haired lead singer said as the last notes of the first song faded out.

"Feel free to play some decent music," someone yelled from a dark corner.

The band continued to forge their own path by playing covers of *I Want Candy* and *Mexican Radio*. The kids continued to stubbornly refuse to dance.

"It's like that, huh?" the singer said, a slight sneer in his voice. Then a lot of the attitude seemed to leak out of him. He counted down and the band kicked out Blue Oyster Cult's *Godzilla*, and a cheer of recognition ran through the students.

One boy ran out onto the dance floor ahead of his girlfriend, waving his hands frantically over his head and screaming "Zillagod!"

The singer and guitarist looked at each other and shrugged. It would be another night of playing the rock classics of the seventies in a small town in Oregon. The edgy stuff could wait until a different gig.

"Do you want to dance?" Anna said, leaning in close, so her lips nearly touched Karl's ear.

That gave him a little frisson of pleasure, but he said, "I can't really dance."

"I've seen your moves on the field," Anna said. She didn't wait for a response but stood and pulled Karl onto his feet. He glanced around, noticing that no one was looking at him. Lisa and Mike were right behind them.

It was almost as if Anna and Lisa were dancing together, and Karl and Mike were just appendages. Both girls swiveled their hips and moved to the beat of the song. Karl and Mike did more of what was called the *white boy overbite*. That is, gripping their lower lip with their teeth, while making some small show of movement with their hands and feet.

It was the way of the world at high school dances in the seventies and eighties.

The rest of the night passed in a blur of punch, dancing, and recuperating on the sidelines.

To his surprise, Karl actually had fun.

When the band played their last song of the night—a cover version of KC and the Sunshine Band's *Please Don't Go*—Anna didn't even ask Karl if he wanted to dance. She stood, grabbed his hand, and led him onto the dance floor.

She seemed to melt into him and laid her head against his chest.

Karl's heart beat so hard that he was afraid that Anna would hear it. If she did, she didn't say anything, but just shuffled slowly around in a circle, two people moving like one.

When the song ended, the singer said, "That's it, Middle Falls. We're Rite of Spring. Goodnight!"

THE TUMULTUOUS LIVES OF KARL STRONG

Almost instantly, the lights overhead came on and the multipurpose room definitely looked like itself.

Some of the basketball team members ran under the streamers, jumping up and tearing them down. Karl looked at Anna and saw that her cheek was slightly red from where it had been pressed so tightly against him.

A few hours earlier, Karl had had a hard time bringing Anna's face into focus in his mind. Now he thought she was one of the prettiest girls he had ever seen.

It's astounding what a small amount of soft, nice-smelling girl pushed against a young man can do to enhance his opinions.

They walked to the car and Anna reached out and took Karl's hand as though it was the most natural thing in the world.

He started the Falcon and said a small prayer of thanks that it fired right up. There were times that it was not so cooperative. He turned out of the parking lot and toward Anna's house. If he'd had a little more going on in the romance game, he might have suggested they find a spot to go parking.

His game was non-existent, though. The thought didn't even pass through his mind.

Anna was proving more adept. She scooted as close as the bucket seats would allow and stretched out so that her head rested on Karl's shoulder. He leaned his head over and inhaled.

"Your hair smells so good."

"Thanks. It's *Gee, Your Hair Smells Terrific.*"

"Really, it does? I just use Prell."

"No, I mean that's what shampoo I use." She spoke without moving her head away.

"Oh," Karl said in a small voice.

"But I do think you smell really good. I love that cologne."

They rode in silence for half a mile as *Longer* by Dan Fogelberg played on KMFR.

"Is your dad home?"

That presented a dilemma to Karl. He doubted that Finley was home. He was more than likely sitting on a stool at the Do-Si-Do, listening to sad songs on the jukebox and crying in his beer. But, if he'd run low on funds, it was possible he'd picked up a six-pack of Olympia Beer and was sitting at home, downing them one after another.

Karl scrunched up his face uncertainly. "Honestly, I don't know. Probably not, but he might be."

"We could drive by and check, couldn't we?"

That simple question, so freighted with meaning and possibility, sent an electrical charge through Karl.

His throat was suddenly thick, but he said, as casually as possible, "Yeah, sure."

He turned right a few blocks before Anna's house. "What time do you have to be home?"

"I told Mom that the dance went longer than it does, so we've got time."

That amount of preplanning might have shocked Karl if he had thought about it, but the truth was, he really wasn't thinking at that moment. He felt like he was living outside himself, watching as he turned left, then right into Crampton Village.

He held his breath to see if Anna would suddenly lift her head and say, "Oh, I didn't know you lived here. Take me home."

She didn't. She hummed along with the song on the radio, which Karl found very pleasant.

He held his breath a little as he approached his house.

It was dark. Finley's truck was not in sight.

He pulled into the driveway, killed his lights, then the engine.

Anna lifted her head up and put her lips against his ear. He had to fight the urge to shiver when she said, "Take me inside."

He did.

Chapter Five

After the sudden, heated rush of Homecoming, either Karl or Anna might have reasonably thought that they had gone from strangers to boyfriend and girlfriend overnight.

It didn't gel that way.

When Karl woke up that Sunday morning after Homecoming, he lay in bed, trying to separate fact from fiction in his mind.

What he knew was fact was that he and Anna had somehow ended up in that very same bed a few hours before. Then he had driven her home and been back to the house before his dad got there.

Finley remained none the wiser that his son had lost his virginity the night before.

There was a swirl of emotions inside Karl. He'd had a wonderful time with Anna even before events transpired the way they did at the end. It had turned out that she was sweet, funny, and caring. The fact that they had inexplicably become sexual partners, almost totally at Anna's behest, shouldn't have altered the way Karl felt about her.

And it didn't, in a way. They were still essentially strangers, though now intimate ones.

And it did, in another way. That physical intimacy carried a tremendous impact and now, a few hours later, he was just starting to get a handle on it.

To say that a teenage boy, pumped full of hormones but lacking the experience to know what to do with them, was confused, was stating the obvious. There is no creature in nature more lost and wandering than a teenage boy.

If Karl had bounded out of bed the next day and called Anna, asking her what she was doing that afternoon and perhaps taken her for a drive or maybe to Artie's to get a burger basket, things might have gone differently.

He didn't do that.

If Anna had rung Karl up to tell him that she'd had a wonderful time the night before and hinting that she was free to spend time together later that day, things might have gone differently.

But she didn't do that.

And so, a relationship at rest stayed at rest.

Karl didn't see Anna at school at all on Monday, which wasn't unusual. Their paths didn't cross on Tuesday or Wednesday, either. By the time they did see each other, as they were going different directions in the hall between classes, too much time had passed. It had become awkward. Neither one was sure if the other one was dodging them or not.

The fledgling relationship died before it had a chance to flourish.

And life went on.

Karl played well the remaining two football games and the Bulldogs won both games. That clinched a spot in the divisional playoff round for them.

The joy of that accomplishment paled when Coach Shield gathered the team together for practice the Tuesday before the playoff game and told them that Coach Bulski had passed away the night before.

It had been serious after all.

He didn't use Coach's death for a rah-rah speech. No *Win one for the Gipper*. There was just a sense of sadness that settled over the team. Coach Bulski had been rough and gruff, and well-loved.

Karl was bothered by his coach's death. He had done a lot for Karl, and Karl wasn't an ungrateful person.

He was also growing into an exceedingly practical person. What was done was done. Coach Bulski was gone. He would pay his respects, the team would go to the coach's funeral and then he would move on.

What other choice was there?

Coach Shield did his best to implement the game plan that he had drawn up with Coach Bulski before he died.

It didn't matter.

The Bulldogs came out flat and lost to Centerville, 42-7. Karl scored the Bulldog's only touchdown, but when you are already behind by five touchdowns, that's not something to be celebrated.

Just like that, Karl's high school football career was over. His father never saw him play a single snap.

Karl felt at loose ends for the next week.

His possible romance with Anna had fizzled and failed to launch. The football season, which filled his hours and his thoughts since two-a-day practices in August, was done.

Karl had heard that there was a scout from Oregon State in the stands watching the playoff game. If so, he hadn't hurt his chances of a scholarship. He'd run for a hundred yards, caught four passes, and scored the touchdown.

The problem for Karl was that he wasn't the type of prospect that the newspapers make a big deal about when they sign a letter of intent.

He was more the kind of prospect that a college makes an offer to when they've won or lost with all the four-star and five-star recruits, who have either accepted the scholarship or gone elsewhere. He knew he would need to wait until after the new year to find out if he was going to be able to go to college the following year or not.

That became a moot point on Thanksgiving Day.

It was possible there had never been a sadder Thanksgiving spread than there was that year at the Strong household. The local food bank cooked turkey and mashed potatoes for the poor of Middle Falls to make sure they had a decent holiday meal.

Finley and Karl Strong ate two frozen dinners on TV trays. They weren't even turkey—they were Salisbury Steak because that was what was in the freezer.

There was a football game on, but it wasn't much of a game, really. The Dallas Cowboys played the Chicago Bears, but there was very little offense.

Still, both men leaned forward as if they cared about the outcome of the game. It gave them every reason not to speak to each other or comment on the meagerness of their dinner.

The game was winding down, with Dallas ahead of the Bears 10-9, when a solid knock came at the front door.

Finley and Karl looked at each other as though they had been caught doing something they shouldn't.

Karl jumped up and scooped up the empty aluminum trays that their dinners had come in and said, "I'll take these into the kitchen." It was a tacit agreement that neither of them really wanted anyone else to see what they were eating.

Karl headed to the kitchen, dropped the forks and knives into the sink and tried to stuff the trays into the garbage, which was already overflowing. He cocked his head and heard the murmur of voices but couldn't make out what was being said.

He gave up on trying to push the trays into the garbage and pulled out the can liner, stretched it, then finally managed to close it. He set the bag by the door to take out to the garbage can, then hurried back to the living room.

He was surprised to see his father talking to a man in an Oregon State Trooper uniform. Both men looked serious, but Karl immediately gleaned that Finley didn't look particularly guilty, so whatever the problem was, it was probably him.

The man in the trooper uniform stood up and Karl could see he was a big man. Beefy, but not fat. The kind of build that, when coupled with the uniform, led people not to want to tangle with him.

"Karl, this is James Masterson. He's Anna Masterson's uncle."

Trooper Masterson did not extend a hand to Karl. In a deep voice, he said, "We need to talk, son."

Karl's stomach sank, but he knew he had no choice but to nod and say, "Yes, sir."

The three men sat down. Karl and his father took a seat in the two ratty armchairs, while Masterson took up a lot of space on the couch.

"My brother William was Anna's father. He died of cancer last year and before he passed, I promised him I would do everything I could to watch over Anna."

Both Karl and Finley nodded.

"Candace called me yesterday with some upsetting news. She said that Anna is pregnant."

A small explosion went off in Karl's head and for a moment, he lost the ability to think rationally. He almost made the mistake of saying, "Why are you talking to me about it?" but managed not to. That might have earned him a deadly look from Trooper Masterson. Instead, he just swallowed hard and nodded dumbly again.

"I'm glad to see you're not immediately denying your part in this. Anna has sworn to her mother that she's only ever been with one person, and it's you."

Finley looked at Karl as if hoping that his son would deny it.

Instead, Karl just said, "Yes, sir."

Masterson looked intently into Karl's eyes, taking the measure of him.

"Now we have to decide what we're going to do about it."

Chapter Six

The wedding was a small affair, held in the Masterson living room on the day after Christmas.

The Mastersons were a Catholic family, but the priest from the local parish would not officiate the ceremony, so Mary Dalton, the local Justice of the Peace agreed to come to the house.

A small Christmas tree still stood in one corner of the living room. Karl and Anna stood in front of Mrs. Tompkins, flanked by Lisa Hanson and Finley Strong, who acted as the bridesmaid and best man, respectively. Finley had been rather surprised when Karl had asked him but had quickly agreed. He managed to arrive at the ceremony stone cold sober, but slightly twitchy.

The only other people at the wedding were Candace and James Masterson and Lisa's boyfriend, Mike. Today, Masterson was not wearing his State Trooper uniform but looked just as physically impressive in a dark suit.

As low budget as the wedding was, there were still a few expenses. Finley didn't have any money to contribute, so James and Candace Masterson had handled it.

Karl borrowed a suit from Mike, which was ill-fitting, but was better than any other option Karl had.

In a tiny bit of irony, Anna wore her homecoming dress as her wedding gown.

James Masterson had taken Karl to Barrington Jewelry in Middle Falls, where they picked out the least expensive wedding ring in the store, which came to a little over a hundred dollars. Masterson paid cash and Karl could tell by the way he pulled the twenties out of his wallet that he didn't throw money around easily. He promised to pay him back as soon as he could.

Weddings should be joyous occasions, but when it's what was commonly known as a *shotgun wedding* between two high schoolers who barely knew each other, any joy felt a bit forced.

Mrs. Masterson made a nice meal for everyone afterward and gifted the newlyweds with a set of pots and pans.

Everyone agreed that there would be no honeymoon.

The biggest decision revolved around where the newlyweds would live. Both Finley and Candace offered to let them stay with them. With no income and both of them still in school, it was obvious that a place of their own was out of the question.

Karl said that he would get a job after school and on weekends to bring in some extra money to help defray the expenses.

In the end, they chose to live in the Masterson house.

They probably would have had more privacy at Karl's, since Finley was rarely ever home, but the clean and neat Masterson home was so much more attractive, it was an easy choice to make.

It didn't take long for Karl to move in. He brought two boxes with his few belongings and carried his clothes, socks, and underwear in Hefty bags.

It was dark by the time he returned to his new home with those belongings. He knocked on the door and Mrs. Masterson opened it. There was a fixed smile on her face, and she said, "You live here now, Karl. No need to knock."

Karl nodded and took his stuff into Anna's room. Now *their* room.

It was painted a pale pink and she had posters of Simon Le Bon from Duran Duran and Rick Springfield pinned above her bed.

Anna glanced at those and said, "I'll take those down. I didn't think."

"No need. This is your room. You should have it as you like it."

Anna stepped tentatively to Karl and laid her head against his chest. "I didn't plan this, you know. I really didn't."

Karl kissed the top of her head and put his arms around her. "I know you didn't. If you were going to plan something like this, it wouldn't be with me."

She took a step back and looked up at him seriously. "You've got to stop saying things like that. I've liked you since junior high."

"What? You have? I didn't have a clue."

"Cuz I kept it to myself. The first time I saw you, you were sitting on the football bleachers during lunch. The sun was shining off your hair, and I thought you were beautiful."

"Beautiful, huh? Never been accused of that before. I thought you always liked Kenny."

"I did, for a while, but..." she trailed off without finishing the thought.

Karl wasn't much interested in what it was that made her stop liking Kenny, so he didn't follow up.

"I feel guilty. This is my fault, and I know it." She laid her head against his chest and quietly said, "If I hadn't asked you to take me to your house, what would we have done that night?"

"I was just taking you home."

"Right. So it's my fault. I can't change that now, though. I'll work really hard to make sure things are good for us." She hesitated, as if there was something she didn't want to tell him. Karl didn't prod her but let her make up her own mind.

Finally, she said, "I think I'm going to drop out of school."

"You don't want to do that. You're too smart."

"I'm smart enough that I can get my GED. I can take the test at the community college."

Karl felt overwhelmed with everything he needed to juggle. Providing for Anna and soon, a baby. He thought about his own future plans. College, getting out of Middle Falls. Those dreams felt like they had evaporated. He knew he would need to go to work at a real job as soon as he graduated. There was no way he would be able to go off to Oregon State and play football for four years.

"I don't want you to do that," Karl said. "I want you to stay in school."

"By the end of the school year, I'll be like out to here." She held her hand a ridiculous distance from her belly, which showed no bump at all. "I don't want to be waddling around school like a duck."

"Let's talk to your mom about it. Maybe we can arrange for you to do your work from home for the last semester or something."

"You are a sweet boy," Anna said, and Karl could see she meant it.

"I am a sweet *husband*." The word still felt strange in his mouth, but he was determined to start thinking of himself that way.

"Yes, you are," Anna said, plopping back onto her bed and pulling Karl down with her. It was a twin-sized waterbed, and they sloshed back and forth.

"Whoa," Karl said.

"I got this for Christmas last year, just before Daddy died. It was the last thing he ever bought me."

"Way to kill the mood."

Anna giggled and removed her top. "I think I can manage to heat things up again."

She did.

《 》

BEING MARRIED HIGH school students obviously had its disadvantages. Both their futures were changed drastically.

Anna had dreamed of going on to college and becoming a veterinarian. Karl certainly had dreams of his own, and those had all crashed.

A few weeks into January 1982, Finley knocked on the door. Karl answered. In his few weeks in the Masterson house, he had become much more comfortable with the situation. Teenagers adapt fast.

"Dad. Come on in."

Finley waved that off. "No, just heading home to get dinner."

Karl was almost certain that was a lie and that his dad's dinner would mostly consist of bottles of beer and a few handfuls of complimentary mixed nuts at the Do-Si-Do.

"You just got this letter at the house yesterday. I wanted to drop it off to you."

Karl looked at the envelope. In the upper left-hand corner was the logo for the Oregon State University Athletic Department.

Finley fixed him with a meaningful look. They both knew this was a definite fork in the road.

Karl didn't hesitate. He tore the end off the envelope and several sheets of folded paper fell out. He unfolded them and the first line read, "We are proud to offer you..."

Karl took a deep breath, folded the papers back up and stuffed them inside the envelope.

"What are you going to do, son?"

Karl studied his father. He wanted to tell Finley that he had forfeited his right to give parental advice when he had essentially abandoned him four years earlier. He thought about it for a few heartbeats and realized this wasn't the time for that conversation.

"What can I do, Dad? I'm going to tell them *Thanks, but no thanks*. There's no way I can make it work. What am I going to do, leave Anna here with her mom while I go off to college for four years?"

"I figured. Just wanted to make sure you got that." Finley stepped off the porch and walked to his truck without looking back.

Karl closed the door and hurried to the bedroom he shared with Anna. His school backpack sat on the floor beside what had become his side of the bed. He opened the pack and shoved the letter inside just as he heard the front door open again.

He walked out of the bedroom and saw Anna and Candace walk in with Safeway bags.

"You guys need help? Is there more to carry?"

"No, this is it," Anna said. She squinted at Karl, sensing something was up. "What's going on?"

"What?" Karl said, trying to look totally innocent.

Candace swerved around them, but Karl reached out and took the bags out of her hand, carrying them to the kitchen counter. When he turned back around, he saw Anna still giving him the fish eye.

"What?" Karl said again, laughing.

If they had been married more than a few weeks, Anna would have relied on her intuition more and pressed him harder.

Instead, she let it go.

The next day, Karl went to Coach Shield's office, showed him the letter, and asked if he could use the phone to call Oregon State.

"I get the feeling that you're about to make a mistake," Shield said. "There are an awful lot of kids out there that would kill to get a letter like that. I know you're in a tough spot, but once you make that call, there's no going back."

"I know, and thanks, Coach. I've got to do this."

Shield shook his head but pushed the phone across the desk to Karl.

Five minutes later, Karl walked out of the office, feeling oddly lighter and heavier at the same time. He found Anna in the hall and put an arm around her neck. She hadn't started to show yet, but of course someone had noticed the wedding ring on her finger and the story had been all over the school their first day back.

Neither Karl nor Anna cared. It wasn't a horrible secret. They weren't the only people attending Middle Falls High who'd had sex. And they certainly weren't the only people attending Middle Falls High who'd had sex *on Homecoming night.*

They were just the ones who found themselves in that perfect storm of a lack of preparation, a strong male figure to look out for Anna and a boy with a conscience in Karl.

⟪ ⟫

THE THIRD MONDAY OF January, Anna said she wasn't feeling well. She decided to stay home from school and rest.

By the time Karl got home, Candace had taken her to the hospital. He found the note on the table and hurried over to Middle Falls General.

By the time he got to Anna's room, she was sitting up in bed, looking forlorn.

Candace hugged Karl when he came in the room, then said, "I'll leave you two alone."

Karl hurried to sit on the bed beside Anna. "Are you okay? What's going on?"

Anna shook her head, struggling to get words out.

Finally, she said, "I lost the baby."

Chapter Seven

Karl Strong startled himself awake. The TV volume seemed to have jumped up when a commercial came on.

He sat up with a bleary, "What?" then looked down at himself.

He had fallen asleep eating Cheetos, and they had spilled down the front of his white wife beater shirt. As he swept them to the floor, he rubbed orangish Cheeto dust into his already soiled shirt.

"Gah..." he said, a wordless summation of how pitiful his world was.

A hopelessly cheerful song emanated from the television, and he glanced at it. Six attractive young people were trying to convince the camera that they were having the time of their lives frolicking in a fountain.

The song, the smiles, the frolicking were all too much for Karl. He fumbled for the cable remote on the table beside him and clicked the TV off. The only other light came from the small light over the stove.

He groped for the bottle of beer on the TV tray beside him. He almost knocked it over but caught it before it tipped over.

"Another brilliant save by Strong, and the crowd goes wild."

He tipped the bottle back and the warm beer slid down his throat.

The combination of half-flat beer, Cheeto remnants caught in his teeth and the dark of his depressing little rental house was enough to make Karl think about ending it right there.

It was just a thought, though. He never came close to actually going through with it.

He put the footstool down on the recliner and stood up. Between the beer and the nap, he was a little woozy and a little boozy.

He stumbled into the bathroom and peed for a long time.

"You never actually *buy* beer, you just rent it," he said to himself. Karl had a lot of little sayings like that now.

He walked into the bedroom without turning on the light. The unmade bed didn't exactly beckon him, but he figured it was the next step in the endless series of mind-numbing lousy days he had experienced.

He fell on his back on the cheap mattress, which groaned under his weight. Karl hadn't gotten on a scale for a very long time, but the way his belly and thighs jiggled told him that it wouldn't be good.

He brushed the long, curly hair out of his eyes. Fifteen years after he had graduated from high school, those curls were almost the only part of him that remained from those days.

He belched—a loud, honking, beer belch—and said, "Excuse me very much," as though there was someone else in the empty house he might have offended.

Unable to fall into merciful sleep, his mind wandered along its well-worn groove of listing and examining every mistake he had made since high school.

The first of those mistakes was always Anna.

The two of them had married as strangers but divorced eight years later as battle-hardened fighters who knew precisely where each other's vulnerable spots were. Neither was afraid to use the sharpest words to exploit those vulnerabilities.

Even though he had immediately said he forgave her for trapping him into marriage, doubts lingered. When things didn't go well, those doubts metastasized into thoughts, then eventually words that he flung at her.

The first few times he did, the obvious hurt in her eyes stopped him from pressing on, hurting her more.

As time passed and their living situation deteriorated, he found it was seeing the hurt in her eyes that he craved. That was the two-edged sword that made Anna retreat away from Karl and made him hate himself a little more each time.

Karl had graduated a local hero. The star running back who had finally brought the Bulldogs back to respectability.

His father, who had been mostly useless in his life for years, stepped up and got him a job at the box factory.

Karl had dreamed of the beautiful campus of Oregon State University and perhaps more gridiron glory. Instead, he got to spend forty hours a week standing at the same machine, turning out cardboard boxes.

Anna's fleeting dream of becoming a veterinarian quickly went away, replaced by a desire to have enough money to pay their rent after they moved out on their own. She did eventually get a job as a receptionist for the local vet, but she would have been hard-pressed to say if it was good or bad to be so close to her dream, but really so far.

Still, between the fights and the regrets, they did what they could to make things work. Karl would feel guilty about being so cruel, so he would stop at Safeway and pick up a small bouquet of flowers on a Friday night. Anna would work all day but hurry home to make something special.

Those were just small oases in a wide desert that neither had the stamina to cross.

They tried to make the same mistake that so many young couples did. They decided that having a baby would complete their family and make all the other problems fade away. That rarely ever works for troubled couples. Instead, it often creates new casualties in the eventual dissolution of the marriage. In the case of Anna and Karl, it didn't matter, because they never got pregnant again.

After becoming pregnant on that first, furtive time they were together, they never caught again.

Over the years, they grew farther apart and farther apart until they rarely spoke.

Karl could not say he was surprised when Anna dropped off the divorce papers at the box factory with a note saying she would be at her mother's. He didn't have the strength to argue and went passively along with the proceedings. It was a bloodless divorce. Neither of them was inclined to fight over the piteously small number of things they had.

One decent trip to *Twice but Nice*—the local second-hand store—would have netted out more treasure than they had between them.

And so the marriage that started quietly in the Masterson living room ended equally as quietly in the Middle Falls courthouse.

It all could have gone differently, but it didn't.

After the divorce, Karl couldn't ever find any part of his youthful energy, any hope for the future. Instead, he lived in a continual loop of the same day, the same week, the same month, and the same year over and over.

He got two weeks' vacation from the box factory, but never used them. It wasn't that he loved being at work, it was that he had no idea how to spend extra free time. Spending more time doing nothing in his small house was not appealing.

Before he knew it, he was thirty-three, overweight, unhealthy, and waking up from a beer-induced haze covered in Cheetos.

《 》

KARL LEANED AGAINST the chain link fence as the players walked by toward the practice field. He was dressed in jeans and an old work shirt and his belly pressed against the fence as he tipped his head back and drained his beer.

As the team moved away, he turned to Mike—who had married and divorced Lisa Hanson—and said, "These damned kids. They're all soft. When you and I played, we had Coach Shield to light a fire under our asses."

"He was a bastard all right," Mike agreed. He didn't look as bad as Karl. He had gone to work for Graystone Insurance out of high school. When he showed up at practices, he was still dressed in khakis and a white dress shirt. "I remember he started every practice off with a mile run and if he didn't like our attitude, he made us do another one." He shook his head at the memory.

"Remember when he used to wear his cleats and walk across our stomachs?" Karl looked into the paper bag at his feet but was sad to see he had just finished his last beer. He squinted at the kids on the practice field. They seemed to be very far away.

He belched, but that didn't make him feel any better. He looked at Mike and said, "Are we having an earthquake?" He grabbed for the fence to steady himself but missed.

Karl Strong crumpled to the ground.

Chapter Eight

Karl didn't come to until the medics were loading him on the ambulance.

"Whoa, whoa, whoa," he said, trying to sit up. "What are you doing? I can't afford this."

The medic over his head bent over him a little. "Where do you work?"

"Middle Falls Box Co."

"You're fine. They might pay lousy, but they've got good insurance. We're taking you in."

Karl tried to protest further but couldn't seem to catch his breath. The ambulance ride was a blur, as was the bumpy exit from the ambulance. Inside the hospital he saw a fast-moving collage of overhead lights and different faces momentarily looming over him. He heard those people talking about him like he wasn't there. He heard the words but didn't understand anything they were saying.

Finally, a young nurse leaned over him and, in a too-loud voice, said, "Mr. Strong? Your vitals are fluctuating. I'm going to give you something to relax you."

A few seconds later, he felt a small pinch in his right arm, then the world faded blissfully away.

When he opened his eyes, he was in a darkened hospital room. He was alone, or at least believed he was. His bed was surrounded by a curtain attached to a rail in the ceiling that cut him off from the rest of the world.

He tried to take a deep breath, but that hurt, so he settled for a series of shallower ins and outs.

Finley Strong had died of a heart attack a few years earlier and Karl thought he had just gotten a better perspective on what that had felt like for his father. It was an experience he wouldn't choose to repeat if given the opportunity.

The door whooshed quietly open and a different nurse stepped through the curtain, pulling it back a bit so he could see more of the room.

"Good evening, Mr. Strong. I'm Nurse Hopkins. I'm glad to see you're awake."

"What's wrong with me?"

"That's a question for Dr. Chin. It's past midnight right now, but the doctor will be in to see you in the morning."

"My mouth is dry."

"Doctor doesn't want you to have too much liquid right now, but I'll bring you some ice chips, and you can suck on those. That will help."

"Could you pour a little Scotch over them?"

Nurse Hopkins smiled faintly, then looked at his chart. "No, but I can get you a little something that will help you rest."

She went out and returned a few minutes later with a small paper cup and a small pill. "I'll give you a sip of water to take this with."

Karl looked suspiciously at the tiny pill. "That's too small to do anything. I'm a big guy."

"You'll be surprised." She filled another paper cup with a swallow of water and watched as he took the pill.

"Think pleasant thoughts now, and the next thing you know, it will be morning."

She was right.

Karl didn't remember going to sleep, but when he opened his eyes again, he saw that the curtain had been pulled back and bright sunlight slanted in through the blinds in the window. He tried to sit up, but soon found that was not a good idea.

"Just tell 'em you're in pain and they'll dig out the good drugs," a voice said from behind another curtain to his right.

Karl jumped. He had thought he was alone in the room. "Who's there?"

"Your roommate, friend."

Karl decided that he didn't need more information than that, so he fell back against his pillow.

An hour later, Dr. Chin came in—an older Asian man who gave off a vibe of having seen it all. He stepped directly to stand beside Karl's bed.

"Mr. Strong," Chin said without preamble, "you had a myocardial infarction last night." He glanced at Karl and saw confusion on his face. "A heart attack. You're not going to feel very good for a few weeks. You'll need to get plenty of rest, and if you can promise me you'll do that, I'll get you out of here in a day or two."

"I've got to get back to work."

"Nurse Hopkins already called your supervisor and told him the situation, including that you would be out of work for a few weeks. He told her that you had enough vacation time saved up to take the rest of the year off if you wanted."

Dr. Chin leaned over Karl to bring home the seriousness of whatever he was about to say. "When was the last time you had a physical exam with blood work and your blood pressure taken?"

"Before yesterday?" Karl asked, trying to lighten the moment.

Dr. Chin frowned. "Yes. Before yesterday."

"Never."

Dr. Chin closed his eyes. "Are you trying to kill yourself? You are this much overweight and aren't getting yourself checked out regularly? Your blood pressure was low when we first took it."

"That's good, right?"

"That is not good. It likely means your heart was damaged and was too weak to push your blood through its system. When the nurse took your BP this morning," he looked at a chart, "it was 190 over 125." He shook his head. "That's stroke territory. I've got my special mix of medications that I'm going to give you through an IV for the next few days. After that, I've got several prescriptions you will need to fill out and take at home."

Karl nodded but stayed quiet.

"You are still a young man, but if you don't address these issues—lose some weight, get your blood pressure under control—you're not going to get the chance to be an old man." He stared intently at Karl to see if the message was getting through. Satisfied that it was, he said, "Before you check out, I'll have them make an appointment for you to see me in my office."

Dr. Chin spun on his heel and hurried on to his next patient.

"Cheerful guy, huh?" the disembodied voice said from the other side of the curtain.

"I guess he thought I needed to hear that." So quietly his neighbor couldn't hear, he added, "And he's probably right."

《 》

THREE DAYS LATER, KARL was allowed to leave the hospital, though not under his own power. As the orderly wheeled him toward the exit, it occurred to him that he didn't know how he was going to get home.

"My car's still at the school," he said to the tall man pushing the chair.

"Don't worry. They wouldn't let me bring you out here if there wasn't someone waiting for you."

They pushed out into a drizzly October day and stopped under the overhang. A moment later, a blue Cadillac pulled up.

Karl recognized both the car and the driver. "Oh, no, no. Just take me back inside. I'll find a different way home."

"No can do, sir. You're already discharged. This nice lady is here to pick you up and take you home."

This nice lady was Anna Keynes, formerly Anna Strong.

Where Karl had let himself go, Anna had stayed trim. She looked like she was ready to go to the country club and play a round of golf or a few sets of tennis. Her hair was long, falling over her shoulders. Her face looked as though it had stopped aging about the time of their divorce.

Perhaps it had.

She hadn't rushed into another marriage after her divorce from Karl. But three years after they had separated, she had become engaged and then married to Seymour Keynes.

Karl, perhaps a little bitterly, had made fun of the union. "What, did she pick out the most boring guy in Middle Falls to marry?"

Karl was right in that Seymour was not exciting. But he was stable. He was also the head administrator of the very hospital Karl found himself in. When Seymour and Anna had married, he had told her that she would never need to work again unless she wanted to.

She had taken to the life of a pampered wife who took care of things around the house quite nicely.

And now she was here, with her Cadillac that cost substantially more than Karl's entire net worth.

"Guess I'm still your emergency contact," Anna said. "Might want to update that one of these days."

"How did they even find you? That had your old number on it." Karl had almost said, *our old number*, but he had managed to catch himself.

"You must be forgetting who runs this hospital. It wasn't hard for them to find me."

"You don't need to do this. I'll call Mike and have him come pick me up."

"I'm here. You need a ride. Don't be silly."

This small conversation was the first they'd had in many years.

"Come on, I don't think I can lift you."

"Is that a fat joke?"

For a moment, Anna looked chagrined, then regained her footing. She smiled. "No, it's an *I'm a small weak girl* joke. Come on, Karl. I've got to get home eventually. Get in the damned car."

Karl got in the damned car.

She turned out of the hospital. "You'll have to give me directions. I don't know where you live."

"Just go to Falling Waters. It's the big house on the right."

"Still the funny boy, aren't you? *Our* house is the big one on the right in Falling Waters and you damned well know it."

Karl nodded wearily. "Do you remember where Dad and I lived?"

"In...Crampton Village?" She had obviously paused to make sure she didn't say *Crapped-on Village*.

"Yeah, the house two doors down from Dad's old place."

Anna nodded but didn't comment. Instead, she said, "I stopped at the store and picked up a few things for you. They told me you had a heart attack, so I'm sure you're not up to cooking right now. I got some instant meals that you can heat up in the microwave real quick."

"Don't have a microwave."

"Then you can heat them up in the goddamned oven. Come on, Karl. I'm trying to help you here. Don't be an ass."

Half a mile of silence later, he said, "Thanks, Anna. I appreciate it."

"No problem."

When they got to the house, Karl saw it through Anna's eyes. The mostly fallen-down fence, the grass that had needed to be mowed for months, the project car that he had bought and never done anything with, now up on blocks.

He tensed, waiting for Anna to say something. *Anything.*

She pulled into the driveway and said, "Door locked?"

"Nothing worth stealing."

"Stay here. I'll run the groceries inside and put them away. Then I'll come back out and help you."

"I'm not helpless, you know."

Anna shrugged. "Suit yourself. I'm not your mother." It took her a millisecond to realize what she had said. Her hand flew to Karl's shoulder. "Oh! I didn't mean that. I'm sorry!"

Karl just shook his head, glad to have any shred of higher ground to cling to. "Don't worry about it. I know."

Anna jumped out of the car, a blush tinging her cheeks. She grabbed the two bags of groceries and carried them up the broken steps and inside.

Sixty seconds later, she reemerged to find Karl struggling to get out of the car.

"Take it easy, man. Come on." She hurried to him, put his arm around her shoulder and helped him up the stairs.

Inside, Karl saw what kind of condition his house was in. It made the yard outside look tidy.

"Oh no," he said in a flat monotone. "Someone ransacked the place."

"You've always been a funny boy." She helped Karl to the chair, and he sank down with a sigh of relief.

She seemed anxious to be anywhere else.

"Go on. Thanks, Anna. I mean it."

She took three steps to the door and turned to look back at Karl. There were tears in her eyes and a look of pity on her face. She nodded and hurried out.

That pity impacted Karl more than anything else she could have done.

Chapter Nine

The next few weeks were miserable for Karl. Part of it was how he felt, of course. Just getting up and going to the bathroom or to pop a frozen meal into the stove wore him out.

He had plenty of time to remember the good times that he'd had with Anna. He couldn't help but think of what this experience would be like if he'd had her with him. Instead of facing this uncertainty alone, she would have worried and fussed over him and done anything she could to make sure he got his strength back.

It's easy to cherry pick memories from the past, especially when the present is bleak.

Karl wallowed in feeling sorry for himself. Over and over in his mind, he replayed the last seconds of Anna's visit. He burned the mental image of her sympathetic, pitying look into his memory.

He ascribed things to that look that were not in evidence, except in his mind.

Oh look, he imagined her saying, *he's let himself go so much that he nearly killed himself. I'm so lucky to have gotten away from this sorry excuse for a man.*

For ten days after he was released from the hospital, Karl did nothing. In that way, those days were just a continuation of what the previous eight years had been.

And then he had enough. He had a talk with himself.

The weakest side of him argued for more weakness. The idea of just continuing to do nothing was so appealing. He could just continue to eat poorly, never exercise, and, when he had recovered enough, go to work at the box factory. Wash, rinse, repeat until he keeled over at his station, dead of another heart attack at fifty or fifty-five.

Somewhere, buried deep beneath the years of ennui, there was a small sliver of a different Karl Strong. A small voice that argued against the idea of returning to his life of slow disintegration.

One day, Karl woke up in his run-down living room—he had been sleeping in his recliner because that was easier—to sunshine coming in around the closed curtains. That unexpected bit of light in a season more known for its endless gray did something to him. In an odd way, it lit a small fire.

He was still weak, and his conditioning was non-existent, so he didn't leap up out of the chair and become a whirlwind of activity.

He did make it to the window, though. He pulled the curtains open and let the sun shine in. He blinked a few times, like a mole coming above ground. A million small dust motes swirled in front of him, lit up by the rays of the sun.

"Enough."

He slowly walked back to the table by his chair, which was stacked high with the containers of all the frozen meals he had cooked. Another pile of the same reached from the floor up to the tabletop. To the left of the chair, there was a pile of Coke cans and beer bottles. He hadn't been able to get to the store, but he'd been stocked up the day the heart attack hit.

He tottered into the kitchen and reached under the sink where the garbage bags were. He pulled two out of the box and returned to the chair. He wanted desperately just to plop back down and fill the bags from there, but something told him that if he did that, he might not get back up again for the rest of the day.

Instead, swaying slightly, he plucked the containers up, one, two, or three at a time and stuck them into the stretchy white bag. The first bag was filled up before he had even cleared all the containers. He went to work on the second bag, getting the rest of the meal packaging and most of the beer bottles and aluminum cans in that one.

He picked the bags up, straining as he did. They were light, but his muscle tone was completely gone. He had the idea that he would take the bags out to the garbage can in front of the garage, but his legs started to give out.

He didn't want to fall and spill the bags everywhere, so he settled for carrying the bags to the door and leaving them there.

"Later."

He returned to his chair with a sense of accomplishment—of setting a goal, no matter how small, and then meeting it.

He was worn out. He closed his eyes and drifted off.

When he woke up, the sun was still shining, and he felt a little better.

He immediately carried the bags out to the garbage can and even managed to wrestle the can out to the curb. Garbage pickup wouldn't be for a couple of days, but at that moment, he was all about checking things off his mental checklist.

He realized it was mid-afternoon and he hadn't eaten anything. He went to the freezer and found it nearly empty. Unless he wanted to make a meal out of ice cubes and a package of meat that had been in the corner so long he couldn't identify what it was, he needed to go to the store.

The problem was, he didn't have his truck. He wondered if it was still parked at the school. He picked up the phone, closed his eyes, and retrieved a number from memory.

A few seconds later, his friend Mike's voice said, "Yeah?"

"Mike. It's Karl."

"Hey, man! Sorry I haven't been by to see you."

"It's okay. I haven't been up to having a lot of visitors anyway. I was wondering if you could give me a lift to pick up my truck?"

"No need. I brought it home for you that same day. It's just sitting in my yard. Neighbors will probably be glad if I move it. I'll bring it over to you."

"Thanks, man. Appreciate it."

Karl pushed the antenna down on the cordless phone and set it in its charging cradle. He looked around the house and tried to decide what was next in his great reclamation project. Then he looked at himself and knew that was the place to start.

He hadn't had a shower or a shave since he'd gotten home. He was pretty sure his sense of smell had turned itself off out of self-defense.

When he climbed into the shower the hot water pouring over him felt so good that he berated himself for not having thought of it sooner. He brushed his teeth and shaved in the shower just like always and felt like a new man when he finally turned the water off.

He looked at the stained, crumpled pajama bottoms and t-shirt that he'd been wearing.

"Those should probably be burned," he said, pushing them into a corner with his toe. He thought better of that, bent over, and carried them into his dirty clothes basket. Like the rest of the house, it was overflowing.

"Soon. One thing at a time."

He pulled a clean shirt off a hanger and found a pair of jeans on the floor that he'd only worn once. The bachelor equivalent of clean. He slipped them on and was pleasantly surprised to find that the waist wasn't quite as snug.

He hooked a thumb in the belt loop and pulled it away an inch or so.

"How did you manage to lose weight, Karl?" he asked himself. "Well, I like to call it the heart attack diet. It's the easiest thing ever," he answered himself.

He grabbed some tube socks out of his dresser drawer and realized he had accomplished more in the last few hours than he had in a long time. It gave him a little boost.

He went into the kitchen and ran some hot water into the sink and washed the dishes. The frozen dinners meant he didn't have a lot to do, but he had run out of silverware a few days earlier and had been reusing the same fork over and over.

He finished that and knew he was at the end of his strength when Mike pushed his head in the front door. He held out a Shakey's pizza box in one hand and a six pack of Rainier Beer in the other.

"I come bearing pizza and beer."

"You, sir, are a gentleman and a scholar."

Mike carried the pizza box into the kitchen and rooted through the cupboards until he found a couple of plates. He slapped two pieces on each one, then opened two bottles of Rainier.

The two of them made small talk for a few minutes. The sad truth was, Mike was probably Karl's best friend—and Karl might have been Mike's—but they rarely spoke about anything.

So, they talked about what men do when they have nothing to talk about. How the Seattle Mariners' season was going and whether they might make another playoff run. The disappointing Bulldogs football team and how they were underdisciplined and poorly coached.

When those conversations ran quickly dry, Mike jumped up, fished a key ring out of his pocket and tossed the keys to Karl, who caught them cleanly.

"You always did have good hands."

"Probably the only thing I've got left these days."

"You left your keys in the truck on the day... the day you..."

"Almost bought the farm? Yeah, of course I left my keys in it. Who's gonna steal that piece of crap truck in Middle Falls? They wouldn't make it to Artie's before someone said, 'Hey, that's Karl's truck!'"

"Can't disagree. So, you feel up to giving me a ride home?"

"Let's go."

Five minutes later, they pulled up in front of Mike's house and Karl saw another possibility for his life. Mike didn't live in Falling Waters, but it wasn't Crampton Village, either. It was a nice little rambler with a neatly mowed lawn and painted shutters on the windows.

"Thanks for the lift," Mike said. He jumped out before the truck even came to a complete stop.

"Thanks for looking out for me."

Mike waved that away. "You'd have done the same for me."

Karl nodded his assent and knew that at least that much was true. There might have been a time when he had small ambitions about Mike's girlfriend and eventual wife Lisa, but that had all passed long ago.

Karl turned toward Safeway and felt lucky to find a parking spot near the front. The activity of the day had worn him out, but he knew that if he didn't pick up some groceries, he would regret it.

He went to the frozen food aisle first. He felt drawn to the frozen pizzas and Hungry Man dinners. That was what he had always eaten.

The words—the warning, actually—of Dr. Chin returned to him.

If you don't lose some weight and take better care of yourself, you'll never be an old man, or something like that.

Karl rolled past the first few freezers and stopped in front of the lo-cal dinners. He picked up one that said it was healthy, although it contained lasagna. The package felt light in his hands, especially compared to the Hungry Man dinners. He shrugged, dropped it in the cart, and picked up one of each of the others.

On the way to the checkout, he even went through the fresh vegetable section and picked up a few ingredients to make a salad.

"First time for everything," he mumbled. He also knew that he was lost and wandering in the wilderness when it came to trying to learn a healthy diet. He made a mental note to call Dr. Chin's office and see if they could recommend some things to him.

He paused in front of the broccoli. He had read a Reader's Digest article that had called broccoli a *superfood*. He started to reach for it but pulled his hand back.

"A bridge too far."

He paid for his groceries by writing a check and then realized that if he didn't get home soon, he was going to fall down. He had done that in public recently enough that he didn't want to repeat the experience.

He made it home without incident.

Over the next few days, he slowly tackled everything he had ignored about his house. He had to dig around in the one-car garage to find the old vacuum cleaner that he hadn't used in forever, but it still ran. He had to empty the bag twice before he finished vacuuming the house.

He didn't go so far as to dust. He wasn't a fanatic about things. He just thought it would be nice if he could let someone come inside without being embarrassed.

Slowly, his strength returned.

He started walking.

When Dr. Chin gave him clearance to return to work, he drove the first day to see how far it was. He was surprised to see that it was only 1.9 miles from his house to the Middle Falls Box Factory.

The next day, he walked to work. On the way home, he was flagging a bit. The work that he did was not taxing, but after a heart attack, it did take a bit out of him. Still, he had walked to work, so he had no choice but to walk home. He had barely gotten out of the gate when Mike rolled up beside him.

"Truck broken down?"

"Nah, just trying to get more exercise and get rid of this." He jiggled his stomach a little.

"Good for you." Mike was quiet for a second, staring ahead through the windshield. Finally, he said, "So, you want a ride home?"

"Yes, I do." Karl climbed gratefully in the truck. "But tomorrow, don't tempt me with a ride, okay?"

Chapter Ten

Karl Strong had spent quite a few years digging a hole and trying to pull it in after him.

If someone had asked him what he cared passionately about, he would have been hard-pressed to come up with any answer.

He had eaten poorly, relying on picking up a Shakey's pizza or stopping at Artie's for a burger basket—or maybe two—almost every night.

The most exercise he ever got was walking from his truck onto the floor of the box factory or pushing a grocery cart through Safeway to pick up his junk food fix for the week.

He didn't even enjoy his time sitting in his recliner watching television. He did it because he had to do *something*.

That all changed after his heart attack. Or to be more specific, after the look of all-encompassing pity that Anna had given him when she had dropped him off.

Karl started walking back and forth to work—at least after that first day.

Dr. Chin gave Karl a pamphlet on something called the DASH Diet: Dietary Approaches to Stop Hypertension. That was a whole new world for him, but he committed to it. He stopped hitting fast food or grabbing junk food on the way home.

He had never learned how to cook. His mother had just started to show him a few things in the kitchen when she died. But salads and fish were not difficult to cook, and he found a book about the DASH diet at the library that came with recipes.

For the first month, he didn't exercise beyond the miles he walked back and forth to work, but that was enough. Those steps wore him out—a little too much at first.

After those first thirty days, though, he felt the need to branch out a little. He tried doing calisthenics in his living room but felt a little foolish and demotivated doing jumping jacks and pushups in between the television and his recliner.

That changed when he got an ad for a new health club that had just opened in Middle Falls. They advertised their state-of-the-art exercise equipment and what attracted Karl's eye was that they had a Grand Opening Special.

Join Middle Falls Health Club today, but don't pay a penny for ninety days!

Not paying fit Karl's budget perfectly.

He drove there after work the next day. The building wasn't much on the outside—a metal pole building with a single entrance, but inside, they had done what they could to spruce it up. Karl wasn't much on appearances, anyway.

What was important to him was that they had treadmills, free weights, and station-to-station workout spots.

There was also a very attractive young woman standing behind the desk when he walked in. She looked like she was just out of high school and was bright and chipper, with her blonde hair pulled back in a ponytail that bounced as she spoke.

"Good evening, and welcome to Middle Falls Health Club. We're glad to see you here!"

Karl glanced around and saw that the place was empty except for one overweight man in the corner doing bicep curls.

"Looks like you'd be glad to see anybody. Is it always this empty?"

"Oh, we just opened this week, so we're still building up our clientele. It gets pretty busy in the mornings, though."

"Wait. You mean people come in here and work out, then go to work?"

"Yes, sir! That's a good way to get the blood pumping. Start your day off right." She smiled at Karl as though he was the cute young boy he had once been and not the approaching-middle-age wreck that he actually was. It made him stand up a little straighter and at least make an effort to suck in his stomach.

The young woman introduced herself as Tammy and walked Karl through the sign-up forms. Fifteen minutes later, he found himself in the men's locker room, changing into what passed for his workout clothes. They weren't much—an old sweatshirt that he had torn the sleeves off of and a pair of sweatpants. He promised himself that if he stuck with this new program, he would buy himself something a little better-looking to work out in.

He remembered some of the machines from the weight room in high school and started there. After twenty minutes, he was sweating profusely, but was surprised that he felt pretty good.

He lifted for another half hour, then spent twenty minutes walking on the treadmill.

When he left there, he felt good about himself. He even managed to whistle a little on the way to his truck. He sat in the driver's seat and looked at his face in the rearview mirror. What he saw was a jowly, unshaven face that looked ten years older than he actually was. What he pictured in his mind, though, was much different. He saw a stripped-down version of himself that would somehow approach the curly-headed young athlete he had once been.

Maybe even someone who deserved the smiles that Tammy bestowed on him.

He was beginning to feel a little sore by the time he got home. His lower back hurt a little and he made a mental note not to push it so hard on the weights the next day.

He thought about frying the fish that he had in the refrigerator and making himself a salad, but his energy was gone. It was enough exertion to push himself out of his recliner and limp into bed.

He fell asleep almost instantly.

When he woke to the sound of his alarm clock radio beeping at him the first day, he thought he must have dreamed everything that had happened since his heart attack, because he felt worse than he had the first day he was home.

He tried to lift his head off the pillow and found that his neck was sore. His back was worse, and his left leg had a charley horse. He felt worse when he tried to actually sit up.

"Oh my God," Karl moaned. "I would feel better if I had died."

He dragged himself out of bed and, bent over like an old man, made it into the shower. The hot water worked its miracle and by the time he stepped out, he was at least able to stand upright.

His stomach rumbled from his skipped dinner the night before, so he managed to pour himself a bowl of Raisin Bran.

He knew that he would never manage to walk back and forth to work that day, so he swallowed three aspirin and took his truck.

The workouts eventually got easier, and he felt less and less like he was mostly dead when he woke up the day after.

Karl lost the pounds, but he gained something much more important—something to care about. Something that he could spend his time doing that had tangible positive results.

Six months after his heart attack, Karl was a new man. He'd dropped forty pounds and although he didn't look all that much like the teen athlete he had once been, he had more energy and felt better about himself than he had in many years.

He even began to feel that Tammy's smiles when she saw him make his daily appearance at Middle Falls Health Club were genuine.

This self-improvement program extended beyond his physical makeover.

He began to tackle all the oft-delayed work that needed to be done on his rental home. He fixed the sagging gutters, weeded the overgrown flower bed and repaired the front steps so they weren't a danger to man and beast.

For the first time in many years, he began to feel hopeful that he could still accomplish something in his life. He went to his boss Allen Ray at the box factory and asked if he could speak with him after quitting time.

At that meeting, Karl sat across from Allen, shifting a little uncomfortably in his seat.

"I don't know if I've told you, Karl, but it's sure good to see you taking care of yourself. You've lost a lot of weight. You look good."

"Thanks. Having a heart attack in your thirties is kind of a wake-up call. Listen, I've been here a long time."

"Fifteen good years," Allen said, tapping Karl's file in front of him. "You've always been a good man."

"I'm just wondering, is there a chance I could move up a little? I don't think I could do your job, for sure, but I watch what the floor supervisor does, and I think I could do that. And I've had just about every job on the line, so I can always fill in if someone calls in sick."

Allen leaned back in his chair, as though he was looking at Karl with new eyes. "I never thought you were much interested in moving up. You always struck me as a guy that came in, put his time in, then punched out. I figured you had a lot of interests outside of the factory here."

"Not really. Like I say, the heart attack is making me look at things differently. I don't want to be like my dad and die in my fifties, sitting at the same station I'd been sitting at for thirty-five years."

"Your dad was a damned good man. Kind of a legend around here."

"Yessir."

Allen tapped the file folder again. "Tell you what, Karl. Let me think about it. We're thinking of moving Bob into a new position and that'll open up a spot as a supervisor. I'll let you know."

Karl jumped to his feet. He had been dreading the meeting since he had asked for it, and he was glad to be done with it and free to go. He stuck his hand out and shook with Allen, then hurried out the door.

He walked home, then, as he still felt energized, hopped in his truck and drove to the health club.

Tammy was off that evening, but he was greeted by Jillian, the other front desk person.

"If it's Tuesday, it must be Karl," she said with a smile.

"Or Wednesday, Thursday, or just about any other day," Karl answered with a shy smile.

"Always good to have you here. You're an inspiration to everyone."

Karl waved, but as he walked to the locker room to change into his gym clothes, he thought about that. Was he an inspiration because he showed how even a fat slob could get in shape using the equipment here? He remembered an old joke he had heard once. If you fall down and everyone laughs, you're still young. If everyone rushes to help you up, you're old.

Karl was pretty sure everyone would hurry to help him up. He shrugged and put on his gym shorts and T-shirt, both of which were two sizes smaller than what he had once worn.

By this time, he had a regular routine. He started with some easy cardio on the treadmill, then moved to the weight machines. After setting the bench press to one hundred and eighty pounds, he decided he would see if he could beat his best number of reps. He felt strong.

He was up to fifteen reps when something felt wrong. He let the weights slam back down, then tried to sit up. He managed it, but just barely. It felt like there were hundreds of pounds of weights on his chest.

He had done his best to block out the memory of his first heart attack, but that same familiar sensation was returning.

"Oh, come on," he groaned quietly. "I've been doing everything I was supposed to. Not fair."

They were the last words Karl ever spoke in this life.

He tried to stand, faltered, and slid off the weight bench.

The light faded from his eyes.

Chapter Eleven

Karl Strong opened his eyes.

He squinted, unable to believe what he was seeing.

He was sitting in his recliner. The television was blaring loudly. Six attractive people dancing in a fountain, pretending to have a good time.

"What?" was all Karl could manage to get out. He sat bolt upright.

The Cheetos that had been scattered across his chest fell into his lap.

"What?" he repeated stupidly. It was all he could say.

He pushed forward in the recliner and looked around in dismay.

He was in his house, but it looked like it had when he hadn't given a damn. Trash was piled everywhere, the curtains were drawn to block out the world, and the whole place smelled pretty awful.

"Okay, hold on," Karl said out loud. Speaking the words gave him a firmer grip than just thinking. "I was working out, doing good, then I felt like I was having another heart attack. It was like I was falling into a weird spiral or something. I got so tired I had to close my eyes, and now I'm here. But I can't be here because this place doesn't exist. At least, not like this."

He looked at the overflowing kitchen trash can, the blind in the window that hung askew at a drunken angle.

"I fixed that."

The horror of the situation got much worse when he finally looked at himself.

"I'm fat!" he said, his voice tinged with hysteria. "Can't be. I'm not fat anymore. I did it. I did the work."

He stood up and felt a little dizzy. He stumbled across the room to his front door and flung it open. Outside, the night air was cool. An old car with a noisy muffler drove by on the street. He saw that the steps that led up to his small porch were broken once again.

He closed the door and leaned heavily against it. Disbelieving what his own eyes were telling him, he reached grabbed his jiggly belly. He lifted it up, then let it drop. The weight of it convinced him that, for the moment at least, this seemed to be real.

Real? he thought. *Real? This isn't real. It* can't *be real.*

He wandered through his filthy house, letting his fingers brush against piles of garbage, dusty windowsills, anything that might tell him this was all a dream.

Karl did his best not to panic.

Dying was bad. Waking up here, at the lowest point of his life, was worse.

He tried to calm his mind. Still, he began to tremble.

One tear slipped down his face.

"I can't do this. Not again."

Zombie-like, he staggered into his bedroom and fell across the tangle of sheets and blankets. He buried his face in the pillow and tried to think himself away.

To anywhere but here.

Within moments, he was asleep. A deep sleep that was like a heavy curtain falling across his consciousness. He slept through the night without stirring.

When he finally opened his eyes again, it was because his clock radio was beeping at him. With bleary eyes, he looked at the time and saw that it was fifteen minutes after he kept his alarm set to go off.

He had been asleep with his head right next to the clock radio as it beeped over and over. It felt as though he was coming off a three-day bender.

When he sat up, he felt logy and disjointed.

"Still here," he mumbled. Then, quietly, "Why? What did I do?"

He buried his face into the pillow once again, continuing to wish all this away. No matter how long he did that, when he lifted his head, nothing had changed.

He sat up and rubbed a hand across his face.

"This is impossible."

Still, out of some long-ingrained sense of habit, he stood up and took off the clothes he'd been wearing when he went to sleep and picked out a shirt and jeans that looked exactly the same.

He wandered into the kitchen and found an open box of Strawberry Pop-Tarts. He tore the foil packaging open and stuffed half of one into his mouth in one bite.

As if to see how far this fantastic, unlikely new world extended, he grabbed his keys off the counter and walked to his truck. Five minutes later, he pulled into the box factory and saw that everyone else already seemed to be there.

"Gotta be a dream, gotta be a dream," he said to himself as he walked in the door where the time clock was. He was fifteen minutes late to clock in.

As though in a dream, he reached out and saw his own time card, his name scrawled across the top of it in his own handwriting. He punched in then headed toward his spot on the line.

There were catcalls.

"Tough night, Karl?" and "Get your ashes hauled last night, buddy-boy?" and "The dead awake!"

Karl ignored them all but took it as another data point that as strange as this new circumstance was to him, everyone else seemed to take it in stride. To them, this seemed to just be another day.

After so many years, Karl didn't have to think about his job, but at least it occupied a part of his brain. He fell into a near fugue state for the next three hours until the whole line shut down for lunch.

He approached Ken, who he had worked with for more than fifteen years. "Anything weird going on today?"

"Like what?" Ken asked. "The sun is shining. That's a little weird. Other than that, no." He looked at Karl. "You okay buddy? You look a little pale."

"Yeah, I'm fine," Karl lied. "Fine." He considered telling Ken, "Well, I died yesterday, and now I'm here. Does that count as weird?" but he didn't.

Instead, he did what he always did. He took his worries, his concerns, and his fears and stuffed them deep down, appearing pretty normal to the rest of the world.

He finished his shift and went home. He was disgusted by what he found. After spending a few months cleaning and tidying up and doing repairs, it felt grossly unfair to find things in this sad state. The same thing applied to himself but having just spent the same amount of time trying to remake himself, he knew that was a long task. Housework could be tackled with obvious rewards much quicker.

He went to work. Three hours later, he had restored things to a state that at least felt like he wasn't living in a pigsty.

That night he went to bed hoping that whatever had caused him to drop into this spot would change. He didn't mind going on to whatever was next after death, but he didn't want it to be this—revisiting the worst moments of his life.

He woke up in his same bed, although it was between clean sheets, since he had changed them the night before.

Small changes add up to big goals.

At work that morning, he checked the calendar and saw that he was only a few days away from when he had his first heart attack.

He had no idea how any of this worked, of course. He had no clue if he would have a heart attack again, or if he could do something to stop it from happening.

What he did know was that he didn't want to be standing along the fence line shouting at the Middle Falls football team when it hit. That had been mortifying. The fatso, out-of-shape former athlete trying to relive a tiny sliver of his glory and falling down with a heart attack.

Instead, he went straight home that day and sat on his recliner. The TV was off, there was no music on the radio. He sat very still, hoping that whatever had stressed him out enough to cause the heart attack wouldn't happen if he was relaxing at home.

Of course, stressing out about whether a heart attack was about to hit wasn't exactly relaxing.

Still, the minutes passed. He drummed his fingers impatiently.

Nothing happened.

"Okay," he mumbled to himself. "So there's that." He stood up to see what was in the refrigerator. The familiar feeling washed over him. It felt like a massive weight had been dropped on his chest. He tried to take a deep breath and found he couldn't suck in any oxygen at all.

"Oh no."

He turned and reached for the cordless phone on the table beside his recliner. His fingers brushed against it clumsily, knocking it to the floor. The next moment, he found himself on the floor as well, staring at the phone under the table.

The pain made him grimace, but he reached his arm out as far as he could manage.

He tried to scoot to his right so he could call 911. He made it far enough that he finally managed to touch the phone.

His reach, however, exceeded his grasp. He only managed to push the phone farther away.

He gave one final effort, then closed his eyes and died.

⟨ ⟩

KARL STRONG OPENED his eyes.

The television was too loud. The dancing people were too fake happy. The Cheetos spread across his chest were too Cheeto-y.

Karl Strong didn't wonder where he was this time. He knew.

He was bereft. He couldn't imagine this happening, or why it might be happening to him.

Karl repeated essentially this same loop more than a dozen times.

They were not all the same, but some things were consistent. He always woke up at the same time, with *Friends* playing on the television and the evidence of his junk food junkie habits spread across his chest. And, no matter what he did, he died on the same day.

He tried to change that. He took several days off before the heart attack was scheduled to arrive so he would be well rested. He ate better for the few days between his waking up and his dying. He tried to exercise. That just felt like he was encouraging the heart attack, though.

No matter what he did, he woke up on the same day and died on the same day.

Each life found him a little deeper in the hole.

Not physically, he was already at his nadir there, but emotionally.

Slowly, the deep blackness of depression was reaching for him, inviting him to fall into it. The life force inside him seemed to dim a little each time he was forced to wake up miserable, live miserably for a few days, then die miserable.

The worst part was the result of living a life with only acquaintances and no true friends. There was no one he could confide in about the strange turn his life had taken. Perhaps the strange turn his *lives* had taken would be more accurate.

Each of these short loops didn't really feel like lives to Karl. To him, a life included choices, a chance to alter a path, to make mistakes and then correct them. What was happening to him offered none of those options.

Still, he went on because what else could he do?

At least he had learned to adjust more quickly. He no longer spent his first few minutes of each life wandering around, asking, "What? What?"

That question seemed to have been answered, though not in a satisfactory way.

What was that he apparently was doomed to repeat a terrible few days of his life over and over. He wondered why it couldn't have been a good section of his life that he was stuck in. Say, the last Christmas he spent with his mother, or the vacation to the ocean he had taken with his mom and dad when he was ten years old.

Even, he sometimes thought, Homecoming night and his date with Anna. When he was sitting on the line at the box factory, he let the inactive part of his brain fantasize about what he might have done differently had he been given the chance.

Would he be bright enough to say, "Nope, I'm taking you home," when Anna asked him to take her to her house. How would his life have evolved if he had made that single, fateful decision?

He didn't get far enough along the path of that idea to think about whether he could just be a better husband and perhaps make it work with Anna. He had the evidence that Anna seemed to be happy in her second marriage to Seymour, so he figured it was him who was the weak link, not her.

What Karl couldn't figure out was, why had he managed to survive the initial heart attack in his first life but had died of the same thing in every life since? He had managed to sit with the phone in his hand several times, and when the heart attack hit, he had quickly dialed 911. Nonetheless, he was dead before the ambulance arrived.

He tested this idea further by going into the Emergency Room of Middle Falls hospital on the day he knew he was going to die again. Limping in, he told them he had sprained his ankle and wanted to get it looked at. That was an innocuous enough malady that he figured he would have to sit in the waiting room for quite a while, waiting to be seen.

He had been correct.

He was in the best position possible, then, when the attack hit. No need for an ambulance, there were doctors and nurses just a few steps away.

And still he died.

And opened his eyes to face this terrible life again.

And again.

And again.

Interlude One
Universal Life Center

Margenta spun her pyxis. A smile so tiny that no one would have been likely to see it played on her lips.

Her pyxis showed a heavy-set man sitting in a recliner. He wasn't doing anything. He wasn't watching television or reading a book. He was simply sitting. Waiting.

Margenta watched as the event the man was waiting for arrived. First, he braced, then stiffened and pushed back against his chair as though a strong electrical shock had run through him. He tried to stand, to turn, to do anything other than flop around in his chair but managed only to crumple to the floor.

Margenta spun the pyxis expertly back, then turned it at a slight angle. The picture displayed within barely changed. Once again, it showed the same man sitting in the same recliner. This time, he was asleep, though he opened his eyes as she watched. Immediately, the man's chin went to his chest and tears began to stream down his cheeks.

The frame around the picture turned a dark gray, then into a harsh black.

"Margenta," a voice came from over her shoulder.

Margenta jumped, as though slightly guilty about something, but she had only been doing her job.

"Yes?" she answered, her fingers flying to her gray hair, which was piled high and stiff on top of her head.

Carrie moved around to where Margenta could see her.

"I notice that you aren't using our ability to reset our people at different points in their life."

"That's right, I'm not. Is that a problem?"

"Problem? No."

"Good. My understanding is that we are still allowed to do our job the way we see fit."

Margenta didn't bother to try to hide the disdain she held for Carrie. They were enemies who had stood on opposite sides of issues a number of times before. Carrie had always persevered and now was the Head Watcher, while Margenta was working under her.

"You are always able to do your job as you see fit."

"And what I see is that my job is to feed The Machine. If you'll look at this person's frame, you'll see he is sending a lot of energy to The Machine."

Carrie involuntarily reached her hand toward the image of the man, surrounded by blackness. She stopped and pulled her hand back.

"Yes, your reports and numbers are always top notch. You do a wonderful job of feeding The Machine."

"Thank you," Margenta said primly, poking once again at her stiff hair.

"But I would consider it a personal favor to me if you would consider trying it at some point. It's always possible you might find even better ways of accomplishing this primary goal."

With one last lingering look at the man suffering in the pyxis, Carrie was gone.

Margenta didn't bother to look around for her. She twitched her mouth, annoyed at the presumptuousness of the request. Carrie's last words rankled her. *You might find even better ways of accomplish-*

ing this primary goal indeed. That was just like Carrie, who always seemed to care more for the insipid souls of the people she watched over than for this much more important aspect of the job.

Still, Margenta did like to be efficient.

While the man sat in his recliner and sobbed, she spun the images of his life backward and forward, backward and forward, looking to see if there might be a different spot that would cause more energy to be fed to The Machine.

Chapter Twelve

Karl Strong lived through this latest incarnation of what he had begun to consider was his personal Hell, though he didn't do it with any verve or joy.

He had stopped bothering to go to work. What was the point? He wondered how many times he had made the same boxes—not just similar, but the exact same boxes?

He had begun to call in on the morning after he first woke up and lay claim to his unused vacation time. It wasn't that he wanted to do something. It was more that he didn't have the energy left to do *anything*.

Instead, he sat at home, the TV on but unwatched, and let the minutes, hours, and days pass while he waited for the next identical loop.

The heart attack came right on time. He had almost gotten used to the massive pain of this experience.

It arrived, he stiffened, he died.

⟨ ⟩

KARL STRONG OPENED his eyes.

He jerked, stumbled, and nearly fell.

He was not in his recliner in Crampton Village, though he *was* in Middle Falls.

THE TUMULTUOUS LIVES OF KARL STRONG 85

He glanced wildly about, trying to figure out where he was. He had no idea *when* he was.

He was in a knot of people all walking in the same direction.

This is right by the Middle School.

He looked at himself and realized that not only was he young but he was wearing his football uniform. Shoulder pads, jersey, pants and all.

He felt youthful and strong. And totally confused.

Although he had become as accustomed as someone can be to the short cycles of his life, this was completely different and totally disorienting.

"Hey, nice game, number twenty-two," a man said, clapping him strongly on his shoulder pads. "You really stuck it to them out there."

"Thanks," Karl said automatically.

"Three touchdowns," an older boy added. "You outscored the other team all by yourself."

"It wasn't just me. It was those guys in front of me opening the holes." It was an automatic response that bubbled to the surface, even in these seemingly impossible circumstances.

Karl looked around and saw other players mixed in among the crowd. They were all cutting to the left to head off to the locker room to get changed.

"Excuse me," Karl said and headed the same way. He got halfway there when something the high schooler said rang in his ears. *Three touchdowns.*

Karl had only scored three touchdowns once in his life. It was in a junior high game. The touchdowns were meaningless.

It had happened the day his mother died.

Adrenaline spiked through Karl's system. Both hope and despair overloaded him at the same time.

He sprinted back toward the crowd, carelessly bumping into people and not caring. A few steps later, he was in the clear.

He hadn't been there when it happened, but he had returned to the spot where his mother had died many times, hoping to commune with her in some way.

The circumstances of that night, long buried, returned to him. His parents had always come to his junior games. He was the best player on the team, and they were proud of him. They also held the fledgling hope that maybe this athletic prowess would translate into at least a partial scholarship to college. That was something they'd worried about for years. How could they afford to send their bright young boy to college on the salary of a factory worker and a teacher's aide?

They had saved everything they could, but it wasn't much.

On this night, Finley had been offered a chance to work a double shift. He took it. Any chance to earn a little extra was gladly accepted.

His mother had come to the game, though.

Karl sprinted beside the band room, then turned right onto the front lawn of the school. His young legs felt like they could run forever, even though he had just played all four quarters of a football game.

Far ahead, he saw her. He recognized her blonde hair from behind.

"Mom!" Karl called to no obvious effect. "Mom!"

She was perhaps a hundred yards ahead of him. The length of a football field.

Karl's heart dropped as he saw her turn to cross the street. She had turned slightly and Karl could see her bright smile. She was waving and saying something to a woman behind her.

Karl had imagined this scene a thousand times. Ten thousand. Somewhere in the back of his mind, he knew he had never come close to getting it right. He had never pictured her smiling just before she died.

Karl pounded his feet against the sidewalk. He was still wearing his cleats and he couldn't get up to full speed as they slipped here and there.

He closed the gap, though.

Everything slowed. His mother, still smiling and waving at her friend. Karl's legs pumping, trying to close the gap. He didn't want to look, but he did. To her right, he saw the death car. An old four-door car that he knew was filled with half a dozen teenagers. They were laughing, cutting up, speeding, and paying no attention to what was going on in front of them.

Karl willed himself to run faster, to close the gap. He didn't waste his lung power on shouting any more. He focused every bit of strength on reaching her.

He watched as his mother stepped off the curb and into the first lane. It was obvious to him now how it had happened. The perfect storm of events that had changed his life.

He could see that he was going to be just short of being able to catch her.

Karl realized with a sinking horror that he was about to watch his mother die.

"No!" he screamed and launched himself into the air.

His jump closed the final few feet between them and he pushed against her shoulders. She stumbled forward, out of the path of the car.

Karl fell to the street, but the front bumper of the car caught him and flung him into the air. He twisted as he flew, and saw that his mother had fallen, but that the car had missed her.

Karl hit the pavement at an awkward angle, scraping his face from chin to forehead.

Things immediately started to go dim.

There was chaos around him.

"Don't touch him!"

"Call an ambulance!"

"Is there a doctor here?"

Karl felt himself hearing less and less of what was being shouted. And then she was there.

She turned him slightly so he could see her face. Beautiful. Unmarred.

"Karl!" she shrieked. Her face was a twisted knot of fear and fright. "Karl, honey. Baby, baby, baby."

Karl wanted to reach out to her. He wanted to tell her that it was okay.

In his confusion, he said, "It's all right. I'll wake up somewhere else."

Tears leaked from the corners of his eyes. He smiled at his mother through broken teeth.

Things went dark.

Interlude Two
Universal Life Center

Margenta watched the scene in front of her. It showed a young boy dressed in a sports uniform milling in a crowd. He looked a little lost and dazed.

Suddenly, as if he remembered he was late for something very important, he began to run through the crowd.

The frame that surrounded the image glowed a white bright. A huge spike of emotions.

Margenta watched, quite satisfied at the intensity of what was feeding The Machine.

"Strong emotions," a male voice said from over her shoulder.

Margenta knew the voice. "Hello, Charles."

"Do you know," Charles said, "the full equation for each life?"

"I am a watcher, not an engineer," Margenta answered.

"Yes. I am both. There is an energy cost in starting each new life."

"Of course. How can there not be?"

"It's a formula, then." Charles began making motions in the air and an equation hung there. It was likely that this formula only meant something to him. He finished the equation and said, "There. As you can easily see, a life such as this, with a strong spike in emotion, but a short duration, does not pay for the energy used to create it."

"Thank you, Charles," Margenta said, though the way she said it showed that she didn't really mean, *Thank you, Charles*. She meant, *Go away, Charles*.

Charles wiped his hands across the numbers and symbols and they all fell into nothingness. "I thought you might like to know that. Since you're not an engineer, I mean." He smiled at her. "I don't want to see your reports go down. No one likes to be reprimanded."

Charles did not disappear. He simply wandered away, stopping to chat with several other people as he walked by.

Margenta sighed. To herself, so quietly that no one could possibly hear her, she said, "I remember when everyone just left you alone."

She tilted her pyxis and scanned through the life in front of her. She set her chin with grim determination and picked out a new starting spot.

Chapter Thirteen

Karl Strong opened his eyes.

What he saw was familiar, though not exactly expected.

He was in his bedroom in the house he shared with his father in Crampton Village.

A few moments before, he had seen his mother's lovely face twisted with worry and guilt. He knew that once again, she was gone.

Or is she? A hopeful thought dropped into Karl's mind. *What if I saved her, and now she will be alive wherever I wake up?*

It was an unlikely thought. If he'd stopped to think about this theory, he would have seen the holes in it. He would have thought that if his mother was still alive, they would not have ended up in this tiny house. They would be living in their previous cozy house, not here.

But hope and logic rarely occupy the same space.

Karl threw the covers back and was relieved to see that it was his lean, athletic body. At least he wouldn't have to worry about keeling over dead from a heart attack in the short term.

With wings on his feet, he ran through the tiny house shouting, "Mom?" over and over.

The only answer was the sound of a car backfiring outside and the settling of the house on its foundation.

It only took him a moment to realize that this was not a place that had ever seen a woman's touch. Clothes were piled here and there, bottles, cans and various food bags and containers were stacked up on the table and falling to the floor. There was a mound of dishes waiting to be done in the sink.

Karl took a deep breath and sat on the couch. He weighed things out in his mind.

His mother was dead again. Even so, he had spent lifetimes without her. He could never say that he had *gotten used* to not having her around, but it was part of his life now.

On a more positive note, he was young and strong again. He tried to recapture the frame of mind he'd had before everything had happened with Anna.

Anna, he thought. *Have we already been together? That feels exactly like what would be happening to me—start a life when it's too late to fix what I messed up.*

Karl wandered through the house, looking for a calendar. There was nothing.

He stepped into the bathroom and looked in the mirror. His own familiar face stared back, with his long curly hair that hung over his ears and down his neck.

He hurried to the front door and flung it open. The Falcon was still sitting right where it always was.

The clock on the wall said it was 7:55. The sun was shining and still coming from the east, so he was at least sure that it was morning.

High school, he thought. *I'm about to be late for freaking high school.*

He ran into his bedroom, flung on whatever clothes he first laid eyes on, and threw on his shoes and socks. His keys were right where they always were – in a bowl on the kitchen counter.

He looked around in a slight panic for whatever school books or homework he might need. He couldn't find anything, so he hurried out to the Falcon.

The sun was warm on his face, and sure enough, when he opened the driver's door, a full blast of the smell of cat pee hit him.

"Good to know that at least some things never change," he muttered.

He still felt lost and bewildered, but he hoped that by going to school, he would be able to figure out *when* he was.

The streets of Middle Falls were quiet, but that was not unusual. The streets of Middle Falls were almost always quiet.

He flipped on KMFR and the disc jockey was saying "...sunshine and a high in the mid-sixties today. Now here's Michael Jackson, all grown up and out on his own." The musical intro to *Rock with You* played over the Falcon's tinny speakers.

Before the song ended, Karl turned into the Middle Falls parking lot.

It was deserted.

He was in such a fantastic situation that his mind began to wander to fantastic theories about how something had happened and all the students and teachers of Middle Falls had disappeared, perhaps vaporized.

Then, the more likely answer hit him. It was more probably a weekend.

He drove a circle around the parking lot, completely at loose ends, when he saw a person standing in the grass, swinging a golf club. He vaguely recognized the boy, though he couldn't have come up with his name under any circumstance.

Karl felt lonely and decided on the spot that the best fix for loneliness was to talk to people. He parked his car at the edge of the parking lot and got out. The boy was perhaps seventy or eighty feet in the grass, facing toward the football field, which was a long ways off.

Carefully, the boy shifted his hips, looked down at the grass, then pulled his club back and swung it in a graceful arc. Karl whipped his head around to follow the ball he had hit, but there was no ball to follow.

The boy repeated this process again and again, but never hit a ball. That piqued Karl's curiosity. As if drawn to this odd activity, he put his hands in his pockets and wandered toward the boy.

When he got closer, he could see that there were indeed golf balls scattered around the golfer. He just wasn't trying to hit them.

The boy was looking down at the ground, again wiggling his hips. Without looking up, he said, "You probably think I'm the world's worst golfer." He swung again and this time Karl saw that a few blades of grass flew up into the air.

"Well," Karl said, "I *was* wondering."

The boy looked at Karl and there seemed a small spark of recognition. "It's more efficient this way. I try to do things efficiently."

Karl couldn't help smiling. Hearing a teenage boy—and one who looked to be a few grades behind Karl—say that he wanted to be *efficient* was a little out there. He studied the boy more closely. He looked more like a mad scientist than an athlete. He was not very tall, with short hair and thick glasses that continually slipped down his nose. His khaki slacks and polo shirt were not exactly the classic early-eighties Middle Falls high school dress, which skewed heavily toward jeans, T-shirts, and Chuck Taylors. When Karl took into account that it was a weekend, it was even more odd.

"What do you mean, *more efficient?*"

"Improving my swing is more about becoming consistent. To reach that, I have to take thousands of swings. But, if I hit a ball every time I swing, I'm going to spend a lot of time walking from one end of my range to the other. Not efficient. But, if I repeat my swing over and over and only hit the ball when I feel like I'm in sync, I can get a tangible result to compare. More efficient."

Karl couldn't help but smile a little. "Cool. I'm Karl, by the way."

The boy looked at Karl frankly. "Oh, I know who you are. You excel at one of the popular sports, so everyone knows you. I'm Eric Swanson." He twitched his mouth a little, as though he was about to share something embarrassing. "My parents call me Eckie, though. So if you ever come to my house, you can get the laughs out of your system now."

"No laughs from me, but I'll probably just call you Eric."

"*Thank you*," Eric said with emphasis. "Parents have no idea how much damage they can do their kids' social life when they hang these names on them."

"Do you mind if I give it a try?" Karl asked, nodding at the club.

"Have you ever golfed?"

"Nope."

"Sure. Really, you should have a longer club, so that will hinder you a little bit. It won't matter much, though. Your natural bad habits and awkwardness will be much worse." He held the club out to Karl.

"Bad habits and awkwardness, huh?" Karl asked.

"Sorry, I don't really screen the things that come out of my mouth. I know I should."

"No, really, no need to screen things with me. I like honesty." Karl squared up to the ball like he had seen Eric do. He even gave a little hip wiggle before he pulled the club behind his head and swung it like he was trying to knock it into the next county.

He whiffed completely. He gaped at the small white ball, sitting mockingly in the same spot.

"Not an unusual result for a first swing," Eric said. "Try again."

Karl rolled his neck and focused. He pulled the club back again, but this time swung it with a little less velocity. The club head hit the ground a few inches behind the ball and sliced a divot that flew a few feet away.

The ball sat in exactly the same place. Again, mocking him.

"Son of a...!"

"Now you just need to be somewhere between those two swings and you'll at least hit the ball."

Karl took a deep breath. He was feeling the frustration that eventually became commonplace to almost every golfer. For such a simple game—hit the ball into the hole—golf was supreme in mentally wrecking those who played it.

Karl did an all-over body shake, gave himself a talking-to and swung again. This time he just focused on making contact and he did. The ball moved in a small arc and landed fifty yards away.

"Yes!" Karl exulted.

"Enjoy those small moments of satisfaction. If you take up golf, they are rare."

"Let me see you hit one, if it's not too inefficient."

Eric shrugged, addressed the ball and pulled the club back and let it drop in one smooth motion. The ball seemed to leap off the club and traveled well past the one Karl had hit. Well past.

Karl chewed on his cheek and nodded. "I get it."

In quick succession, Eric moved from one ball to another and another, sending them all in the same parabolic arc as the first. They all landed within a few yards of each other. "See? Efficient."

Another jock might have been insulted to be so outplayed by someone so much smaller than them. Karl was more amazed than ticked off, though.

"Could you teach me to do that?"

Eric shrugged. "If you committed to practicing regularly, sure."

"Well, I don't have any clubs."

"Oh, that's no problem. My dad is the club pro at the country club. I can get some scrub clubs that have been left behind for you to practice with."

"Really? Your dad is the pro?" Karl wanted to ask if that meant that Eric's family was wealthy, but he knew that was rude.

Eric nodded, then squinted at Karl. "People usually think that means that we're rich, but we're not. It just means that Dad's good enough that he qualified for the Tour, but not good enough to make a lot of money at it. That's why he's a club pro now."

"Is that what you want to do too? Be a golfer?"

Eric made a face and said, "No. I want to be an engineer. That's a lot more consistent than being a golfer."

"You're a smart dude."

Eric shrugged, picked up a metal basket and walked to where the balls were clustered. He stopped on the way and picked up Karl's lone ball. He dropped them into the basket. "Gonna head for home."

"Want a ride?"

"Let's see, walk home or take a ride. Which is more efficient?" Eric put his clubs in a small leather golf bag and hooked it over his shoulder.

"You walked all the way here carrying that stuff?"

"Dad didn't want to loan me his golf cart, so yeah."

Karl squinted at him, unsure if he was joking or not. He decided he probably was.

They walked to the Falcon and a stray thought ran across Karl's mind. *Had this kid been here all the time I was in school and I never noticed him? How many cool people are there that I just never paid any attention to?*

Eric pointed the direction for Karl to turn until they ended up in a nice neighborhood not far from the school. It wasn't Falling Waters, but it was a nice place. There were trees on both sides of the street that had branches that almost touched. It felt like driving through a woodsy tunnel.

Eric pointed to a two-story house with white columns in front. Before he climbed out, he said, "Are you sure you want to learn how to golf?"

"Yeah, why?"

"Because you're already good at a sport that people care about around here. That's enough to make you popular. There is no golf team at Middle Falls."

"I don't care about any of that."

"You are an unusual jock."

"And you are an unusual brainiac."

Eric thought about that, then smiled. "True. See ya!" He pulled the clubs and basket out of the back seat and ran toward his front door.

Karl had just met Eric, but already felt at least a little less lonely.

Chapter Fourteen

When Karl got back to his house, he saw that his father's truck was parked in the driveway.

Finley had died three years before Karl. Still, he was a little surprised that he didn't really feel any strong surge of emotion thinking about seeing his dad again.

Even when Finley was alive, he had been a ghost for the last twenty years of Karl's life.

Still, when Karl walked in the house and saw his dad sitting in his recliner watching television, he felt a pull of happiness. He reminded himself that in Finley's mind, he had seen Karl very recently, so he didn't make a big fuss about it.

"Hey, Dad."

Finley tipped a squat Olympia Beer bottle in Karl's general direction.

More than anything, Karl wished he could have told his father that he had just seen his mother. That in some life, somewhere, she was still alive. He wondered what that life looked like after he died. Would the two of them have been consumed by grief like he and his dad were after losing his mom? Or would they have found a way to pick up the pieces and go on?

He thought it was more likely that it was like it was now between him and his dad. Distance. Not great communication. A divide that couldn't be breached. Suddenly, he didn't feel so good about saving his mother. Was he dooming them both to a bad life?

These were questions that he knew he could never answer.

Karl felt lost and at loose ends the rest of the day. He still wasn't even sure if it was Saturday or Sunday. He decided to find out at least that much. He grabbed his keys out of the bowl and said, "I'm going to the store. You need anything?"

"Got everything I need," Finley said, lifting his beer bottle slightly.

Karl drove to Sammy's Corner Grocery and went inside. He felt a sense of nostalgia for this little store. Sammy had died and the store had been torn down to make room for a U-Store-It a few years later. Now it was here again.

Karl dug a quarter out of the Falcon's ashtray and headed inside. Just inside the front door, there was a newspaper rack. He saw the date on the front page: *Sunday, September 27,* 1981. It also said that the Sunday paper cost fifty cents, so he picked up a Snickers candy bar instead.

If it was 1981—then he was right at the beginning of his senior year. He had finally been dropped at a point where he could do something about the way his life had gone. Where it had gone wrong, more specifically.

For the first time since his first death, he let himself feel a little optimistic. The next day he would turn eighteen again. He remembered that was when Lisa Hanson had trapped him into taking Anna to Homecoming.

He thought about that on the ride home and off and on for the rest of the day.

What was the best way to approach that?

He thought the safest thing would be to stay away from Lisa altogether, or just tell her *no* when she buttonholed him.

At the same time, he thought it would be safe to go to the dance with Anna and just not sleep with her. Nothing bad should come out of that, and as much as he hated to admit it, he really did miss Anna.

Plus, he would have the secret advantage of knowing so much about her while she knew nothing about him.

This time, he knew how much she liked him.

When he went to bed that night, he still wasn't sure what he wanted to do.

He soon fell into the deep, almost trance-like sleep that always visited him during his first sleep in a new life.

His alarm woke him the next morning, though it had obviously been going off for an extended time when he finally regained consciousness.

It was Karl's eighteenth birthday and there was nothing in the house to eat. Unlike his first trip through this birthday, he didn't stop and get a snack at Smith and Son's. He didn't want to be any later to first period than he already was.

This day, he didn't arrive close to the opening bell and Mr. Polk was well into his lecture. The door squeaked when he opened it and though Karl made an exaggerated tiptoeing motion across the back of the classroom, Polk called him out.

"Late again, Mr. Strong?"

"It's my birthday today?" Karl said. It was the only excuse he could think of.

"Charming. Happy birthday. My gift to you is an hour's detention. Can you fit that into your celebratory schedule?"

"Yessir," Karl said while the class roused momentarily from their lecture-induced stupor to giggle at him.

Karl soon joined them and tried to plan a strategy to get through this day. He knew he could fake his way through English and he wouldn't have any trouble with the shop classes. But he had long since forgotten any of the math or science he had learned in high school. He hadn't needed any of it while he sat on the line at the box factory.

In between classes, he decided to hurry to the office and make up a story about losing his locker combination. And his locker number. He wasn't sure what the story would be, but he figured he would come up with something. It wasn't like he was trying to do anything wrong, he just needed access to his own books.

Somehow, he had forgotten that this was the exact time that Lisa Hanson was lying in wait for him.

"Hey, stranger," a girl's voice said from behind. "You ignoring me?"

A small shudder ran down his spine.

"Hey, Lisa. No, why?"

"Just wondering who you are taking to Homecoming. Big football star such as yourself shouldn't go stag."

"I'm not going."

"I think you need to take Anna."

Karl didn't feel the need to play dumb and say *Anna who?* this time. He glanced over Lisa's shoulder and saw Anna standing there, shifting nervously from one foot to the other. Seeing her so uncertain and vulnerable did something to Karl.

At the point of decision, he made up his mind. "Okay, I'll ask her." He didn't even try to get away as he waited for the second half of the trap to close on him. Lisa didn't need to reach out and grab him this time.

Instead, she leaned back a little and said, "Anna? Karl's got something to ask you."

"Oh really?" Anna said, hurrying over as though this hadn't been part of some well-laid plan. "What's that?"

Karl felt suddenly warm standing so close to Anna. He couldn't help but hold this moment up against the first time it happened. Anna was a stranger then, but not now. The pain of slowly devolving into a divorce washed away. What remained—at least for that moment—was what he had grown to feel about her.

He took an almost involuntary step toward her, so he was standing less than a foot away. He didn't reach out and touch her, but there was a noticeable charge of electricity in the air.

"Anna Masterson, will you go to Homecoming with me?"

Anna looked away, suddenly shy at the intensity with which Karl asked the question. Lisa gave her a quick elbow to the ribs.

"Yes," Anna said. "Yes, of course I'll go with you." She smiled broadly and, as if remembering her next part in the charade, she started to fumble in her jeans pocket, looking for something.

Now Karl did reach out and touch her, laying a soft hand on her arm. "I'll pick you up at six that night. We can go to Artie's before the dance. And what color is your dress? I want to get a corsage that matches it."

Anna's mouth fell open.

Lisa took a step back, fanning herself. She made a *whoo* sound, then said, "Karl Strong, you're a surprising boy. I never knew you had it in you."

Karl patted Anna's elbow and smiled. "I don't need your address. I can find you." He turned and walked away, leaving a small coterie of teen girls gaping at him.

He felt a little lost for the rest of that day. He was surprised at how much he had forgotten. Not just his studies, but his schedule, where classes were held, who people were. He had led multiple lives since then, but each was short, lasting only a few days. It had been less than sixteen years since he had attended Middle Falls High, but many of those memories had apparently leaked out his ears while he slept.

He did manage to solve his pressing problems, though, such as where his locker was. He waited until a freshman girl was working as an aide in the office. He approached her and said, "Do you know who I am?"

The young girl's eyes grew a little wide and she nodded vigorously. "Karl Strong."

"Good. I need you to pull my file and give me my locker combination. It's a little sticky and I wonder if I've gotten the numbers mixed up."

She didn't hesitate. She whirled around, pulled a cabinet drawer open and ran her fingers along a row of files. After she pulled one out, she looked inside and said, "38-12-24."

"Yep, that's right," Karl said. "Lock must have gotten a little sticky. I'll bring some WD-40 tomorrow." Casually, he wrote the number on a piece of scrap paper. "And that is locker number…?"

"417."

Karl winked at her and said, "You pass." He jotted the locker number on the same sheet of paper and stuck it in his pocket.

If the girl thought it was weird that he had to write down information he said he already knew, she didn't show it.

Chapter Fifteen

Karl had football practice after school. He saw Coach Bulski in the coaches' office, talking on the phone. Karl couldn't help but wonder if he was getting the phone call from his doctor at that very moment. He wished that there was something he could do but knew full well that there wasn't.

By saving his mother, he had realized that he could change other people's fates, but there was nothing he could do for Coach Bulski.

He dressed in his practice uniform and ran out onto the track. Coach Shield was waiting for the team, clipboard in hand. He ran the team through their normal calisthenics regimen, and Karl reveled in how strong he was, how much stamina he had.

Even the hated leg lifts felt fine. Nothing like dying over and over to make you appreciate being healthy.

Shield focused in on Karl before they ran their laps, but Karl took it good naturedly. He let Coach Shield lead the pack around the first corner, then easily pulled up beside him and quietly said, "Come on, old man," then zoomed away.

That inspired Shield to sprint after him, but it was no use. Karl easily outdistanced him and breezed across the finish line a dozen strides ahead of anyone else.

Danny Jenkins finished second behind him and poked Karl in the chest when he crossed the finish line. "What got into you, boy? Was there something chasing you?"

"Just want to work on my conditioning!"

"Just want to work on my conditioning," Danny said, mockingly. More quietly, he said, "You're making us look bad, brother."

Karl slapped Danny on the back and said, "So you're saying you don't want to race over to the practice field?" Danny's answer was muffled, but Karl thought it might have been an invitation to commit an unlikely act.

Karl shook his head as he jogged over to the practice field. He slowed when he saw the working men leaning up against the fence, offering commentary as the team passed. He had a new perspective on them.

"Good hustle out there, Strong," one of the men said as Karl jogged past.

"Youth is wasted on the young, isn't it?" Karl said with his lopsided grin.

Everything about the rest of the practice felt good to Karl. Even the scrimmage, where he got hit hard on every play was a miracle of sorts. He would take a helmet to the thigh or ribs and then bounce right back up, ready for more.

After practice, he got in the Falcon to drive home and noticed that the gas tank was on empty.

"How the hell did I keep gas in this beast when I didn't have a job?" he muttered to himself. He pulled out the ashtray and saw some coins there. When he added them all together, the total came to just over a dollar.

He pulled into the 76 station and saw that gas was $1.29 per gallon. A guy that Karl vaguely recognized as someone who had graduated the year before came out and said, "Hey, Karl. Fill 'er up?"

"You're funny. This is the sum total of my wealth."

The pump jockey nodded. Pumping less than a gallon of gas for a teenager wasn't completely unheard of.

He unscrewed the gas cap and quickly put the gas in.

Karl turned the engine on and saw that the fuel gauge barely moved off of empty.

"Anything else?"

"Yeah, you guys hiring?"

"Nah. There's barely enough hours to keep me and my brother working."

"How did you guys get on here?"

"Our uncle owns the place," he said with an apologetic shrug.

"You've got your own vehicle, though. You should check with Pizza! Pizza! Pizza! I heard they're looking for a delivery driver."

"Thanks, man." Karl tipped a salute and pulled away. He thought about asking his dad if he could get him on at the box factory, but he knew that wouldn't work. They didn't have any part-time jobs, and they didn't hire kids that were still in high school. With Homecoming coming up, he knew he would need at least a few bucks. He didn't want to be caught without a corsage again, especially since he'd told Anna he was buying her one.

He dreaded having to go through his dad's closet looking for something to wear, too.

Pizza delivery driver was not a dream job by any means, but Karl could see the advantages of it. He thought he would get a salary, but while he was waiting for that, he guessed he would probably get some tips, too. Looking at his gas gauge, he knew he would need that.

Karl and his dad had always been Shakey's Pizza customers. They liked it better than what everyone called 3P—Pizza! Pizza! Pizza! But customer loyalty had nothing to do with getting a job, so Karl pulled off the main drag and into the parking lot of 3P.

He saw the immediate contrast between Shakey's and 3P. Shakey's was on the main drag as you headed out of town toward the Silvery Moon Drive-in Theater. It was a newer building with a great atmosphere.

3P was in an old building off a side street. Most of its business was takeout and delivery, but there was a sitting area where someone could eat their pizza if they wanted. There was no atmosphere, though—just plain white walls and scarred-up wooden tables and chairs.

Karl sighed, then got out of the Falcon and pushed inside 3P. A red-headed kid that looked like he was still in high school said, "Welcome to Pizza! Pizza! Pizza! Can I take your order?" His lack of enthusiasm was noticeable.

"Is the manager in?"

"That's me," the kid said. "Why, did we mess up your order? If you ate part of the pizza, there's no refund."

"No, I just heard you were looking for a driver."

The kid glanced out the front window at the Falcon and said, "That yours?"

"Yep."

"Got insurance?"

"Yep."

"Can you prove it?"

Karl didn't answer but went out to the glove box and fished out his proof of insurance. He went back inside and laid it on the counter.

"Want to start right now?"

"What?"

"I said, do you want to start right now? My driver just called and said his car broke down. Is your car broken down?"

"No."

"Do you want to work? Minimum wage, but you get to keep your tips. Oh, and you'll need all this." He laid a thick magnetic pad with the P3 logo on it on the table, then dropped a bright red shirt and hat, also with the logo.

"The magnet goes on the side of your car. Whenever you're delivering, you need to have it on there. You can leave it there all the time if you want. Great way to pick up chicks."

Karl wrinkled his brow. "Really?"

"No, dummy, not really. What girl wants to be seen with the pizza delivery driver. So what do you say? Want the gig?"

Karl was feeling a small nag of regret. Any job so easy to get probably wasn't a huge opportunity. On the other hand, it would solve his immediate problem of needing gas and money for Homecoming.

"When do I get paid?"

"Every Friday." He reached under the counter and produced a single sheet of paper. "Here. Fill this out, but don't take too long. I've got a pizza in the window waiting for delivery. I'm Red, by the way. From now on, I'm your boss."

Karl was at least five inches taller than Red and figured he was probably a year or two older, but that didn't bother him. "What would you have done if I hadn't come in just now?"

"I don't have to worry about that, do I?" Red said, pushing the application and a P3 pen across to Karl. "Just fill in the top section for right now. I've got you started on the clock," he looked up at the P3 clock overhead, "ten minutes ago. Let's go!"

Karl leaned over the counter and quickly filled in his name, address, phone number and social security number, then slipped off the T-shirt he had worn to school that day and put on the P3 shirt. He noticed it was a little stained around the neck. He put the bright red hat on and said, "I guess I won't be sneaking up on anyone."

"That's the idea," Red said, returning from the kitchen with a zippered red container. "Address is on the receipt. You know your way around town?"

"I guess so. Pretty well."

"If you get lost, find a payphone and call me. I've got a map in the back, and I'll help you find it."

Karl saluted, picked up the insulated bag, and headed for the Falcon.

"You forgot your magnet!" Red called.

"Right, right." Karl grabbed the magnetic sign and pushed out into the night. He felt a little dizzy. He'd been in this life for less than two days and he was already changing things. When he thought about the way his previous life had gone, he decided that was not a bad thing.

He headed for his delivery and soon realized it was a familiar street. In fact, he had been on it just the day before. He followed the house numbers and soon saw that he was driving to the exact same house where he had dropped Eric off.

"Huh. Well, it was bound to happen that I delivered to someone I knew." He hopped out of the car with the pizza bag and walked up the driveway to the front door. He rang the doorbell and listened as the sound echoed through the house.

A minute later, the door swung open and Eric looked at Karl in surprise. "Sweet gig."

"Is it?" Karl asked.

"Do you get free pizza?"

"I dunno. Maybe."

"If so, it's a sweet gig."

"You're my first delivery." Karl unzipped the bag a little awkwardly, trying to balance the boxes while he opened the bag. "$8.72."

Eric handed over a twenty-dollar bill.

"Oh, crap. I just started and they didn't give me anything to make change with. Got anything smaller?"

"Nah," Eric said. "But it's okay. It's my dad's money. He won't care."

Karl had a hard time understanding not caring where eleven dollars went, but he shrugged and said, "Cool. I can give it to you at school."

"Don't worry about it. Thanks for the pizza. Still want to learn how to golf?"

"Sure do."

"Meet me at the school on Saturday morning, maybe around ten?"

"Howsabout I come and pick you up here, so you don't have to walk all the way there?"

"Sounds good. I'll have some of my dad's old clubs for you."

Karl waved and hurried back to the car. He drove straight back to the 76 station. The same guy came out. He looked at the magnet on the car and the way Karl was dressed.

"Weren't you just in here?"

"Life moves pretty fast," Karl said, quoting a movie that wouldn't come out for another five years.

"I'd say so!"

Karl handed him the twenty-dollar bill and said, "Put five dollars in."

This time, when Karl turned the engine over, the needle actually moved to between a quarter and a half-tank.

Karl turned out of the gas station and headed back to P3.

Don't You Want Me by The Human League was playing on KMFR. Karl sang along, changing the words slightly. "Don't, don't chew on me..."

At least early on, this life was shaping up pretty well.

Chapter Sixteen

Karl was busy over the next few weeks. He was optimistic about his future for the first time in many lifetimes, and so wanted to make sure that his grades stayed up. The thing that rankled him the most about his first life was that he had met his goal. He had earned the athletic scholarship that he had worked so hard for but had been forced by circumstances to give it up. Keeping his grades up meant he had homework most nights. He also had football practice for two hours after school, then drove straight to Pizza! Pizza! Pizza! when practice let out.

In addition to that, once or twice a week, he picked Eric up and they drove to the school to hit golf balls around. Eric said that Karl wasn't exactly a natural, but he had good size and strength. He even said that if he could learn a better swing and be consistent with it, he would be an okay golfer.

In some ways, this killer schedule was good for him. It kept him constantly moving and didn't give him a lot of time to worry about the many strange turns his lives had taken.

He made a point of finding Anna in the halls a few times and even started to eat lunch with her. He knew her very well, of course, but he kept in mind that he was still a stranger to her. He thought it would be better if she felt like she knew him at least a little.

He hadn't decided on whether or not he wanted to continue to have a relationship with her after Homecoming, but he wanted to build a better foundation in case he did.

He built up his bankroll enough that he had a few dollars put away. He never got a tip as big as the one he'd gotten on his first delivery, but almost every house he dropped off at gave him a dollar or two. Along with his wages and the fact that he didn't burn much gas since Middle Falls was so small, he managed to put more than fifty dollars away.

The Wednesday before the dance, he stopped at Newman's Clothing in between practice and reporting to work.

It was early October and Middle Falls had moved into autumn. Leaves collected against buildings or swirled around the streets, blown by cars and trucks. The temperature had dropped into what Coach Shield had called *real football weather*.

Inside Newman's, it was quiet. In fact, the front of the store was completely empty when he walked in. The door made a soft bong that sounded at the rear of the store, though, and a nicely dressed woman hurried out around the counter.

"How can I help you?"

"I've got Homecoming this weekend. I could use a new shirt and maybe a pair of slacks, but I don't have a lot of money."

The woman, who appeared to be in her late twenties, took in Karl at a glance. "Medium shirt? Twenty-nine-inch waist, or thirty?"

Karl looked a little helpless. He had no idea.

"No problem." She reached for a cloth measuring tape and stepped close to Karl. "Won't take but a second." She stretched the tape around his waist at the hipbones and said, "Thirty. Well, those are what we call our *heart sizes*, which means that they don't often go on clearance. But there are a few things that I've been thinking about marking down anyway. Let's see if they fit you."

She went to a round rack toward the back of the store and pulled off a pair of dark slacks and a white shirt. "Here. Try these on."

Karl accepted the clothes and went to the very back of the store, where the dressing rooms were. He had showered after football practice, so he wasn't worried about getting the nice new clothes smelly. He slipped on the shirt and pants, then stepped out and looked in the mirror. If he ignored the fact that he needed a haircut, he looked like a whole new man.

"I thought so," the woman said, a note of pride evident. "Perfect."

"They look great, but how much are they?" Karl had looked at the price tags and saw that between the shirt and pants, they would take almost all the money he had saved.

"I could let them go for thirty-five dollars."

Karl did some calculations in his head. By the time he put gas in the Falcon, bought the corsage, and took Anna out to Artie's, he would be in the hole.

The woman saw his expression and smiled. "I could reduce them a little more, if that would help. How about thirty dollars?"

Karl smiled and said, "Sure. Thank you." He went back to the dressing room and put on his jeans and P3 T-shirt.

Two minutes later, he was lighter in the wallet, but had a slick plastic bag with the Newman's logo on it sitting beside him as he drove to work. He felt good about having the biggest item checked off his Homecoming to-do list. He glanced at his watch and saw that if he stopped at the florist's shop, he would be late to work.

He did it anyway. The idea of having everything set for his date with Anna that Saturday was worth getting chewed out a little by Red. It went much quicker than he had guessed with the florist—who had already processed dozens of similar orders in the previous few days—and he was only two minutes late arriving at P3.

His first order of the day took him to the Covington Arms condos. He had delivered there before and knew the drill. Park in the basement garage, take the elevator to whatever floor the delivery went to, then look for the right condo.

For this delivery, he had a large cheese pizza to deliver to the third floor. He knocked on the door and when it swung open, he could smell marijuana and incense even stronger than the pizza he was holding.

"Pizza delivery."

The man in front of him looked like a holdout from the sixties. He wore faded old Middle Falls High School P.E. shorts and a tie-dyed shirt. He had a bushy beard and long black hair that stuck out at odd angles.

"Right on," the man said, and the picture was complete. He sounded a lot like Tommy Chong. "Hang on, I'll get my wallet."

The man retreated back into his condo but left the door open. Karl leaned a little to his right and saw the source of what he was smelling. An oddly shaped bong sat on the coffee table, a curl of smoke still rising up.

Karl looked a little nervously to his left and right. Marijuana was illegal in all fifty states in 1981, and though he knew the scare movies they played at school were baloney, it still made him a little nervous.

He glanced at the receipt on top of the bag. *Masterson, Large Cheese.*

The man returned with a smile and some bills in his hand.

"$8.05, Mr. Masterson."

"Just Moondog. Mr. Masterson was my father." He handed a ten-dollar bill and two singles to Karl. "Thanks, man. Much appreciated."

Karl handed the pizza over and said, "Thanks. Uh, Mr. Masterson? I mean...Moondog?" Karl's tongue stumbled over that offbeat name.

Moondog was starting to close the door, but stopped and said, "Mmm-hmm?"

Karl blushed a little and wished he hadn't started this conversation. "Umm, I'm taking a girl whose last name is Masterson to the Homecoming dance tomorrow."

"Far out. That must be Anna? I didn't know she was old enough to go to a high school dance."

"She's a junior," Karl said a little defensively, as though he had been accused of robbing the cradle.

"Time flies," Moondog said. "She's my cousin. Her father was my dad's brother. They're both gone now."

"My condolences."

"Ah, neither was a very nice person. Anna always seemed like a sweet girl, though." He paused for a moment, then said, "Hang on just a second." He turned, put the pizza on his kitchen counter, then hurried away again. When he returned, he put a ten-dollar bill in Karl's hand. "No need to tell her who it's from but take her out to Artie's or something on me."

Karl couldn't pinpoint exactly why, but this unexpected gesture of kindness from this strange man moved him. His throat felt thick, and he had a sudden fear tears were going to form.

"Really nice of you, Mr...., I mean, Moondog. Thank you."

Moondog waved the thank you off and closed the door. With fourteen dollars in a single tip, Karl felt suddenly wealthy and whistled his way to the elevator.

〈 〉

THE FARTHER KARL GOT from the point where he woke up in this life, the more things changed.

The Homecoming game, for example. Everything about the game was different, though the end result was the same.

This game, Karl did manage to get into the endzone—twice. Part of that was that as long as it had been since he had played this game the first time, he remembered number forty-five. Every time Danny Jenkins tossed him the ball, he kept his eye out for the hard-hitting safety.

The final score was 21-0, and the Homecoming crowd went home happy.

Walking off the field, dirty and sweaty and with his long hair hanging in his face, Karl saw Anna coming off the grandstands. He jogged over to her, reached down, and kissed her cheek.

Some wit in the crowd crowed, "Number twenty-two scores twice on the field and once off it."

That embarrassed Karl, but not Anna. She looked at the man who said it, then stood on her tiptoes, put her arms around Karl's neck, and kissed him on the lips. She even raised one foot for effect.

That really did embarrass Karl, but it also sent an electric shock through him.

"See you tomorrow night," Anna said. The way she said it promised many good things, but Karl was intent on having a chaste night. As long as his brain was the organ in his body that was working, everything would go according to plan.

As he walked through the crowd on the way to the locker room, he got slapped on the back and received a dozen cheers and well wishes. In Karl's mind, though, he was four years younger and he remembered sprinting after his mother, trying desperately to save her. Succeeding, yet failing.

Karl shook his head to clear out that memory, which was lost in time. He had been forced to reevaluate how time worked. He no longer believed it was a one-way stream flowing from the past to the future. He knew he could be plucked from one point in time, picked up, and dropped in at any earlier point.

What he had no idea about was how it worked, or why.

Karl showered and changed back into his jeans and flannel shirt. He was still overheated from the game, so even though it was a chilly night with temps in the low forties, he slung his jacket over his shoulder and stepped into the parking lot.

Anna was standing nervously beside the Falcon. When she saw him come out of the locker room, she brightened and said, "This is your car, isn't it?"

"Such as it is," Karl agreed.

"I like it. It's cute. Like you."

Karl reached up and ruffled his wet hair self-consciously.

Anna stepped toward him, stopping only when she was less than a foot from him. "You are, you know. Cute."

Karl had been intent on playing things completely cool until they got past Homecoming. Standing in the darkened parking lot, with Anna in front of him, a flood of memories poured through him. The good ones. The fun they'd had when they were first married and living in her mother's house. How beautiful she was, lying naked across their bed in the moonlight.

All the other bad thoughts couldn't find any purchase in his mind.

"I think you're beautiful." It was the only thought in his head and he meant it.

Anna's dimples showed as she smiled. She didn't contradict him but looked at the ground, suddenly shy.

"Thank you." When she raised her chin again, her eyes were burning with intensity. "Can you give me a ride home? My friend flaked out on me."

Karl didn't ask which friend. He knew she was telling him a lie so she could spend more time with him and he didn't want to make her lie more.

"Sure." Karl opened the passenger door for her. This time, there was no mixture of cat pee and cologne, it was pure, unaltered cat urine. "Sorry for the smell. It's always that way. I've tried to get rid of it..."

"It's fine," Anna said, softly laying a hand on his arm. "I appreciate the ride."

Karl hurried around to the other side and climbed in. "I'll get some degrees going in here," he said, starting the engine and turning the heat on high.

Anna didn't make a quip about "I'll give you some degrees," or anything silly like that. Instead, she reached out and pulled him to her. She kissed him with soft, parted lips.

It had been a very long time—any number of lifetimes—since Karl had been kissed. And kissed like that? He wasn't sure he ever had been.

Anna pulled back and looked searchingly into Karl's eyes. He had never thought he would be so close to her beautiful hazel eyes again and at that moment he felt like he was falling into them.

Without realizing it, Karl pressed down on the gas and the engine roared, or as much as a Falcon's engine could roar.

This time Anna couldn't resist. "That got your engine going, huh?"

"Umm, yeah." Now it was Karl's turn to search Anna's face. "Maybe I better take you home."

"Oh, sure, that would be great," Anna said, reaching into her small purse for her lip gloss. She uncapped it and rolled it across her lips. "Or, whatever." She glanced at Karl. "We could go up to the Falls."

That was a new twist. In their eight years of marriage, they had never been up to the great make-out spot of Middle Falls. Things had progressed too quickly for them. They skipped right over the steamy windows part of teenage love and jumped straight to matrimony, where they calmly discussed school work and rumors while getting undressed before jumping into bed.

Karl tried not to think about kissing Anna like he just had. He tried to think about anything other than Anna and the lip gloss she was still applying.

He knew any excuse he might make would sound lame. What teenage boy is *too tired* to go make out with a pretty, willing girl?

"I think we should maybe save that for tomorrow night."

"I might have something else planned for tomorrow night." She reached out and laid a hand on Karl's thigh.

His brain was rapidly shutting down.

He shook his head and made a funny sound with his lips.

That made Anna giggle and the moment—the heat—was momentarily broken. She removed her hand from his leg, though Karl could feel the warmth linger there.

Karl let the lopsided grin fade from his face. "I really do like you, though."

"I'll take that for right now." She sighed. "Okay, take me home."

Karl did.

Chapter Seventeen

Karl woke up early the next morning. It was probably his imagination, but he swore he could still feel the warmth of Anna's lips on his and the tingle of her touch on his leg.

He jumped out of bed and without even brushing his teeth, he picked up a bag of cleaning supplies he had bought the day before. He looked outside and saw that it was a typical fall day.

He really wanted to be able to throw both doors of the Falcon open and get some airflow through the interior. The rain was blowing sideways, though.

An idea hit him and he grabbed his keys out of the bowl and carried the cleaning supplies out to the car. The cold weather had tamped the cat smell down a little, but it was still noticeable. He slid behind the wheel and drove to the elementary school. A gravel road led behind the school to a covered play area. There were monkey bars and basketball hoops, but also plenty of open space.

He never would have gotten away with parking on the asphalt surface during the week, but unless a janitor was inside, the school should be empty. It was still chilly, but at least he was out of the rain. He threw the doors open and left the car running.

Now that he had a job, he was able to keep gas in the car and wasn't constantly worried about running out. He cranked the radio up and KMFR was playing a commercial. "Come on, come on," he said, wanting some tunes. At that moment, he thought of buying an

8-track player and installing it so that he wasn't so dependent on the radio station for music.

KMFR came through for him after the commercial ended, though. Boston's *Foreplay/Long Time* played, and that seemed like excellent car cleaning music.

Karl had tried to eradicate the cat smell a number of times before, but this time he was serious. He pulled the carpeting up and revealed the floor underneath. Sure enough, there was a stain on both the underside of the carpet and a brown residue on the floorboards.

He dropped the carpeting on the asphalt and sprayed 409 on the stained floorboards. He almost wished he'd thought to bring some bleach, but that would likely be replacing one strong smell with another.

For the next ninety minutes, Karl attacked the car with a vengeance. He had bought some spray carpet cleaner and used that on both sides of the carpeting, scrubbing it vigorously. When he thought he had done all he could with the carpet, he detailed the rest of the car, using Windex and Armor All.

After he was done, the Falcon shined like it never had before. He put everything back in place and for the final touch, hung a scented Little Trees Air Freshener from the rearview mirror.

He stood back and looked at his handiwork, satisfied.

That smell might come back someday, but for now, it's gone, and that's good enough.

He gathered up the cleaning supplies in the Safeway bag and headed for the only car wash in Middle Falls.

There was no fancy drive-through car wash in town, just a small two-bay affair where you dropped a few quarters in and a hose sprayed out soapy water. The weather was so crappy, Karl thought it was possible that the owner of the Sudsy Clean Car Wash might have shut it off for the winter, but instead found that it was just empty.

Karl hopped out, put four quarters into the slot, and did his best to knock the accumulated mud and dirt off.

When he got home, he was surprised to see that it was still before noon. His dad's truck was parked in the driveway, so Karl pulled in behind it.

The house was dark, lit only by the flickering light of the television. Finley sat in his recliner, watching a golf tournament.

"You like golf, Dad?" Karl was a little surprised but had a sudden vision of the two of them playing a round on the municipal course.

"It's the only thing on other than gardening shows. Weekend television is the worst."

Karl nodded and retreated to his room. He had hours to kill before it was time to pick Anna up for dinner and he had already accomplished everything he needed to. He still had a lot of nervous energy, though. He didn't want to just sit around the house and watch golf with Finley until the time came to get in the shower.

He popped up off the bed and went to the kitchen. He picked the phone up, dialed a number and said, "I'm bored. Wanna hit a few balls around?"

On the other end of the line, Eric said, "I'm no weatherman, but it doesn't look like good conditions for golf."

"I've got a spot. You game?"

"Sure, I guess."

"Grab your clubs and your bucket of balls and I'll see you in ten minutes."

Karl headed for the front door, saying, "See ya, Dad."

"You a golfer now?"

"No, not really. I've just got a friend that's showing me a few things. I'm terrible."

"Too bad. You should see what those guys earn when they win a tournament. It's ridiculous."

"I might be able to earn a few bucks as a caddy, but I think that's the only way I'll ever get any money from golf."

"Stick to football. You're good at that."

"Thanks, Dad," Karl said as he pushed out the front door. He had considered saying *How do you know I'm good at football when you never come see me play?* but he wasn't interested in having that conversation. His dad had made his choices and Karl didn't think there was anything he could do about it.

He picked Eric up at his house and drove them back to the covered play area at the back of the elementary school.

Eric gave Karl the side eye and said, "Won't we get in trouble?"

Karl opened his eyes wide and looked left and right. "From who?"

"Whom," Eric corrected. "Okay, let's see what we can do. Maybe we can practice our putting or our chip shots."

They created a few different games to play. One, where they stood under one basket and tried to chip a ball across the play area and hit the basket on the other side. One point for hitting the backboard, five if you managed to put a ball through the hoop.

Eric waxed Karl at that game and every other bastardized game they could think of. Karl took it all in stride. All he was interested in was killing some time and if he wasn't staring at his ceiling in his bedroom, he felt like he was ahead of the game.

They had been goofing around under the cover for almost two hours when a yellow pickup pulled up behind the Falcon. The door of the truck read *Middle Falls School District*.

A middle-aged man got out of the truck. "You guys heading to the golf course and took a left turn at Albuquerque or somethin'?"

"Yeah, I guess so. Probably shouldn't be here," Karl said.

"Probably not." The man looked at the two of them a little closer. "Hey, you're that Strong boy, aren't you?"

"Yep."

"Good game last night. You're having a good season. Now it's time to move along, right?"

"Right!" Karl and Eric said together and ran around like madmen picking up the scattered golf balls.

Fifteen minutes later, Karl was home and it was finally time for him to take his shower and get ready to pick up Anna.

His father was gone again, and Karl didn't have to wonder where. It gave him the house to himself, though.

He went to the old record player that they'd had in the family for a decade. Karl had never bothered to buy any albums of his own, so the musical selection was pitiful, at least by his standards.

He flipped through albums by Nat 'King' Cole, The Lettermen, Herb Alpert and the Tijuana Brass, and was just about to give up and turn his clock radio on in his bedroom, when he saw *Meet the Beatles*. He shrugged, pulled the vinyl out of the sleeve, and dropped it on the turntable.

He wasn't sure it would even work. He couldn't remember if he or his dad had played it since his mom had died, but he didn't think so.

He dropped the needle and a static-y hiss came through the speakers, though. The volume was turned low, but *I Wanna Hold Your Hand* was not the kind of song that should be played quietly. He cranked it up until the speakers distorted a little, then backed it up a notch.

Karl tried singing along, but didn't know the words, so settled for singing the chorus and leaving the rest to The Beatles.

He jumped in the shower, still attempting to sing along with every song. When he got out, the first side was finished. He flipped it over while he got dressed. He didn't like that side as well, so flipped it back over and listened to Side One again.

By the time it finished a second time, he was dressed in his new clothes and his hair as combed as it ever was. He hadn't had enough money to buy a pair of dress shoes, so he laced up his Chuck Taylors. He thought that added a slightly irreverent look to the dress clothes anyway.

He had picked up Anna's corsage at the florist's the day before and stored it in the refrigerator, next to the milk and the case of Olympia Beer. He was sure his dad had seen it but hadn't mentioned it. Karl tried to imagine what it would be like to be in what he pictured as a normal family, where parents talked to children and were at least a little involved in their lives.

He shook his head and put that thought down as non-productive, then grabbed the small plastic container that held the corsage and hurried out the door.

He pulled up in front of Anna's house at 6:00 on the dot and looked inside, remembering the scene the first time he had picked her up. Remembering how he had moved in as a new groom on their wedding day.

He took a deep breath, reminded himself how he wanted the night to go and stepped up to the front door.

Chapter Eighteen

Things were different on this night, right from the get-go. For one thing, Karl had told Anna that they were going to go to Artie's before the dance, so he was there an hour earlier.

This time when he knocked on the door, Anna didn't answer. Instead, it was her uncle, James Masterson. He wasn't wearing his State Trooper uniform, but he was every bit as intimidating. Karl reminded himself that he had never met him in this life.

"Hello, I'm Karl Strong. Is Anna here?"

James held out a hand that engulfed Karl's. "Nice to see a polite young man that introduces himself. I'm Anna's uncle, James. I wanted to be here to see her off. Come in, make yourself comfortable."

Karl looked hopefully around for Anna, but she was nowhere to be seen.

"You know how it is," James said. "Young ladies always take a bit longer to get ready, but it's always worth it, isn't it?"

"Yes, sir."

James pointed Karl to a seat on the couch, then sat at the other end. Karl looked straight ahead.

"Son," James said. "I don't know if you're aware, but Anna's father passed away last year. It's been very difficult for the family."

Karl had already heard this lecture once before, albeit under slightly different circumstances. He turned his attention to Mr. Masterson and nodded gravely.

"That's why I'm here. I promised my brother I would help look out for her. My instinct is to be overly protective. I never cared much for that boy she was seeing before. Kenny, something or other. He didn't seem respectful."

Anna walked into the room wearing the same pale green dress she had the first time.

Both Karl and James jumped to their feet automatically.

Anna went to her uncle first and reached up to kiss him on the cheek. He leaned down so she could reach him. "Thank you for being here tonight. It means a lot to us."

"I'll always be here," James answered.

Anna turned to look at Karl, who held the plastic container out like an offering.

"You've got to put it on me, silly."

Karl risked a quick glance at James who was looking on with interest.

"I should have practiced this on my dad at home," Karl said, which earned at least a pity chuckle from the towering Mr. Masterson.

Anna tilted her head away and Karl did his best not to stare at her long hair that fell across her neck.

He pinned the corsage on, managing to do it without copping a feel in front of her uncle. Karl had carried the rock over a hundred times for the Middle Falls Bulldogs that season without fumbling once. He managed the same with the corsage.

Candace Masterson emerged from the back of the house and took in the young couple. "Karl, you look so handsome."

"All he needs is a haircut," James offered helpfully.

Candace stepped forward and pushed a curl out of Karl's eyes. "This is the style these days, Jim."

Chastised, James stepped back and it was apparent he would not be offering any more fashion or grooming tips on this night.

Anna and Karl posed in front of the same curtains and Karl once again managed to smirk instead of smile, saved for posterity by the Kodak Instamatic.

Karl glanced at this watch, sure that at least two hours had passed while he was in the house. It had been a little less than fifteen minutes.

Candace noticed Karl's gesture and said, "Oh, fine, you've been good sports. You can go." She looked at Anna. "What time is the dance over again?"

"12:30, but I have to stay after and clean up since I'm on the decorating committee."

Karl put part one of his plan into action. "Oh, you mustn't have heard. When I bought the tickets, they told me the dance ended at 11:00."

Anna turned and looked at Karl as though he had just grown two extra heads. She tried to recover quickly, but not so fast that Mrs. Masterson didn't notice. "Is that right, honey?"

"Must be," Anna said.

"Good boy," James said, clapping Karl on the back and making him take an involuntary half-step forward. "A man should always keep track of things like that."

"Yeah, he should," Anna said, but Karl could see she meant it in a completely different way.

"You're not going anywhere after the dance, are you?" Mrs. Masterson asked.

Anna and Karl looked at each other. "I guess not," Anna said, then corrected herself. "I mean, nope, we're coming straight home."

"If you have to clean up after the dance, I'll give you until 11:30, then. I'll leave the porch light on and wait up for you."

"That's great, Mom."

Karl smiled and nodded. "I'll have her home, don't worry."

Anna cast one more sidelong look at Karl to make sure he hadn't been abducted by aliens, then gave up, went with it, and just laughed a little.

Outside, Karl opened the passenger door for her. When he got in beside her, Anna opened her mouth, but stopped. "Hey. The smell's gone."

"Only a date with you would make me spend two hours scrubbing that smell out."

"That's sweet. So then, you *do* want to spend time with me?"

"Of course. That's why we're going out."

"Then what was the whole Boy Scout thing with Mom and Uncle Jimmy in there?"

"Oh, that. I just wanted us to get off on a good foot. I didn't think lying to your mom was a good start."

"I thought jocks were supposed to have just one thing on their mind."

Before he pulled away, he turned slightly in his seat and looked at Anna. "I'm a little different." Karl didn't like the way that sounded in his ears. "I mean, not *too* different. I do think about that too, of course. It just seems like we should take our time and get to know each other, right?"

Anna raised her eyebrows and said, "Ooookay. Sure."

Karl shifted into gear and acted as though that conversation was closed, even though it obviously wasn't. "I bet Artie's will be crawling with people tonight. We better get going."

"Can't argue with that. I skipped lunch today just so I can have Artie's tonight."

"Gotta watch your girlish figure, right?"

"I've gotta watch it so you'll want to watch it, right?"

"Right," Karl agreed with a laugh.

Karl's prognostication skills were strong. When they pulled into the Artie's parking lot they had to wait for a place to park.

"Look," Anna said. "There's a spot over there without a speaker. Want to just go in?"

"Done." Karl wheeled the Falcon into the parking spot and looked up at the darkening sky. There were heavy clouds, but no rain at that moment. He hurried out and opened Anna's door, then took her hand. They walked into Artie's holding hands and acting like they'd been a couple for a long time.

To Karl, they had been. Anna seemed happy to go along with it.

As busy as the parking lot was, the small dining room was almost empty. One middle-aged couple sat in the corner, silently eating their burgers and fries.

The jukebox was playing an old Elvis Presley song that neither Karl nor Anna knew. While Anna sat in one side of a booth, Karl went to the jukebox and dropped two quarters in. Over his shoulder, he said, "Man, these are old songs! Wait a minute, here we go."

"What did you find?" Anna asked. "Something good?"

"Something that's not a million years old, anyway."

A young woman came out from behind the counter carrying a tray loaded with food. She saw Karl and Anna and said, "When I get back, come on up to the counter and I'll take your order."

"What do you want? Burger basket and a chocolate shake?" Karl asked.

"Yes, but I want a vanilla shake instead."

That stopped Karl cold. In his memory, Anna had always taken a chocolate shake at Artie's. He gave her a look very similar to what she had given him in her living room.

"Really? Vanilla?"

"Yeah. What's wrong with that?"

"I didn't even know they made vanilla shakes at Artie's."

"Of course they do. They're good, too."

Karl chewed on this turn of events as he walked up and stood at the counter. When the waitress came back at a jog, he said, "Two burger baskets and two shakes. One chocolate, one vanilla."

The waitress didn't bother to write anything down, but she shouted the order at the fry cook, who raised his spatula in acknowledgement.

"Maybe we should have gotten here a little earlier," Karl said.

"What's the worst that will happen? That they'll crown the Homecoming Queen without us?"

"Are you really on the decorating committee, so we have to stay after to clean up?"

"Yes and no. Yes, I am really on the decorating committee, but no, we don't have to clean up tonight. We're all meeting tomorrow morning to do that."

Karl let his mouth hang open in shock. "You *lied* to your mother."

Anna slapped his arm. "I was trying to buy us some time to be alone."

"I know," Karl said, grinning. "We're young. We've got our whole lives ahead of us."

"You don't sound so young. You sound kind of old." She didn't mean it badly, it was more like a sudden realization.

Karl curled his arm and flexed his bicep. "Does this look like the muscle of an old man?"

Anna put her hand on his arm and fluttered her eyes. "No *suh*, Mr. Strong. You are strong indeed."

The song Karl had picked out came on the radio. It was *Turning Japanese* by The Vapors.

The fry cook leaned back and stared out into the dining room. Karl waved at him and the guy grinned and went back to his burgers and fries.

"I don't think I even know this song."

"Then I better not tell you what it's really about."

"Is it about turning Japanese?"

"Kind of," Karl said with a shrug and a smile.

The song faded out, then started up again.

"Is this the only song you played?"

"It was the only song I knew!"

Karl was rescued from his total lack of musical diversity when the waitress brought their burger baskets. She set the shakes on the table, saying, "Chocolate for you, and vanilla for you."

"How did you know the vanilla wasn't for me?" Karl asked.

"I just knew. Six-seventy-five."

Karl handed her a ten-dollar bill. She counted his change out, but Karl held up a hand. "Keep the change. You're gonna serve a lot of teenagers tonight and wear yourself ragged. They're not famous for being good tippers, so I'll do what I can."

The woman smiled broadly and said, "Then I suppose I'll have to forgive you for playing this same song over and over."

"I suppose you will," Karl agreed. "By the way," he said to Anna, "this is courtesy of your cousin."

"Wait. How is that possible? Moondog?"

"I'm a man of mystery."

"Moondog never leaves his condo."

"But he does order pizza."

"Ah," Anna said, understanding.

"He seemed like a really cool guy and he gave me the money to buy this spread for you."

"I love him. Mom won't let me go see him by myself, though. She's afraid I'll come back a drug-addicted tea lover."

Karl thought back to the bong he'd seen on Moondog's coffee table. Even growing up in the seventies and early eighties, he was innocent about such things. As an athlete, he'd never wanted to experiment with anything. Even in his thirties, when life had gone to hell for him, he just turned to his father's escape—beer.

Some girls just nibbled at their food when they were on a date, but not Anna. She bit into the soft bun and made a groan of pleasure. "That's what I've been dreaming about all day." She plucked up two of her French fries and dipped them in her vanilla shake.

Karl looked at the shake curiously. "Can I try a little?"

Anna smiled mischievously. "I'm warning you. You'll never go back to chocolate."

"I'll be the judge of that." Karl tipped up the cup and the thick liquid eventually touched his lips. He made a smacking sound and set the shake back on Anna's tray. "Not what I expected. It's got something else in there. Almost like a banana flavor."

"It's Artie's greatest secret."

Karl smacked his lips again and said, "Good, but I've gotta stick with my chocolate."

"I'm so disappointed," Anna said, continuing to smile.

When *I'm Turning Japanese* came on for the fourth time, the fry cook came around the corner and slapped two quarters down in front of Karl. "Sorry, man. Can't take it anymore." He stepped to the jukebox and unplugged it. "I'll turn KMFR up in here."

Karl felt a little embarrassed, but said, "Deal."

"Did you know," Anna asked, "that there used to be a big tower out in front of Artie's and the radio station broadcast from it every Friday night?"

"You're kidding, right?"

"Nope. My mom told me about it. Sometimes I wonder if all the good stuff has already passed us by."

Karl reached out and laid his hand on hers. "Nope. The good stuff is just getting started."

Chapter Nineteen

Karl and Anna held hands as they walked into the dance. Across the room, Karl saw Kenny, Anna's boyfriend until just a few days earlier. He had brought some girl that Karl didn't recognize, which meant she had to be from out of town. Everyone knew everyone else in Middle Falls. Kenny caught Karl's eye and shook his head. Anna did a wonderful job of ignoring him.

Karl considered asking Anna if she knew the girl but decided that probably wasn't necessary.

Just as they had at the first dance, the two of them joined Lisa and Mike, who were the high school equivalent of an old married couple. They had been together so long that everyone just assumed they would get married.

Karl had no idea if history would repeat itself or not, with them getting married, having two daughters, then getting divorced. After all, he was here with a girl who had once been his ex-wife, and he was hoping to find a way to change that future. Karl wasn't interested in marrying Anna. He wanted to go to college and build a life. But he was determined to change the way this night went and then see what happened in their future.

Right on schedule, the lead singer of the band stepped to the front of the stage and said, "We're Rite of Spring. Thanks for having us." The bouncing bass line of the B-52s *Rock Lobster* once again echoed through the empty dance floor.

"That music's never going to work here," Karl said.

"Oh really, Mr. *I'm Turning Japanese?*"

Karl had no answer for that, so they all sat and watched as the band tried another New Wave song, before giving up and playing the classic rock songs the kids wanted to hear.

So many things had changed for Karl since he had woken up in this life. He'd gotten a job at P3. He'd made a new friend in Eric and was picking up a hobby for the first time. But some events, like this Homecoming, seemed to be playing out in a very similar fashion.

Karl thought of how the previous version had ended and once again promised himself that would not happen tonight.

One thing that hadn't changed was that neither Karl nor Mike were very good dancers. Anna and Lisa dragged them out on the dance floor again and again, but it was the girls who really danced.

It didn't matter. They were young and engaging in the important tribal ritual of the high school dance, and they had fun.

The band played a different slow song for the last number of the night—*Always and Forever* by Heatwave, instead of *Please Don't Go* by KC and the Sunshine Band. The music might have changed, but the dance was the same.

Anna melted into Karl. She put her arms around his neck and laid her face against his chest. She pulled him tight, and she felt so warm that Karl hoped the song might go on for an hour or two.

It was a normal-length song, though, and when it ended, Anna stepped away and Karl felt the loss of her. He swallowed hard and said, "Whoo."

"Yeah, whoo. You may not be light on your feet, but you're a good slow dancer."

The dance was over. The lights turned on and everyone headed for the exits. Mike leaned over to Karl and said, "We're going up to the Falls. What about you guys?"

"I promised Anna's mom we'd go straight home."

"Poor you, dude. It looks like Anna's really into you."

Karl looked at Anna, her hair a little damp from sweating while they danced and thought about how beautiful she looked. "Maybe so," was all Karl could say.

They walked out into the cool night air and the two couples went their separate ways. Karl looked up at the sky and saw that the rain clouds had moved on. The stars were out and an almost full moon lit the night, bright enough to cast a nighttime shadow.

"Now," Anna said, taking Karl's hand, "don't you wish you hadn't told Mom we'd be right home?"

Karl didn't answer.

Anna looked at the small silver watch on her wrist. "You know, if we hurry, we could still go somewhere. Is your dad home?"

If we hurry. There was portent and meaning in those words.

"I don't want to hurry anything with you," Karl said honestly.

Anna took a half-step back and said, "What kind of a teenage boy *are* you, Karl Strong?"

"The different kind, I guess. Does that bother you?"

"Well, I like that you're different. That's what makes you *you*, right? It's just not what I'm used to."

"Kenny, you mean?"

"Yeah. He put a lot of pressure on me."

That was the first time Karl had ever heard her mention Kenny, even through all the years they were married.

"You mean about sex?"

"Yeah. He was my first boyfriend, so I guess I just assumed all boys were like that."

"Is that why you guys aren't together anymore?"

"I guess you could say that."

Karl compared that information to what he remembered about their first Homecoming date. Anna was saying that she had broken up with Kenny because she wouldn't have sex with him. But on their first date, it was Anna who was the aggressor. He would have had to be a lot stronger than the average teenage boy was to *not* have sex with her.

None of it made sense.

Then Anna took two steps toward him and hugged him tight. She smelled so good, she felt so good, that whatever thought process he might have had was derailed.

She put her soft lips against his throat and said, "We could at least go up to the Falls for a few minutes, right? Mom won't care about that."

"Yeah...yes, let's do that."

Anna rewarded him with a long, lingering kiss that promised more to come.

Karl opened the door for her and lifted his face up to the cool breeze as he walked around to his side. He was feeling overheated and that was the last thing he wanted. He knew he needed to stick to his guns this first night.

He got in the car and turned to Anna.

"No. Sorry. I just can't. I promised your mom I would bring you straight home. No matter how much I want to go somewhere and be alone with you, I just can't."

Anna had been reaching for Karl's hand, but now she turned her face away and looked out the window. "Is there something wrong with me?"

"God no. Anna, I love you."

Time seemed to stop at that moment. That was the absolute last thing Karl had wanted to say. As far as Anna knew, this was their first date. What kind of weirdo would declare their love so quickly?

But to Karl, things looked different. In the early years of their marriage, he had grown to love Anna. Then things piled up and he withdrew into himself and their long battle of attrition had started.

By the time they had been divorced for a few years, Karl had realized that they had made a mistake. If they had worked a little harder at their marriage, he thought they could have worked things out. By then, it was too late. Anna had moved on and was married to Seymour. When she had come to pick him up at the hospital, it had driven home how much he missed her. He knew he would never have a second chance to make things right. Losing Anna was just a pain he would have to live with.

Then that second chance arrived. He wanted to do everything he could to make the most of it.

And now, he had just blurted out that he loved her on their first date.

Anna spun around, eyes wide. "What did you just say?"

Karl just shook his head, unwilling to repeat it.

Anna's eyes narrowed. "Did you just say that you loved me? How? You don't even know me yet?" Her words held both accusation and, somewhere, a small sliver of hope.

"I didn't mean to say that."

"So now you're saying you don't love me?"

Karl felt the sand shifting under his feet. This was a familiar feeling whenever he started to argue with Anna. He took a deep breath.

"I'm not saying either. That would be kind of crazy if I told you I loved you on our first date, wouldn't it? It's just that..." Karl groped for the right words. "It's just that I really do like you, and I don't want to mess things up."

"And you think us being together would mess things up?"

"I think it's wrong that you say you broke up with Kenny because you didn't want to have sex with him and now..." Karl was beginning to feel he was in deep water and didn't know how to get out of it.

As had been so often the case in their marriage, Anna had no interest in letting Karl off the hook. "And now...what?"

"And now…I don't know. I'm sorry, Anna. I just wanted this to be a fun night together. A chance to get to know each other. And now I feel like maybe I've messed that up."

This was a strategy that Karl had often relied on. Apologizing for something, even though he didn't really have any understanding of what he had done wrong. He tried to get things back on track.

"But I really do like you."

"Not love me?" Anna asked, but she was smiling, at least a little.

"We can talk about my tendency to run off at the mouth later. For now, how about if we plan on going to the movies next weekend? *Escape from New York* is playing at the Pickwick. A friend of mine said he saw it in Portland this summer and that it's really good."

Anna drew a deep breath and let it out slowly. She looked at her watch again. "Well now we've talked for so long, you *have* to take me home. Was that your plan all along?"

"As you get to know me, you will find out that my plans typically include stupidity instead of cleverness." Karl leaned forward and kissed Anna gently, then started the car.

He drove her home and walked her to the front door well within the time frame he had promised. Standing on the small front porch, under the porchlight, he wondered if maybe Candace Masterson was watching through the curtains.

Or worse, James Masterson.

Karl leaned forward and planted a very chaste kiss on Anna's cheek. A kiss even a mother or uncle might approve of. He smiled and winked, then hurried back to his car.

Driving home, he felt good about the night. He'd had to work harder than expected to not be alone with Anna and he still didn't understand that. But he had negotiated the night without putting his—or their—future in danger.

There was plenty of time for everything else.

Chapter Twenty

Karl went to work at P3 early the next afternoon. He had become Red's most reliable delivery driver and found he liked both the money he earned and doing the job.

It was nice having enough money to be able to ask Anna out on a date and not have to worry about how to pay for it.

Meanwhile, his plate was full. Beyond delivering pizzas, he had finals coming up, a term paper on an ancient civilization due, and a few more football games to play.

Plus, as he realized the day after Homecoming, he wasn't sure whether he had a date with Anna the next weekend or not. She hadn't really answered him.

On Monday, he tracked her down in the hall to ask her. He snuck up behind her and put an arm around her shoulder. After the intimacy they had experienced a few days before, he thought that was okay.

But Anna gave him a bit of a cold shoulder. She didn't push his arm off her, but she didn't snuggle up to him either.

Karl was good at interpreting signals and dropped his arm. Anna was talking to three other girls, but once Karl arrived, their conversation wound down quickly, and the other girls drifted away.

"Sorry, didn't mean to break up the group. We just didn't decide if we were going to go to the movies this weekend or not. *Escape from New York?*"

"I remember," Anna said non-committally. "I'll think about it. Gotta go to class."

As she moved away, Karl stood dumbfounded. In his first life, he had not seen Anna for a few days after Homecoming. He was starting to think that was the better plan. He was having a hard time adjusting to the way she ran so hot and cold. If she didn't like him and wasn't interested, that was fine, Karl would gladly leave her alone. But those certainly weren't the signals she had been sending out on Saturday. It would have been possible for him to have pushed down the feelings he had for Anna. To have not taken her to Homecoming at all. To have left the feelings he had for her buried in the past.

Instead, he had tried to rekindle things, but to do it right in this life.

The fact that they had gotten married so young had ruined so many things for both of them. Anna had bounced back, but Karl had not.

He thought back on their marriage and tried to remember if Anna had been emotionally all over the place then. Those memories said she hadn't been. She had been consistent. When things had gone sour, they had just slowly drifted apart.

Karl gave up on trying to figure the situation out. He decided to just back off and let Anna approach him if she was interested in going out. He was good at being alone. He had done it for so long, it was like second nature.

The bell rang and Karl came out of his daze to see that he was the only person in the hall. He sprinted for the back door and off to woodshop. Mr. Lasky never took roll. All he cared about was, did you manage to finish your project on time with all your fingers intact?

Karl was working on a gun rack for his big project. It wasn't for him, of course—there was no room for a gun rack in his Falcon. It was something that he could give Finley for a Christmas present if it turned out well. He went to the back room where his project was stored and ran into Kenny coming out.

He and Kenny had never really spoken. Each of them was just another in the sea of faces you saw floating through the halls in high school. But now, Kenny seemed interested in him. It looked like he was going to say something as they passed each other, but then shut his mouth and walked on by.

"Hey, Kenny. Everything cool? Is there something wrong?" Karl wondered if maybe Kenny was regretting his breakup with Anna. Maybe, even, that he had tried to get back together with her and that was why Anna was so suddenly cold to him.

Kenny turned around and looked at Karl. "Just be careful, man." That felt vaguely like a threat. Kenny wasn't very big, and he didn't have a reputation for being tough, so Karl found this weird.

"What are you trying to say, man? Just spit it out."

"Nothing. Forget I said anything."

"Do you have a problem with me going out with Anna? She said you guys had broken up."

"I don't have any problem with that. You're doing me a favor." He glanced up at Karl as if he might have gone too far and maybe Karl was going to take a swing at him. "Never mind. I shouldn't have said anything."

He turned around and headed off to the main shop.

"Why is everyone so weird today?"

A long-haired boy with a reputation as a stoner walked by. "That's the same question I ask myself every day, man. Why is everyone so weird, and I'm so normal?" He let out a high-pitched giggle and walked away.

Karl finished out the day. He had adjusted remarkably well to being a high school student again. Perhaps it was because once he graduated, he had never changed, never moved on emotionally, really. He traded in his hours at school for the hours at the box factory. It was possible that his marriage to Anna might have helped him grow and change, but that had disintegrated and he had retreated into the most dull, boring life imaginable.

Lying in bed that night, he ran the scenes with Anna and Kenny through his head. He felt like there was an answer somewhere, but it was just outside his grasp.

That weekend, he went to see *Escape from New York*. He didn't see it by himself, though. He and Eric went together and that was fine with him. Both of them loved the movie, and after seeing it, Karl wasn't sure that Anna would have liked it. For the next few weeks, every time Karl and Eric saw each other, they spoke in Snake Plissken's raspy delivery.

The weather was lousy, so they didn't have a lot of time for Eric to give Karl golf lessons, but on days when it wasn't raining and Karl wasn't delivering pizza, he would go to Eric's house and practice putting in their backyard. They had a practice putting green there, so at least Eric could give him tips on that aspect of his game.

After they were done, Eric's mom would often have a snack for them. Tuna fish sandwiches, or some cookies she had just baked. It was no wonder Karl preferred to spend as much of his free time at Eric's instead of at home.

They were an odd pair. Karl, tall and athletic. Eric, short and bespectacled. It frustrated Karl that he couldn't just outmuscle the smaller boy when it came to golf. Strength was great, but technique was everything.

The Bulldogs once again won their final three games of the season and once again lost badly in the first round of the district playoffs. Karl had another great game in the loss. He was hoping that he would get that same envelope in the mail inviting him to Oregon State that he had received—but been unable to use—in his first life.

As Thanksgiving approached, Karl couldn't help but remember what had happened on that day. He had an irrational fear that James Masterson would show up on his door again and accuse him of impregnating Anna. He had buried that thought each time it wormed its way to the surface, though. Anna had told him in their previous life that he was her first and only lover, so there was no way she could be pregnant.

Karl was at Eric's house the Sunday before Thanksgiving. He and Eric had planned on putting in the backyard, but it had rained all afternoon.

Eric's father had just brought home an Atari 2600 video game system. It was hooked up to the big TV in the family room, so they were more than happy to content themselves with playing Space Invaders and Asteroids.

Ellonyia Swanson brought a plate of cookies in for them. "Scoot back, boys. You'll ruin your eyes sitting so close to the TV."

"Aw, Mom," Eric started, but looked up to see the expression on her face. Both boys scooted back against the couch. "Thanks, Mom," Eric said.

"Yeah, thanks, Mom," Karl said with a small giggle.

"Dork," Eric said, pushing Karl in the ribs.

Away from the Swanson house, Karl was a quasi-adult, with a job and a car. But when he hung out at Eric's, he regressed a little, perhaps to a time when he had a mom himself.

Mrs. Swanson said, "Boys, can you pause your game?"

They couldn't, but Eric just let it roll on, as the Space Invaders slowly moved down the screen to crush their blurry little firing mechanism. Karl and Eric both looked up at her expectantly.

"Karl, we'd like you to come have Thanksgiving dinner with us. What do you say?"

Karl was torn. He already knew that Mrs. Swanson was an excellent cook, and he was sure that the Thanksgiving spread at their house would be epic.

At the same time, he felt guilty about leaving his dad alone. He thought back on the miserable TV dinners they had eaten while watching the football game and how they had ignored each other until James Masterson showed up and changed Karl's life forever.

He tried not to think about his dad too much—how he had essentially abandoned him after his mom died. But sitting in the Swanson's bright and happy kitchen, it was impossible for him not to compare and contrast.

Finley didn't need to be both father and mother to Karl, but he could have continued to be involved in his life. They could have bonded together, two men doing the best they could against the world. Instead, Finley crawled deep inside his grief and left Karl completely alone to try and find his own way through the darkness.

Karl let all these thoughts play through his mind in a matter of seconds, then made a decision.

"That would be great, Mrs. Swanson. Thank you."

"We'd love to have your father, too, if he'd like to come."

"I'll ask him, but you can at least count on one more teenage appetite showing up."

"I better get shopping then, before all the big turkeys are gone."

Karl waited until she left the room, then said, "Your mom's cool."

Eric made a face and said, "She's a mom." Immediately, he realized that might be a bad thing to say to someone who didn't have a mom at all. "Sorry."

"Don't worry about it. If I still had a mom, I'd probably think the same thing. Come on, let's crush those damned Space Invaders. They're kind of pissing me off."

Chapter Twenty-One

Karl was almost sure that Finley wouldn't want to go to the Swansons' for Thanksgiving, so he kept putting it off. He rarely saw him anyway, so that made avoiding anything that might be unpleasant easier.

He got out of school early on the Wednesday before Turkey Day and put in an extra-long shift at P3 that afternoon and evening. There were a surprising number of people who had no interest in cooking that day, and he was busy driving from one end of Middle Falls to the other. By the time he got home, he had an extra twenty-five dollars in his pocket and was feeling flush. He stopped at Safeway on the way home and bought a small bouquet of mixed flowers to take with him the next day, then got home around 10:00.

Finley was nowhere to be seen, but since Karl didn't have to be up early the next day, he decided to stay up and wait for him. He knew he would have a hard time sleeping that night if he hadn't at least mentioned it. The invitation to dinner already felt like it was last-minute, and he didn't want to spring it on Finley just a few hours before they were supposed to be there.

The Magnificent Seven came on after the news on Channel Four and Karl was immediately hooked. Just before the climactic final battle, the front door opened and Finley stepped in, obviously surprised that Karl was waiting up for him.

"Don't you have school tomorrow?"

"It's Thanksgiving, remember?" Karl's tone was more acidic than he had intended. He did his best to keep things neutral with his father, but he wasn't always successful.

"Yeah, I knew that," Finley said with a little wobble in his voice. "I was just checking to see if you did."

That made no sense to Karl, but he let it pass. "I waited up because I wanted to tell you that we've been invited to my friend Eric's house for dinner tomorrow."

Finley looked at Karl with that particular focus the long-time drunk can sometimes have. "What did you tell them? Are you going?"

That was a canny way to ask the question, and it would reveal a lot. If Karl said he didn't know, that would mean he waited for his father's approval. If he said yes, then that approval wasn't important to him.

"I'm going, but I'd like it if you came, too." That was a lie, but he told it with good intentions. The truth was, he had an unsettling fear that Finley would do something to embarrass him, maybe even make it so he couldn't go back.

The harder truth was, he would have rather given up going home than going to the Swansons.

"It's like that, huh?"

'What do you mean, Dad? They invited us and I said yes. They said they were hoping you would come too."

"It's a pity invite," Finley said, but quietly. Even more quietly, "I'll bet they won't even have the game on."

"Didn't mean to make a big deal of it, Dad. Just thought it would be good not to be eating a frozen dinner on Thanksgiving." As soon as he said it, Karl realized that he had made a mistake.

For just a moment, Finley stood up straighter and seemed a little more sober. "I understand. You go on without me. I'll stay here with my frozen dinner and watch the game. Have a good time." Before

Karl had a chance to say anything, Finley hurried into his bedroom and closed the door firmly behind him.

"Gah..." Karl said to himself. He plopped back down on the couch and saw that things weren't going well for the Magnificent Seven. They were dropping like flies. Karl had lost his appetite for the battle. He switched off the TV and sat in silence until he fell asleep stretched out on the couch.

He woke up when he heard Finley messing around in the kitchen. He was doing the dishes and setting them to dry. Karl looked at him with bleary eyes. Seeing his father in the kitchen was a rare sight.

Finley started opening and shutting the cupboards, bent over as if he was looking for something.

Karl knew what was in those cupboards, and it wasn't much. "Looking for something, Dad?"

Finley stood up but didn't look at Karl. "Stores all closed today?"

"Yeah, it's Thanksgiving."

Finley went back in his bedroom, grabbed his coat, and headed for the front door. "Have fun with your friends." He slammed the door on the way out, then Karl heard his truck start up and back out of the driveway.

Karl sat on the couch, still half-asleep, trying to figure out what was going on.

"Where you gonna go, Dad? The Do-Si-Do is closed on Thanksgiving. Maybe you can find a gas station open that will sell you a half rack of beer, though."

The best he could figure was that his father had decided suddenly to make a Thanksgiving meal to compete with the Swansons at the last minute. That was ridiculous, unless he was going to make a gourmet meal out of corn starch, Wheaties, and the small tub of sour cream in the fridge. There wasn't much else in the kitchen.

Karl tried to work up a sympathetic feeling for his father. When he put himself in Finley's position, he could see the loneliness, the guilt, the self-destruction. He'd been wallowing in that soup of regret for more than four years now and showed no sign of doing anything different.

Karl picked up the phone in the kitchen and dialed Eric's number. Mr. Swanson answered and called Eric to the phone. Karl had considered canceling altogether and staying home waiting for his father, but as soon as he heard Eric's voice, he changed his mind.

"Will you let your folks know not to set a place for my dad? He's not gonna make it."

"Sure. You're still coming, though?"

"I'll be there."

"Good, I've got a bet with Dad that the Bears are going to beat the Cowboys today."

Karl closed his eyes and tried to remember what the score had been in the game when he and his father had watched it. He couldn't remember that, but he did remember that there hadn't been a lot of scoring. "See if you can get your dad to give you three and a half points."

"Okay. You want in on the action?"

"How much are you betting?"

"Twenty-five cents."

"Hey, big spender. Yeah, I'll take that bet if he'll give the points."

"See you here."

"Bye, doofus."

Karl jumped into the shower and when he came out, Finley was back, sitting in his recliner. He must have found something open somewhere. He had a bag of fried pig skins on his lap and an Oly beer on the table beside him.

Karl got dressed quickly—wearing the same clothes he had when he had taken Anna to Homecoming—and stepped into the living room. He didn't bother to ask his dad if he had changed his mind. He'd bloodied his nose against that wall enough for one day.

"See ya, Dad. I won't be home late."

He closed the door quietly behind him.

Karl felt down as he drove across town. It had rained overnight, so the streets were wet and overhead the skies were a threatening gray.

He parked at the curb in front of the Swanson house because the driveway was already filled with cars. Karl was apparently not the only guest for Thanksgiving.

He grabbed the flowers and hurried up the walk. Before he could knock, Eric answered the door, saw the flowers, put his hands under his chin and said, "Oh, my, are those for me?" in a terrible faux-southern belle accent.

"These are not for you, my young dweebish friend," Karl said. "These are for the lady of the house."

Mrs. Swanson poked her head around the corner, saw Karl, and her face lit in a smile. "So sorry your dad couldn't make it. We were looking forward to meeting him."

Karl thought about making a cover story for Finley but found himself too exhausted with the whole thing to do that. Instead, he said, "Thanks for inviting him. I brought these for you."

"Oh, how lovely!" she said, as though it was a gorgeous bouquet, instead of a $2.99 collection from Safeway. "I'll go get these in water right now."

"Come on, Dad's got the game on."

Eric led Karl into the family room where they normally played video games or watched videos on the VCR. The room was overflowing with people. Eric introduced Karl to everyone, and Karl immediately forgot everyone's name. Eric saw the confusion on his face and said, "And there *will* be a test later, so I hope you've got all this."

Karl had met Eric's dad, Don, a few times, but it was always in passing. He put in long hours as the pro at the country club.

Today, Don sat on the couch with a cocktail in his hand and surrounded by friends and family.

"So you're the gambling shyster who insisted that I give three and a half points."

Karl glanced at the screen and saw that there was still no score early in the second quarter.

"I thought it was going to be a low-scoring game, so those points might be valuable."

"I might need to take you with me to Vegas the next time I go," Don said, then returned his attention to the game.

There was nowhere left to sit, so Karl and Eric sat on the carpet at the edge of the room and watched the game for a few minutes. At least Eric watched the game.

Karl just sat, soaking in the atmosphere of a family gathering and trying hard not to think about *What if?*

Chapter Twenty-Two

Time passed and Karl stayed focused on his primary goal. He wanted to keep his nose clean, keep his grades up, and wait to see if he was once again offered a scholarship to Oregon State.

In mid-January, he had just finished another school day and was walking toward the Falcon to go to work at P3. Snowflakes blew around the parking lot and he turned up the collar of his denim jacket against the weather.

Christmas was in the rearview mirror, and he hadn't been sorry to see it go.

He had been mostly adopted by the Swansons and had spent Christmas Eve, Christmas Day, and New Year's Eve with them. It was wonderful to have a place to go, but there were times when their warm and fun family gatherings were just a reminder of how pathetic his own family life was.

After Thanksgiving, he had stopped even inviting Finley to go with him. Karl could see the finish line of his high school days, and he had come to think of that as the likely end of his relationship with his dad, too.

With no girlfriend and no expensive habits, he was socking money away from his job delivering pizzas and he thought he would have enough saved to be able to move out right after he graduated. He was one of the oldest kids in his class, so he was already eighteen. He was hoping that if he took as many shifts as possible, he would be able to maybe move out even earlier.

He wasn't one of those kids who wanted to get a place of his own so he could party. He just wanted to make a break from the life he had lived the first time. If he could find a room to rent or a small one-bedroom apartment, he could live there until, he hoped, he went off to Oregon State.

He had just opened the Falcon's door when he heard his name. He turned around and saw Lisa Hanson hurrying toward him.

"What's up, Lisa? Where's Mike?"

"We're not joined at the hip, you know," she said, slightly out of breath.

"Okay," Karl said, putting up his hands in surrender. It felt to him that no matter what he said to Lisa, it was the wrong thing. "What's up?"

Lisa's eyes were alight, and she was obviously excited or upset about something. She hurried to where Karl was standing beside the Falcon and stood close to him, like she was afraid someone might overhear what she had to say. She leaned in close to complete the effect.

"Did you hear about Anna?" There was no one anywhere close to them, but she still spoke in a low voice.

Karl shook his head and tried to appear as uninterested as possible. He had seen Anna from afar several times each week, but he hadn't spoken to her since asking her if she wanted to go to the movies. Since she had never bothered to give him a real answer, he figured that was an answer in itself. He still had no idea why she had been so coquettish over Homecoming weekend, then cold as ice since.

It bothered him, but he wasn't going to show that to anyone.

"No, I haven't heard anything, why?"

"She's dropped out of school."

That set Karl back. He remembered that she had planned on dropping out when they had gotten married because she didn't want to be hugely pregnant and have everyone gossiping about her. Then she had lost the baby and hadn't followed through with that plan.

"Why would she do that?"

"She's pregnant."

That really staggered Karl. He opened his mouth to speak, but nothing came out. Finally, he managed to say, "What?"

Lisa shrugged. "Why else would she drop out? She's a straight-A student, belongs to a bunch of clubs, plays volleyball."

"Right," Karl said absently, trying to fit things together.

"You didn't have anything to do with that, did you?"

This was very different from when he had sat in his living room with his father and James Masterson, but there were echoes of it in his head.

He didn't overreact here, but just shook his head sadly and said, "No, not possible."

Lisa seemed to believe him. "Just wondered. You guys were all over each other on Homecoming night. I thought something might have happened that night. Then you both cooled off so fast afterward that I was surprised."

"You're not the only one."

Realization dawned on Lisa's face, at least a few beats ahead of Karl.

"Oh, Karl, I'm sorry. I didn't mean to...to... set you up."

"Sure you did. You knew exactly what you were doing."

Concern was suddenly etched on Lisa's face. "I mean, you're right. I knew that I was setting you up to take Anna to the dance, but I didn't know..." she trailed off.

"Didn't know what?"

"Come on, Karl. You're not a dumb guy. At least I thought you weren't."

"I guess I'm dumb about stuff like this."

"Think about it. She broke up with Kenny and then came to me to help get you to take her to the dance. It seemed like fun, and I've been thinking I should set you up for a long time. You're too good a catch to always be on your own."

"Right..." Karl said, still not following. "When we went out that night, she told me that she had broken up with Kenny because he was putting pressure on her to have sex."

"Well, first, you need to learn not to believe everything a girl tells you, okay? What if that was true, kind of, but that after being together for so long, she went along with him? What if they had sex and she got pregnant? What do you think Kenny would do about that?"

Karl thought about what he knew about Kenny. He'd always thought he was selfish, way more concerned about himself than he was about anything or anyone else.

"Kenny's a selfish prick. He would bail on her."

Lisa put her finger to her nose and said, "Ding, ding, ding. You win the prize. So if you're in Anna's position, pregnant and abandoned by your boyfriend, what do you do? Maybe you look around and see if there's someone else that might take his place. Maybe you look at that cute, lonely boy that you've always kind of liked anyway."

"Is that what I am? The lonely boy?"

"Not always," Lisa said, putting a hand on Karl's arm. "But since your mom died, yeah, you've kind of kept away from everyone."

This whole conversation was awful for Karl. The thought that Anna had really and truly trapped him in their first life together, changed his whole life for the worse, was too much for him to take in all at once. He needed to get away and think about that. Finding out that Lisa—and obviously others—thought he was just the lonely freak wandering the halls of the high school was the rotten cherry on top.

He decided not to debate that. There wasn't much he could point to that would prove she was wrong anyway, and he knew it.

"So what you're saying is, if Anna and I had sex after Homecoming, she would suddenly pop up pregnant and see if I would do the right thing, instead of running for the hills like Kenny did."

"Yeah," Lisa said. "I knew you'd get there eventually."

"I just don't think about people doing stuff like that in real life. That's more like what people do in movies or on television."

"It's a bad thing to do, no doubt, but I feel for her. I'm sure she was desperate."

"But you didn't know?"

"I swear. It was just in fun. It was just to get you a date for the dance." She reached out and hugged Karl.

Mike, Lisa's boyfriend and likely future husband and future ex-husband jogged up. He had seen Lisa hug Karl, but if that upset him, he didn't show it at all.

"What's up?" Mike said. "Somebody die?"

Lisa let go of Karl and explained what was going on to Mike.

"Looks like you dodged a bullet, bro."

Lisa smacked Mike on the shoulder. "Way to be sensitive, big guy."

"Sorry," Mike said, shrinking back. "That's what I get for saying the first thing that pops into my head." He seemed to search his mind for a long moment, then said, "Sorry you dodged the bullet, bro?"

"You're so bad," Lisa said. "Why do I love you?"

"You love me cuz I'm big and strong, not because I'm sensitive. Seriously, though, that sucks man. Can't believe Anna would do that to you."

Karl just felt overwhelmed and wanted to get away. "Thanks for telling me, Lisa. See ya, Mike, I gotta get to work." He climbed into the Falcon and pulled out of the parking lot a little faster than he had intended.

He drove toward P3, but halfway there, he felt shaky and knew he couldn't go in. Instead, he turned around and drove home.

The house was empty, of course. He picked up the phone in the kitchen and called the pizza place. When Red answered, Karl said, "Sorry to call in so late, but my car's broken down and I couldn't get it to start."

"What's wrong with it?"

Karl knew that Red knew absolutely nothing about cars, so he could have made anything up. "Something's got the carburetor fouled, so it won't start. I've got it torn apart right now. I'm sure I'll have it up and running by tomorrow."

He didn't feel too bad about lying to Red. It was the first time he'd ever failed to show up. Worst case scenario was that Red might have to make a few deliveries himself.

Karl looked around the dark, empty house. He didn't really want to be around people, but he found that he didn't really want to be home, either. He decided to go for a drive.

There was always the risk that he might run into Red in town, but he was sure he could handle that if he did.

He initially thought about taking the short drive out to the Falls. That was always a good spot to think.

At the edge of town, without really thinking about it, he turned around and headed back into Middle Falls.

He almost felt like he was in a dream. He wasn't really conscious of where he was going, but after a few turns, he pulled up in front of Anna's house.

Chapter Twenty-Three

"What am I doing here?" Karl muttered to himself. Almost like he was being controlled by something else, he found himself getting out of the car and walking up to Anna's house. He knocked softly on the door.

Candace Masterson answered the door. Over her shoulder, Karl could see that it was dark in their house, too. It was that kind of day.

"Sorry to bother you, Mrs. Masterson. I just wanted to see if I could talk to Anna for a minute."

"I don't think so," Candace said. "It's not a very good day here, and—"

"It's okay, Mom," Anna's voice came from her right. "Let him in. Might as well."

Karl looked at Candace, waiting. He had grown to care about her and even love her during his marriage to Anna. She was always kind and never the kind of monster-in-law he heard other people talk about. He wanted to reach out and hug her, but he knew that was crazy in this circumstance.

Candace took a step back and nodded toward the living room. "I'll turn some lights on. It gets dark so early these days." She went ahead of Karl, turning on first the overhead light, then several lamps.

Anna was sitting on the couch. She was wearing jeans and a long sleeve sweater that she had pulled down over her hands. She didn't have any makeup on, but to Karl's eyes, she was still beautiful. She was looking out the window, so she had obviously seen him pull up.

Her face was wet with tears, and she made no effort to hide or wipe them away.

"I'll leave you two to visit," Candace said and walked toward the back of the house.

"You're pretty much the last person I expected to see today."

When he had driven away from talking to Lisa, Karl had felt completely pissed at Anna and thought that if he never saw her again, that would be great. But something had made him come to talk to her, so he searched his mind for something to say.

"I wish you'd done this differently."

"Thanks, man. I was just sitting here thinking I'd done everything perfectly and wondering how I'd ended up in such a shitty place anyway."

"Can I sit?"

"Do what you want. Did you just come here to tell me what a crappy person I am? You'll have to get in line behind my uncle and mom." She paused, then said quietly, "And me."

"I don't want to make you feel any worse about yourself."

She turned and looked at him. Really looked at him. "What's up with you? You're the one person that really *should* be making me feel bad." She turned away and stared at the rain outside again. "I know what I tried to do to you wasn't very nice."

"I really did like you," Karl started, but then got lost.

"Excellent use of the past tense there, Mr. Strong," she said, imitating Mr. Davidner, their English teacher.

"Everything feels so confused right now, that it's hard for me to even know what I'm feeling."

"Welcome to the club."

"I know you're dropping out of school," Karl said.

"News is pretty much instantaneous in a small-town high school, isn't it?"

"I don't think you should drop out."

"You think I should just get bigger and bigger, so I can't even fit behind the desks in class? Maybe they'll buy a special maternity desk for me?" Her voice was bitter. She had made all the choices that had led her to this place, but it was clear she wasn't ready to accept her share of the responsibility for that.

"No, but look at you. You're not even showing yet."

"You should see me naked." The tears started again. "Oh, wait, I gave you that chance and you weren't interested, right?"

"That's not fair, Anna. I was really trying to do the right thing, that's all."

"That's what I get for choosing a Boy Scout as my backup plan. Any other boy in school would have jumped on me."

The room was nearly silent for a long time. The only sound was the soft ticking of a grandmother clock in the corner.

"And then I would have ended up married to someone that I didn't like at all, and I would have been stuck here in this little town forever. Would that have been a big improvement over the situation I'm in now? Maybe, maybe not."

"But what if your plan had worked? What if we had slept together and then you convinced me the baby was mine? I think I'm going to get a scholarship to play ball at Oregon State. I would have had to give that up. I probably would have ended up being one of those guys that works forty hours a week at the box factory and never gets out of town either."

Whatever façade Anna had been trying to keep up slipped away and she sobbed, dropping her head so Karl wouldn't see. When she looked up, her face was a mask of pain.

"I know. You're right. I really am sorry, Karl. I just always liked you, too."

"Then why did you cut me off after Homecoming?"

"Because I had convinced myself that Homecoming was my last chance. I was already almost two months pregnant. It would have already been very weird if you thought the baby was premature and then came out at eight pounds, or something. After Homecoming, I just figured it was too late."

Karl opened his mouth to say something, but Anna cut him off.

"You were a good thing. I didn't feel like I deserved good things anymore. And I knew that you would have just left me after you found out I was pregnant anyway." She looked at him with a certain desperate hope. "Wouldn't you?"

"I don't know. You didn't give me the chance to find out." He tried to put himself in that situation. If he and Anna were going out but hadn't slept together and he found out she was pregnant, what would he have done? He tried to think he would have done the kind thing and stuck with her, but he realized that wasn't true.

He wanted that scholarship, that escape out of Middle Falls, and having a pregnant girlfriend, whether it was his baby or not, wouldn't have worked.

"No, that's not true. I do know." He didn't have to finish that thought.

"And I wouldn't have blamed you. Who wants a sixteen-year-old girlfriend pregnant with some other guy's baby? You've got a better life than that ahead of you."

It was Karl's turn to smile a little bitterly. "Maybe, maybe not. But, no matter what, I don't think you should drop out of school yet. Maybe you're showing a little, but you can wear slightly looser clothes for a while, right?"

"What's the use of that? What good is an extra month or two of geometry or English going to do me?"

Karl tried to remember exactly what the date was when Anna had gone in the hospital, when she had lost the baby. It was a sad, momentous day in his life, but he couldn't remember exactly when it was. He knew it couldn't be that much in the future, though.

At the same time, he didn't want to say, "You shouldn't drop out of school because you might lose the baby next week." He wasn't even sure if that would happen in this life. So many other things had already changed between this life and that.

"Did you already drop out?"

"It's not like it's a big, formal process. Mom and I just went in and talked to Mr. Tilden. We told him I wasn't going to be coming to school anymore." She narrowed her eyes a little, thinking. "How did you find out already? Mom and I were just there a couple of hours ago."

Karl felt put on the spot. He didn't want to throw Lisa under the bus, but he didn't want to lie to Anna, either.

"Doesn't matter. Someone told me."

Anna shrugged. "You're right. It doesn't matter. Everyone in school will know by lunchtime tomorrow. This is good, juicy gossip. I've been part of telling people about this stuff before. Now it's my turn."

"You can do what you want, but I think that if you just went to school like normal tomorrow and met with Mr. Tilden again, he wouldn't care. He'd still be glad to have you in school."

"So what are you saying I should tell him? *I know I told you I was pregnant and dropping out yesterday, but today I've changed my mind?*"

Karl felt his frustration rising. He was trying to do the right thing, but Anna wasn't making it easy. And, looking at it from her perspective, he got it. If he was in her place, he wouldn't want to go back and tell them he'd changed his mind.

"I get it. You've got to do what you think is right. So what are you going to do now?"

"No idea, really. I don't have a plan. Mom says she'll help me with the baby, so maybe I can go back to school next year. Or get my GED and take some classes at the community college. Everything seems so hard right now. I can't think of anything past having the baby."

"Kenny's not going to help at all?"

"Kenny's an asshole."

That seemed to close off that avenue of conversation. The truly odd aspect of this situation settled in on Karl and he felt suddenly self-conscious. From his perspective, he was sitting talking to the woman he had once loved, married and divorced. Someone he knew well.

He knew, though, that to Anna, this was just some boy she had tried to involve in a scheme to rescue herself. He didn't really have any standing in this situation.

"I know to you, I'm the asshole, and I accept that," Anna said. She looked at Karl, almost begging it not to be true.

Karl smiled a little, his little lopsided smirk. "I was pissed when Lisa told me." He stopped and shut his mouth so hard it made a popping sound.

"I can't believe I did that."

"It's okay, I knew it was probably Lisa. If the situation had been reversed, I would have been the one to tell you."

Karl shook his head. "I'm never going to work for the CIA, obviously." He let a breath out. "Anyway," he started again, "I was pissed when I first found out."

"Like an hour ago, so you've had a lot of time to process your feelings?" Anna asked sarcastically.

"I don't know. It's hard for me to stay mad at you."

"I should have picked you to begin with, instead of Kenny."

"Is that the way it is with girls? You just pick who you want, and it all works out?"

Anna pointed to her stomach and said, "Yes, it all works out. But yes, if you're a cute girl and you really like someone, it's not that hard to make it happen. I would have picked you, but you always seemed so distant that I wasn't sure I could break through. I did try sometimes, you know. Before I started going out with Kenny."

"You did not!" Karl said. He searched his memory, trying to remember any interaction at all with Anna.

"That's what I mean. You were hard to reach. I would literally bump into you in the hallway and you would just say, "Oh, sorry," and move on. When most boys bump into a pretty girl, they at least look at her. You never did."

"I guess I've been pretty distracted for a long time."

For the first time, Anna seemed to look beyond her own misery. "I know. I'm sorry about your mom."

Karl nodded. "I know you understand. I'm sorry about your dad, too."

When he had walked up and knocked on the door, Karl had really had no idea what he was hoping to accomplish. Now, perhaps having accomplished nothing, it felt like everything that needed to be said, had been.

"I guess I'll go, then," Karl said, standing up.

Anna startled him by standing and hugging him. She didn't melt into him as she had at Homecoming, but it was still a real hug.

Karl was surprised to see that it made him emotional. His throat grew thick, and he swallowed hard.

Anna laid her head against his chest, not unlike when they had slow danced.

"I'm sorry," she murmured.

"It's okay. All is forgiven."

Karl was surprised to find that he meant that.

Once he left Anna's house, Karl felt like that whole chapter of his life was finished. He still felt a certain attraction to her, especially when she had held him close, but he knew there was nothing ahead for the two of them.

A relationship that started with secrets and betrayal could never grow into something long lasting and meaningful. At least, that was what Karl believed.

He was surprised, though, to see Anna in the hall between classes a few weeks later. He saw her coming toward him and noticed that people ignored her until she passed them, then put their heads together, gossiping. He couldn't help but wonder why she had to bear up under that, while Kenny got a free pass.

In Middle Falls Oregon in early 1982, it was easier to be male than female.

Anna saw him and waved. She approached him and said, "I should have listened to you that day." She moved closer, so only he could hear and said, "I lost the baby just a few days later."

"I'm sorry, Anna."

She shrugged. "I felt empty after that, so I thought I'd just stay out of school. Mom wouldn't allow that, though. No one gets to stay home and feel sorry for themselves on her watch. So here I am." She glanced around and caught two girls looking at her and whispering. "It's lots of fun, as you can see."

"High school. It will pass."

Anna nodded. She looked up at Karl, a serious expression on her face. "I suppose it's too late for us?"

Karl felt that old pull. He resisted.

"Yeah. It is."

"I don't blame you."

"Hey, I know a boy who really likes you, though."

"I think I might take the rest of the year off from boys if we can't go out."

"No problem."

Curiosity got the better of her, though. Before she walked away, she said, "Who?"

"Seymour Keynes." Karl couldn't remember ever talking to Seymour. He ran with the Science Club kids. But Karl assumed that since he had married her once, and they seemed to be happy, maybe he had been carrying that torch for a long time.

Karl thought Anna might reject him without really considering it. She didn't, though. She looked thoughtful and said, "I've seen him looking at me in class. Maybe I'll give him a chance."

Chapter Twenty-Four

A few weeks later, Karl got the letter from Oregon State that he had been hoping for. Once again, he went into Coach Shield's office and showed it to him. This time, it was to ask for advice.

"What do I do now?" Karl asked.

"It's pretty simple," Coach Shield said. "We should call Coach Andrews and thank him for the offer. Then you should sign the forms they sent you before they change their mind." He was smiling, though. Getting a player a full scholarship was a feather in the cap for any small program high school coach.

"Coach Bulski did a lot to help you. He and Coach Andrews were old friends."

"I know he did. I was able to tell him how much I appreciated what he did that last day he was with the team."

Coach Shield dialed the number for Coach Andrews, but he wasn't available. Instead, Karl got to speak to an assistant coach who worked with the running backs. "We're excited to have you on the team next year, son," that coach had said.

Karl had a feeling that the assistant coach had never heard of him.

"Just wanted to let you know that I've signed all the forms and I'll get them in the mail to you today."

'Thanks, Coach," Shield said, taking the receiver from Karl. "You've got a good one here. I know he's going to do well for you."

He hung up the phone and said, "Now, just don't do anything to mess things up between now and then."

"Like what?" Karl asked.

"Like get arrested for drunk driving, or something dumb like that. I've seen them pull scholarships over things like that."

"No problem. I don't drink, and I'm doing my best to avoid doing stupid things this life."

That was a kind of odd way to phrase it, but it flew right past Coach Shield.

Karl walked out of the locker room feeling good about life in general. He wanted to tell someone about what had happened. He really only had one friend, so he turned left and walked to the freshman end of the school.

He saw Eric at his locker and clapped him on the back. Kids around him scattered, as though Karl might be there to haze them.

Eric looked up at Karl and grinned. "It's okay, Karl's like my big brother."

"I wish I had a friend on the football team," a tall, gangly boy said. He had thick glasses and a buzz cut that hadn't really been in fashion in several decades, even in Middle Falls.

Eric grinned. "Karl, meet Grayson. Maybe we should start a business where I rent you out to keep these guys safe from the bullies."

"Nobody really bugs you guys, do they?"

The small group of boys looked at each other, then back at Karl. The tall boy spoke first. "Are you crazy? Look at us. Of course they do!"

Karl shook his head. "That's not right. If someone is bullying you guys, just tell me. I'll talk to them."

"Yeah," the smallest boy said, smacking a fist into his hand, "you'll *talk* to them."

"Karl's not like that," Eric said. "He's non-violent. Right?"

"Right."

"Hey," Eric said, "it's supposed to be nice this weekend. Want to go out to the municipal course and play a round?"

Karl had been wanting to get onto a course and play a real round for months. All they had done so far was practice their swings and their putting.

"Yes! Finally."

"I'll call and get us a tee time. What's best for you?"

"I've gotta work in the afternoons and evenings. How about morning?"

"That's best. If we go early enough, it won't be crowded, and we won't hold anybody up."

"You mean *you* won't hold anybody up," Karl said, grinning. "I plan on crushing this."

"Says the man who's never stepped foot on a golf course," Eric said. "This game has a way of humbling people. Even big strong jocks. Pick me up about 7:00, okay?"

"How much is it?"

"Don't worry about it. The guy who runs the course knows dad. If we go early, they'll probably just let us play for free."

"The best price! See you there." Karl wandered back up the hall, but not before the tall, gawky boy high-fived him.

It was a good day to be Karl Strong.

《 》

ERIC WAS RIGHT. GOLF was humbling.

After many hours of practice, working on his swing over and over until he felt like he had a grasp on it, it all fell apart the first time Karl approached the tee box.

He had grown confident while he was hitting balls in the field behind the school. But standing there, looking at the long fairway stretching in front of him, everything Eric had taught him fled his mind.

He tried to calm his mind, but instead of sending a perfect arc onto the fairway, he shanked the ball, hitting it sharply into the rough on the right.

"Glad you got that out of your system," Eric said with a grin. He teed up his own ball and swung just like he did during their practices, sending the ball straight ahead. "Come on, I'll help you find your ball."

They managed to get eighteen holes in, but Eric mercifully suggested they stop keeping score after the third hole.

Somewhere about the fifteenth hole, Karl said, "I don't get it. Why am I so bad?"

"It's your first round ever. Don't worry about it. I think you're doing better than I did my first time."

"How old were you then?"

"Five."

"That's a big comfort."

"Like I said, being strong is helpful, but technique is everything. And you know how to get technique?"

"Practice," Karl answered. "I mean, I knew I wasn't going to be great, but..."

"I think you did pretty well. You didn't throw your clubs in the lake back on Thirteen. Don't worry about this round. Weather will be getting nicer, and we'll be able to come out a couple of times a week if you want."

"I want."

Karl had been naturally athletic his whole life. When he played Little League, he was the best pitcher and hitter on the team. In Pee Wee football, he could run rings around the other kids his age. He never played organized soccer, but every time he stepped on the field during gym, his burst of speed and coordination stood him in good stead.

And then there was golf.

There weren't many sunny weekends in March, or even weekends when it wasn't raining and blowing. But every time one rolled around, the two of them were out on the course early in the day.

Slowly, Karl got a little better. His muscles weren't as tight. He started to remember the tips that Eric had given him. After that first round, they always kept score. Eric beat him by more than a dozen strokes every round, but at least it gave Karl something to measure his progress against.

By April, Karl felt like he had enough saved to be able to move out on his own, if he could find a place cheap enough. He hadn't talked to Finley about it, but he figured that even if he moved out without telling him, it might take him a week or two before he noticed.

He couldn't remember the last time he and his father had a real conversation about anything.

For a few weeks, Karl picked up a copy of the *Middle Falls Gazette* and looked through the classifieds, hoping to find a room for rent. There always seemed to be apartments at the Crestview, but even their one bedroom was out of his range. He started to think that he would have to just suck it up and stay where he was.

On nights when he got off early enough from P3, he just naturally gravitated toward Eric's house. Mrs. Swanson had come to expect him and often kept a plate of whatever they had for dinner aside for him.

One night, Karl and Eric sat in the kitchen. Karl was eating the meatloaf and mashed potatoes Ellonyia had made that night and Eric was going on about a Dungeons and Dragons game that he was going to play with his friends that weekend. Eric was the Dungeon Master and so was in charge of planning the adventure out.

He had been trying to talk Karl into joining their D&D group for months, but Karl always resisted. While Eric was going on about the terrible traps he was going to set for his friends, Mrs. Swanson laid her hand on her son's shoulder, waiting for him to wind down. When he did, she said, "Eric said you're looking for a place to rent."

"Mmm-hmm," Karl said around a bite of mashed potatoes. "Everything's pretty expensive, but I'm still looking."

Eric smiled widely, as though he knew what was coming.

"We've been talking about it," Ellonyia Swanson said. "We've got a room over the garage that we're just using for storage right now. If you want to help us clean it out, we've got an extra bed and dresser that we could put in there for you."

"I have this feeling you're going to say that you don't want any money for that either."

"Of course not."

Karl shook his head. "I already know that I eat you out of house and home. You're a good cook," he said with a grin.

"I like to watch a young man eat. This one," she tapped Eric on the shoulder, "eats like a bird."

"My budget is a hundred dollars a month. If you would take that from me, I would love to take you up on your offer."

"I told you," Don Swanson said, coming around the corner of the kitchen.

"We don't want to argue with you, Karl," Ellonyia said.

"Good. Then if you'll take my hundred dollars on the first of every month, I will happily accept your very kind offer."

Don Swanson walked across the kitchen and extended his hand to Karl. When Karl reached to shake it, Don said, "We'll take fifty bucks a month, but not a penny more."

"And for that, you can bet I'm going to feed you, too," Ellonyia said.

"Just like most days," Eric said with a broad grin.

Karl wanted to say no, but the offer was so kind that he shook Don's hand. "Deal. But you've got to let me do more to help out around here. Mow the grass, take out the garbage, weed the flower beds."

"If you do all that, you'll put our gardener, Eckie Swanson, out of work."

"Yes!" Eric said agreeably.

"No," both Ellonyia and Don said together.

"Seriously, you've got a lot going on, Karl," Don added. "School, staying in shape so the coaches at Oregon State don't kill you, a job..."

"Golfing terribly," Eric chipped in helpfully.

"You better watch out, Eckie. One of these days, Karl might make you eat those words."

"Not until he tames that slice on his driver," Eric said helpfully. He looked at Karl and said, "Come on, let's start moving stuff out of that room. You can move in tonight!"

Karl shook his head. "We can move stuff right now if it's okay with your folks, but I've got to talk to my dad. He doesn't know I'm leaving yet."

Chapter Twenty-Five

The way Ellonyia had talked about cleaning up the room above the garage, Karl thought it would be a few days' work to clear it out. It was really only a few stacks of boxes, though.

The bed and dresser that were going into the room were stuck in a corner of the garage, so the boys carried them upstairs, then stacked all the boxes in the now empty corner. In less than an hour, the upstairs room had the bed and dresser, but nothing else.

Karl and Eric put the twin bed together. Just as they finished, Ellonyia came in with sheets, pillows, and a comforter.

She looked around the room. "It's pretty plain in here. We've never used this room for anything except storage. We can paint it if you want."

"Black. All black walls," Eric said.

Ellonyia shook her head. "He always wants to paint things black. We never let him, but he always wants to. If you've got any posters or anything you want to bring, feel free. This is your room now."

Don Swanson walked in carrying a small television and set it on the dresser. "There's no cable outlet here, but we've still got our old antenna on the roof, and we can hook you into that. You'll be able to get the Portland channels at least."

"Hey!" Eric said. "I don't have a TV in my room!"

"Right. Start paying me fifty bucks a month and I'll get an old black and white TV for your room too."

"Pass," Eric said. "I'll just hang out in here with Karl."

"That's what I figured," Don said. He reached into his pocket and took out a small key ring with a single key on it. "This is for the side door that goes into the garage. That way you can come and go as you please. You're an adult, and we're going to treat you like one."

"I swear to God, if I knew I could get all this stuff for fifty bucks a month, I would have gotten a job."

"Really?" Don asked.

"Well…no, probably not," Eric admitted.

"That's what I thought," Don said. He tossed the key ring to Karl. "The place is yours now. No need to check in with us, but if you need anything, let us know."

Don and Ellonyia left, closing the door behind them.

Eric looked around and said, "Your room is a lot bigger than mine. I think we should have our D&D sessions in here. There's a folding table and chairs in the garage. We can bring it up and set it up over there." He pointed to an empty spot.

"Sure, I don't care. That would be great."

"Of course, you'll have a lot of freshmen in your room then."

"I can handle it."

"Now if only we knew someone that worked at Pizza! Pizza! Pizza! that could bring us something to eat on Friday."

Karl got a free pizza every day he worked more than four hours, so he just said, "Whatever. I won't let you guys starve." He looked around the room, which had walls that sloped inward at the ceiling. There was a window at each end of the room, so he would get both morning and evening sun.

"This is so cool of your parents."

"It was my idea," Eric said casually, "but I didn't have to twist their arm. They really like you. Dad says we'll have to drive to Corvallis and catch some Oregon State games this year."

"That's a long ways to go just to see me sit on the bench. I doubt if I'll get on the field much my freshman year." Karl sat on the bed and bounced a little. "Comfy. Nice." He took a deep breath and said, "I guess I better go talk to my dad."

"I know that's not easy, man," Eric said. "But while you're gone, do you mind if I get everything set up for the D&D game in here?"

"Way to stay focused."

"It's just one of my many talents."

"This room is your room too, as far as I'm concerned, so go ahead."

"Cool."

"Just make sure to leave your twenty-five bucks on the dresser on the first of every month." Karl ducked as the pillow Eric threw sailed over his head, then closed the door behind him.

It was only a little after eight, and Karl knew that if he went home to wait for his dad, it would probably be sometime after closing time before he got there. For the first time in his life, he thought he should go to the Do-Si-Do.

He wasn't old enough to get in legally, yet. The drinking age in Oregon was twenty-one. But he didn't want to drink, he just wanted to go in and tell his father what he had to say.

He pulled into the poorly lit parking lot and parked beside his dad's truck. There were only four other vehicles parked in the side lot. Not too surprising for a Tuesday night.

Karl's stomach hurt, and he felt a sudden urge like he needed to go to the bathroom. This place, this little run-down bar, had become almost a weirdly mythical location. The thing that had swallowed his father.

There were no windows in the Do-Si-Do, so he anticipated it would be dark inside. He pushed the front door in and was surprised to find that it looked almost exactly like he had suspected it would. It was dark, all right, with most of the light coming from a single strip of lights over the bar on the right-hand side, and a dozen neon signs advertising Schlitz Beer, Budweiser, and, oddly enough, Champion Tools.

What he hadn't been prepared for was the smell of the place. It smelled musty, but with a combination of stale beer and the wax from the bar. Karl thought the combination was a smell he would likely never forget.

There were no women inside, just half a dozen men, including the bartender, who looked at Karl.

Karl had often tried to picture what it was about this place that drew his father in like a magnet. Looking around now, he still had no idea. He spotted his father immediately, but he looked like he was part of a painting, not a living, breathing person. From where he stood, Karl couldn't tell where his father ended and the barstool began.

There was a glass in front of him with several inches of beer still in it, but Finley wasn't touching it. He stared straight down, perhaps seeing something other than the polished surface of the bar.

"Hey, son, you're gonna need some ID if you want to drink."

The five men who sat along the bar turned to look at Karl in unison. Finley blinked owlishly in Karl's direction, then rocked backward and nearly fell off his barstool when he recognized him.

"He's not here to drink," Finley said. "Or at least he better not be. He's my kid."

The barkeep waved a towel at Karl, having lost all interest in him.

Finley seemed to make an effort to pull himself together, to make the whole scenario seem a little less sad. He shrugged his shoulders, adjusting his work shirt into place. When he had first turned toward Karl, his eyes had been dead. Now he blinked, trying to rejoin the world as it was, not how he was wishing it to be.

Finley glanced at his watch. "What are you doing out so late? Don't you have homework or something?"

Karl didn't even bother to answer that. It was ridiculous. He could have been staying out until midnight every night and Finley would have no idea. He hadn't asked him about his schoolwork in the four years he had been in high school. Karl was tempted to say, *Why the sudden interest in me and my life, Dad?* but he bit that back. He hadn't come to fight or argue.

He closed the distance between the two of them in just a few steps. The Do-Si-Do was not a large place. There was an empty stool beside his father, but Karl had no interest in sitting on it. He just wanted to be close enough that their conversation was at least mostly among themselves. He glanced at the bartender, who found something to do at the other end of the bar.

"I want to let you know that I'm moving out."

Karl was shocked to see that his father was shocked.

"What? No. Why?"

"Why, Dad? Seriously? Why not? What's there for me? When is the last time I saw you long enough to have a real conversation about anything? Did you even know that I got the scholarship to Oregon State?"

Finley nodded. "Saw the letter."

"Right. The biggest moment of my life and I never got a chance to tell you about it, so I left the letter out where you might see it."

"I thought I was doing the right thing by giving you some space. I would have loved that when I was a kid."

"No, you wouldn't have. I guess that's what you tell yourself, but it's not true and you know it. I wish you'd stop lying to yourself, Dad. The more you lie to yourself, the more you lie to me, too."

"I never lied to you."

"There are different kinds of lies, Dad, and you know it." Karl took a half-step away from his father and drew a deep breath. "I didn't come here to argue with you. Why would we argue now? It's all over. I'm leaving."

Karl would have guessed it was impossible, but he saw a new level of grief in his father's eyes. "When will I see you?"

"Tell you what. You tell me when you won't be sitting right here holding that barstool down, and I'll come home and see you. When would that be, though?"

There seemed to be a battle inside Finley. Finally, he picked up his glass and poured the last of the beer down his throat. He looked at the bartender and twirled his finger. The man went to the tap and began to draw another glass of beer.

"I figured that was the answer. Goodbye, Dad."

Karl turned quickly away because he didn't want anyone to see the tears that were forming in his eyes.

He had meant to move into his new room the next day, but after talking to Finley, he knew he didn't want to stay in that house another day.

It was 10:30 by the time he put the last of his stuff into the trunk and backseat of the Falcon. It hadn't taken much. He carried his few clothes out on their hangers, threw his socks and underwear into one box and his bathroom stuff into another. He took the picture of his mom and dad off the top of the dresser. It showed a different life. The farther away he got from it, the more it seemed like a dream, but he wanted to keep the souvenir of that time.

He looked around the rest of the house and couldn't find anything else he needed to take. He wondered briefly if Finley would even bother to stock groceries once he was gone, or would he just stock the refrigerator with half racks of Rainier and Olympia Beer?

Shaking his head, he let go of that thought. Finley had never been his responsibility and now was the time to completely let go of that idea.

He looked around the living room and kitchen one last time. There were no good memories in this place that he wanted to take with him. He was just happy to be leaving.

When he opened the door, he was illuminated by the headlights of his father's truck pulling into the driveway. Finley got out of the truck, glanced in the backseat of the Falcon and saw the boxes of stuff.

He brushed past Karl and into the house. "Tonight, huh?"

"No sense in putting it off."

Finley nodded, then said, "Tuesdays."

Karl couldn't puzzle that out. "What? Tuesdays what?"

"I'll be here on Tuesdays. I'll come straight here after work. If you want to come see me, I'll be here."

"Good enough, Dad." Karl was dismayed to find that his voice broke a little. He had looked for something from his father for so long that even this tiny consolation prize stirred something in him. He wrapped his father in a hug. He felt the stubble from his cheek and smelled the beer.

"I love you, Dad."

"I'm sorry, Karl. Really, I am."

There was nothing left to be said. Karl turned away, got in the car and backed slowly out of the driveway.

《 》

THE NEXT TUESDAY, KARL worked his normal shift at P3, then picked up a pepperoni pizza and drove straight to Finley's.

He wasn't surprised when his father's truck was not there.

He opened the door and set the pizza box on the table.

On the way home to the Swansons', he passed the Do-Si-Do.

Finley's truck was parked where it always was.

Chapter Twenty-Six

Spring arrived in Middle Falls. That meant that Karl and Eric were able to golf more often at the municipal golf course.

Karl managed to remember more of what Eric taught him each round they played. He still wasn't able to beat Eric, or even come close, really, but he was closing the gap.

They had started to get eighteen holes in on Thursday afternoons after school. That was Karl's day off from P3. Getting two rounds a week in meant that Karl accelerated the growth in his game by leaps and bounds.

Don Swanson had even agreed to start taking the boys out on the Middle Falls Country Club course and give them both a few pointers, though that hadn't happened yet.

He did ask Karl if he wanted to give up his pizza delivery job and start caddying on the weekends at the country club.

It was hard for Karl to think about not driving for P3. That job had been there when he needed it and it felt wrong to abandon it. At the same time, he knew he would learn a lot more about his new hobby if he was carrying clubs around for the wealthy of Middle Falls.

His compromise was that he asked Red if he could drop the weekend shifts and just keep driving after school during the week. Weekend shifts were easier to find drivers for, and Red was glad not to have to replace Karl completely, so he agreed.

Karl was nervous when he caddied his first foursome. That group included Don Swanson, though, so that helped him stay calm. By the end of that round, he saw that he had built the whole experience into more than it was.

As Don had said, "These guys don't really want anything from you other than to carry their clubs. For the most part, they're terrible golfers, but they think they're good, so they don't want club advice, especially from a kid."

At the end of the round, the man who Karl had caddied for gave him a twenty-dollar bill, so he figured he had done okay.

Ultimately, delivering pizzas during the week and caddying on the weekend meant that Karl earned more money and he felt flush for the first time in his young life.

The last few months of his senior year were flying by. Any trouble Karl had once had about waking up as a high school student again were gone. He was back in the swing of his classes and, more than anything, looking forward to heading off to college in September.

He had just come out of the lunchroom when Lisa Hanson saw him and waved. Grinning, she said, "So Karl, who are you taking to Prom?"

Karl looked at her disbelievingly. "You've got to be kidding me."

Lisa couldn't hold her serious expression anymore and said, "Yeah, I am. Just wanted to see how you'd react."

"Well, now you know, and it's not good."

"I know, but hey, if you do want a date, I know some really cute, sweet girls that haven't been asked yet."

"Thanks, I'll pass, matchmaker. I will happily be home watching TV that night."

At that moment, there was a disturbance in the crowd as someone pushed people out of the way. Karl turned to look and it was Grayson, Eric's tall, gawky friend.

Grayson spotted Karl and ran awkwardly toward him. He brushed against a senior boy, who glared at him and pushed him, nearly making him fall down.

Karl caught him and said, "Yo, Grayson, where's the fire?"

"It's Eric. They're hurting him."

Karl started to ask *Who?* but knew that it didn't matter. If someone was hurting Eric, they would have to deal with Karl first.

Instead, he said, "Where?"

"Down at the freshman lockers," Grayson said. "I'll take you."

Karl didn't wait for Grayson. He knew where the freshman lockers were. He sprinted away, gracefully missing the flow of lunchtime traffic the way he had made tacklers miss on the football field. The freshman lockers were clear at the other end of the school from the lunchroom, but Karl got there in record time.

Sure enough, he saw Eric being held up in the air by Dink Gregson. Dink was one of the defensive linemen on the football team and the biggest guy in school. He looked like he could have wrestled the average bull to a standstill. He was also one of the few guys on the team that Karl didn't even have a passing friendship with. They had gotten into a tussle in junior high and hadn't really spoken since then.

Still, they were teammates. Karl relaxed a little.

"Hey, Dink. That's my little brother. Put him down."

Karl glanced up at Eric who was resting against the sloped tops of the lockers, pinned by Dink's meaty hand. He was trying to keep his composure but looked to be on the verge of tears. A boy crying when he was bullied was the worst mistake that could be made. It was like an invitation to being bullied for the rest of your life.

Dink looked at Karl, slightly confused. "You don't have a brother."

"*Adopted* brother." Karl took two steps toward Dink. He was almost as tall as him but gave up a good seventy-five pounds.

Dink looked up at Eric, who was looking up at the ceiling, still trying not to cry. The confused expression on Dink's face seemed to be part of his permanent makeup.

"When we were freshmen, the senior boys put us up on the lockers and watched us roll off. Now *I'm* a senior and I'm just carrying on the tradition. But, if this little squirt is a friend of yours, I'll let him down and do it to one of these other little freaks."

"No. That's not gonna happen. We're not rolling freshmen off the lockers anymore."

Dink turned toward Karl, letting go of Eric, who immediately rolled off the locker and plunged toward the floor.

Karl jumped forward and managed to mostly catch Eric. He picked him up and set him on his feet, then moved him away from Dink.

"I don't think you're big enough to tell me what I'm not gonna do," Dink said, taking a step forward and jabbing a finger into Karl's chest.

"Come on, Dink. We don't want to do this. This is the stupidest thing in the world to fight over."

"You calling me stupid?"

Karl drew a deep breath and sighed. "No, *this* is stupid. Not *you're* stupid."

Dink frowned and was obviously having a hard time putting those two thoughts together.

"Whatever, Dink. Just leave these guys alone, all right? They're not the ones that rolled us when we were kids. They didn't do anything to us." He turned to look at Eric, who seemed to have himself under control now. "Let's get out of here."

"Where?" Eric asked.

"Anywhere that's not here, okay?" Karl turned his back on Dink and took a few steps up the hall.

"Nuh-uh," Dink said and rushed forward. He slammed into Karl and sent him sprawling forward.

It wasn't really a fight. It was a single shove.

Karl hurtled forward, trying not to fall. When he saw that he was going to hit the deck anyway, he reached out with his right arm to catch himself.

He rolled over and sat up, stunned. When he looked down, he saw that his right arm looked completely wrong. His thumb, instead of pointing away, was turned back on his wrist. Blood dripped from a compound fracture on the right side of his arm.

"Holy shit," Dink said and immediately turned and ran away.

It was Eric who knelt beside Karl. "Oh man, oh man, oh man." He looked up at Grayson who was staring at Karl with his mouth hanging wide open. "Run. Run to the office and tell them we need an ambulance."

"We don't need an ambulance," Karl said, but it was obvious that he was in shock. His face had gone pale and a pool of blood was gathering in his lap. He tried to stand, but the floor was slippery with blood. His knee slipped and he slipped back onto his butt, which caused a wave of pain and nausea to wash over him. Karl winced and sat still, trying to come up with a new plan.

"Karl," Eric said, now deadly calm. "You're hurt really bad. Just sit here. Grayson went to get help. They'll be here soon."

The rest of the crowd had dissipated. As fascinating as the disaster in front of them was, no one wanted to be there when the teachers showed up.

That happened almost instantly. The door to a classroom opened and a teacher stepped out. It was Coach Shield., who doubled as the Civics teacher. When he saw it was Karl on the ground, he sprinted toward him. He looked at the damaged limb that had been Karl's right arm just a few minutes before and shuddered.

"I sent Grayson to the office to call an ambulance," Eric said.

Shield nodded and knelt helplessly beside Karl. He closed his eyes in frustration. "There's nothing we can do for you here. We'll get you to the hospital."

Wave after wave of pain washed over Karl. He tried to take deep breaths, but the pain wouldn't let him.

It felt like hours passed before two EMTs hurried down the hall pushing a gurney.

One knelt in front of Karl and took in the extent of the injuries at once. He looked up at his partner and said, "Nothing we can really do for him here except try to immobilize it."

The other EMT lowered the gurney until it was just a few inches off the ground. As gently as possible, they helped Karl onto it, then covered him with a thin blue blanket. They raised the gurney and pushed back down the hall.

Fifteen minutes later, he found himself once again in Middle Falls Hospital, watching the overhead fluorescent lights blur one by one.

He was pushed into a small emergency room where an older nurse said, "I'm nurse Nancy. Let me see what we're dealing with." She pulled back the blanket and saw the damage to Karl's arm. She winced and looked away for a moment before doing a more thorough visual examination.

"Probably not good when the ER nurse looks like that," Karl said between gritted teeth.

"It's going to be fine," nurse Nancy said. "We'll get you patched right up. For now, I'm going to give you something for the pain."

She brought an IV drip bag beside the gurney and inserted a needle into Karl's left arm. A moment later, she pushed a hypodermic needle into the tube. "Give that just a minute."

It didn't take a minute. Warmth and calm relief flooded up Karl's left arm. It hit his heart and was pumped through his whole body.

"Oh," Karl said, smiling slightly. "Oh, that's incredible."

"I gave you the good stuff," Nancy confirmed.

"I get it now."

"What?" Nancy asked, puzzled.

"This feeling. This is why people do drugs."

"Don't go getting any ideas now."

Karl didn't even hear her. He laid his head back, relaxed, and drifted off into a drug-induced haze.

Chapter Twenty-Seven

When Karl opened his eyes, he was in a hospital room. It gave him the sense of déjà vu from when he had his first heart attack in his previous life, but at the same time, this was different.

This time, there were people in the room, waiting for him.

Don, Ellonyia, and Eric Swanson sat in chairs at the foot of the bed. Their expressions told the story of their worry.

As soon as Karl opened his eyes, Ellonyia stood up and approached him. She smiled at him, but he saw there were tears in her eyes. She brushed a lock of his curly hair off his face.

"Glad to see those baby blues," she said. "We've been a little worried."

Karl tried to speak, but his throat was too dry. His head ached, but it felt like part of him was missing.

They amputated my arm, he thought wildly.

He strained to look down and saw that his right arm was there, it was just encased in a heavy cast that ran from his knuckles all the way up to his shoulder. It was completely numb, which was almost certainly a blessing.

He looked back at Ellonyia.

"You broke your arm pretty bad," Ellonyia said.

Both Don and Eric were standing at the end of his bed.

"And it was because of me," Eric said. This time, tears did run down his face. "I'm so sorry, Karl. This is because of me."

Karl strained to clear his throat and Ellonyia lifted up a paper cup with a straw that she held to his lips. "Just little sips for now."

"You didn't do anything." Karl said to Eric. "Nothing."

"They kicked Dink out of school for the rest of the year," Eric said. "The police came and said that if you want to press assault charges, you can."

"Doesn't matter," Karl said, still trying to take in his new circumstances. "It was mostly an accident."

Ellonyia smiled at Karl. Her normally beautiful face was creased with worry. "We know you did this to protect Eric. We'll do whatever needs to be done for you. You're a good boy, Karl Strong. We love you."

That maternal love washed over Karl, and it was so strong, he had to turn his head away, but only for a moment.

The door to the room whooshed open and Karl tried to lift his head to see who it was.

Finley Strong stepped into the room. He saw the people gathered around the bed and stopped just inside the door as if he was intruding on something.

"Dad," Karl croaked.

Finley stepped to Karl's right side, careful not to get too close to the cast.

"The school called me at the factory. I came right over."

Karl nodded. "Dad, this is Mr. and Mrs. Swanson and their son, Eric."

"You must be the folks that Karl's talked so much about." It was a lie, because Karl and Finley never spoke to each other enough for him to have talked *so much* about anyone or anything. But it was a white lie, told for social reasons and no one would have dreamed of calling him on it.

"How long are they going to keep you here?"

Don Swanson cleared his throat and said, "They're going to keep him overnight. He had a compound fracture of the ulna. They did surgery on that and put four screws in to hold it in place. The bigger problem is that the radius not only broke but was badly separated from the wrist. They said they're going to have to wait a while before they can do surgery to repair that."

"You're going to be good as new in a few weeks, though, right?" Finley said, searching Karl's face.

Karl had no idea. He looked at Don, who seemed to have the information. He shifted a little from one foot to the other. "I'm sure he will be, but it might be more than a few weeks."

Finley looked from Don to Ellonyia, then back to Karl. "Okay. I'm going to take off, then. I'll come back when it's not so crowded."

Ellonyia took her cue from that. "Oh, no. We were just leaving," she lied. "You should stay here with your son."

"No," Finley said firmly. "I'll come back later."

"We're going to set Karl up in Eric's room, at least for a while," Ellonyia said. "So he doesn't have to climb the stairs and jog that arm. But we'd love for you to come by and see him anytime."

"I'll do that," Finley lied, then hustled himself out of the room.

"You favor your father," Ellonyia said kindly.

"I hope not," was all Karl could say.

As soon as Finley left, the door opened again and a somewhat younger version of Dr. Chin walked in wearing a white coat.

"Hello, Dr. Chin," Karl said automatically, forgetting that he had never met him in this life.

Dr. Chin cocked his head to one side and frowned, as if he was trying to place where he might have seen Karl before. "Surgery went well. There is a metal plate and four screws that will hold the ulna in place. I'm a little worried about the dislocation of the radius. We tried to slip it back into place during surgery, but the joint is badly damaged. I'm afraid we'll need to refer you to a specialist who can deal with that."

"We'll take care of that for him," Don said quietly.

"Oh? I never worry about the billing. I leave that to the bureaucrats." He looked back at Karl and said, "You're going to feel out of it for a few days, and that's okay. I'm going to send you home with a prescription that will keep you feeling pretty tired. Just rest and get plenty of liquids while your body recovers from the surgery." He paused and looked at Karl's charts. "Your vitals are all good now. You're a healthy young man. We'll get you as close to back to normal as we can."

That phrase rang ominously in Karl's mind. *As close to back to normal as we can.* That didn't sound good.

For the first time, a new worry settled over Karl. The scholarship to Oregon State. He already knew he wasn't at the top of their list. If he wasn't able to present himself as a hundred percent healthy, would they rescind that scholarship?

That worry settled over him like a heavy weight. He had done everything right in this lifetime, or as close to everything as he seemed to be capable of. The idea that he might lose the chance to get out of town again, and only because he was standing up for a friend, seemed too unfair.

Ellonyia seemed to be tuned in to what Karl was thinking and feeling. "Don't worry right now. That won't help you get better."

Karl nodded, but that seemed to cause a small wave of pain to ripple through his arm.

A nurse came in with a small paper cup. She turned it over in her hand and two small pills fell out. She looked at Karl and opened her mouth slightly, miming what she wanted him to do as though he was a baby being fed. He opened his mouth and she put the pills on his tongue, then picked up the cup with the water and put the straw to his lips.

"That's gonna knock you out," she said. She turned to the Swansons. "This is probably a good time for you to leave. He's going to be out for a few hours. More likely through the night."

Ellonyia looked reluctant to go but nodded her head. "We'll head home and get everything ready for when they let you leave tomorrow. We'll be back first thing in the morning." She leaned over the bed and kissed Karl gently on the cheek. Her blonde hair fell across his face and tickled him. She stood, obviously reluctant to go, but Don touched her arm and she turned away.

A moment later, Karl was alone in the room. He didn't feel any pain, but he did feel a wave of sleepiness come over him.

He closed his eyes and gave into it.

《 》

WHEN KARL WAS WHEELED out of the hospital, he was not alone. Ellonyia and Eric flanked him on either side of the wheelchair. When they got outside, there was a blue Cadillac waiting for him. This time, of course, it was Don behind the wheel instead of Anna.

Eric ran ahead and opened the front passenger door. Ellonyia hurried forward and picked up a fluffy pillow that she had brought. She handed it to Eric, then gently helped Karl stand up from the wheelchair.

He hadn't walked in several days and with the drugs still in his system, he was a little wobbly on his feet. Ellonyia put an arm around his waist and said, "You just watch your cast. I'll take care of you. Don't bump it on anything."

Karl slid gratefully into the passenger seat. Ellonyia helped him lift the cast up ever so gently, then slipped the pillow under it.

"Thank you," Karl said. "That's great."

Ellonyia made sure the injured arm was well out of the way of the door, then closed it carefully.

Don took the back roads to their house and backed into the driveway so that the passenger side was just a few steps away from the front door. Eric hopped out and opened Karl's door, then Ellonyia helped Karl out of the car. He blinked in the sunshine.

"It's nice out," Karl said. He looked at Eric and said, "Too bad we can't go play eighteen. I think I was about to catch you."

"I don't think so," Eric said honestly. "But maybe in another year or two."

Ellonyia once again put an arm around Karl. He kept the pillow resting between his arm and his body. It lessened the jarring of each step.

There were three steps up to the house, but with Ellonyia's help, Karl managed it. They went down a short hall and turned left into Eric's room.

"When you're better able to navigate the stairs," Ellonyia said, "we'll move you back into your room. For now, though, this is best."

"And there's a bathroom right across the hall," Eric said. "It's handy."

Karl lay down on top of Eric's bed and saw that they had moved the small television from his room.

"It's going to be tough for you to read, and we didn't want you to go stir crazy, so Eric had the idea to bring it down," Don said.

"I knew I'd get that TV in here eventually," Eric added, smiling.

"How's your arm feel?" Ellonyia asked.

"It's fine."

She stood over him, with as close to a stern look as she could muster. "Listen, fella. You being in pain doesn't help you heal up. You've got to be honest with me about when you're hurting."

Karl nodded. "You're right. It hurts a little."

"We got your prescription filled, so let me go get a glass of orange juice and some of your pills." She hustled out of the room.

"Let me know if you need anything, okay?"

Karl nodded and did his best to smile at Don through the pain. "You don't need to do anything else for me. You've already done too much."

Don waved that off and left the two boys alone.

"I really am sorry, Karl. I didn't mean for this to happen."

"You didn't mean for Dink to use you like a free weight and roll you off the lockers? Come on."

"He's an asshole."

Karl looked at his damaged arm and said, "I think I agree with you."

"Want me to turn the TV on?"

"Sure, but can you turn the volume down? I think after your mom brings the pills, I'm gonna sleep for a while."

Eric turned the TV on, Ellonyia brought Karl his pills, then they cleared out.

Karl lay back and tried to think. He looked around Eric's room. There was a castle built out of Legos, posters for *Star Wars* and *The Empire Strikes Back* on the wall. It was a good room.

Karl couldn't wait until he was strong enough to get out of it.

《 》

KARL WAS OUT OF SCHOOL for two weeks before he felt well enough to go back. He had stopped taking the Percodan Dr. Chin had prescribed and was now strictly on acetaminophen instead.

He still had the cast on that ran from his knuckles to his shoulder, but the bones were knitting together well enough that a small jostle here or there didn't cause tremendous pain.

Of course, the cast caused Karl to stand out like a glowing beacon when he walked down the hall. He wasn't back in the building for more than two minutes when the first kid approached and asked if he could sign it.

Karl kind of liked the pristine white, but wasn't great at telling people no. So the kid whipped out a Bic and drew a signature on it. That opened the floodgates, and soon there was a line of kids waiting to immortalize themselves on the cast.

By lunch, there wasn't any space left and kids were having to use Sharpies to go over the top of what other kids had done.

It did make Karl feel kind of good in the end.

Because it was his right arm, Karl was unable to write anything that was legible at all. This dismissed him from having to do a lot of his homework, but he had taken a pretty easy slate of classes the last quarter of the year anyway. The teachers were supportive and gave him oral quizzes.

On his first day, he reported to the gym for P.E. Coach Shield called him into the office while he had the rest of the class run laps around the gym.

"How's the wing?"

Karl shrugged. "They're gonna take this cast off in a couple of weeks and put on a smaller one, I hope. Unfortunately, the doctors say I'm going to need another surgery to fix my wrist. They say the way it is right now, I won't be able to do this." Karl held out his left hand and made a *so-so* motion.

"When are they planning on doing that, do you think?"

"They're hoping to do it in late July, but it might be August. Depends on how quickly this fracture heals."

"Did they tell you the recovery time on that surgery?"

"No, but they said this one is more complicated than the other one."

Shield took a piece of paper out of his desk drawer and put it on the table. "This is from Oregon State. Pretty standard stuff. Just a form I need to fill out that says I still think you're a good kid and a good student." He looked up at Karl. "And whether you're still healthy."

"Which I'm not."

"Which obviously you're not."

"What will that mean?"

"It probably means they'll pull your scholarship for this year."

Karl let his head drop. It was news that he had been dreading, but there was nothing he could do about it, so he tried his best to put it out of his mind.

"Is there anything I can do?"

"Well, we can reapply for a scholarship for next year. You'll be all healed up by then."

Karl nodded. "I hope so. I don't know if I'll ever be completely healed again." He paused, then asked, "Have you ever seen anybody do that? Lose their scholarship and then get one the next year?"

"No," Shield admitted. "But I don't have a lot of experience with these kinds of circumstances. I'm going to have to fill this form out and send it to Coach Anderson, but I'll write a letter that goes with it and plead your case."

"Thanks, Coach." Karl glanced out at the gym, where the class had essentially stopped running laps and was just standing around. "I know you've got to get out there."

"Yeah, they're standing around with their thumbs up their butts. Typical." He stood and picked up his coach's whistle and dropped the loop over his head. "Hey, listen. I heard about how everything went down. You did the right thing."

"Dink's a monster. I couldn't let him pick on those kids." Karl got a sudden flash of insight. "Just tell me that he didn't get a scholarship somewhere."

Shield sucked in his breath and looked away. "He did. He lost it when they found out about his suspension from school. You kids have got to keep your noses clean." He jogged out onto the gym floor, blowing his whistle shrilly.

Chapter Twenty-Eight

Even after he got the shoulder-to-knuckles cast off, Karl still couldn't work either of his jobs. The new cast ran from his bicep to his wrist, but it was restrictive enough that he couldn't deliver pizzas or schlep golf bags at the country club.

That left him with time on his hands. Too much time, really. He spent much of the summer of 1982 trying to plan a future that suddenly had a big hole in it where a college education had once been.

After the accident, the Swansons refused to accept any money from him, and Ellonyia continued to stuff him with food, so making money wasn't a huge concern. But boredom was.

Several times a week, he would go with Eric to the big field behind the high school and hang out with him while he hit golf balls. It was the sports equivalent of watching paint dry, but at least it got him out of the house.

During the weeks and months of recovery, Karl never saw his father. Several times, he drove by his old house—luckily the Falcon was not a stick shift, so he could drive with one arm—but Finley's truck was never there.

The Swansons felt guilty about the fact that Karl had lost his scholarship while sticking up for Eric. They were a solidly upper-middle class family but not well off enough to be able to afford to cover a four-year education for Karl. They did volunteer to let him continue to live rent-free and said that they would pay for him to go to Middle Falls Community College for two years.

Karl was grateful, but when he looked over the programs offered at the local college, he couldn't see anything that appealed to him. He could have gotten an AA in accounting or something like that, but he just couldn't see himself sitting in an office somewhere pushing numbers around all day.

The one thing he was certain of was that he didn't want to go to work at the box factory again. That job, that life, had led him to a bad place, and he didn't want to repeat it.

He got the cast off right after the fourth of July. It was a glorious feeling to be able to take a shower without having a bag over his arm. The first thing he did when he got home from the doctor's office was jump in and scrub that arm, which had itched off and on since the break.

The compound fracture had healed nicely, and the doctor made an appointment with him to remove the screws and plate in a few months.

There was no real pain in the arm, but his movement was definitely restricted. He had never thought about all the times during the day that he made a turning motion with his hand. But every time he had to zip up his pants, or open a doorknob, he was frustrated.

Dr. Chin had given Karl a referral to a wrist and shoulder specialist that had just opened a clinic in Middle Falls.

As much as he would have liked to have had full range of motion in his right arm, he wasn't ready to go through another surgery that would have put him back in a cast for three or four months.

The deciding factor for him was whether or not he could still swing a golf club with his arm as it was.

The first day he got the cast off, his right arm was almost unrecognizable. It was like a small, pale baby brother of his other arm.

Dr. Chin gave him a series of physical therapy exercises, though, and after a few weeks of doing them religiously, the tendons loosened up and it looked normal aside from the surgery scars.

As soon as he felt up to it, he and Eric drove over to the empty field and unloaded their clubs and bucket of balls.

Karl nervously lined up for his first shot. He feared that his first swing would result in a terrible pain, or worse, tearing something that had just been fixed.

He needn't have worried. His first shot was a terrible slice, but it was pain free. Karl looked at Eric, expecting him to say something about the lousy shot, but all Eric could do was smile and say, "Let's go back to work."

They did. They practiced every morning and started going back to the municipal course two or three times a week.

Karl's arm did restrict him in some ways. He had lost about a third of the strength in his arm and it was likely that would never return. But hours of swing practice helped him find workarounds to everything. By August, he was shooting at least as well as he had before the accident.

As soon as he was able, Karl went back to work at both jobs. Neither one was a good long-term fit for him, but he felt the need to be doing *something*.

Red was glad to have him back at P3 and Don Swanson got him into the regular caddy rotation at the country club.

Since he was still living with the Swansons, it almost felt like he was still in high school, but he didn't have to go to classes.

Somehow, three years passed that way.

Karl delivered thousands of pizzas, caddied hundreds of rounds, and lived in the room over the garage.

Eric grew taller and started to look more like his golf pro father. Then he graduated and was accepted into Berkeley.

Karl knew that had to mark a change. As long as Eric was living in the same house, Karl felt comfortable just spinning his wheels and watching the calendar turn. When he realized that he would be alone with the Swansons starting in September, he knew he needed to find a new path.

That was facilitated when Red lost his job at P3. It turned out that there had been small amounts of money missing from the nightly counts over the years. A woman named Nancy Spall managed the pizza parlor for the owner, Hart Tanner. She eventually got suspicious and put in a hidden security camera in the manager's office. Soon, she had the evidence she needed and Red was fired and charged with theft.

Pizza! Pizza! Pizza! needed a new manager, and who better to turn to than the trustworthy Karl, who had been working for them for four years already.

Again, managing a pizza parlor—especially the second-best pizza parlor in town, behind Shakey's—was not a dream job. It was practical, though, and the salary gave Karl enough income that allowed him to get a one-bedroom apartment at The Crestwood.

Don and Ellonyia had never made any mention of him moving out and when he told them his plan, they both seemed distraught at the thought of him leaving.

"Let's just wait a while before you do this," Ellonyia had said. "First Eckie leaving, now you? The house will be so quiet!"

It was slightly ironic that Karl felt like it was harder to move out of the Swansons' house than it had been to leave his own father behind.

Ellonyia elicited a promise that Karl would stop by for dinner at least twice a week so she could make sure he was eating something other than pizza.

Karl was planning on finding some used furniture to fill his new place at the Crestwood, but Don wouldn't hear of it. He helped Karl load the bedroom set onto the rented truck, then told him to start carrying the family room furniture out.

Karl laughed and said, "I'm not taking your furniture."

"Oh yes you are," Ellonyia had said. "I've already bought a new living room set and it's coming from Coleman's this afternoon. I've been wanting something new in there for years. If you don't take this old stuff, it'll be out on the curb for anyone to take."

Karl knew this was just one more thing they were doing for him, but it was already done. He hugged her and kissed her on the cheek and said, "You guys are too much."

Most of the people living at the Crestwood were either young people just starting out or divorced men starting over. In both cases, the furniture that they started with was typically not very nice. As it turned out, the Swanson's old furniture meant that Karl had the best stuff in the complex.

Not that many people ever saw it. With Eric gone, Karl was back to just having Mike as a friend. Mike and Lisa had gotten married a few years earlier, though, so he wasn't around much.

In some ways, this life was similar to the one he had led the first time. He went to work, he came home, he kept to himself. Aside from that one fortuitous meeting with Eric, Karl had never mastered the knack of making friends.

One difference in this life was that he had learned it was important to take care of himself. Even though he worked at a pizza parlor, he still ate healthy, and he exercised.

Though Eric had gone away to college, he still hit the municipal course at least once a week. He had hopes of being able to beat Eric when he came home over the summer vacations.

Eventually, Eric graduated and came back to Middle Falls. He knocked around town for a few months, then started his own business. He opened an auto parts store right in downtown Middle Falls. There was one competitor, but that store had been in business for more than forty years and wasn't current with the times. Eric brought his new ideas about how to handle inventory, including a count-reorder system that allowed him to carry a smaller amount of inventory that still had what his customers needed.

Within two years, his company—*Sav-Mor Auto Parts*—was the only store in town. Eric didn't stop there. He soon added car washes and auto detailing to the services he offered.

It was natural for him to offer Karl the job of manager of the main store.

Karl had been dealing with pizzas for so long—either delivering or overseeing them—that a change was welcome.

The new job came with a better salary again, and that allowed him to move out of the Crestwood—still with the Swansons' old furniture—and into a house in a decent part of town.

Karl golfed regularly with Eric and eventually managed to beat him more than half the time. When he got the technique down, his natural athletic ability finally took over.

So, it wasn't a bad life, but it was still lonely. Eric was his lifetime best friend, but he had a life of his own. He got married in the summer of 1988 and he and his wife had three kids over the next four years. It was natural that he and Karl spent less time together.

Karl managed the auto parts store for Eric for twenty-five years.

It wasn't unusual for Seymour Keynes to come in to the store. Once or twice, he even had his wife, Anna, with him. That always made Karl happy.

Karl kept his vow to stay in shape. When the date of his first heart attack approached, he was nervous, but a different lifestyle led to a different result. He flew right past that date.

He was pleased when he broke into new territory. New movies, new books, new world events that he hadn't seen before.

In September of 2012, Karl left the auto parts store for lunch. It was his forty-ninth birthday and he had been gifted a beautiful sunny day. He made the decision to walk across the street to Artie's for a burger. He didn't eat at Artie's as often as he would have liked—part of that lifestyle change—but when he did, he always walked. He told himself that offset the calories of the burger, fries, and shake.

On this day, it was the sunshine that did him in. A woman coming down Main Street in a green Aerostar minivan was distracted by her children arguing behind her. She turned to scold them and when she turned around again, the sun momentarily blinded her.

She never did see Karl, but she felt the impact as she hit him.

Chapter Twenty-Nine

Karl Strong opened his eyes.

He was in bed, but it took him a minute to recognize the room. He had died and woken up often enough that he had come to expect it to happen again, but he knew immediately that he was in a place—or more accurately, a time—that was different than what he had started in before.

He felt a small movement to his left and turned his head.

Anna.

He was in bed with Anna, and that brought the whole room into focus. This was the house they had lived in after they had moved out of her mother's place in 1982.

Karl tried not to move. He needed time to orient himself.

They had moved into this house after he had graduated and started work at the box factory and had lived there until they separated. That meant that he could have woken up at any time during those years.

It also meant that so many of the crucial events of his life were already behind him. His mother was already dead. He had already married Anna and passed on the scholarship at Oregon State. He had already gone to work at the box factory.

He couldn't help but let a long sigh escape, which caused Anna to stir. She opened one eye and looked at Karl, then closed it again.

"It's early, isn't it?" she mumbled.

Karl looked around the room for a clock, finally found one on the table on Anna's side of the bed.

"It's 6:15."

"Shit," she said quietly. "It's not early then."

"Do I have to go to work today?"

"Unless you came into millions while we slept, Mr. Rockefeller, yes, you have to go to work today."

Karl had meant, *Is this a weekday or a weekend?* but he realized he had phrased it poorly. He was used to waking up alone, where he could take a little time to compose himself.

Anna sat up, stretching. She was wearing an old T-shirt with a faded print of Tigger on it. Her hair was a tangled mess. But when she stretched, the shirt pulled tight against her breasts and Karl felt the old attraction. She looked beautiful to him.

"You still mad at me?" Anna asked.

"What?" Karl was completely lost, coming into a series of events that he had no idea about.

"You were mad at me when you went to bed last night. Remember? You said, 'I don't want to talk about it, so I'm going to bed,' even though it was only nine o'clock."

"No, I don't remember that," Karl said honestly.

"But you *are* still mad at me?"

"I'm not mad at you at all. I'm just trying to get my bearings." Karl made a mental note not to be quite so honest about what he was thinking and feeling.

"Good," Anna said. "I don't like it when you're mad at me." She leaned over and gave him a quick peck before looking away and saying, "Morning breath."

Karl didn't know if she was talking about him or her. Could have been either, or both.

"You better get in the shower first, or you're going to be late."

"Right," Karl said. "Another day saving the world through building better boxes."

Anna gave him an odd look. "I know it's not exciting, but we need to keep these jobs for now."

Jobs, plural. That meant Anna was working, too. No doubt as the receptionist at the veterinary clinic. Karl was starting to tune in to when he was.

He jumped out of bed and said, "Damn, it's cold out here."

"I know. That's why you get up first and turn the heat on." Anna pulled the covers back over her. "And if you were a really good husband, you'd not only do that, but you'd start the coffee, too."

Karl nodded and went into the living room. He couldn't remember where the thermostat was, but he soon found it and cranked it up. Immediately, the baseboard heaters began to tick and put out heat. He quick-stepped into the kitchen and saw that the coffee pot was already set up, he just needed to plug it in.

He headed toward the bathroom—he still had the general layout of the house in his head—but poked his head into the bedroom first. "Coffee's on."

"Thank you, sweetie. Love you."

"Love you too," Karl answered automatically. He kept walking, but wondered, *Is that true? Do I love you?*

He turned the shower on and waited for the old hot water heater in their one-car garage to work, then climbed in and let the water run over him for a few seconds.

From the bedroom, Anna yelled, "Don't use all the hot water. I need a shower too!"

Karl had lived alone for many years in his previous life, and for a moment, he missed that. He had never been responsible to anyone. He never had to tell anyone where he was going. Now he had Anna telling him to take a short shower.

He wet his hair and poured some Prell shampoo into his hand, then lathered up.

His whole previous life already had taken on the golden glow of nostalgia. He had missed out on college, but he'd become part of the Swanson family. Right up until he had gotten hit by that damned minivan, he had spent every holiday with them. He was godfather to Eric's children.

He didn't know if he could say he was *happy* in that life, but he was at least content.

"You almost done?" Anna said, pushing into the bathroom. She pulled down her panties and sat on the toilet.

"Yeah, almost. Just let me get the shampoo out."

Anna stood up unselfconsciously and flushed the toilet.

Karl screamed as the water turned blistering hot.

"Oh, sorry," Anna said with a grin that said she wasn't really sorry at all. "I'll go pack your lunch so you're not late. You better get a move on, though."

Karl dried off and found that Anna had laid out his work clothes on the bed. She may not have been self-conscious around him, but he didn't feel the same. He kept the towel wrapped around him and closed the bedroom door behind him. Just as he dropped the towel and was picking up his underwear, the door swung open and Anna offered him a cup of coffee.

Karl reached for the towel first, but Anna said, "No need for modesty, big guy. I've seen it all before."

Karl felt embarrassed, but let the towel drop. Anna stared at him, bug-eyed, then laughed a little. "Here's your coffee, dufus." She went to the closet and picked out her clothes for the day. After she set them on the bed, she pulled off her T-shirt and panties. She picked her clothes back up and squeezed past Karl, bumping him with her bare butt as she did.

Karl closed his eyes and wished the strong attraction away as best he could.

This was going to be a challenge.

From Anna's perspective, she had successfully pulled off her deception back in high school. She had convinced him that the baby she had been carrying was his. The way she still acted flirtatiously with him, he guessed they were in the first few years of marriage. By the end, she wasn't bumping her naked behind against him as she walked to the bathroom.

He had never discovered her lie during that first lifetime, so it had never been a factor between them.

As he dressed, he tried to figure out how he was going to act toward her, knowing that truth. Should he try and maintain the charade of the marriage? Or just tell her that he knew what she had done, though he had no evidence to offer? Or maybe, he could try to make the marriage work this time.

He knew he needed to get away by himself and think. He finished dressing, pulled on his work boots and knocked on the bathroom door. He heard the shower shut off as he said, "Going to work. See you tonight."

"Hey! You said you weren't mad at me! Where's my kiss?"

Karl took a deep breath, pushed open the door and saw Anna standing naked in the shower. He did his best not to look at her but stepped inside and gave her a chaste kiss.

"Thanks, Mr. Excitement," Anna said, but she didn't seem to be too bothered.

"See you tonight."

"Remember, we've got dinner at Mom's."

"Right."

Outside, he saw his same old work truck. He climbed in, started it up, and turned toward the box factory. The closer he got, the more his stomach knotted.

His last life might not have been perfect, but at least he had managed to avoid the box factory. Now, here he was again, and he could see no escape.

It had been many years since he had driven through the gates of the factory, but it was all still familiar to him. He parked in the lot and waved at guys who he had once known, but now had a hard time coming up with their names.

He found his time card, punched in, then automatically made his way back to his station on the line.

It spoke of how non-challenging his job was that it took him all of thirty seconds to remember what he needed to do.

He lowered his head and, once again, went to work making boxes.

Chapter Thirty

Karl found a little time to think during the day. By the time he had been at work for an hour, he was so back in the groove of what he needed to do that he was able to let his mind wander a little.

That didn't mean that he came up with a solution to his dilemma. His marriage was based on a lie.

Anna knew that, but had no idea that Karl knew. It was a secret so long buried that Karl was willing to bet that she only rarely thought about it.

That was the rub.

The more Karl thought about it, the more he began to believe that, over time, that secret knowledge would begin to wear on him. He would do his best to keep it deep inside, but he was sure it would leak out in various ways, much like his almost missed kiss goodbye. That would probably put them on the same long, slow road to divorce that they had been on the first time around.

When he and Anna hadn't had the pressure of him knowing the truth, they had failed even then.

But Karl had gone through a lot since then. He had learned a lot and thought that he had come up with some changes he could make in himself, mostly including being a better communicator, that would have made some big differences in their marriage.

Concealing a secret as big as, *I know you trapped me into marriage*, is not normally the key to good communication, however.

And so, round and round the ideas went in Karl's mind.

At the end of the shift, he had mostly come to a decision.

He needed to leave Anna.

When they had divorced the first time, she had bounced back very nicely, marrying Seymour Keynes and, at least to all outward appearances, having a happy life.

Once that decision was made, the question became, *how* and *when*?

The *how* part of that equation was pretty easy, really. He just needed to say, "Anna, I want a divorce."

The trickier part of that would be when she asked, "Why?"

Why, when they were still at least mostly happily married, would he drop a bombshell like that?

He knew the other questions that would soon follow. *Are you having an affair? Who is it with?*

The fact that Karl was completely innocent might help, but he knew he would still be put under the harsh spotlight of suspicion, and she might not believe the truth of the matter.

Then there was the question of *when*.

Sooner would be better than later, if only to salve his own conscience. Leading Anna on, to make her believe everything was all right when he knew it wasn't, seemed cruel and pointless.

On the way home, he decided it was best to have that tough discussion that same night. That decision made, he thought about what would happen next.

If Anna threw him out, which seemed likely, where would he go? He couldn't show up on the Swansons' doorstep again. They had no idea who he was in this life. He considered his father, but he had virtually never spoken to Finley after he had married Anna. In fact, he couldn't remember when he had talked to him after he had dropped off the scholarship letter.

Karl had no idea where he and Anna were financially, but he remembered that they had always lived paycheck to paycheck, so there probably wasn't anything in the bank to cover first month's rent and a deposit on a second place.

He pulled into the driveway of the house and muttered, "Why is trying to do the right thing always so damned hard?"

Anna's little Ford Escort was already in the driveway, so he knew she was home. It was a few years old, and was the most stripped-down model available, but they had still needed to make payments on it for quite a few years.

When Karl stepped inside, Anna was already standing there with her coat on. "Come on, let's go. Mom's making lasagna."

Karl felt like he was standing on a precipice. Was this the right moment? Or should he wait until after dinner with her mom? Whatever courage he had built up during the day dissipated and he said, "Should I change my clothes?"

"You're so weird today. *Should you change your clothes to go to dinner at Mom's?* The woman who did your laundry and washed the stains out of your underwear for so long? No, I think she won't be shocked to see you in your work clothes. Let's go, I'm starving."

That brief conversation showed Karl that any thoughts he had to talk to Anna probably wouldn't go as planned. He was remembering now how she often steamrolled right over the top of him.

Just gonna have to be strong, he thought. Somewhere, deep in the back of his mind, he heard a tiny voice that said, *Yeah, right.*

Dinner at Candace's house was fine. Good, even. She was a great cook, and the lasagna was as tasty as he remembered it. Conversation was easy, especially between mother and daughter. If they noticed that Karl was a little quiet, they didn't say anything.

Maybe, Karl realized, he had always been quiet and just didn't think much about it.

They stayed at Candace's for three hours. After dinner, they watched *Highway to Heaven* and *The Facts of Life,* though Karl couldn't focus on any of it. The closer it got to time to leave, the more his stomach knotted.

Karl hated conflict. He didn't want to hurt Anna, he just thought that separating from her was the right thing to do. The conflict raged inside him.

As they put their coats on to leave, Candace kissed him on the cheek and said, "Karl, next week you've got to quit talking our ear off and give us a chance to get a word in edgewise."

He wanted to say, "I'll read a book this week so I have something to talk about," but he didn't. He knew that if he carried through on his plan, he had just eaten his last dinner in this house.

They had taken Anna's Escort because it got better mileage and when you were young and broke, every penny counted. That meant that Anna drove.

When she turned the car on, KMFR was playing *Billie Jean* by Michael Jackson. Anna sang along with it absently. That didn't seem like the right moment to start the conversation. Karl, as he had all night, just stayed quiet.

At home, Anna threw her coat on the back of the recliner. Karl picked it up and hung up both of their coats in the hall closet.

Anna disappeared into the bedroom and Karl sat on the couch, waiting for her to come out so he could have the big talk with her. He wished they had some hard liquor somewhere in the house, but a quick search of the kitchen showed that there wasn't even a beer in the fridge. He was going to have to do this without any liquid courage.

He sat on the couch again, his leg bouncing up and down nervously.

A few minutes later, the bedroom door opened and Anna emerged. She was wearing another faded old t-shirt, this one with a barely visible British flag on it. Her legs were bare, and she didn't even have socks on. As she drew closer, Karl realized that she was probably only wearing the thin shirt and nothing else.

He ignored that fact and steeled himself. *Here we go. This is it. Will I even have enough money to pay for a room at the motel tonight, or will I have to sleep in my truck?*

"I'm sorry about last night," Anna said.

"It's okay," Karl said, and it was, because he had no idea what that argument had been about.

Anna stood in front of Karl and said, "I really do love you, Karl."

This was not going at all according to plan.

Still facing Karl, Anna climbed onto his lap and kissed him. This was no chaste goodbye kiss. This was a firestarter.

Karl couldn't help himself, he moaned a little.

Anna broke off the kiss and smiled. She had liked that response.

She started to unbutton Karl's shirt and kissed his neck and chest.

Karl did not ask Anna for a divorce that night.

Chapter Thirty-One

After that first night, Karl lost his momentum in ending the marriage.

He felt too guilty to have sex with Anna and then the next day break up their marriage. Just when he felt enough time had passed that he wouldn't feel too guilty, the same thing happened again.

Karl knew he could have fixed that by not giving in, but each time that Anna rolled over in bed and touched him gently, that didn't seem like an option.

He felt guilty about it, almost as though he was having an affair with his own wife, but perhaps that was part of the thrill of it.

In the meantime, Karl did make a few other changes.

For one thing, he really missed playing golf. Even so, he didn't have the funds at his disposal to pay for a round at the municipal course, let alone enough to get even a lousy set of clubs.

He thought he would remedy that by getting a second job. That would be tough to explain to Anna, of course.

Hey, honey, I'm going to get a job on the weekends, so we won't be able to spend any time together. Oh, and once I get a little money ahead, I'm going to be buying some golf clubs and then I'll be playing golf. No problem, right?

Karl took the coward's way out and just didn't tell her at first. He started by going to Pizza! Pizza! Pizza! Apparently, Red had already been given the boot, as a middle-aged woman named Barbra was now the manager.

"Do you guys ever need an extra delivery driver?"

"I hire a new driver about once a month, the way things work out," Barbra said, looking Karl over.

"That your truck out there?"

"Sure is."

"Delivering pays minimum wage and whatever you get in tips. People usually drive smaller cars that get better gas mileage."

"I've got an Escort too," Karl said, though he wasn't at all sure how Anna would feel about him using her car to deliver pizzas.

"When are you available?"

"I work full time at the box factory over on Center Street, but I get off at 4:30, and I can deliver any time after that. Weekends are clear, too, but I haven't asked my wife about that yet."

Barbra nodded. "I'm doing okay on the weekends right now, but that's always subject to change." She looked Karl over again. "Tell you what. I'll give you Tuesday and Thursday nights from 5:00 to close. How will that be?"

"That'll be great."

She went into the back room and came back with an application, a P3 hat, and the magnetic sign that went on the side of his vehicle. "I don't have any T-shirts in stock, but I'll order you one. In the meantime, just don't wear anything with profanity on it."

Karl grinned and said that wouldn't be an issue.

"See you tomorrow night, then. You'll get one free medium pizza every night you work, too."

"My wife will like that. Save her from cooking. See you tomorrow!"

When Karl got home, Anna was in the kitchen. She was making Hamburger Helper, which was a staple of their diet. She had not inherited Candace's flair for cooking.

"You're late. Got a little girlfriend on the side somewhere?"

Karl shook his head. "Listen, I need to talk to you."

Concern flashed across Anna's face. "Words no wife ever wants to hear from her husband."

"Or vice-versa," Karl agreed. "But it's nothing bad, I promise."

Anna gave him a look that said, *I'll be the judge of that*, then started to scoop brownish hamburger and pasta onto plates. She handed one to Karl and they both sat at the tiny table in the space that passed for a dining room in their house.

"Okay. What?"

"I want to take up golf."

Anna couldn't help it. She giggled. "If you had given me a million guesses, I never would have gotten that one. I might have guessed, *I won the lottery and didn't tell you* before I would have thought of that."

"I know, it's weird. I used to practice a little with this kid at school, and I really miss it." That was only a half lie. He *had* practiced with Eric; it had just been in a different life.

"Okaaaaay..." Anna said. "Isn't that expensive?"

"Well, it doesn't have to be, but yeah, it's more money than we've got."

"Which is basically nothing."

"Right. So, I went to Pizza! Pizza! Pizza! tonight and applied to be a driver."

Anna squinted at him as though she was having a hard time believing all this.

"So you want to work all day at the factory, then go deliver pizza all night?"

"Just until 10:00. That's when they close. Barbra said that they're usually pretty slow that late on weekdays, so she'll let me go early if that's the case."

"Barbra?"

"She's the manager."

"How cute?"

"Not at all."

"I'll need to verify that."

"You can come with me any time. Oh, and if you don't mind, I'd like to use your Escort to deliver. That way I can save on gas."

"You better not leave me without enough gas to get to work."

"You know me. That will never happen."

Anna looked up at the ceiling, as if she was trying to find an angle to all this that she had missed. Finally, she picked up a forkful of Hamburger Helper and said, "Whatever. I don't get it, but whatever."

It didn't take long for Karl to prove himself to be so reliable to Barbra that she made him the full-time driver during the week.

That required another conversation with Anna, and there was more eye-rolling and questions, but having already agreed to two nights a week, she couldn't find a reason to say no to five nights.

It took Karl a few months to have enough to pick up a used set of clubs that were listed in the paper. Once he had the clubs, he had to work another few weeks to get enough to cover the green fees, too.

Not to mention that Karl was no dummy. He knew that if all Anna got out of him working nights at P3 was that he would be golfing on weekends, too, eventually that would wear on her. He made sure to spread the wealth, such as it was, a little. He bought small presents for Anna every few weeks and remembered to stop and pick up a few flowers on the way home at least once a month.

All that being so, he still had enough left over to play once a week at the municipal course.

Even though he had not played in this lifetime, he was pleased to find it didn't take him long to round back into form. He supposed that he couldn't really call it muscle memory, since these muscles had never swung a club. But he had at least managed to bring something with him from that other life.

He hoped that he would see Eric around the municipal course. He thought that maybe he could hook up with him on a round. Karl missed him and wanted to give a natural friendship a chance to develop again.

He never saw him, though, and he couldn't come up with another way to casually run into him without seeming creepy. He realized that he was just going to have to let his friendship with Eric go unless some golden opportunity presented itself.

Karl was stripped of most of the things that had made his last life good. His only friend, his adopted family, a job that was at least palatable, if not wonderful.

With all of that gone, he focused on what remained from that life: golf.

If he had a different perspective, if he had looked at this life as a new opportunity instead of an extension of the last life, he would have seen things differently.

Instead, exactly what he had initially feared would happen, did.

He didn't do anything *wrong* in his marriage as time went on. He didn't start going to the Do-Si-Do. He didn't flirt with other women or ever entertain an affair.

He just stopped being so *present* in the marriage. The small gifts and occasional flowers dried up, but that wasn't the real issue. It was more that when he *was* home with Anna, he didn't engage with her.

Their conversations became all about schedules and things that were not important. They never teased each other or talked about things that really mattered any more.

One night, Anna dropped a bombshell.

They were sitting down to tacos—another easy to cook meal that she could handle. They had abandoned eating at the dining room table and had taken to eating as they sat in the living room watching TV.

They were watching *Wheel of Fortune*, but when it ended, Anna picked up the remote and clicked the TV off.

Karl looked at her, puzzled. *Jeopardy!* was on next. It wasn't his favorite program, but it was part of what they did on Saturday nights.

"I think we should have a baby."

That threw Karl for a loop for a number of reasons. "Have you been using birth control?"

"Not for quite a while now. Two years probably."

"Then, what else can we do?"

"Well, we could have sex more than once a month. That would help."

Karl flushed but didn't have any answer to that. The decline in their sex life had paralleled the decline in the overall intimacy of their communication. For them, at least, the two seemed to go hand in hand.

Anna leaned forward. "It's not your fault. You're working two jobs, you obviously love playing golf, but those things don't leave very much time for us."

"If you're off the birth control, though, it should still happen eventually, right?" Karl realized that probably wasn't enough. "And you're right. We should be together more often."

Anna smiled ruefully. "I don't want it to be another chore for you to check off your list." She looked at him hopefully, waiting for him to say that it wasn't like that at all.

Instead, Karl sat there silently, thinking.

Anna reached into the folds of the couch and pulled out a brochure. She didn't say anything, but just laid it on the arm of Karl's chair.

It was a glossy trifold brochure. At the top, it read *Mountain Ridge Fertility Clinic*. Below that was an address in Eugene.

"I know it's expensive, and that we don't have the money, but Mom said she'd help. She's still got most of the life insurance from when Dad died. And, you know, the urge to be a grandma is strong."

Karl picked up the brochure but didn't open it.

He knew he needed to do what he should have done a long time earlier. Before he had a chance to overthink it again, he blurted it out.

"I'm sorry, Anna. I want a divorce."

Anna looked at him, disbelief etched on her face.

"Who is it?" Before Karl could issue a denial, she grabbed the brochure and stuffed it back into the couch cushions as though its very existence was an embarrassment. Tears sprang to her eyes and she said, "I trusted you. When you told me you were spending all that time golfing, I believed you. But you weren't doing that, were you? I should have known."

"It's not that. There isn't anyone else."

"Then why?"

"I know you lied about the baby."

Those two short statements—*I want a divorce* and *I know you lied about the baby*—were like a punch to the gut and a slap in the face to Anna.

She blanched. Karl thought, *Even if I didn't know already, I would know now. Her expression gave it away.*

"Listen," Karl said, his voice soft and conciliatory, "I don't want to make a big deal about this. I don't want to fight about it. But I need you to know that I know about what happened in high school."

Anna opened her mouth, but no words came out. Finally, when she did speak, it was an admission. "How?"

"Does it matter?" Karl shook his head. "It doesn't. Not really."

"I need to know. How?"

"I can't tell you." Karl almost added *And you wouldn't believe me if I told you*, but he knew that would only encourage Anna to continue to press him for an answer.

Anna turned her head away. The moment was too shocking, too painful for Anna to make eye contact with Karl.

"Why did you wait so long? If you knew, why did you go ahead and marry me? Why did we stay married all this time?"

"I don't have any good answers, Anna. Except to say that no matter how this started, I grew to love you. I still do."

"Wow." Anna shook her head and that caused her tears to overflow and run down her cheeks. She said it again. "Wow. So that's it, then. That's all she wrote for us." She turned back to Karl. "I just don't understand, why now?"

Her hand dropped and touched the brochure. "Never mind. That's a stupid question. I forced this out of you by bringing this up." She pulled the crumpled brochure out and tossed it on the coffee table. "You didn't want to risk getting tied to me anymore. You've been wanting to leave for a long time."

Karl didn't deny that. How could he, when he had been trying to find a way to ask her for a divorce since the day he had woken up here?

Anna took a deep, shuddering breath, trying to get herself under control. "One thing I've got to know. Was it Mom? Did she tell you?"

That surprised Karl. "Did she know?"

His answer was so genuine that it was obvious to Anna he had not heard this from Candace.

"Had to be Kenny then. That son of a bitch." She spat the words, vehement.

Karl considered being truthful and denying that it was Kenny, but he realized that he didn't owe him any favors. If he didn't deny it, that would, in a way, be confirming it. That would make it easier for Anna to accept. He stayed quiet.

"It wasn't enough that he abandoned me. He had to tell you about it, too." Quietly, under her breath, she said, "Son of a bitch."

"So what's next?" Karl asked. He had dreaded this very conversation for so long, he was surprised that now that it was happening, it wasn't as terrible as he had feared. In fact, clearing the air, telling Anna what he knew, felt like a tremendous weight was lifted off his shoulders.

"What's next?" Anna mused. "No idea. This was not the way I thought this conversation would go. I thought you might be excited and then we'd go to bed and make love. Instead, I'm starting over."

"I can leave," Karl said. He wasn't sure where he would go, but he knew that worst case scenario, he could go and park somewhere and sleep in his truck.

"I need to know something," Anna said.

"Anything. This is the time for truth."

"Can you forgive me for what I did? All of it? I tricked you. That made you lose your scholarship, and wrecked your future. Now you've worked a job you hate just to keep us alive. Can you forgive me for all of that?"

Karl thought back to another time. Another life, another Anna. He remembered sitting in her living room the day she had dropped out of high school, telling her that he knew what she had done.

He answered honestly. "I already have. Not forgiving you hasn't been the problem. The problem has been that knowing has been like a wall between us."

Anna wiped tears away and sniffled. She scooted down on the couch so she was closer to Karl. "If that's true, if you've really forgiven me, can we try a fresh start? You say you've grown to love me. I've loved you from the beginning."

That was a new idea to Karl. He had always associated telling Anna what he knew with the end of their relationship.

Anna was staring at him intently, which made it hard for him to think, but he did his best.

He tried to envision what his life would look like after they divorced. He would have more time to himself. He wouldn't feel guilty about taking time to golf.

And he knew he would be lonely.

The time he spent with Anna was quiet, maybe even a little too quiet. But what if he didn't feel the need to retreat into himself anymore when he was around her? What would things be like if he was open and honest with her? It seemed like things could be better.

"Tonight is all about honesty, so I'll tell you the truth," he finally said. "I don't know for sure."

Anna nodded, willing to accept that.

"But maybe, yes. Maybe we can have a fresh start."

Now Anna's tears really came and she couldn't hold back a sob. Feeling sorry for yourself can cause strong emotions. But, forgiveness? Grace? Much more so.

She slipped off the couch and sat on Karl's lap. She laid her head against his shoulder and continued to cry softly.

Karl wrapped his arms around her and held her tight.

They didn't talk any more for a long time.

For once, they had let their guard down and said everything that needed to be said.

They stayed huddled together like that for a long time.

Finally, Anna stood up and reached a hand out to Karl and led him to the bedroom.

They made love and it was the best it had ever been.

Chapter Thirty-Two

Life was different—better—for both Karl and Anna in almost every way after that night.

It wasn't that they lived in some fairy tale romance where he swept her off her feet every night when he got home. It wasn't even that they never argued or fought.

It was that when they had disagreements, they were honest ones. They said what they felt, without a hidden agenda or buried resentments.

Those arguments were few and far between, though.

Mostly, they just lived their lives and tried to plan for a good future.

They tried the fertilization treatments in Eugene, but they never took. After several tries—and a large influx of money from Candace Masterson—they came to accept that they were a two-person family unless they wanted to adopt.

They did some initial inquiries into that, but it was a long and complex process, exacerbated by the fact that they didn't make very much money.

Once they were able to talk honestly about things, it made planning for the future easier.

Karl remembered that many lives ago, he had asked Allen Ray about the possibility of advancement at the box factory. He had seemed inclined to give him a shot, but then Karl had died before it happened.

This life, he tried it again. He was much younger, but he already had a track record with the company and was given the chance to be a line supervisor.

He still didn't love working there, but with increased responsibility, the job wasn't as boring. And the money was better, which meant that he got to stop delivering pizzas. That gave him more time at home with Anna, but he still had enough money to golf on Saturday mornings.

With several lifetimes of practice and hundreds of rounds of golf behind him, Karl had become an excellent golfer.

Good enough that when he saw a poster for a tournament, he talked to Anna and ponied up the fifty bucks to enter.

He didn't win the tournament, but he was in contention until late in the second day, when it was possible that the pressure had gotten to him a little bit. He wasn't used to having eyes on him as he lined up a putt or calculated a chip shot.

Still, third place paid out $250.

He used the money to take Anna to the coast for a nice overnight stay in Lincoln City.

Time passed, and the two of them never spoke of divorce again. They never needed to. They became each other's partners and support team, instead of two people living separate lives under the same roof.

The fact that he started out in a small supervisory role at the factory in his twenties meant that by the time he was in his thirties, he was the most senior line supervisor. When Allen Ray decided to retire, he was the obvious candidate to replace him.

All those years, he worked in the same building with his father, but rarely spoke to him.

Finley couldn't understand why Karl avoided him but never tried to bridge the gap.

Karl had the neglect of a number of lifetimes as evidence, though, and could not find a reason to seek a relationship with someone who wasn't interested in him.

Karl made sure he stayed in shape again this life. He bought a treadmill and put it in the garage for those long, rainy Middle Falls winters. He and Anna took cooking classes together at the college and, as it turned out, he was the better cook. He eventually took over most of the cooking duties for them.

After years of watching him go off to the golf course every weekend, Anna finally asked him if he could teach her.

It was a long road, but it was a good excuse for them to spend time together. Karl remembered the lessons Eric had given to him lifetimes earlier and taught Anna the same way.

She was never great, but over a few years, she became good enough. She liked the social aspect of the game and even joined a woman's group that golfed every Tuesday evening.

It was in that group that she met Danica Swanson, Eric's wife. They became friends and eventually Anna asked Karl if he would be interested in going to a barbecue at the Swanson house.

He said he wouldn't mind that at all.

That Saturday, they turned up at the Swansons and Karl was almost overwhelmed with a sense of déjà vu. It turned out that the barbecue wasn't actually at Eric's house. It was at Don and Ellonyia's Swanson's.

Karl did his best to keep a neutral face when Don Swanson, in his mid-sixties but still as trim and fit as ever, answered the door.

Ellonyia was still beautiful, her blonde hair gone to a natural silver. When Karl gave her a surprise hug, he had a hard time keeping the tears out of his eyes. He felt that he owed them so much.

Of course, they had no memory of knowing Karl, but as people drifted in, the four Swansons gravitated to Karl and Anna. By the end of the barbecue, Eric had invited Karl to golf as his guest at the country club.

It was an unexpected bonus in this life. Karl and Eric didn't become the same kind of friends that they had been as teenagers, virtually sharing a room, watching TV and playing Dungeons and Dragons. But just knowing Eric again, once more being a small part of the Swanson family, was a reward in itself.

That was one of the hardest parts of the repetitive lives. The people that he knew so well, the people he loved learned about him all over again and he had to pretend to do the same.

Finley Strong once again died of a heart attack while at his station at the box factory.

Everyone tiptoed around Karl for weeks after, but it affected him very little. Finley had been gone from his life for as long as he could remember, so having him completely gone again didn't make much of a difference.

Karl again passed the farthest point he had ever lived. He always looked both ways and waited patiently before crossing Main Street.

Still, life eventually catches up to everyone. Some people like to say that Father Time is undefeated. To many of those who live in Middle Falls, though, they know he can at least be fought to a standstill.

But not in each individual life.

In March of 2023, Karl was fifty-nine years old. He was the plant manager at the box factory and was looking forward to his retirement in a few years. He had built up a nice pension and was planning on retiring when he turned sixty-two.

When he finally reached that milestone, he and Anna planned to do what they had talked about for many years. They were going to buy an RV and drive around the country. Neither of them had ever been very far from the place they were born, and they wanted to rectify that.

Life had other plans.

The third Tuesday in March started just like every other day.

Karl kissed Anna goodbye, told her that he loved her, and drove his two-year-old Cadillac to the plant.

He met with a salesman who pitched a product that he said would increase productivity on the line by fifteen percent and would pay for itself in three years. Karl heard sales pitches like that with regularity.

He touched the button on the same old-fashioned intercom he had used for more than twenty-five years. "Helen? Can you send up John? I need to run something past him."

Those were the last words he spoke in this life.

His heart gave out and he fell forward, dead before his head hit the desk.

Chapter Thirty-Three

Karl Strong opened his eyes.

His death had been so sudden that he jumped as though he was falling.

He looked around in a slight panic.

He was alone. He was lying down on the bed in his rented house in Crampton Village.

He tried to sit up and found that was an effort.

"Oh, no. Come on."

He threw the sheets back and saw that he was fat again. He closed his eyes, wishing that he was anywhere other than where he was, but after this many lifetimes, he knew that was for naught. No matter what, the only way out of this life was death.

He rolled that idea around in his brain.

Death seemed so attractive to him. He wondered if he had it in him to roll the dice again. He had come to believe that the point where he woke up was completely random. Sometimes he had a chance to change things, to build a better life. Others, like when he woke up here, it seemed hopeless.

Hopeless or not, he knew he couldn't do himself in. Even if no one in particular would miss him, he just didn't have that in him. Not to mention that as random as his reawakening points were, he might just keep waking up in the same spot.

The alarm on the clock radio began to beep. He turned it off but made no effort to get out of bed. He didn't know exactly what point he was at, but he had decided not to play this life. He wouldn't go to work, he wouldn't do anything.

What can I change from this point? he thought. *Not much, really. College is long past in the rearview mirror. I'm so fat and out of shape that my heart is liable to give out again any day.*

Those thoughts fled and were replaced by one word: *Anna.*

She had been, in so many ways, the central figure in many of his lives. Avoiding her. Marrying her. Asking for a divorce, then having a wonderful marriage with her.

It was that last that was the rub.

In his last life, Karl had not just had friends, he had made a small two-person unit that he knew would always be there for him.

Now he knew that she wasn't just gone from him, she was, almost certainly, *irretrievably* gone. She was married to Seymour Keynes. She lived in a beautiful house in Falling Waters. There was no path he could see to be with the woman who, just a few moments earlier from his perspective, he had loved and shared a life with.

Even if he could manage to somehow get in shape and avoid the heart attack that was probably barreling toward him at that very moment, it didn't matter.

Anna was gone.

He swung his legs over the bed and stood up, swaying a little. He had been fifty-nine years old just a few minutes earlier, but he felt much older in this thirty-something body.

He stumbled out into the living room, which was nearly as dark as the bedroom. He looked around, trying to determine more precisely when he had been dropped into this life.

Things were filthy and messy. That meant that it was some time before he had made the decision to turn his life around.

Beside his recliner, there were stacks of boxes from instant meals. He bent over and peered closely at them. He saw movement. It was an entire line of small black ants transporting tiny bits of food from the boxes down the table leg and under the baseboard.

"Gross," Karl said, but didn't do anything about it.

Those were the dinners that Anna bought me, so I'm somewhere between the first heart attack and the one that finished me off. I had time to get back into shape, though, so that's got to be a ways off.

Karl knew, then, that he had time to make a change in this life. He also knew after living through this stage of his life so often, that there really wasn't any chance at making serious, long-term changes.

"To hell with it." He sat heavily and turned on the television. *The Today* show was on and Matt Lauer was interviewing Sharon Stone about her new movie. Karl couldn't have cared less. He wasn't really watching anyway.

He had chosen to wallow in his misery.

He did that for a few hours, then realized he was hungry. Wallowing was fine, but wallowing with hunger pains was not to be done.

Looking down at himself, he saw he was wearing a stained T-shirt and underwear. He considered going out in just that but decided that might have negative consequences that he didn't want to face.

He switched on the overhead light in his bedroom and fished around the dirty clothes on the floor until he came up with a pair of blue sweatpants.

Ugly, dirty, and with a tear in one knee, but Karl knew that they would at least count as being dressed.

He didn't bother to look in the mirror, where he would have seen that his hair was sticking out at greasy angles and that he desperately needed a shave. When Karl didn't shave for a week, he didn't get sexy stubble like George Clooney or John Grisham. He just looked like he needed to shave.

He didn't care.

He scooped his keys out of the bowl and opened the door. It was bright and sunny outside, which felt completely at odds with Karl's mood.

He grumbled something unintelligible to himself, then got in the truck and drove to Safeway. He parked as close as he could to the front and walked slowly toward the automatic door. A woman in her late twenties was just emerging from the store. When she saw Karl, she put a protective hand on her daughter and hurriedly moved aside.

Karl didn't notice. He grabbed a shopping cart and went up and down the aisles like he was preparing for a winter storm.

He grabbed bags of chips and pretzels by the handful and tossed them in the cart. Down the candy aisle, he snatched up multiples of M&Ms, Reese's Peanut Butter Cups, and Kit Kats. He really hit his form when he got to the frozen food aisle.

He cleaned out much of the frozen pizza, then moved on to the Hungry Man dinners and eventually, the ready-to-bake pies.

When he finally turned his cart toward the checkout line, it was heaped high.

If the first woman who saw him had moved out of the way with alacrity, that reaction was even more pronounced once he was pushing a cart filled with frozen food and empty carbohydrates.

Again, Karl didn't care. He was at a point where, a few hours earlier, suicide had seemed like a momentarily viable option, so the fact that people looked at him with disgust didn't even register.

The cashier did her best to be pleasant and make conversation with Karl as she rang up his purchases.

"Got a big party coming up?" she asked with a smile.

"Nope."

"Oh," was all she could muster, but she did shoot a wide-eyed look at the boy who was bagging up all the food at the end of the conveyor belt.

Eventually, she said, "That will be $269.47."

Karl pulled out his checkbook and painstakingly filled out a check.

He had no idea if he even had that much money in the account.

Again, he didn't care. If Chief Deakins wanted to come arrest him for kiting a check, he would be the county's responsibility and they could feed him.

The cashier ran the check under the scanner, put it in the drawer, and handed the long receipt to Karl. "Thank you, Mr. Strong."

Karl didn't answer. Since he had woken up, it had begun to feel like he was the only real person in the world. Everyone else almost seemed like caricatures, people who would blink out when he inevitably died again.

He drove home and found that though the freezer was empty to start with, he had bought too much food to fit into it anyway.

He shrugged, stuffed as much as he could inside, then started stacking boxes in the refrigerator. He turned the oven on to four hundred degrees and decided that he would just keeping baking pies and frozen pizza until there was room for everything.

The assembly line of bad food kept him tied up for the rest of the afternoon.

While it was baking, he went into the living room and looked at the empty boxes that were stacked on the table beside his chair. He knew he would need room, so he swept them all onto the floor and left them there.

When he finally turned the oven off, there were three pizzas, two apple pies, and a tinfoil pan full of lasagna on the kitchen table.

"Good enough," he said with a nod. He picked up the pan of lasagna, which was intended for a family of four, and sat heavily in his recliner. He twisted the top off a two-liter bottle of Pepsi and took a long drink.

He turned the TV on and an episode of *Roseanne* came on. Machine-like, Karl began to shovel lasagna into his mouth.

Roseanne gave way to *Grace Under Fire*. By then Karl had polished off the lasagna. He dropped the tin into the pile of other boxes on the floor, then grunted as he stood up again. The pepperoni pizza was cool enough that he picked it up whole and sat back with it on his lap.

He had sliced the pizza into only four slices. He folded each of them in half and methodically chewed his way through the entire thing.

Karl followed essentially this same path day after day until he ran out of food.

When he had finally consumed the last of what he had bought, he grabbed his checkbook and prepared to leave the house for the first time in ten days.

This time, when he finally peeked outside, it was raining. He was still dressed in the same clothes, only much more stained and ruined.

He made it to his truck when the heart attack hit. He fell forward, smashed his face into the driver's side window, and fell onto his back.

He lay in the muck and the mud for quite some time, waiting to die.

《 》

KARL STRONG PLAYED out the same life in the same way seventeen more times.

Interlude Three
Universal Life Center

Margenta tilted her pyxis and paused the image. She saw a heavy man sitting in a recliner, gasping for air. He was obviously dying but did not seem upset about it. Instead, he lay back as though he had expected this very thing, taking small sips of oxygen like a goldfish pulled out of its bowl.

The frame around the picture was a neutral taupe.

"I think you've had him repeat that sad little life so often that you've completely broken his spirit."

The voice came from over her shoulder, and it made Margenta jump. She whirled around and saw Carrie and Charles standing behind her.

She opened her mouth to reprimand them, but then looked closer and saw the small blue bird sitting on Charles' shoulder.

Whatever she was planning to say died in her mouth. She reconsidered and said, "Well, yes, I believe that this experiment has perhaps gone on a few lifetimes too long."

"Those lives are no longer feeding Me," the small blue bird said. Its voice came from nowhere and everywhere, a soft gentle tone that chimed like a bell but had to nonetheless be obeyed.

Margenta had never been rebuked directly by The Machine. When she had been the Head Watcher, she treated things more like a bureaucracy, handing out harsh words and perhaps kicking a complaint up to the next level, but not all the way to the top.

The blue bird was the top.

It was The Machine.

Odd that such an all-powerful entity would choose such a small and innocuous way to present itself, but that was the way it often was with the truly powerful. Appearances are not important when you control the universe.

"I...well...I mean..." Margenta could not get a sentence out.

Instead, sentence was passed.

"I love you, Margenta," The Machine said. "And I want to see you be the best version of yourself."

Carrie looked at Charles.

"Can you take over her caseload?"

"Of course," Charles answered. When he reached for Margenta's pyxis, she was gone. Only the pyxis remained.

The gentle voice said, "Margenta needed to see things from a new perspective. I am helping her with that."

The bird didn't exactly disappear, but almost seemed to shrink into itself until it could no longer be seen.

Carrie touched Charles' shoulder. "See if you can find a better starting place for this soul."

"I'll need to create some equations for this, but I'll get him started again in a better spot."

《 》

IN THE MIDDLE FALLS, Oregon hospital, a red-faced baby was born. The parents had been sold on the name *Julia* for her, but when the mother looked at the baby, who was squalling heartily, she said, "Her name is Margaret. We'll call her Marge."

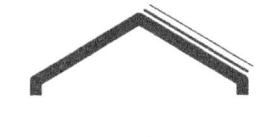

Chapter Thirty-Four

Karl Strong opened his eyes.
He stumbled slightly but someone caught him.
"Sorry," he said automatically.
"It's okay," a girl's voice said from very near.
Very near. As in, just a few inches from his ear.

He had gotten so used to dying and waking up in the same nightmare scenario over and over that he had essentially given up. Each life was dedicated to one focused idea: death by gluttony.

Now he was here. Wherever or whenever *here* was.

The girl who had spoken to him was close. In fact, he realized that she was laying her head against his shoulder.

Anna?

It took him a moment, but he got his bearings. He was in the multipurpose room. Music was playing and he was, apparently, dancing. He listened carefully to the music, hoping that would give him a clue.

It was The Brothers Johnson's version of *Strawberry Letter #23*.

He glanced around without moving his head too much. Everyone was dressed just like they did for school. No leisure suits or tuxes, so it wasn't a formal dance like Tolo or Prom.

The song ended and Lisa Hanson looked up at him shyly.

Lisa Hanson? Mike's wife Lisa Hanson?

But of course she wasn't Mike's wife yet. Or, perhaps, not even his girlfriend, judging by the way she had been snuggled up to him during the song. He looked nervously around to see if Mike was going to come blasting out of nowhere and clean his clock for dancing with Lisa.

No such blasting occurred.

Instead, Lisa smiled and said, "Thanks for the dance," then walked back to the wall to stand with her girlfriends. She looked so young. Just a girl, really.

Karl was dazed. This was a place he had not ever revisited before. It must be a sock hop at the high school. One of those informal dances they held after basketball games so that kids wouldn't be so likely to go off somewhere and get drunk or pregnant.

I don't remember ever slow dancing with Lisa Hanson, Karl thought. *But there's the evidence, and I guess I did.*

He looked around the room to see if Anna was anywhere in sight. She wasn't, which told Karl that this might be his freshman year. Since Anna was a year behind him, if he was a frosh, she would still be in eighth grade and not invited to high school dances.

There wasn't a real DJ at these dances. The school would never go for an expense like that. Instead, there was a single turntable hooked into the room's sound system. Not great, but no one was there for the perfect sound. Everyone tended to go to these dances hoping for, as Journey would soon put it, some *Lovin' Touchin' and Squeezin'*.

That meant there was twenty or thirty seconds of dead air while one 45 was taken off and another was put on.

That time passed with Karl standing motionless in the middle of the dance floor. Then Jimmy "Bo" Horne's *Dance Across the Floor* came on and he was jostled by dancers.

That was Karl's cue to exit the dance floor. He backed up against the wall and looked around, trying to get his bearings.

I guess I'll never understand how this whole thing works, he thought. *Make me repeat the same miserable life again and again, then toss me into someplace I barely remember and see what I do. It doesn't make any sense.*

The fast song ended and Mr. Davidner, the English teacher who must have drawn the short straw and ended up chaperoning the sock hop, picked up the microphone.

"That's it, folks. Ten o'clock. You don't have to go home, but you can't stay here. Wait, that's a joke. You're kids. You most definitely have to go home."

Karl headed to the exit, unsure of what was next. A young-looking Mike Tomkins put a shoulder into him and grinned, showing off a set of braces that Karl had all but forgotten about. "Slow dancing with Lisa, huh? She's kinda cute, isn't she?"

"Yeah, sure," Karl said, then took mercy on him. "But I think she's more your type than mine."

Mike's eyes lit up. "Really? You think she likes me?"

"I think you'll never find out if you don't ask her to dance some time."

Mike grinned in such an aw-shucks sort of way that Karl couldn't help but like him. He could have said, *Mike, you're gonna work up the nerve. You'll be together through the rest of high school, then get married, and ten years later get divorced. Enjoy. Have a good time.*

He did not, of course. He had never considered ever telling anyone about the strange time looping that was happening to him. He did wonder, from time to time, if it was also happening to anyone else he knew and maybe they were just keeping it to themselves as well.

"You still want a ride home?" Mike said, pulling Karl out of his reverie.

"What?" Karl felt a small flood of relief. He wasn't sure *how* he was supposed to get home. He knew that he didn't have the Falcon yet, but he wondered if maybe he had ridden his ten-speed bike there that night. "Oh, yeah, that'd be great."

"We better go, then. Dad will be waiting outside, getting more impatient every second."

"I'll follow you," Karl said. For the life of him, he couldn't remember what Mike's dad looked like or what he might be driving.

They stepped out into the crisp night and that helped Karl zone in on when he was. He could see his breath in front of him, so it was at least October. The sock hops were always after a varsity basketball game, so that meant it was likely November or December.

What year was I a freshman? he wondered. He had to do the math. I *Graduated in '82, but it was '81 at the start of my senior year. If I'm a freshman, it's gotta be November or December 1978.*

He tried to pull any more specific memories about that time but couldn't remember a thing. His mom would have been dead for a little more than a year, then. Everything after that felt like a blur for years and years. Almost the rest of that life, really.

"There he is, smoking a stogie," Mike said, pointing to a Ford pickup. "It's the only place he can smoke them without Mom getting on his case."

Mike climbed in first, scooting over on the bench seat enough to make room for Karl.

"Thanks for giving me a ride home, Mr. Tomkins."

"No problem." Dale Tomkins took a deep drag on the cigar he was smoking, then rolled his window down and blew the smoke outside. "Your mom's got a nose like a bloodhound for these things," he said to Mike.

Mike didn't answer, just grinned at Karl.

Mr. Tomkins put the truck in gear, pulled out of the parking lot, and turned right, toward Crampton Village. Karl was glad that he hadn't asked for directions because he wasn't a hundred percent sure whether they had already moved into that house or not. Since that was the direction they were heading, he guessed they must have, and Mr. Tomkins knew it.

There was music playing, but it wasn't KMFR. There was an 8-track player in the truck and Johnny Cash's *At Folsom Prison* was in the player. *Flushed from the Bathroom of Your Heart* was playing, and Mike sang along.

Before the song was finished, Mr. Tomkins turned the truck into Crampton Village and slowed down. "Which one is it again?"

"That one," both Mike and Karl answered, pointing at the run-down house that looked unchanged from the last time he had seen it.

"Your dad's not home?" Mr. Tomkins asked. There were no vehicles in the driveway, and the house was completely dark. His ten-speed leaned up against the house. Karl remembered that Finley would still be driving the Falcon himself at that point. He wouldn't buy the truck and give the car to Karl for another two years.

"No, he had to be somewhere tonight," Karl lied. "It's okay. I knew about it. The door's not locked."

"Okay, I'll wait until you're inside to make sure."

Mike bopped Karl on the shoulder and said, "See ya."

Karl hopped out and hoped that what he had said was true and that the door was unlocked. If not, he wondered if he might have a key stuck deep in his jeans pockets.

The doorknob turned easily, though, and the door pushed open. He turned and waved at Mike and his dad, then gratefully slipped inside. For once, he was glad to be alone in the house. He needed to think.

He switched lights on in the living room, kitchen, and then the bathroom, trying to banish the deep shadows.

He looked at the mirror and gasped a little at how young he looked. His hair was much shorter than he could remember it ever being in high school, but that wasn't the oddest thing. It was his face, which was still child-like, with a little baby fat. Not to mention that he had to stand on tiptoes slightly to see himself in the mirror over the sink.

"Guess my big growth spurt is still coming."

He rubbed his hand over his short hair and concluded, "Gonna have to do something about that."

He wandered through the rest of the house and found that it wasn't much different from any other time he had been there. It was like it was stuck in a time capsule. He opened the refrigerator and cupboards and saw there was a little more food than he was used to. Finley must not have slipped as far into his alcoholism as he eventually would.

There was no junk food and that sat well with Karl. After his last round of repetitive lives, he hoped to never see another pie or bag of chips again. Just the thought of what he had been doing to himself made him a little queasy.

He decided to go to bed before his dad came home from the Do-Si-Do.

After turning off all the lights, he took off his clothes and dropped them on the floor. He fell into the same deep slumber he always did on his first day in a new life.

Chapter Thirty-Five

He woke up to see Finley standing over him. He was surprised at how good his father looked. The years of too much drinking, not enough sunlight and too many hours spent on a barstool had taken their toll on his father in previous lives. It was easier to see when he dropped back in suddenly like this.

"Just wanting to check and see if you're alive," Finley said.

"Why?"

"Because it's ten o'clock. You've slept most of the day away."

Karl sat up, trying to shake the sleep from his brain. "It is? Geez, I don't know why." He did, but telling his dad that he always fell into a semi-coma the first night after waking up in a new life wasn't on the agenda. "I'll get up."

"It's a free country," Finley said. "But I want you to rake up all those leaves I told you to do last week before you go anywhere."

"I'll do it right now."

Finley waved at him in a *calm down* gesture. "Go ahead, get some breakfast first, then do it."

Karl nodded and Finley left, shutting the bedroom door behind him.

Karl felt a surge of energy. Other than his brief five-minute life when he had saved his mother from dying, he had never woken up this early. He had a chance to stop so many of the things that had gone wrong.

The last time he had been a freshman, he had been so devastated by the loss of his mother that he had sleepwalked through the entire year. He had gotten horrible grades and had to work hard just to get his grade point average into decent shape to be eligible for college. But now, the loss of his mother—while still devastating and painful—was a distant and unchangeable pain.

If Finley wanted him to rake leaves, that probably meant that it was only November. By December, the leaves were all gone. That meant he had more than half the year to buckle down and get his grades headed in the right direction. That was one mistake he could fix.

Any possible entanglement with Anna was still years away, so he didn't need to worry about that yet.

He thought of Eric and his parents. If Karl was a freshman, then Eric was only a sixth grader. It had not seemed too out of place for Karl to be friends with Eric when they were both in high school. It *would* be weird for a high schooler to be friends with an elementary school kid, though. So, he would have to wait to find a way to reestablish that relationship.

He let his mind wander over the possibilities that were ahead for him. After the spiraling depression of so many lives when he couldn't change anything, he felt like a weight was lifted off him and he could do anything.

His mind settled on an idea.

Golf.

In his last full life, he had further refined his game and had almost reached the goal of many lifetimes: to be a scratch golfer. He hadn't quite gotten there in his most recent life with Anna, but he had gotten close. He wondered if, with a number of lifetimes of lessons and practice behind him, plus getting such an early start this life, he could do even better than that.

He toyed with an idea that had been in the back of his head for lifetimes without ever being fully expressed. If he really focused and practiced, could he maybe qualify for the Pro Golf Tour? It was a distant dream, but if things worked as they had in previous lifetimes and he carried much of his ability with him, it was at least possible.

There were roadblocks, of course. He was barely fifteen and didn't have a car, a job, or clubs. He couldn't see Finley pitching in a lot for something like golf clubs, so he would have to solve that problem for himself.

He threw the covers back and jumped out of bed, feeling energized. In the kitchen, he poured himself a bowl of Wheaties with milk and gulped them down in record time. Once he'd dressed in warm clothes, he hurried out to the one-car garage. He grabbed the rake and attacked the leaves with an energy rarely seen in a teenager doing chores.

Forty-five minutes later, the leaves were raked and bagged, and the rest of the day stretched out before him. He went inside and saw that Finley was putting his shoes on.

"Got called in to work," he said. "Damned factory."

Karl knew that was a lie. If Finley had to work on a Saturday, he would have been up and gone well before noon. There were some indications that Finley was paying a little more attention to the world around him at this time. Food in the cupboard, caring about whether the leaves were raked. But being unable to go an entire day without visiting the Do-Si-Do and getting drunk showed he was on the same path as always.

"Sorry, Dad. That sucks."

"Part of being a grownup," Finley said, slipping out the door. Slip sliding away.

Karl didn't care. His father hadn't been part of his life for so many decades, so many lives, that he was a non-factor in any plans Karl might have had.

He gave Finley time to get out of the driveway, then went outside and pulled his bike away from the house. It had been a very long time since he had ridden a bicycle, but the old saying proved true. He hadn't forgotten how.

But he *had* forgotten how damned cold the hard plastic seat could be after sitting out overnight. He rode the first mile or two standing up on the pedals.

As he made his way through town he saw that it was essentially the same Middle Falls he had last seen. There were a few changes. Safeway hadn't gone in yet, so Smith and Son's was the only grocery option. Everything else seemed to be essentially unchanged, though.

He took a quick tour through town, then turned toward his real destination—the municipal golf course. It was built on the edge of town, toward the Silvery Moon Drive-in. By the time he had gotten there, he was warmed up, but hadn't begun to feel tired yet. There was no substitute for being a teenager.

He rolled past the wooden sign that read *Middle Falls Fairways*. This course wasn't nearly as nice as the Middle Falls Country Club, but it was well-maintained and Karl had come to think of it as his home course.

Even in the dead of winter, there were quite a few cars in the parking lot. It was a sunny day and though it was cold, duffers were dreaming of a distant spring. They were out to get one last round in before the rains and snow arrived for real.

Karl walked into the familiar clubhouse. Jake Farley, who had run things every time Karl had ever been at the course, was behind the desk. He was taking money from two middle-aged golfers and making change for them.

Karl tried to be as unobtrusive as possible. He wandered through the small shop area looking at golf balls, towels, clubs, and bags.

When the two men left to head out to the course, the little shop was empty except for him and Jake.

"Can I help you with something, son?" Jake asked.

"I'd like a job."

Jake smiled but said, "I like your attitude, but there aren't a lot of jobs here. Me and my son mostly run things. Have you tried looking in town?"

"No. I want to work here."

"Now why in the world would you have your heart set on working at this golf course?"

"Because I want to be a golfer."

That seemed to amuse Jake. "Have you ever golfed?"

That was a tricky question, of course. Karl had spent thousands of hours over his lifetime with a golf club in his hands. But in this life, he had never so much as picked up a putter. Still, he thought it was okay to stretch things a little.

"Yes, sir. A lot."

Jake raised his eyebrows and said, "A lot, huh? Well, that's a good start. How old are you?"

"I just turned fifteen."

"Well, sorry, son, but I just don't have anything for you."

Karl stepped to the counter and looked up at Jake. "I'll bet there are things around here that you have to do that you'd rather have someone else do instead."

"Yep, that's true. That's pretty much true of every job, though. You'll find that for yourself in a few years."

Karl tried another tactic. "I don't want money, but I'll do a lot of those things for you. I'll keep the sidewalks swept, I'll run the vacuum over the carpet in here, I'll go out and pick up all the range balls for you. I'll work hard and never be in the way."

Now Jake was definitely amused. "If you don't want money, what do you want?"

"I want to borrow an old set of clubs, and I want to be able to golf whenever I've caught up on everything else."

Jake shook his head. "I wish my other son had half the ambition you do. He's about your age and I can't even get him to show up here. I'm sorry, though. I just don't think I can do it."

Desperation fueled what Karl said next.

"I'll bet I can drive a ball farther than you can."

That was a risk on Karl's part. When he was in his full, adult body, he had been able to outdrive most everyone at the course. But now he was fifteen, and he hadn't ever attempted a drive since he had woken up in this life. Not to mention that Jake was a pretty fair golfer.

Jake looked at Karl, then looked around as if someone might be having him on. "Is this one of those *Candid Camera* kind of shows?"

"Nope," Karl said. He had started down this road, he felt like he might as well see it through. "If I can't outdrive you on two out of three shots, I'll get on my bike and go away. I won't come back until I have money in my pocket and clubs on my back. But, if I *do* beat you best two out of three, then I get to do all the work you don't want to do in exchange for borrowing some clubs and golfing a round when there's room on the course."

Karl hadn't heard it, but a threesome of men had come in behind him.

Jake looked away from Karl, then said, "You gentlemen ready for your tee time?"

Karl stepped away so Jake could conduct his business.

The oldest of the four men, who looked like he might be in his early sixties, said, "I'm more interested in the wager this young man offered. I'll tell you what. If he can do what he says, I'll put up his green fees for a round and he can golf with us today."

Karl said, "Thank you, mister," then grinned up at Jake. "Whaddya say?"

Jake raised his voice and said, "Junior, come in and watch the desk for a few minutes. I've got to step out."

A teenage boy, who appeared to be seventeen or eighteen, and who Karl assumed was Jake Junior, stuck his head around the corner and said, "Okay, Dad. I've got it."

Jake stepped into a back room and emerged a few seconds later with a bucket of balls and two drivers. One looked brand new. The other looked like it had been rescued from the junk heap. He handed the second one to Karl and said, "Let's go."

The older man who had offered to front Karl a game said, "I think he's nervous. Anyone want to bet against the kid?"

The youngest man said, "What kind of odds?"

"I'll take two to one."

"Done," the younger man said. He fished a twenty-dollar bill out of his wallet and said, "Let me see the color of your money."

The older man took a ten spot out and both men handed their money to the third. He looked at Karl and smiled. "Don't let me down, son. I love betting on an underdog."

Karl grinned and said, "I'll do my best."

The five of them hiked out to the driving range. Jake set the bucket of balls down and fished around until he found three orange balls and three green ones. "Any preference?"

"I'll take the ones that fly the farthest," Karl said. That made everyone laugh.

Jake handed him the orange balls and said, "I'll go first."

"Last chance for more action," the older man said.

No one took him up on it, including Jake. If he'd had any money in his pocket, Karl would have bet on himself.

Jake addressed the ball, took a cleansing breath and took a smooth, powerful swing. The ball carried well out into the field.

"I'll let you out for half price," the younger man said.

"The coward's way out," the older man said. "Never. Your turn, kiddo."

Karl looked up and saw that a few more golfers had gathered to watch. "No pressure," he said, grinning.

Karl stood over his ball, measuring the length and weight of the club he had been given. It was a little longer and heavier than he would have liked, but he thought he could make do. He adjusted his stance, said a little prayer for muscle memory, and lifted his club. He swung, made good contact with the ball, and it flew out onto the range.

It came up about ten yards short of Jake's ball.

"Oooh," the older man said. "Good effort, kid. I like your chances."

Jake's eyebrows crawled up his forehead in surprise. "Where'd you learn to hit like that?"

"Practice, consistency, and technique will overcome strength every time," Karl said, quoting Eric.

Jake might have been slightly rattled by the fact that Karl had come so close to his ball. His second swing did not send the green ball nearly as far down the course.

"You've got him on the run, kid," the older man said.

Karl grinned but let the smile slip from his face. He quieted his mind so everything he had learned could flow around him. He stopped thinking at all and rocketed his ball twenty yards past Jake's.

"Holy..." the younger man said.

"I'll let you off for half price, if you want," the older man said gleefully but received no answer.

"Nice shot," Jake said, shaking his head. "I'll say you've golfed somewhere before." He smiled, stood over his ball, and sent a shot in between his first and second ones.

"Piece of cake," the older man said.

And it was. Karl was relaxed and confident now. He shifted his feet, settled into his stance and enjoyed the feeling of holding the club in his hands and the pressure of the moment. He hit it even farther than his second shot.

The older man whooped and collected his money. He slapped Karl on the back and said, "My son will pay for your round." He handed the ten-dollar bill to Jake. "We'll be a foursome today."

If Jake was chagrined at being outdriven by a young boy, he didn't show it, at least much. He grinned ruefully and said, "Guess you've got a job."

Chapter Thirty-Six

Karl had to go through all the normal charades of waking up in a new time. He had to figure out what his schedule was, where his locker was, and what the combination was. He wasn't able to dazzle a young girl with his semi-celebrity this time, but he was able to play the dumb freshman who had somehow forgotten everything.

He found that he and Mike hung out more often than he had remembered. They ate lunch together and sat next to each other in quite a few of their freshman-required classes.

In his other lifetimes, Karl had come to think of Mike as a more distant friend than that. He couldn't help but wonder if it had been him that had slowly drifted away over time and not Mike.

The week after he had woken up in this life, he had come home to find a handful of what Middle Falls High School called *Poor Work Slips* in the mailbox. These were mailed out mid-semester to parents to tell them their kids were either failing or almost failing their classes. They had to be signed by the parent, then sent back to school with the student.

Karl opened all four of them—one each for English, Algebra, History, and Science—signed Finley's name in a reasonable facsimile of his signature and carried them back to school the next day.

He wasn't worried about ramifications. For one thing, he couldn't remember Finley ever looking at his report card. For another, he had decided that he would bear down, make up whatever missing homework he could, and pull his grades up before the end of the semester.

There wasn't much else for him to do on days when he didn't go to the golf course. He came home to an empty house, made himself a box of Macaroni and Cheese or some Top Ramen, then had the rest of the night to himself. He may have learned to cook in his lifetime with Anna, but there wasn't much he could do with cans of soup, boxed dinners, and white bread.

Jake told him he could come in once during the week and twice on the weekends, but that once the weather got nicer, he could increase his hours if he wanted. He was as good as his word. There was a spot in the back room where he kept a set of loaner clubs for Karl and let him go out on the course whenever there was a lull in the schedule.

Karl found that the work of all his previous lifetimes came back to him quickly, and he was immediately outshooting most of the more established golfers that came through. Jake even suggested that maybe Karl should start giving lessons.

Karl loved the idea but wasn't sure if adult golfers would take well to being coached by a kid that looked too young to get into an R-rated movie.

He had gotten good at adapting to new situations—at least the ones where he felt he had a chance to make some changes to his fate.

He was still lonely, though, and that started at home.

Finley hadn't quite fallen so far down the rabbit hole of alcoholism that he spent every waking hour that he wasn't at the box factory away from home. He was trending in that direction in 1978, but it still felt like he at least made an effort to occasionally be home for Karl.

Karl hadn't seen that side of him in a long time, and it tugged at his heart a little to see even the smallest of efforts from his dad. He tried to do what he could to encourage spending more time together, but he soon realized he had probably done that in his first life too and had failed.

He felt sure he would fail again.

Things changed one Saturday morning when he was using the carpet cleaner in the shop at the golf course. Karl was a mind-your-own-business kind of a guy, but on that morning, he overheard Jake and another man talking. He couldn't make out everything they were saying, but a few phrases caught his ear, like *One day at a time,* and *Let go and let God.*

He stuck to his work and tried to stay out of the way, but when the man left, he approached Jake about it.

"Didn't mean to spy on you guys, and I'm sorry if I'm butting in, but can I ask you what that was about?"

Jake looked at him carefully. He liked Karl, and had, in some ways, become a father figure for him. It was obvious he was trying to decide whether to tell Karl to buzz off or to be honest with him.

Karl waited quietly. He knew that this was either something Jake would want to share with him or not. Nothing he might say would make any difference.

Finally, Jake waved him in a little closer. "It's not something I talk about here in the shop, but that's my sponsor."

"Like a golf sponsor?"

"No, like an AA sponsor. But it's not very anonymous if we talk about everything when other people are around."

"Sorry. What does a sponsor do?"

"They're someone who's been in the program for a while. When they feel comfortable in that, they can choose to help someone else along. It's like a coach, only it's for staying sober instead of working on a golf game or something."

Karl let that roll around inside his brain. He felt like he had blundered into an area where he didn't really belong, but now that he was here, he had questions. More accurately, he had one question.

"Could somebody like that help my dad?"

Jake said, "Ah," as if many things had suddenly become clear. He thought about it for a time, then said, "No one can really help anyone else until they want to be helped. No matter how much you might want to help someone else, you can't really. They have to want it for themselves."

Karl nodded. If he had thought about it, he had already known that. It was why he had never tried to throw himself between his father and the Do-Si-Do.

"But there is something else. You can't control what anyone else can do, but you can help yourself."

"Oh, I think I'm okay with that. I don't even drink."

"That's not what I meant." He opened a drawer to his right and pulled out a small, orange book. "Children who grow up in an alcoholic household often have issues of their own to work out." He pointed at the book. "This can help."

The cover read, *Courage to Change*. Jake pulled a bookmark out of the same drawer and said, "This has an address and schedule for the local Al-Anon group. It's a support group for people whose lives are impacted by addiction. They meet three times a week, if you want to go."

Karl took the book and looked at the back cover. "You think I might get something out of this?"

"That's not for me to say. Look it over. Anyone is welcome to attend. If you don't like what you hear, you can leave and never go back."

"Thanks, Jake. I appreciate it. Didn't mean to snoop on you."

"I know you didn't. Now if you want to go pick up all the range balls, there will be a solo golfer that I can put you with for a round."

When he got home, Karl tried to read the book, but it didn't really resonate with him. He stuck it up on his bookshelf and attempted to forget about it.

Over the next few weeks, he kept coming back to it and thinking about some of the things that were in the book. Finally, he decided to attend one of the meetings.

That Thursday evening, Finley didn't come home after work and since that was one of the weekly meeting times, Karl hopped on his ten-speed and rode to a small white church on the edge of town.

There were just a few cars in the parking lot when he got there, but the door was open and a sign directed him to the basement.

Downstairs, he definitely felt like the new kid in town, emphasis on *kid*.

Everyone else that was there was at least thirty or forty years older than he was. They all seemed to know each other and were standing around holding Styrofoam cups of coffee and tea. When Karl walked in, everyone smiled at him.

One man, tall and balding, came over and said, "Glad to see you here. I'm Chris."

"Karl."

"Come on in, Karl. We're just about to get underway. Would you like something to drink?"

"I'm good. I don't know if I'll stay for the whole thing."

The man smiled. "Exactly what I said twenty-two years ago, and now here I am."

There was a rectangular table that everyone sat around. Karl saw that several of the people had the same orange book sitting in front of them, only their copies looked old, bent, and a little dog-eared.

As it turned out, Karl stayed for the whole meeting. It wasn't anything like he had expected. Mostly, it was just people talking about their lives, and it was interesting. They talked about situations they found themselves in and how they might have handled them well, or poorly. When they admitted to handling things poorly, they usually shared some insight that might help them do better the next time.

Karl expected to have almost nothing in common with these people, but he found that much of what the meeting had come down to was *control*. What they could control, and what they couldn't but tried to anyway.

That made a lot of sense to Karl.

He was in a situation where he was repeatedly spun out of control, and there was nothing he could do about it. But there were things that he *could* control. How he reacted to things. How he got tangled up or not.

At the end, Chris said, "That'll wrap things up for tonight, then. Anything that you heard in here tonight that makes sense to you, take it with you. Anything that doesn't, leave it here."

What had struck Karl was how intimate the conversations were. As if there was a cone of silence that hung over the meeting, guaranteeing that the things that were said there would not leave the room.

When the meeting broke up, several people broke off together, talking about more mundane things.

Karl was struck by the contrast.

Chris approached him and said, "I didn't call on you to speak tonight. I know how hard it can be at your first meeting. Especially when you're so young. If you decide to come back, though, let me know if you'd like to talk. We'll listen. We might not offer a lot in the way of advice, but you can usually hear what not to do in our own stories."

"Thanks," Karl said and hurried back to his bike. He had come with no idea of what to expect and left with a lot to think about.

He did return the next week, and the next and the next. He found comfort in being in an environment where people shared their stories so honestly.

Karl wished that he could have shared *all* his story—dying, waking up, and repeating that over and over—but he sensed that was a bridge too far. Instead, he eventually opened up about his mother dying and how Finley had reacted to it. Just talking about it felt like it lifted a weight off him.

After he had been attending a couple of months, Finley came home on Thursday night and Karl was faced with a dilemma. He knew he could easily skip the meeting, but he had come to look forward to it. If he went, though, he would either have to tell Finley why or make up a story.

Making up a lie about going somewhere to tell the truth of things didn't seem like a good idea. Neither did skipping the meeting.

A few minutes before he normally left, he looked at his dad. Finley had brought home a pizza from Shakey's that night and they had eaten while watching the evening news.

"Dad, I've got to go somewhere."

"Oh? This late? Where?"

"It's a meeting at a church over on Elm."

"You a churchgoer now?"

"No, not really. It's not a church meeting."

"What, then? Some cute girl got you going?"

"No, not that, either. It's an Al-Anon meeting."

Karl had no idea if Finley knew what Al-Anon was or not.

"You know what that is?"

"Yes," Finley said. He frowned. This was an unpleasant truth, and he wasn't sure what to do with it.

Karl thought he might say something like, *What do you need that for?* but he didn't. If he knew what it was, he knew why Karl was going.

"I thought we could watch some TV tonight, but if you'd rather do that, go ahead."

If this was Karl's first life, that manipulation might have had an impact. Now, Karl had a much better perspective.

He thought, *If you wanted to spend time with me, Dad, then where are you all the other nights?*

Finley stood up and said, "That's okay, though. I've got somewhere else to be, too."

They left at the same time, but they were definitely not together.

Chapter Thirty-Seven

After that, Finley essentially gave up on coming home after work. Once again, Karl was living with a ghost.

One of the things Karl had learned at the Al-Anon meetings was The Serenity Prayer: *God grant me the serenity to accept the things I cannot change, the courage to change the things I can, and the wisdom to know the difference.* He put Finley's accelerated drinking under the category of being one of those things he had to accept, as he could not change it.

One thing that Karl noticed was that attending the meetings—hearing the successes and failures as people fought against being codependent—had brought other changes to his life.

He found it was easier to open up to people and stopped being quite so alone all the time. He and Mike became better friends than he could ever remember in his past lives.

He even gave Mike the courage to ask Lisa out. He knew he would have gotten there sooner or later, but Karl's push got them there a little earlier. Of course, that also meant that soon Mike was either with Lisa or being all moony-eyed thinking about when he could spend time with her again.

On some Saturday mornings before he pedaled to the golf course, Karl would swing by the school to see if maybe Eric would be out there with his bucket of balls, working on his swing. He never saw him, though, and thought that he might still be too young for his parents to let him walk that far. Karl knew he would be there eventually, and they could become friends again.

A small miracle happened a few weeks before Christmas. A massive snowstorm—unusual for Middle Falls, even in December—buried the city in more than a foot of snow. Since the town rarely got that kind of snowfall, the highway department wasn't really prepared to clear the roads. Middle Falls had one snowplow, and it was old enough that it only ran when it wanted to.

The town essentially ground to a halt, and that included the box factory and the Do-Si-Do.

Karl and Finley were together in the house, whether they liked it or not.

Finley had seen the storm coming and so had at least stocked up on easy-to-cook meals and plenty of Rainier Beer. In fact, he left four half-racks out in the one-car garage and two more in the fridge. He made sure he would not die of thirst during the great storm.

The first night, the two of them ignored each other, so it was essentially the same as it was every night—they were alone, they just happened to be alone under the same roof.

The second day, Finley made toast and scrambled eggs for both of them for breakfast. He checked the thermometer and saw that it was still below freezing and knew they were inside for at least another day.

He dug around in a kitchen drawer and came up with a deck of cards. "How about a game of cribbage?"

That should have been an easy, fun request, the most natural thing in the world while they were snowed in. But they had been so distant for so long, the gap between them was so wide, that Karl could see how much effort it had cost him.

"Sure, Dad. Board's in the bottom drawer there."

"You still remember how to score?" Finley asked.

It had been a long time—lifetimes, really—since Karl had played, but somehow the scoring was still in his memory.

"Yeah, I think so. Fifteen-two, fifteen-four, fifteen-six, and a pair is eight, right?"

"You might need to help me a little, but we can figure it out."

Karl remembered something and went into his room and poked around on his shelves. He came back with a battered copy of *Hoyle's Rules of Games*. He thumbed through it until he found the information on cribbage scoring and read it out loud to his father.

Karl shuffled the cards and dealt. Half an hour later, he pegged out and Finley asked for a rematch. "First, though, I'm gonna put some potato soup on. You want to peel for me?"

Karl jumped up and washed the potatoes, then said, "That enough?"

"Maybe one more," Finley said, eyeing the pile. "I'll make enough that we can get two or three meals out of it." He put six strips of bacon to fry in the cast iron frying pan and the aroma of bacon filled the air.

"I wasn't even hungry until I smelled that," Karl said. He kept his head down, looking at the potatoes as he peeled them. He tried to remember the last time he had actually done something with his dad and came up blank.

"Got a loaf of that French bread from Safeway, too. That'll go good with this."

The fact that there was potatoes, bacon, milk, and French bread in the house told Karl that Finley had put some planning into this whole thing.

When the soup was done, they sat at TV trays and ate. Karl ate two bowls and said, "Might not be any left over after all."

In the afternoon, they played three more games of cribbage and Karl had a sad thought that wrapped around his heart and wouldn't let go: *This is what it could have been like. It's not the same without*

Mom. It never could be. But if we had gone a different way, if we had stayed together, it could have been okay.

It was possible that Finley was thinking the same thing. After the third game—Karl won all three—Finley said, "I want to talk to you about something."

"Sure, Dad. What's up?"

For a moment, Finley looked like he'd rather be anywhere than where he was at that moment. "I know I've let you down. When you told me you were going to those Al-Anon meetings, I knew why. I just didn't want to do anything about it. That was a road I didn't want to even look at, let alone think about walking down."

"You mean not drinking?"

"I mean the whole thing. Not drinking...everything."

There was a world of unspoken pain in Finley's pause. Karl could fill in the blanks about Finley not facing the world, not being a real father, everything.

Karl didn't say anything. He had given up on the idea that they were ever going to have this conversation, so he hadn't thought about how to respond. He decided to just let go and be honest.

"I know it's hard, Dad. I get it. And nothing is going to happen until you decide you want to do it. That's why I never mentioned anything to you. I figured I would do what I could for me and you would make up your own mind about things."

"Sometimes I think you're the mature one and I'm the kid. It wouldn't have mattered if you had tried to talk to me about it then. I wasn't ready."

Karl wanted to ask *Are you ready now?* but stopped himself.

"How did you find out about Al-Anon anyway?"

Karl told the story of overhearing Jake's conversation with his sponsor.

"That makes sense, I guess. Everybody needs a little help, right?"

"Right."

"Are the phones working?"

"I don't know, Dad." Karl got up and went to the kitchen. He picked up the phone and heard the strong buzz of the dial tone. "Yep."

"I feel like if I put this off, I might never do it. Do you think your boss would talk to me?"

"Honestly, I don't know how any of that works. But I'll call him if you want."

Finley swallowed hard and nodded.

Karl looked up Jake's phone number in the Middle Falls phone book and dialed it. A woman's voice answered. "This is Karl Strong. I work for Jake senior. Is he there?"

"He sure is, honey. There's nowhere else where he can be right now."

A few seconds later, Jake's voice said, "Karl? I'm pretty sure you know the course is closed. It's hard to golf what you can't see!"

Karl laughed a little, but then said, "That's not why I'm calling. My dad asked if he could talk to you."

"Oh," Jake said. "Hang on just a second." Karl heard the phone clunk as Jake laid it down. In the distance, he heard, "Hon? I'm going to take this in the bedroom. Will you hang this up for me?"

Eventually Karl heard a click and Jake said, "Got it! Thanks, hon. Okay, now we've got some privacy. Sure, I'll talk to your dad. Put him on."

Karl held the phone out and said, "Dad, this is my boss, Jake. He said he'll talk to you."

A flicker of regret passed over Finley's face, as though he wished he had never brought this all up. He nodded, though, and reached for the phone.

"I'll be in my room. Let me know if there's anything I can do."

Finley took the phone and said, "Hello?" Then, a few seconds later, "Yeah, he's quite the kid."

Karl didn't hear anything else as he shut his bedroom door behind him.

⟨ ⟩

IT WOULD HAVE BEEN nice to think that Finley poured out all that beer he had brought home and then never drank again. That's the way things work for some alcoholics, but certainly not all.

He didn't pour that beer out but did become a little more surreptitious about drinking it. He moved it to the back of his truck and stopped drinking in front of Karl.

Finley spoke to Jake for a long time that night—more than an hour. He agreed to meet with him at Marv's for a cup of coffee when the snow melted.

He blew that off and went to the Do-Si-Do instead. The next day, he apologized and asked for another chance.

Jake had walked that same road and understood. He agreed to meet him the next day.

That time, Finley showed up.

What followed was two steps forward, one step back.

Many chapters of Alcoholics Anonymous give colored chips to commemorate milestones. The first one is silver, and that's for being sober for twenty-four hours. That seems like it should be the simplest, but it isn't. For many, that first twenty-four hours is the most difficult day of all.

There are other chips—red for thirty days, gold for sixty, and a bronze for a year of sobriety.

Finley fell off the wagon a few times before ever getting that bronze chip.

Karl had gotten in the habit of starting dinner when he got home from school ahead of Finley. There were days when his dad just didn't show up for that meal and he knew he was gone again.

The key was that each failure didn't mean that it was the final failure. It just meant it was time to start again.

One day at a time.

Chapter Thirty-Eight

Karl had learned that everything he believed about time in his first life was incorrect. He had thought of time as like a river, constantly flowing in one direction. Now, he knew that was not true, at least for him. Every once in a while, he was pulled out of that river and dropped in a different place well upstream from where he had been.

Another thing was that the more lives he lived, the faster time seemed to pass. Karl applied himself to all the tasks he had set, but the days, weeks, months, and even years seemed to melt into each other.

He had already accomplished a lot in this life that he never had before.

His relationship with Finley was so much better, there was no comparison.

After his freshman year, Anna had once again appeared in the high school. It was a little shocking to Karl how young she looked. The last time he had seen her, she had been in her late fifties. She had still been beautiful, but now, she was fourteen and coltish. He knew she was the same person in some ways, but in others it was so very strange for him.

He had thought that perhaps he could ask her out during his junior year. That was when she had started dating Kenny, and he knew that would stop all that and give her a better chance at accomplishing what she wanted.

He hadn't done it, though. He already felt like he had so many balls in the air—keeping his grades up, continuing to attend Al-Anon meetings, working on his golf game—that he thought adding a girlfriend was one thing too many.

At the same time, he didn't want Anna to get into the same bind she had in all his other lives.

He watched her in the halls and figured out what locker was hers. Before she ever started dating Kenny, Karl wrote a note and slipped it in her locker.

It was a simple note, written in block letters that even a handwriting expert wouldn't be able to link back to him.

Kenny has VD. Anyone who goes out with him will have VD too.

It wasn't elegant. It wasn't true. But Karl felt that in this case, the ends justified the means.

He wasn't around when she opened her locker and found the note. He couldn't even be sure that she had read it.

But he did notice that she didn't start going out with Kenny like she had in all her previous lives. In fact, none of the girls in school would go out with Kenny. It soon became obvious that if he wanted to date, he would have to look farther afield.

Soon, Anna started going out with other boys. That was hard on Karl, but unless he was willing to ask her out, there wasn't much he could do.

Before he knew it, it was once again the summer between his junior and senior year.

Earlier that year, Finley had given him the title to the Falcon. That meant that Karl was able to retire the bicycle and get around more easily.

He had long since graduated into a paid employee at the golf course. Jake's son—Jake Junior—had left for college and his other son, Frankie, showed no interest in golf at all. Karl stepped into Junior's role.

The hours he spent at the course were happy ones. None of the tasks ever felt like work. He had lifetimes' worth of memories of working at the box factory, so he was able to keep a good perspective about what constituted work and what didn't.

As August of 1981 approached, Karl started to think about something that once would have been unthinkable. He was unsure about whether he wanted to play football or not. On the one hand, he knew it was his only real chance at getting a free ride at a real university. At the same time, he knew it would put a crimp in the development of his golf game.

One thing that Karl had found was that his football ability seemed to be capped from lifetime to lifetime.

He had made the varsity team both his sophomore and junior years and had been the starting tailback since midway through his sophomore year.

He had accomplished both those things in his first life, though. He was a good player, bordering on great, but he didn't think he would ever get that final push.

It was different with golf, though. Every life, he got a little better. With another three years of practice and tips from Jake, he was already better than he ever had been before, and he was only seventeen.

He still harbored the secret dream of being a professional golfer.

He had made it through seasons of high school football uninjured in his previous lives, but he knew that was no guarantee he would again. If he blew his knee out or sustained a serious back injury, that wouldn't just knock him out of a scholarship, it would seriously hinder any dreams of golfing professionally.

The Middle Falls football team started what they lovingly called *two-a-days* the third week of August. That meant an early practice in the morning, then a late-afternoon practice around 4:30.

For the kids who worked in the hayfields—and there were a lot of them—that made for very long days.

Karl had never hayed, and he wasn't planning on starting that summer, as it would have severely limited his time at the golf course. Jake didn't mind the two-a-days. He had always been supportive of Karl's football and had even started coming to the games to root him on. It had been a very good thing when Karl scored a touchdown and looked up to see both Jake and Finley in the stands, screaming their approval.

There was nothing in particular that was stopping Karl from playing. It was Karl himself. He just wasn't sure he wanted to play anymore.

The week before two-a-days started, he made up his mind. He decided to drop out of football and focus on golf. With another year of working on his game, he thought he would be in good shape to start working toward getting his card to play on the tour.

Even then, it was a long shot, and he knew it, but it was something he wanted to try.

He drove to the high school and saw that there were only a couple of cars parked there. Not unusual when school was out. He looked out into the field and his heart leaped when he saw a small, skinny boy with a sweet swing hitting a golf ball. Karl was tempted to abandon his mission and run straight out to talk to Eric.

He reminded himself that Eric would be out there for quite a while, and he wanted to take care of business first. Karl pushed into the empty locker room and knocked on the door to Coach Bulski's office.

"Karl!" Coach Bulski said. "Good to see you. You look like you stayed in shape over the summer. Good, good. You're a little early for two-a-days, though."

"Hey, Coach. I need to talk to you for a minute." He sat in the folding chair opposite Bulski.

Coach waved at the chair and said, "Sure, sure. Always have time for you. We're going to have a good team this year. I think we might make the playoffs. You deserve that. You've worked hard."

Karl knew that maybe the team might make the playoffs, but Coach Bulski would not.

"I need to tell you something, Coach. I'm not going to play this year."

Bulski blanched and actually pushed back from his desk a little. "I know you wouldn't kid around about that, Karl. Is everything all right? Everything good at home? I saw Finley at all the games last year. He looked good, too."

"Everything is fine, Coach. Dad's doing good. I just don't have it in me to play anymore."

"I don't understand." Bulski shook his head. "You're one of the cornerstones of the team. Maybe the best running back I've had since I've been here. I've got a call in to Coach Anderson at Oregon State to tell him about you. I think we've got a real chance to get you a scholarship next year."

"I know, Coach, and I really do appreciate everything you've done for me. I just can't do it."

Bulski seemed to recover from the shock of Karl quitting the team. "Well, if you're really feeling that way, then you shouldn't play. That's how guys get hurt. I wouldn't want that to happen to you." He stood up and stuck his hand out. "Thanks for what you gave the team."

"You're a good man, Coach, and I appreciate it. Thanks again for everything you did for me." Karl fought an urge to tell him to go see a doctor right now. He had gone round and round with himself the last few years but had stayed silent all that time because it never felt like the right time, and it always felt awkward.

Karl left Coach Bulski sitting in his office, at least a little befuddled. One of the strengths of his team had just become a big question mark.

Outside, Karl turned his face to the warm summer sun and grinned. In his first life, he never would have dreamed of dropping off the team. Now, all he felt was relief. He jogged out to the open field until he was ten yards away from Eric.

The smaller boy lined up a shot and sent a ball arcing against the clear blue sky.

"Nice shot," Karl said. "You've done that before."

"A few thousand times," Eric agreed. "You golf?"

"Yeah," Karl said. "Wish I had my clubs with me. I'd hit a few with you."

"Be my guest," Eric said, holding out his driver.

Karl couldn't help but smile a little. He could tell by the slightly superior grin on Eric's face that he thought Karl was just another dumb jock. He was probably already loading up his *Technique is greater than strength* talk.

"Thanks, I'll give 'er a try. I'm Karl, by the way."

"Yeah, I know who you are." Eric cupped his hands around his mouth and in a loud voice said, "Number twenty-two in your program, ladies and gentlemen, it's Karl Strong!"

"And the crowd goes mild," Karl answered, squinting at him. "And that's *former* number twenty-two to you, I'll have you know. I just told Coach I was dropping off the team."

"Why in the world would you want to do that?" Eric asked, shaking his head. "If I was in your spot, I would wear my jersey to school and around town every day. I'd make sure everyone knew who I was." He waggled his eyebrows a little suggestively. "Especially the ladies."

That made Karl laugh, but he still lined up over the ball.

"That club is a little short for you."

"I'll make do," Karl said, placing his hands high on the grip. He wiggled his hips and swung. It was the complete opposite of the swing he had first shown Eric many lifetimes earlier. This was smooth and practiced. It was also powerful.

The ball exploded out of the grass and flew high and straight, forty yards past the ball Eric had hit.

"Holy shit," Eric said, his mouth hanging open. "What the hell, man?"

"I like to golf," Karl said simply.

"I like to golf," Eric said mimicking him. "I hope to Arnold Palmer you like to golf. How can you hit it like that and I've never seen you before?"

Karl liked that. For just a moment, it was almost like they were best friends again, living in the room over his parents' garage. He had really missed this young, kind of smartass Eric.

"Do you know who my dad is?"

Karl did, of course, but remembered that in his first life, he had not. "No, why?"

"He's the pro out at the country club. I think he'd like to see your swing. How's your short game?"

"Probably a little better than my drives. I've really been focusing on that the past few months."

"Where do you play? Out at Middle Falls Fairway? I've never seen you at the country club."

"Yeah, I work for Jake. He lets me golf pretty regularly, so I get a lot of rounds in."

"Based on that swing, I'd say it's paying off. You must be able to beat everybody who shows up at the place, including Jake."

"Most days, yeah."

"You ever think about trying out for the Tour?"

Of course Karl had. He thought about it, dreamed about it, lusted after it.

"Yeah, maybe. That competition is pretty tough."

"That's true. My dad is the best golfer I've ever seen in person, but he was never able to get off the bottom of the tour standings. Never finished better than twentieth at any of the big events. That's why he's a club pro now. He mostly helps rich old people with terrible swings be a little less terrible."

Eric looked at Karl, sizing him up. "You're not some sort of ringer, are you? Like a thirty-year-old guy pretending to be a high schooler?"

"I promise, I'm seventeen. Turn eighteen in a couple of months."

"You got a car?"

Karl pointed toward the Falcon. In this life, he hadn't given it the incredible scrubbing he had when he took Anna to Homecoming, so it still stank like cat pee in the summer heat. "It ain't much, and it kind of stinks inside, but it runs."

"It beats using my shoe leather. If you want to give me a ride home, I can introduce you to my dad. I think he'd like to meet you."

Karl thrilled a little at the thought of seeing Don and Ellonyia again.

"Let's go."

Chapter Thirty-Nine

Karl woke up each day feeling optimistic. He knew that wherever he might wake up in his next life might not be ideal, so he resolved to just enjoy this life and live it to the fullest. If he woke up fat and covered in Cheeto dust again in his next life, he would just bear down and get through it.

One of the things that was new in this life was that he was able to bring Finley and the Swansons together. In previous lives, Finley had always felt threatened by this new part of Karl's life. But now that he was more present, more on solid ground, that wasn't the case.

Karl knew that it was likely that the Swansons would eventually get around to asking them to things like holiday meals, so he decided to strike preemptively.

One weekday night just before school started again, Karl and Finley were standing in the kitchen doing the dinner dishes. Karl asked if he could invite a friend and his parents over for a barbecue that Sunday.

Karl remembered how nice the barbecue was that he and Anna had attended at the Swansons in a previous life. He knew he couldn't match that, but that wasn't the point. What he wanted to establish was that having each other over for a meal was something normal and accepted.

Finley looked around their small house—which wasn't as run down as it had been in previous lifetimes but was still small and cramped—and professed his doubts.

"We're not really in a position to entertain. We don't have any room."

"We've got the backyard. I'll work hard this week to get it in shape," Karl countered. "And we've already got a barbecue."

That was true, as far as it went. They did have something that had once been a barbecue, though it had sat outside in the weather for several years and was now as much rust as anything else.

"I'd really like you to meet these people, Dad. Eric is great, and so are his parents. It would be nice to have friends again."

That was more of a pointed barb than he had intended, and he worried that he had pushed his father too far.

Instead, Finley sighed and said, "You're right. I'll pick up some steaks and I'll make the foil potatoes recipe that your mom loved."

That marked a big change. The ability to occasionally mention her name, to continue to bring her back into their lives was a new thing.

Karl surprised his dad by wrapping his arms around him in a hug. Finley hugged him back.

Karl was up and at it early the next morning. He started by mowing and raking the backyard, then fixing the gate that led out the back. The flower beds didn't contain any flowers, and since it was the end of August, it was too late to plant any. Still, he spent a few hours yanking all the weeds up.

After two days of hard work, the backyard looked pretty respectable.

He tackled the barbecue next, but soon found it was a lost cause.

Finley came out the sliding glass door and looked at what Karl had accomplished. "I guess we should have had people over for a barbecue more often." He looked at the barbecue that Karl was trying to rescue through sheer willpower and elbow grease and said, "Come on, let's go."

They drove to Coppen's Hardware and went inside. Mrs. Coppen was behind the register and said, "Anything I can help you find?"

"Believe it or not, we're looking for a new barbecue."

"Season's almost over for that, but I think we've got a few my husband was just getting ready to put into storage until next spring. He'll probably make you a good deal on one just so he doesn't have to haul it up there."

She was right. Mr. Coppen offered to sell it to Finley for cost plus ten percent, which knocked twenty bucks off the price.

They drove home with a new—not fancy, but new—barbecue in the back of Finley's truck.

Karl realized that in his other lifetimes, they wouldn't have been able to afford even a small spur of the moment purchase like that. The fact that Finley wasn't donating a sizable portion of his income to the Do-Si-Do made quite a difference.

He hadn't been sure the Swansons would accept their invitation, but they liked Karl, and liked that Eric had a new friend, so they agreed.

"But only," Ellonyia had said, "if I can bring my macaroni salad."

There was no lawn furniture at the Strong house, but Finley and Karl fixed that by hauling the small kitchen table and chairs outside for everyone to sit on.

Finley looked around the backyard and said, "What kind of people are these? I suppose I should have asked earlier."

Karl knew what his dad meant: were these wealthy people or poor folks like them? He chose not to answer that question. Instead, he said, "They're good people, Dad. They're not snooty at all."

"I should have bought some new furniture," Finley fretted, but it was too late. They heard a car pull up in front of the house.

Karl ran through the house and saw that the Swansons were getting out of Don's Cadillac. They all had something in their hands.

Ellonyia had her macaroni salad, Eric had brought a game of lawn darts, and Don was lugging a cooler.

"You didn't have to bring all this!" Karl said.

"My grandmother," Ellonyia said, "taught me to always arrive at someone's house with one arm longer than the other."

Karl looked a little confused by that, as he'd never heard that expression.

"See, your one arm is longer because you're carrying something," Eric said. "It's another one of their old people expressions. Come on, I'll wax you at lawn darts."

Karl had a sudden nightmare scenario flash through his mind. What if the cooler was full of beer, the temptation was too much for Finley, and the barbecue started him on another binge that he might or might not recover from.

He felt panic rise up inside him, then the lessons of many Al-Anon meetings floated through his brain. *Let go and Let God.* He had to remember that he was not responsible for his father's sobriety, although he would never choose to put him in a bad position.

Any worries he might have had were immediately allayed when Don said, "I brought some pop, too. That's about all I'm trusted to 'cook.'"

Karl led them through the gate to the backyard and introduced the Swansons to his dad. He still felt a little unsure about whether they would hit it off, but he shouldn't have worried.

The Swansons were wonderful people—Karl's adopted family—and Finley, at least in this life—was charming and friendly.

Karl and Eric set up the lawn darts. In the early eighties, these were still the real lawn darts—heavy and capable of inflicting serious damage if they hit someone. Karl soon discovered that not unlike golf, lawn darts was another one of those games where skill and technique counted more than brute strength. Eric beat him in game after game.

"My son, the lawn dart hustler," Don said from the sidelines.

Finley put on the steaks and foil-wrapped potatoes and peppers. He kept turning his head and watching the boys throwing the yard darts until Ellonyia approached him.

"Would you like to challenge the boys to a game? I can watch these for you."

Finley took her up on that and soon all four of the men were playing a round robin tournament.

As Don observed, Eric was a hustler, and ended up beating everyone.

"Anyone want to play for a quarter a game?" Eric asked.

"A good hustler loses a few," his father reminded him. "Once you show everyone your best game, it's a lot tougher to get money out of them."

"Duly noted in my *How to be a hustler* notebook, Dad."

When they sat down to eat, Finley finally asked Don what he did for a living.

Don could have said, "I'm the club pro at the country club," and that would have been the truth. Instead, he said, "I work out at the country club."

"You a golfer?"

"Sure am."

"You should see Karl golf. He lives for that stuff. Even dropped off the football team this year so he could focus on it."

Don nodded. "I was going to talk to you about that. Karl is one of the best junior golfers I've ever seen. Would it be all right if I worked with him some? I think he's got real potential."

Finley chewed on that for a minute, then said, "That would be great. What would we owe you for that?"

"Oh no, no," Don said. "Not like that. I'd just like to give him a few unofficial pointers here and there."

Finley relaxed a little and said, "I sure can't teach him about that. Never held a club in my life."

"If you'd ever like to come out to the club and play a round, let me know."

"I think I'm a little too old to pick up a new hobby, but if you want to help Karl, I would appreciate it."

After a few hours of small talk, the Swansons thanked Finley and Karl for their hospitality and left.

There had been a few potential landmines. Finley might have reacted to the Swansons like he had when he'd met them in a previous life. Instead, that had all been avoided.

⟨ ⟩

DON SWANSON WAS AS good as his word. He invited Karl out to the Middle Falls Country Club for a few lessons.

They played eighteen holes and Don waited until the round was over before he gave any tips to Karl.

They headed over to the driving range and Don said, "You're one of the most natural golfers I've ever seen. I don't know how you've got such good technique at such a young age without any lessons, but good for you."

Karl knew it was lifetimes of practice but couldn't say so.

"There's still things to work on, though." Don grinned at him and said, "There will always be things to work on. Even Arnold Palmer and Jack Nicklaus still work on their games every day."

"I appreciate you taking the time to help me. I want to get better." He squinted his eyes at Don and said, "Is it crazy to think I might make the tour someday?"

"It's not impossible, but the odds are against it. If you think about how many golfers there are in the world and then realize that there are only a hundred and twenty-five people on the tour at any given moment, that brings it into focus. Of course, there are different exemptions for past wins and sponsors, but you need to have already had some pretty good success on the tour to get that."

Karl nodded. He wasn't daunted by those numbers. He knew it was a long shot, but also knew that if he didn't succeed with it in this life, he could always go back to football the next time he woke up around this time.

He had repeated his lives so often, he had come to accept that this was his lot in life.

Chapter Forty

Dreaming of the pro tour or not, Karl still had to finish high school.

His schedule was a little easier without having football practice and games to worry about.

At the start of his senior year, things were going well. He and Finley were getting along, spending time together, and he had his friendship with Eric and his parents.

Still, he felt a certain loneliness.

Each time he saw Anna in the hall, he felt a twinge that pushed him toward talking to her, but to that point he had resisted.

Seeing Anna so young, when he felt so old, had put a crimp into how he felt about her. They both looked like they were close to the same age but were definitely not in terms of life experience.

The situation in this life was so different, he thought it was likely that Lisa wouldn't be cornering him into asking Anna to Homecoming.

He spent a lot of time debating with himself about whether it would be right or wrong for him to be with Anna. Finally, he remembered the life where they had stayed married until he died. That had been a good life, one of his best. He knew that unless he took the first step, he would likely lose her to someone else.

He made up his mind to ask her to Homecoming without any prompting from Lisa. He thought that was the right thing to do to give them a clean start.

He kept his eyes open and finally saw her at her locker, kneeling and sorting through her books.

He stood behind her, waiting for her to see him, but she seemed lost in thought and didn't notice him. After a few seconds, he started to feel like a creeper, so he cleared his throat and said, "Hey, Anna?"

She jumped a little. She had been a million miles away. "Oh!" She quickly stood up and faced Karl. "I didn't see you standing there."

"Sorry," Karl said. At that moment, he realized something. As well as he knew Anna, they had virtually never spoken to each other in this life. Approaching her like this must seem completely out of the blue. He remembered something she had told him when they were married in their first life—that she had always liked him—and persevered.

"Hey, I was wondering if you'd like to go to the Homecoming dance with me."

He watched her face carefully and saw a whole swirl of emotions. Happiness, excitement, but also frustration. "Are you serious?"

"Yes, sure. Of course I am."

Anna squinted her eyes shut and seemed to be talking to herself. Finally, she looked at Karl again and said, "Karl Strong, you have the worst timing in the world."

"You're not the first person to tell me that. Why?"

"Someone else just asked me and I said yes."

"Who, Kenny?"

"Ew, no. I wouldn't go out with him. Not after the things I've heard."

At least not in this life, Karl thought. *Thanks to me.* He didn't feel bad about that. Then, the answer came to him in a blinding flash.

"Seymour. Seymour Keynes."

Anna's mouth fell open. "Yes, how did you know? He just asked me a few minutes ago."

"Just a wild guess. I've seen the way he looks at you."

"That's funny, because you never seem to see the way I look at you."

That caused a little tingle to run up and down Karl's spine. That old feeling of love and longing mixed with the feeling of being so close to her that he could reach out and touch her.

Karl felt a heat rise on his cheeks and said, "Well, that's what happens, right? You snooze, you lose." He turned to leave. He just wanted to be somewhere that Anna was not.

She reached out and touched his arm. When he looked back, she said, "I would have said yes."

Karl did his best to smile, but he knew it didn't really make it all the way to his lips.

He hurried off to class, berating himself for waiting too long.

Later that day, Lisa Hanson again approached him in the hall between classes. "Heard you asked Anna to Homecoming."

"And now you're here to just pour salt in the wound?"

"No, of course not. Have you ever thought about Denise Watson? She's a pretty girl, and she doesn't have a date for the dance yet."

Karl let how sick he felt about not getting to take Anna show on his face.

"Oh, it's like that, is it?" Lisa was always perceptive. "Well, then you should have asked her earlier. She's liked you forever, man, and you've always ignored her. I thought she just wasn't your type. Boys. You are all so frustrating. So how about Denise? She's a sophomore, but she's sweet and funny and pretty."

"I don't think so. Thanks, Lisa."

"Don't wait so long next time!" Lisa said, flipping her long hair over her shoulder as she walked away.

At least for me, Karl thought, *I'm pretty sure there will be a next time. But I'm eighteen. Unless I get struck by lightning or run over by a van crossing Main Street, that next time is probably a long time away.*

He thought about what Lisa had said about Denise. He couldn't have picked her out of a lineup and not having any history with her, he didn't feel any interest. After having so many memories, so many lifetimes—both good and bad—with Anna, he wondered if he would ever feel that way about anyone else.

Then he thought of the intensity in Anna's eyes as she had reached for him. *I would have said yes.* That was painful, but it was also hopeful. Maybe she would go to Homecoming with Seymour and that would be it. He had shown her he was interested by asking her, at least. *Now that she knows, maybe she'll feel the same pull that I do. If she does, she'll let me know.*

Karl decided to wait and find out. He didn't go to the dance at all.

That next Monday, he saw Anna in the hall again.

She was holding hands with Seymour Keynes.

Karl turned the other way.

Chapter Forty-One

There were so many things going right in this life, Karl did his best not to beat himself up over one aspect going wrong.

He remembered back to when he felt that being with Anna had cost him the chance to go to Oregon State to play football. Now he was giving up that opportunity on his own just to have a chance to play golf at a higher level.

We often tell ourselves things to make us feel better.

Even so, what was he to do? Slip another note in Anna's locker to warn her away from Seymour as he had with Kenny? He felt that torpedoing Kenny was fair game. He had earned that. But not Seymour.

What would a note say about Seymour Keynes?

Seymour is boring and solid and is going to have a really responsible job at the hospital someday.

No, as with so many things in his life, he had to just let go and let it work out the way it was going to.

In the interim, he focused on things he could control. He knew that rainy weather was coming and that would hamper his ability to practice his swing for the next six months.

He approached the high school basketball coach and asked if he could come in early on school days and practice his swing in the gym. It was the only building in Middle Falls that was big enough to hold anything more than a chip shot.

The high school had installed a new high-tech rubber floor two years earlier, so he wouldn't have to worry about scuffing up the polished hardwood with any errant swings or shots. His plan was to set up on a mat at one end of the gym and knock drives against a mat against the wall at the other end.

One day after P.E., Karl caught up with Coach Carlson. He was a young teacher—less than ten years older than Karl. He had just taken over as the basketball coach the year before.

"Whadya say, Coach? Can I use the gym for the next few months while the weather's lousy? I won't hurt anything; I just need a place that's dry and out of the rain to practice."

Carlson looked at Karl—tall, lanky, and athletic—and said, "You were a damned good football player, Strong. Maybe had a shot at a scholarship. But you didn't play this year. Why?"

"It's golf, Coach. It's in my blood, but Middle Falls doesn't have a team. If it did, you can bet I'd be on it."

"No, you're right. We don't have a golf team. But we do have a basketball team."

Karl saw where this conversation was going. "Oh, come on, Coach. No way."

"Can you shoot?"

"Nope."

"Dribble?"

"Nope."

"Rebound?"

"Nope."

"Play defense?"

"Nope."

"That's perfect. You'll fit right in with this team. The whole program is kind of starting over. We've got five juniors and five sophomores on the team right now. You'll be our only senior."

"I would be your only senior if I was playing basketball, but I'm not."

"Come out for the team, and I'll give you your own set of keys to the gym. As long as you don't break anything and clean up after yourself, you can come in whenever you want."

"You're killing me, Coach."

"It's not blackmail, Karl. You don't have to play if you don't want to."

"I don't want to."

"Good enough. Good luck with your golf career." Carlson turned and walked away.

Karl ran after him, grinning. "You are a hard man, Coach. What time is practice?"

"Every afternoon after school. 3:30 to 5:30. When the season starts, we'll have two games a week."

"If I come out for the team and practice and play as hard as I can, that's my end of the deal, right? Even if I suck, I still get to use the gym, right?"

"Right. But I saw you on the football team last year. I don't think you'll suck. An athlete is an athlete. You may not have a grasp on the finer points of the game, but you'll bring a lot anyway."

As it turned out, they were both a little right.

Karl was a natural athlete with good stamina, grace, and strength. He also hadn't played basketball in any serious way for years. There were times, both at practice and in the games, where he looked like he might be the best player on the floor. Other times, he looked completely lost.

He did what he said he would, though, and he gave it his all. He didn't make the starting five, but he did work his way up to where he was the first man off the bench. Since he played limited minutes, he didn't hold anything back. He jumped half out of the gym, his dark, curly hair bouncing. He loved to play defense because that was easier to focus on. He dove for every loose ball and sacrificed his body. He soon became a fan favorite. When he went to the scorer's table, the crowd would begin the chant, "Strong, Strong, Strong."

Karl did his best to ignore that, but inside, he liked it and even played to the crowd a little. When he had played football, he was buried under pads and a helmet. On the basketball court, he got to let his light shine a little more.

He also had his own small rooting section yelling for him every time he did something positive. The three Swansons came to every game, often swinging by to pick up Finley on the way. Jake from the golf course made most of the home games, too.

He even saw Anna sitting with her friends at a few of the games, cheering him on. When he made a basket or ripped a rebound down and whipped an outlet pass downcourt, he liked to jog by and give her a little wink. He couldn't help himself.

That was all just a little side trip for Karl. He had joined the team to get access to the gym and he took full advantage, showing up to school early and staying late after practice to work on his swing. It didn't take long before Eric discovered his deal and showed up with his own clubs.

A few of the other guys on the team even hung around and asked Karl to show them a few things. Eventually, the after-practice sessions grew until he had to put a cap on the number of participants.

Coach Carlson stood on the sidelines, watching. "If you guys have enough energy to hit that little white ball around the gym, I think I'm probably not running you hard enough during practice."

"I told you we should have a golf team," Karl hollered back. "Think how great we'd be!"

By the time spring arrived, Coach Carlson knew that Karl was about to take his game outside. Carlson showed up early one morning with buckets of paint, brushes, rollers, tape, a ladder, and a stack of tarps.

He pointed to the far wall where they had been peppering shots for the previous four months. "You said that you would put the gym back in the condition you found it when you were done."

Karl hadn't really noticed the small dings and smudges as they had occurred. Looking closer, he had to agree that it needed to be done.

When he showed up that afternoon, the rest of the basketball team that had practiced with him all winter was already there. As much as he ever had with the football squad, Karl felt like he was part of a team.

They were not professional painters, but Coach Carlson was—it was what he did during the summers to make ends meet. He stuck around and supervised to make sure the job was being done right.

⟨ ⟩

THE REST OF THE SCHOOL year passed quickly. He had been through it enough times, he had the rhythm and pattern down.

When graduation arrived, Karl had the same cheering section that he'd had at the basketball games.

Ellonyia had volunteered to throw a small graduation party for Karl since their house was more accommodating for entertaining.

Most of his basketball teammates showed up, along with Jake from the golf course and his wife. Mike and Lisa, and all of the D&D warriors that Eric hung out with were there, and of course, Finley.

It was a low-key affair, at least until Don Swanson stood in the center of the living room and clinked a spoon against his glass and said, "I've got something I'd like Karl to see."

All conversation died and everyone turned to look. They all had the same look on their faces: *Was he going to pull some sort of a rabbit out of a hat?*

"Karl gave up a promising shot at a football scholarship this year so he could concentrate on golf. Well, it paid off. The first time I ever saw him play, I thought I'd never seen such a natural talent. His swing, his power, his accuracy, were all so far beyond where I was at the same point that there's no comparison."

Everyone around the room beamed at Karl.

"And then...well, and then, he worked as hard on his game as anyone I've ever seen. Unfortunately, Middle Falls is not exactly a hotbed of golfing activity. I thought Karl had too much talent to waste, though, so I've been doing some work behind the scenes."

He turned and looked over his shoulder at Ellonyia, who handed him an envelope.

"The last few weeks, I've had Eric following Karl around with an 8-millimeter film camera as he golfed and practiced. I told him a small untruth, but it was all for a good cause."

Karl's brows knitted together in confusion. He truly could not see what direction this might be going in.

"I'm not much for keeping up with technology, but Eric here is. He spent a lot of hours in the AV room at school and edited together some of Karl's best moments. I sent that tape off to my old college roommate, who just happens to be Harrison Jenkins." He paused and looked around the room. "If the name isn't familiar, he's the golf coach at Oregon State University. Karl, he sent this letter to you here." He handed the envelope, which was unopened, to Karl. "You don't have to read it out loud if you don't want to."

Finley stepped beside Karl and put his arm around his son. Tears glinted in his eyes.

"Did you know about this, Dad?"

Finley didn't answer. His throat was thick. He settled for a nod.

Karl carefully opened the envelope, then read it over to himself. His mouth fell open.

"What's it say, dufus?" Eric said from the back of the room. The tension broke and everyone laughed.

A chant of "Read it, read it, read it," went up from Karl's friends.

Karl tried to clear his throat and speak, but his voice didn't come out right. He turned away, covered his mouth and coughed, then turned back to face everyone.

"Dear Karl," Karl read, then looked up at the crowd. "That's me."

The chant went up again, "Read it, read it, read it."

"Dear Karl, Don Swanson sent me a tape of your swing and perhaps the most glowing recommendation I've ever received. Ordinarily, I might dismiss that kind of effusive praise, but I've known Don for thirty years and never heard him gush like that."

Karl looked at Don and mouthed, *Thank you.*

Looking back at the letter, he continued.

"I don't have quite the same scholarship program that the football program does here, but I'd like to bring you to Corvallis to talk about what I do have to offer. We expect to field a competitive team and I can promise an excellent education at OSU. Please call me at your earliest convenience and we'll arrange for your visit. We can go out on the links and hit a few balls around."

Karl looked up and said, "It's signed Harrison Jenkins, OSU Golf Coach." He shook his head and a tear leaked out of his eye.

Finley grabbed him hard around his neck and whispered, "I'm so proud of you. Your mom is too."

That pushed Karl over the edge and he sobbed into his father's shoulder. It wasn't just the possibility of the scholarship. It was being surrounded by so many people he loved and cared about after so many lonely lifetimes.

It was overwhelming, in the best way.

Chapter Forty-Two

Karl made the trip to Corvallis the following week. He didn't go alone, though. He rode up with the three Swansons and Finley. Luckily, Don Swanson's Cadillac carried five comfortably.

The few days he spent at Corvallis went by in a blur. Twice, Karl golfed with Don Swanson and Harrison Jenkins. They were close matches, but Karl shot one under on each round, edging out both of the older men.

When the five of them drove back to Middle Falls, Karl had a signed scholarship offer in his pocket and big dreams in his head.

He started school in Corvallis in September, just in time for the fall golf schedule. Karl had a lot to learn. Not just about being on a golf team, but also about how to be a college freshman. He had lived a number of lives where his goal was to get to that very spot, but this was the first time he had actually made it.

Harrison Jenkins put Karl on the reserve team that first year to let him become acclimated. That allowed him time to practice and become friends with several of his teammates.

His classes that year were mostly the basics—Psychology 101, English Literature, that sort of thing. He knew he would need to pick a major soon, but now that he was here, he wasn't completely sure what he wanted to study.

Corvallis was only an hour's drive from Middle Falls, which meant that Karl could go home over the holidays and even some weekends.

There were plenty of attractive college girls at OSU, and Karl even dated a few. This was another area of his life where he was inexperienced and really had no idea how to handle himself. By some measures, he was old and experienced. By others, he knew nothing. He'd been married to Anna in a number of lives but had never actually been on many dates.

After a few times going out, though, Karl decided it wasn't for him. It felt like so much work to try and get to know someone and he felt that most of the time, they were showing him the face they thought he wanted to see. He had a hard time putting his finger on it, but in his heart, he longed for that frictionless communication he'd had with Anna after they had let all their walls down. It was hard for him to admit, but the girl he had originally been trapped into marrying was the woman he carried the torch for.

When he returned to Middle Falls, he asked Eric if Anna was still seeing Seymour Keynes. She was.

That knowledge helped Karl focus on his golf game and his schoolwork. College was so much different than anything he had experienced in high school.

It wasn't just that the classes were tougher—they were—or that the professors had much higher expectations—they did—but more that he felt completely on his own.

In high school, if he cut a class, he would hear about it. Probably even get a detention or two over it.

At OSU, no one seemed to care if he came to class or not. No one took roll, and he could even buy notes for each class at the Student Union Building for just a couple of dollars.

He fell into that temptation for a few weeks, as many freshmen did, but soon ended up on the carpet in Coach Jenkins' office for what Jenkins called a *come to Jesus* meeting.

Karl apologized profusely and promised it wouldn't happen anymore. As he walked out of Jenkins' office, he berated himself.

How many lifetimes did it take for me to get to college, he thought, *and now I'm blowing it.*

It turned out that no matter how many lives you've lived, a college freshman still tended to act like a college freshman.

He got himself back on track and back in the good graces of Coach Jenkins.

By his sophomore year, he made the traveling team and was able to play in both the fall and spring tournaments.

Karl had high expectations when it came to his golf game this lifetime. He had sacrificed a lot to get this good and now he wanted to make it pay off.

And it had, in some ways. Less so in others.

It got him a good education. He finally elected to study Business and go for his BA in Business Administration. He thought that was a good general-knowledge degree that would help him with whatever he wanted to do.

He wasn't sure what that was yet, but he was sure what it *wasn't*. He didn't want to have to return to some dead-end nine-to-five job that sucked the life out of him one day at a time.

That was good.

What surprised Karl was that, as happy as he was with his game, there were others on the team who were just a little bit better.

He thought that might pass over time. He redoubled his efforts. He took extra sessions with Coach Jenkins, he added a strenuous weight program, he tried yoga, he tried everything he could think of to get the last few drops out of his natural ability.

In all likelihood, he did. And he was good.

But he had to face a certain reality. With all the time, work and effort he had put in, it was possible—likely, even—that he wasn't going to get much better.

At his first collegiate tournament, OSU traveled to Stanford. Karl was a little nervous, but he'd practiced enough that when he needed it, everything kicked in.

He played well. Maybe not his very best, but not far off.

At the end of his first round, he had shot slightly better than his average.

And he was third on the team and fourteenth in the tournament.

That's when the harsh reality began to settle over him. He was good, bordering on great, but he still wasn't the best golfer on his team. Over the next three years, he placed in the tournaments, but he didn't live in that rarified air with those that might go on to play on the Tour.

His dreams of traveling the world, playing golf and becoming rich and famous began to seem unreachable. Karl didn't like to give up on things, but he also wanted to be realistic.

He had always told himself that making the Tour was a long shot, but in his secret heart, he thought that having the advantage of a number of lifetimes to hone his game might get him there.

A stray thought occurred to him then—*what if some of those great athletes were playing out the same thing he was, but they had started with just a little more natural ability?* He filed that thought away, because whether it was possible or not, there was nothing he could do about it.

During his senior year at OSU, Karl changed his goals. He had initially thought of his four years as a stepping stone to something bigger. That he would go on to play in the Qualifying School and then on to smaller tournaments before working his way up to the PGA tour.

Once Karl realized that wasn't likely to happen, he focused more on just enjoying the experience of being in college. He walked around the OSU campus with different eyes, taking in the beauty instead of looking past it.

He went out with his teammates more. Paid more attention in class. Spent more time with friends.

Karl had no idea what his next life would be like, but he knew that with the question answered about whether he could make the big time, he wouldn't likely be back here.

The one thing he had found he could carry with him from life to life was knowledge and perspective. He decided to make the most of that.

Karl graduated from OSU in 1986 with that BA in Business Administration.

Back in Middle Falls, he went to stay with Finley while he planned his next move.

When he had first moved away, he'd had some fear that his dad might start spending his evenings at the Do-Si-Do again, but it hadn't happened. Finley had his meetings, which he still attended. He hadn't had a relapse in six years. Still, he didn't take his sobriety for granted. He continued to take things one day at a time.

Karl went and visited Jake at the municipal course. They played a round and Karl beat him by five strokes.

The fact was, Karl could drop in on just about any small course in the US and likely be the best golfer there. That just wasn't good enough to get him to the next level that he had dreamed about.

When they finished their round, Karl and Jake sat in the shade of the back patio.

"So what's next in the exciting life of Karl Strong?" Jake asked.

"Honestly, I'm not sure. Maybe I'll travel across the land as a golf hustler."

Jake closed one eye and squinted at Karl with the other.

"Okay, okay, that's probably not the plan. I'm not sure what's next. I've got the education now, but I don't have a lot of money to put into starting a new business. I'm going to look around and see what I can find that can get me started."

"I've got a suggestion for you, if you'd like."

That surprised Karl a little, but he leaned forward and said, "Sure. Shoot."

Jake waved his hand around at the course.

"Not sure I get what you're talking about."

"I'm talking about the splendor that is Middle Falls Fairways."

Karl looked out over the first tee and said, "I love this place, but like I said, I don't have any money to invest right now."

"You already have years of goodwill built up with me. I still remember that day the scrawny little teenager walked in and said, *I can outdrive you.* I could have slapped you." Jake grinned at the memory.

"I was a little full of myself," Karl admitted. "But I had to do something to get your attention."

"Listen. I'm getting old. Old enough that I can start collecting my Social Security if I want. I'd like to do something other than come in here every day and watch other people golf. I'd like to travel around the country with the missus. See some things I've never seen before." He leaned in toward Karl and said, "Here's what I have in mind. We go in partners. You do all the work, but over time, you can pay me off until you own the place by yourself."

"That's incredibly generous," Karl said. "But what about Jake Junior?"

"He never loved this place like you do. He's out of college, got a job up in Portland and he's settled down with his wife and kids. He doesn't want to come home."

"There was a time when all I wanted was to get out of Middle Falls," Karl mused. "Now, it looks pretty good to me."

"I took the liberty of having some papers drawn up," Jake said. He pulled a manila envelope up off the chair beside him. "There's a young kid in town that just hung out his shingle. Thomas Weaver. He's pretty green, but I figured he could draft something like this for us."

Jake pushed the envelope across the table. "There are a bunch of other lawyers in town if you want to have one of them look it over for you. Or you can ask your dad and Don Swanson to go through it. You know they'll have your best interest at heart."

"I know you won't do anything squirrelly." Karl picked up the envelope. "But one of the main things I got out of that four-year education was, *Use the other guy's brain*."

Karl stood up and walked to the edge of the patio, scanning the course.

"I can see the wheels turning already. You're making changes to the course and it's not even yours yet."

Karl turned and grinned. "Guilty. But then, I see the faraway look in your eyes and figure you're probably off on some road trip somewhere."

"Guilty," Jake agreed. "Take your time. No hurry."

Karl conferred with Finley and the Swansons that night.

After they took turns reading the agreement over, Finley whistled and said, "Looks like a sweetheart deal to me. What do you think, Don? You know a lot more about these things than I do."

"I don't know about that, but this looks like your chickens coming home to roost in a good way. He's giving you a chance to outright own the course in fifteen years. Hard to beat a deal like that. If I was a young man of...?"

"Twenty-three," Karl said, filling in the blank.

"...of twenty-three, I'd do the math and figure I'd have a pretty damned nice asset completely in my name before I was forty." He glanced at Finley. "Remember when forty seemed old?"

"Yep," Finley said. "*Old* becomes a moving target. Right now, I'd say it's fifteen years older than whatever I am at the time." He looked at Karl. "Jake's been a good friend to you for almost ten years. I trust him."

The next day, Karl and Jake met at the cramped offices of Thomas Weaver, Esq. Half an hour later, Karl Strong was a partner in Middle Falls Fairways.

Being a partner in the golf course didn't make Karl a wealthy man at an early age. It was probably never going to be a huge cash generator. It did give him a chance to save money, though. There was a room at the back of the clubhouse that Karl decided would be just right to live in for a few years. He and Finley remodeled it over the course of a month and made it nice, then Karl moved in.

With no real expenses, he was able to save most of the salary he paid himself each month. Even after he paid Jake what he was owed, there was still money left in the business account, and Karl started making small improvements around the course.

Within a year, it looked better and attracted more players.

Karl also had the idea to start a small golf school for the kids of Middle Falls. That wasn't a big profit center, as he kept the courses inexpensive. But what it did was build for the future. The more young golfers there were in the eighties, the more older golfers there would be in the decades ahead.

Besides which, running the lessons became Karl's favorite thing.

The third year after Karl took over running the course, Eric graduated from college and came back looking for something to do. Karl remembered the life when he had opened the auto parts store, the car washes, and the detailing company.

He approached Eric and pitched the idea to him. He was not surprised when both Eric and Don liked the idea.

They went in as partners.

That meant that Karl was busier than ever, but that was okay. He had plenty of time to spend with those he was closest to.

That enterprise made enough money for Karl that he was able to help Finley retire from the box factory a little early.

Karl decided that he had lived at the golf course long enough and bought a nice house in the same neighborhood they had lived when his mother was alive. Not fancy, but solid. He invited Finley to come live with him and they became bachelors together again.

On lazy afternoons when Karl sat on the back patio of the club house, he often thought back over this life and decided it was good. He had wonderful friends, he had a real relationship with his father, and he had finally been able to find out where his golf would take him. It wasn't as far as he wanted, but at least he knew.

There was a certain part of him that was lonely, but after the overriding loneliness of his previous lives, it was manageable.

Once again, Karl paid attention to his diet and never gained weight as he had in his first life. Working essentially two full-time jobs between the golf course and his business with Eric kept him active.

Finley lived longer in this life than he had in any of Karl's other incarnations. He had a heart attack and passed away in 2014. Karl and the Swansons were with him in the hospital when he died.

Karl once again lived longer than he ever had before.

He lived to be sixty-nine in this life, but never retired. With Finley gone, there was nothing he really wanted to do but work, so that's what he did, right up to the end.

He was mowing his backyard in the spring of 2032 when an aneurysm in his brain killed him. He was dead before he knew what had happened.

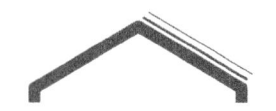

Interlude Four
Universal Life Center

Charles turned his pyxis left, then right, tilting it at odd angles, looking for information. He had gone over this particular life more often than any other that he could remember.

He felt a deep responsibility toward the souls he watched over. This one, he felt, had not been handled optimally.

He wanted to make sure to correct that.

He did extensive calculations in the air in front of him, wiped them away, then did them again.

Finally, his thin lips pulled back in a smile.

"Of course. I should have known."

He spun the image in the pyxis back until he found the spot in the life he was looking for.

Chapter Forty-Three

Karl Strong opened his eyes. He was jostled from behind and stumbled.

Where am I? he thought.

There was a crowd around him. He looked down and saw that he was in his football uniform.

His stomach clenched. He had been here before.

He did not hesitate. He knew exactly what he needed to do.

He dropped his helmet and tore out of the crowd, bumping carelessly into people as he did.

"Hey, watch it, kid," one man said as Karl nearly ran him over.

Karl did not even hear him. He ran as fast as he could. He ran alongside the band room, then turned right, his cleats digging into the grass as he pushed harder.

A junior high football game didn't attract a crowd like the varsity did, but a fair number of people came out to root their kids on. The sidewalk was busy.

Ahead, Karl saw his mother and his heart leapt. He didn't waste time or breath calling out to her. It was too early.

He avoided the people on the sidewalk and ran parallel to it, whizzing by family after family slowly making their way back to their cars. It was a lovely fall evening and no one was in a hurry.

Except for Karl. For him, it was life or death.

He craned his neck and saw her ahead. He recognized her coat, her hair, the way she walked. He had never forgotten.

Finally, he judged that he was close enough.

"Mom!" he screamed as he ran. "Mom!"

Other mothers between Karl and her heard him and stopped to look. He ran past them.

"Mom!"

She had reached the spot where she stepped out onto the street. Coming from the other direction was the car with the teenagers.

"Mom!" Karl shouted so loudly that he strained his voice.

Christina Strong stopped and turned. She looked over her shoulder, saw Karl, and smiled broadly. She waved.

Karl sprinted toward her. He wanted to grab her, to hold her, to keep her out of the path of the car he knew was coming her way.

"Honey, honey, it's all right!" Christina said. "I was just going to get the car. I'll come back and..." Her words were cut off as Karl reached her. Slammed into her, really, forcing her to take a step back.

"Ooof," Christina said. "Hold on there, tiger. You're supposed to tackle the other team, not your old mom."

Karl looked up at her. Sweat poured off of him and mingled with his tears. He tried to speak but found he couldn't.

"Honey, what's wrong?" Christina asked, alarmed. "Are you all right? What is it?"

Karl wrapped his arms around her and held her tight.

"Way to tackle 'em," a man said as he passed them.

Christina gave the man a look that sent him on his way, then put her finger under Karl's chin, lifting his face up. "Tell me what's wrong."

Karl finally found his voice. "Nothing," he said, and smiled through his tears. "Nothing is wrong. I just thought you were about to step in front of that car, and I didn't want that to happen."

Christina narrowed her eyes at Karl. She looked out at the now empty street. The death car had disappeared down the road. "You ran all the way here because you thought I was going to get hit by a car?"

Karl nodded. He knew he couldn't make it all make sense, and he didn't care. He was holding his mother. She was alive.

"That's it for you, mister. No more of those crazy science fiction movies you like to watch on Friday nights. Your imagination is too good." She ruffled his hair and said, "It could be worse, I suppose. An imagination is a good thing to have. Now, go change out of that uniform and..."

Karl shook his head vehemently. "I'll walk with you to the car, then you can give me a ride back to the locker room, okay?"

Christina looked out over the empty street. "Still worried, huh? Okay, come on, help the old lady across the street then."

Karl had been almost seventy just a few minutes before, so his mother, who was thirty-nine, looked incredibly young to him. He nodded and put a protective arm across her, looking both times before they crossed the street.

Cars coming out of nowhere had affected both of them at various points in their lives and he was taking no chances.

They crossed the street and found the Falcon parked on a side street. When they climbed inside, Christina wrinkled her nose and said, "Do you think that smell is ever going to go away?"

"I know how to get rid of it," Karl said.

"You do?"

He nodded. "I'll do it this weekend. I'll just need you to buy me a few things at the store, okay?"

"Sure. Give me a list," she said and looked down at Karl, who was still a good three inches shorter than her. "Are you sure you're okay? Didn't get hit in the head during the game or anything?"

"Nope," Karl said. "I guess I'm just happy we won."

Christina laughed and said, "You lost 28 to 21. Now I know something's wrong."

"Just kidding, Mom. I know. Come on, take me to the locker room so I can get changed and we can go home. I'm starved."

Christina turned the key, put the Falcon in gear, and headed down the street they had just walked across. The crowd had mostly all departed now, and she drove right up and parked in front of the locker room. "Hurry up now, I've got a surprise for you."

"Be right back!" Karl said as he hopped out and ran for the locker room.

Mike was waiting for him, holding his helmet. "You dropped this when you took off like a rocket, man." He grinned and Karl saw that he'd already had his braces put on.

"Thanks," Karl said. "I forgot to tell Mom something and I had to catch up to her."

"I don't think I've ever needed to tell my mom something that bad." He handed the helmet to Karl. "I didn't want you to get in trouble for losing it."

Karl smiled at him and sat on the bench in front of his locker. He took his jersey off, then his shoulder pads. Looking down at his skinny chest, he thought, *I've got some growing to do, I guess.*

For the first time since he had opened his eyes in this life, he took a breath and thought, *Everything is in front of me. I can do anything I want.* He smiled, pulled his thigh pads out of his pants, and stripped.

He had to look in three different lockers before he found the one that had his clothes in it, but he did find it eventually. He hurried and got dressed, dropping his pads and uniform in the proper places.

Outside, Christina had the car all warmed up. KMFR was playing *I Like Dreamin'* by Kenny Nolan.

Everything seemed good in the world, but it got better.

"You're starved, huh?"

"Yep." Karl couldn't keep the grin off his face. "What have we got in the fridge at home?" It made Karl warm to think about that home. Modest, but a real home, with a real family. *His* family.

"The usual, but that's not for us tonight. You scored three touchdowns!"

"Oh, right, I did," Karl said as though he had forgotten that because he really had.

"That calls for Artie's."

"Oh, yes!" Karl pumped his fist. He had some worry about being able to remember how to act fourteen again, but Artie's sounded so good that he didn't have to pretend enthusiasm.

"Let's go, then, they'll be closing soon."

Christina turned out of the school parking lot and toward Main Street. She hung a left and pulled into Artie's. The parking lot was mostly empty. She looked at Karl and said, "The usual?"

"If *the usual* is a burger, fries, and a chocolate shake, then definitely."

"What else could it be?" Christina pressed the red button and ordered two burger baskets and two chocolate shakes, then added another burger basket to go. She looked at Karl and said, "Wouldn't be fair for us to come home smelling like Artie's and not have one for your dad, right?"

"For sure." Karl tried to remember what his parents' relationship had been like, but he came up pretty blank. They had just been his parents. He had mostly ignored them, thought they would always be there for him. And then she was gone.

A few minutes later, the neon sign overhead turned off. Just then a young woman came out with their order.

Christina rolled the window down and the waitress put the tray on the window. Christina opened her purse and took out a ten-dollar bill. The waitress made change and Christina handed her a nice tip.

"Just flash your lights when you're done and I'll come get the tray." She hurried away, no doubt to start on her closing cleanup duties.

Christina took the white bag and set it on the seat between them, then handed Karl his basket and shake.

He stuck the shake between his legs and held the basket to his nose. "Nothing smells like Artie's."

Christina did the same. "Right you are. We'll replace that horrible smell with Artie's, at least for the ride home."

Karl hadn't been lying when he said he was starving. He demolished the burger in record time and Christina said, "Slow down, it's better when you taste it!"

Karl just grinned and stuffed french fries in his mouth.

He looked at his mother, alive, and taking much more decorous nibbles at her burger and fries.

He thought he had never been so happy.

When they got home, the house was still dark. Christina flipped on the lights and looked at the clock.

"Your father won't be home for another hour." She turned the oven on to low and put the paper bag with his dinner on the lower rack. "It won't be as good as what we got, but I've never seen your father turn down Artie's in any form."

Karl yawned and felt the familiar exhaustion that always accompanied each transition into another life.

"I'm tired, Mom. I'm going to go to bed." He stepped to his mother and wrapped her in a huge hug, wanting to feel the realness of her again. "I love you, Mom," he murmured as he held her.

"I love you too, Karl. You are the sweetest boy."

Karl let her go and said, "Tell Dad I love him too," and toddled off to bed.

He hadn't seen this room since his first life, but everything in it was familiar. The same orange bedspread, the curtains with dinosaurs on them that he had wanted when he was eight, and a toy chest in one corner. The bedroom of a child just on the cusp of being an adolescent.

He clicked off the lamp on the bedside table and slipped between the cool sheets. He rested his head on his hands and stared up into the darkness.

For the first time in many lifetimes, he said a small prayer.

I don't know who or what is doing all this, but thank you.

He closed his eyes and was out.

Chapter Forty-Four

The next morning, Karl opened his eyes and Christina was standing over him.

"I know that was a hard game last night, but it's getting late. Your father is talking about taking us to the movies tonight, but we've got chores to do first."

Karl felt the familiar fogginess, but still couldn't help smiling. Sometimes the transitions from one life to another seemed like a dream, but he was happy that it was as real as any other life he had lived.

"Sorry, Mom."

"Nothing to apologize for. You're not normally a slugabed." She laid some clothes on the end of his bed. "Get up and get dressed. I'll make some pancakes for us."

Karl nodded, hopped out of bed and got dressed. In the living room, Finley glanced up from reading his paper and said, "The dead arise!"

Karl glanced from Finley to Christina. To them, it was just another Saturday morning. One in a seemingly endless series. To Karl, it was a miracle.

Christina bustled around in the kitchen, mixing pancake batter and scrambling some eggs.

Finley leafed through the paper and pulled out the Arts and Entertainment section of *The Oregonian*. He folded it over so that the comics section showed. Without a word, he held it out to Karl.

Karl took it and sat on the couch, reading *Peanuts* and *Garfield*. At least he *looked* like he was reading the comics. What he was actually doing was marveling at the scene around him. Finley, young and healthy-looking, complaining about the government. Christina cooking in the kitchen, saying "Mmm-hmm" every few seconds and totally ignoring what Finley was saying.

A stray thought popped into Karl's head—a quote he had read that was attributed to Kurt Vonnegut. He gave voice to it. "If this isn't nice, I don't know what is."

Finley lowered his newspaper and looked at Karl, then over his shoulder at Christina in the kitchen.

They looked at each other for a few seconds, then both burst out laughing.

"Did you go to sleep last night and wake up an old man?" Finley asked.

Karl looked up, suddenly self-conscious. "Umm...It was in something they had us read in English."

"Was it now?" Christina asked. "Well, breakfast is ready. Come tell us all about it."

Karl managed to avoid that by playing dumb and soon his honest but out of place observation was forgotten.

Everyone had chores to do that day. Christina had to do the weekly shopping, and Finley and Karl were going to clean the gutters and rake up the leaves.

By late afternoon, all the work was done.

Christina made chili burgers for dinner. That was a tradition that Karl had long forgotten about. On shopping days, they usually had chili burgers because they were quick to make.

Whatever the reason, they were delicious and Karl almost asked for two, but remembered what his mom had said about going to the movies.

Finley wandered into the living room and sat down with the Mariners game on. Karl jumped up and cleared the dishes, then said, "Go sit down, Mom. I'll do the dishes."

This was obviously another extraordinary statement and Christina held a hand against Karl's forehead to see if he was feverish.

"You work too hard, Mom. I'm going to start doing the dishes."

Christina smiled and ruffled Karl's short hair. "I don't know how long this attitude is going to last, but I'm going to take full advantage of it while it's here."

Karl did the dishes and Christina sat curled up on the couch with her feet up reading *Redbook* magazine.

Karl plopped down beside her and watched a couple of innings of the Mariners game with his father. It was the first season for the expansion Mariners, and they weren't very good. They were winding down a season where they would finish almost forty games behind the Kansas City Royals in the American League West. Their only point of pride that year was that they managed to finish half a game ahead of the well-established Oakland A's, which had won the World Series just a few years earlier.

As they had so often, the M's went down to defeat and Karl couldn't resist testing his dad a little.

"It's just the first year, Dad. We'll be better next year, won't we?"

Finley thought about that for a few seconds, then said, "I'm not so sure. We're old and slow. Our pitching's not very good. I'm not sure if we're gonna get better at either of those things over the winter."

"Sure would be cool to see a game at the Kingdome though, wouldn't it?"

"Maybe we'll have to plan a trip up to Seattle and do that next year."

Karl grinned and Christina gave Finley a look that said, *Don't go promising the boy things we can't afford to do.*

Finley took the silent rebuke in stride and said, "But for now, we'll have to settle for a movie. Your mom told me all about your game last night. Three touchdowns! Sorry I wasn't there."

"That's all right. We lost anyway. Maybe you can come next week."

"No overtime for me next week. Not gonna miss another of your games."

They all put on their coats and climbed into the Falcon, with Karl in the back seat.

Christina wrinkled her nose, then looked over at Finley. "Karl said he can get rid of that terrible smell."

"If he can, then he's a better man than I," Finley said, looking at Karl in the rearview mirror.

Christina half-turned in her seat and said, "I stopped at the auto parts store and got you the things you asked for."

"Great! I'll tackle it first thing in the morning."

They drove past the Pickwick Theater, but all the spots in front were already filled. They had to turn down the next block to find a place to park.

Christina and Finley walked together, she with her arm slipped through his. Karl followed along behind, grinning a little and shaking his head.

I suppose, he thought, *that I'll get used to this eventually, but for right now, it's the best thing I can imagine.*

When they turned the corner, Karl saw that the movie playing was *Smokey and the Bandit*. He realized that he had not seen it in any of his lives, then thought that perhaps they were planning on seeing it as a family this same weekend, but then Christina was killed.

Karl hurried a few steps and put his head against his mom.

"I think someone wants some popcorn."

"He worked hard on the leaves and gutters today. I'd say he deserves some," Finley said.

Finley paid for a large bucket of popcorn and a small pop for each of them. They were there twenty minutes before the movie started, but the theater was filling fast. They found seats on the aisle about halfway down and settled in for the show.

On the way home, they played the game they always did, asking each one in turn what their favorite part was.

Karl's real favorite part was just sitting in the theater with his parents, but he picked one of the times when Burt Reynolds had made Buford T. Justice look silly.

When it was Christine's turn, she said, "I liked the movie, but my favorite part was just being together with my boys."

Karl and his dad looked at each other and said, "Sappy!" together, then laughed.

It was a good day, a good night.

《 》

IT WAS A LITTLE EASIER for Karl to reacclimate himself to being in eighth grade. He had a single home room where he left all his stuff, so he didn't have to pretend to have lost his locker combination.

As a college graduate, the eighth-grade material wasn't too tough to handle, though he did find that he had forgotten a few things.

Karl wasn't looking too far into the future in this life. Like his last year at Oregon State in his previous life, he was committed to just enjoying things as they came.

Some of his predictions from that first weekend came true. He did become accustomed to the fact that they were once again a whole family. He never did take it for granted, though. Good as his word, he did start doing the dishes every night so Christina could sit and relax.

Finley was also as good as his word. The summer of 1978, he managed to put things together so that the three of them could drive up to Seattle and watch a Mariners game.

In all of Karl's previous lifetimes, Finley had stayed at his position on the line at the box factory until he died or retired. In this life, he had more ambition. This time it was him who went into the office upstairs and talked to Allen Ray about moving up a little bit. By the spring of '78, he still worked on the line, but also spent time as a part-time floor supervisor.

He took some of the extra money and stashed it away for the trip to Seattle. They made a weekend out of it, going up in the Space Needle, seeing a show at Laserium—where music played while laser images bounced around on the ceiling—and, of course, the Mariners game.

The Kingdome was almost new then. It was something of a concrete monstrosity and would be imploded in just a few decades, but to Karl's eye, it was special. The idea that something as huge as a professional baseball stadium could be under a roof was still relatively new. It might have been ugly, but it was *their* ugly.

The Mariners even did them the favor of winning the game, so they made the six-hour drive back to Middle Falls happy. Karl fell asleep in the back seat before they got to Portland.

Chapter Forty-Five

Karl's freshman year flew by. Unlike his first few trips through that year, he wasn't mourning the loss of Christine, so he decided to get really good grades. He wasn't completely sure that he wanted to go to college again but thought that he might as well give himself the option. He knew he could get straight A's after several trips through school, but he decided against that.

He knew who the valedictorian and salutatorian of the class would be, and he didn't want to interfere with that, so he made sure to scatter a few B's through his transcript.

He did take new and different classes whenever he could, particularly English classes. He took *Great Religions*, hoping that it might provide him with a clue about what was happening to him. When they studied Hinduism and the concept of reincarnation, that was close, but not quite. He wasn't being recycled back into different people, or different beings. He was just being returned to his own life over and over.

Still, the basic idea of reincarnation—that we live over and over until we become our best self—fascinated him.

Looking back at his first life—divorcing Anna, falling into depression, then dying so young—Karl knew that had not been his best life.

He hadn't stepped back and looked at the big picture of his lives before, but sitting in that class, he let his mind wander over his journey. With the likely exception of the times he felt stuck in an out-er circle of Hell—being reborn over and over at a time when he couldn't change anything—he realized that each life had gotten a little better.

That *he* had gotten a little better. He was nowhere close to the same person that he had been in that first life.

He was happy in this life, at least in part because he wasn't having to grieve the too-early loss of his mother, but he was happy in his last life too. He hadn't had Anna or Christine with him, but he had been happy. He had made progress, learned the lessons he needed.

He had time to think about what he wanted and didn't want in this life.

In his previous life, he had dedicated everything he had to develop his golf game. He had become an excellent golfer. But in focusing with such intensity, Karl felt like he had probably maximized that ability. Even if he used the same laser-focus in this life, he didn't feel he would progress anymore.

That didn't mean he wouldn't golf. He had come to love the game. The beauty of a perfect parabola of a drive, reading a green precisely to predict a break on a putt. It all made him happy. He just didn't think that he would put so much time and effort into it. He would let it slip into the background a bit.

He also had to decide about football. He had let that fall by the wayside in his previous life. He had done that because he didn't want to be injured and risk losing his chance at becoming a golf pro. With that goal gone, he had to decide if he wanted to continue to play the game for its own benefit.

When he closed his eyes and thought about whether he would be happier playing or not, he realized that he had missed the game.

He played varsity football for three years. Again, he became the starter halfway through his sophomore year.

This time, he did something he had considered doing in each of his previous lifetimes.

He didn't know if it would do any good, but he wanted to see if there was anything that could be done to help Coach Bulski. He considered the best way to warn him.

Karl pictured himself sitting in Bulski's office and saying, "I can't tell you how, Coach, but you need to go in and get checked out. Get tested for Leukemia."

He knew that would not go well, so he resorted to something he had done to keep Anna away from Kenny in their previous life.

Just before spring break of his junior year, he decided the time was right. Karl snuck into the typing room. The lights were off, and it was shadowy inside, but he could see well enough to sit down at one of the IBM Selectrics.

Middle Falls High School had not jumped into the computer age yet. In fact, half the typewriters in the room were still old manual Underwoods.

The Selectric, with its rotating head that spun and jumped up at each letter, was the closest thing the school had to technology.

Karl didn't turn on the lights. Students were not supposed to be in the typing room when the teacher was not present.

He rolled a piece of paper into the IBM. He put his feet flat on the floor and his fingers on the home row, just as he had been taught. He had thought about what he wanted to say in the letter for a long time, so the words came easily. He hoped they would be persuasive.

The letter told Bulski that he needed to make an appointment as soon as possible and told him exactly what tests to ask the doctor to run. Or at least what tests within the framework of Karl's knowledge, which was limited.

He tri-folded the page, then stuck it into an envelope that he had typed Coach Bulski's name and the school's address on. He stuck a stamp in the corner and stopped at the Middle Falls post office that afternoon.

It wasn't much, but he couldn't think what else he could do to help.

That summer, he met Eric again and once again impressed him with his golf game. Eric took him home to meet his parents—again—and Karl was thrilled to have the three of them back in his life.

Of course, Karl's overall situation was different this life. Before, the Swansons had offered him a safe port in the storminess of his life. When Finley had disappeared, they did their best to step in and become a substitute family. This life, Karl didn't need that, but he loved them and wanted to be in their lives.

To that end, he organized another barbecue. It was much easier in this life. The house that he lived in with his parents was nicer and though they spiffed things up for the barbecue, it didn't require major surgery.

The Swansons once again showed up with macaroni salad, a cooler full of pop, and a game of yard darts. It was their go-to move for barbecue invitations, apparently.

It was an odd feeling for Karl when he saw Christina and Ellonyia meet each other for the first time. He had grown to think of Ellonyia as his second mom and he kept his fingers crossed that the two women would like each other.

He needn't have worried. They hit it off like old friends and spent most of the day away from the men, huddled in conversation.

Karl made a bit more of a game of the yard darts, but Eric again prevailed.

《 》

WHEN KARL SHOWED UP for two-a-days, he found that he had made a difference. On that first day, it was Coach Shield who greeted them.

"Coach Bulski has a health issue that's going to keep him out for the season. He's asked me to stop in and take over the team until he can get back."

Karl leaned forward, listening intently.

"Coach will be undergoing treatments up in Portland, but the good news is that they caught whatever it is early, so they think he's going to be fine. Now, let's start whipping you boys into shape. I can see that you've been sucking down too many shakes at Artie's over the summer. Let's start working those off."

The season was different without Coach Bulski being there from the start. The Bulldogs started 0-2 while they got used to Coach Shield's playbook and style.

Meanwhile, the Homecoming game approached.

Karl had used the same technique to stop Anna from going out with Kenny during his junior year. This time, several lifetimes removed from what he had done to Anna, he felt a little guilty, but he did it anyway.

When the dance was still a month away, Karl sprang into action. He found Anna at the same locker she always had.

He had seen her in the halls over the previous two years and this time he had made a point of paying attention when she *accidentally* bumped into him. He had even taken to eating lunch at the same table she did. It wasn't the same thing as eating lunch together, but in this life, he didn't want to go into Homecoming cold.

Anna saw him coming and smiled at him as she so often did.

"Homecoming's coming up," Karl said casually. He watched Anna carefully.

She didn't show a lot of reaction, but her eyes did widen.

"Is it?" she asked innocently.

"I thought I'd ask you to go with me before someone else beat me to it. You are the prettiest girl in school, after all."

That might not have been strictly true, but it was for Karl.

"So are you going to?"

Karl was momentarily confused. "Am I going to what?"

"You said you thought you'd ask me to go, but you didn't actually."

"Oh, right." Karl realized that no matter how many lifetimes he had on Anna, she would still be able to tie him up in knots. He cleared his throat and then, as if making an official announcement, said, "Anna Masterson, will you do me the honor of attending the Homecoming dance with me?"

"You know, I probably would have if you weren't being such a dufus." She watched Karl's crestfallen expression, then said, "Karl Strong, of course I will do you that honor." She dropped the act and more quietly said, "I thought you were never going to get around to asking me."

Karl drew a deep breath and let it out. It seemed a little odd, but somehow this Homecoming dance, either with or without Anna, had seemed to be a pivotal moment in each of his lives.

Having Anna with him hadn't always been a positive thing, but in his last life he had discovered that not being any part of her life hadn't been ideal either.

That first life, where she had trapped Karl—though he hadn't known it at the time—had been tempered by expectations and a sense of loss when he had to give up his scholarship. This life, he wasn't at all sure whether he would accept that scholarship even if it was offered.

Living multiple lives had given him the freedom to plan different lives and he hadn't decided what path he wanted to follow on this go-round.

"So, what color will your dress be? I want to get a corsage to match."

"I'm impressed! Most boys don't think that far ahead."

"I'm not most boys or even most men," Karl said, flexing his bicep a little.

"Oh, brother, I'm going to have to work on teaching you how to accept a compliment."

That simple idea—Anna thinking she needed to *work on* Karl, might have been a turn-off, but he didn't see it that way. To him, it showed that she was already thinking of a future for the two of them, and that sounded good to him.

Chapter Forty-Six

This Homecoming was different from any they'd had before, though of course only Karl knew the differences.

In the other times, Anna had come on like a young temptress, trying to get Karl to sleep with her so she could find a possible husband and father for her baby.

This time, everything was different. After Karl asked her to the dance, they became more obvious about their relationship. Karl started carrying Anna's books between classes, they found a quiet table to eat lunch at together, and Karl started coming over to Anna's house after football practice one or two nights a week.

Two weekends before the dance, Karl sprang an idea on her as they walked between classes. "How would you like to come to dinner at my house on Saturday?"

"Whoa, and meet the parents? That's a big deal."

"I think you're a big deal."

Anna made a slight gagging sound and said, "Sweetness overload." But the way she smiled showed Karl she liked the idea.

"Oh, and it's not just my parents. It's our friends the Swansons and their son Eric. He's a freshman and we hang out. We both like to golf."

"I heard through the grapevine that you like to golf, and that you're pretty good at it. You've got a lot of layers to you, Karl Strong."

"And here everyone thinks I'm just a dumb jock."

"I don't." Her expression was serious. "I know who you are." She looked up and to her left, as if trying to decide whether or not to say something. "Have I ever told you that I've liked you for a long time? A long time ago, I saw you sitting on the bleachers outside. You were smiling and laughing and the way the sun shone on your hair, I thought you were the best-looking boy I'd ever seen."

Anna *had* told him that, of course, but it was lifetimes ago and it was always nice to hear it again.

"And just think, now you get to go to Homecoming with me, you lucky girl."

"I knew I would regret telling you that as soon as the words were out of my mouth."

Karl grinned his lopsided little smile and said, "But you can't stay mad at me, right?"

"Right."

"So, dinner at my place Saturday? I'll come and pick you up around 5:30."

"Okay, but what should I wear?"

"Oh, you should wear your Homecoming dress. I'll be in a suit. It's a formal dinner."

"My God, you've gotta be kidding."

Karl kept his face serious for two heartbeats, then let it crack. "I should have let you come like that. Everyone else would have been casual, and—"

"—and I would have had to kill you."

Karl sobered momentarily. "You are small but mighty."

"Best you keep that in mind!"

Having seven people for dinner stretched the ability of what passed for a dining room at the Strong house. Karl and Christina had to pull the dining room leaf out of the back of the closet and three people were going to sit on mismatched chairs, but it all worked.

Karl picked Anna up at her house. It wasn't until he knocked on her door that he thought that maybe he should have invited Candace, too.

That would have probably been overreaching, though.

More than anything in this life, Karl wanted to focus on the people around him and he wanted to bring them all together as much as possible. To dive headlong into a pool of family and friends and only come up for air when he had to.

At the same time, he knew there was a time and a place for everything. Asking your freshly minted girlfriend's mom to dinner with a bunch of strangers was, he realized, not a great idea.

On the way to his house, Anna was quiet, which was kind of a departure in itself. Karl saw that she twisted her hands together in her lap and he laid his hand over hers.

"Really no need to be nervous," he said sincerely. "Just dinner with the folks."

"And their friends. And your friend."

"Right, that too. Oh," Karl said, a little too casually, "did I mention that Mrs. Swanson writes the etiquette column for the *Middle Falls Gazette*? You're up on all your fine dining rules, aren't you? Which fork to use, and all that?"

Anna blanched, then closed her eyes, realizing she had been had. "Sometimes I hate you."

"And perhaps this is one of those times, but I'm sure you'll want to seem like the perfect future daughter-in-law when we get there, right?" Karl shut his mouth and it was his turn to be chagrined.

Anna's head whipped around, and she stared a laser at Karl. "What did you say?"

Karl tried to think fast, which was not one of his specialties. "Like the perfect future—" he groped for something that sounded like *daughter-in-law* and came up understandably blank. Finally, he gave up and giggled to himself a little. "I have no idea what I meant by that. My brain just went on vacation for a minute there."

"Tell me this dinner is not some excuse to meet your parents so you can ask me to marry you."

"It is most definitely one hundred percent not that."

Anna looked at him out of the corner of her eye. "Good, because that would be ridiculous."

"Ridiculous." Karl agreed. He patted her hand. "Sorry, I really didn't mean that. Sometimes I think I've been hit in the head once too often on the football field."

"That would explain a few things, all right," Anna agreed, but she smiled and laid her cheek on his shoulder.

Just like Karl knew it would be, the dinner was wonderful. When he introduced Anna to Christina—for the first time in this or any other life—it felt momentous.

Anna was a little overwhelmed, as any young woman might be when thrown into a situation like that, but that mostly just caused her to hang on to Karl like a life preserver, and he enjoyed that.

When he drove her home afterward, KMFR was playing romantic music like *Girls on Film* by Duran Duran and *Just Can't Get Enough* by Depeche Mode. MTV had come to Middle Falls and KMFR's format had adjusted to the new reality.

Nonetheless, the mood in the car was cozy. It was as if the rest of the world was far away. Anna had met Christina and Finley and all had gone exceedingly well. They had the Homecoming to look forward to the following week.

And there was the magic of the first kiss still to come.

Karl walked her to her door and couldn't help but think back on when he had stood with her on that same porch in another life. This felt completely different.

At that time, he had known a secret that Anna was desperately trying to keep. It had formed a wall between them that couldn't be breached.

This life, there was nothing but the two of them and whatever the future held.

Underneath the single light bulb of the porchlight, they held hands and stared into each other's eyes.

Karl bent and kissed her softly.

He had kissed this same person, young and old, passionate and not, but this felt different.

This was not the young woman looking for something. Instead, it felt like two young people finding something like they might have in all their earlier lives if things had been different.

Karl had the strangest feeling that he was falling, falling into her.

He lifted his head up and said, "Whoa."

Anna didn't speak at all. A small smile lit her face, and she reached up and touched her lips.

Karl guessed that she was feeling the same thing he was.

Love.

A continuation for Karl.

The spark for Anna.

Chapter Forty-Seven

It didn't take long for Karl and Anna to progress from their Homecoming date to going steady.

In his previous lives, Karl had waited too long, or was afraid that a commitment to Anna would take his focus away from trying to win a scholarship.

He had no such worries this time, as he didn't care if he got a scholarship or not.

Did it feel a little strange to *go steady* with someone Karl knew so well over lifetimes? Yes. But he was committed to slowing down and enjoying this life and letting the future take care of itself. He had missed Anna terribly for an entire lifetime while he pursued golf and business and she was with Seymour. This time, he would take things as they came and enjoy their time together.

By January, Karl had mostly forgotten about ever hearing about a scholarship when the letter came from Oregon State University. His first instinct was to turn it down, but when he told his parents that, he thought their heads might explode.

There was no way Karl could tell them that he already had a college education. Neither Finley nor Christina had gone to college and the idea that their son could go for free was a dream to them. Karl felt like he couldn't let them down.

So even though he wasn't as fired up about playing college football as he had been before, he once again went to the coach's office at the high school.

The previous times he had made that visit, it had been Coach Shield who had helped him.

This time, it was Coach Bulski who sat behind the desk. He had returned from his treatments midway through the school year. Seeing him once again sitting behind the scarred-up old desk in the coach's room cheered Karl immeasurably.

It wasn't always possible to tell when he had made a difference in someone's life, but the fact that Bulski was still on the right side of the dirt showed him that he had done exactly that.

Karl laid the letter on the desk and said, "I think I owe you for this." Just because Karl wasn't as fired up about the opportunity as he had once been didn't mean he shouldn't be grateful.

Bulski picked the envelope up and weighed it in his hand, grinning. He admired the OSU Athletic Department logo. "I've seen a few of these in my time, but not many. Congratulations, Karl. Sorry I couldn't be here to see you through your senior year."

Karl nodded at the envelope. "I know you had a lot to do with getting Coach Anderson to give me a look. I wouldn't have gotten that if not for you."

Bulski waved that idea away. "It was what you did, the film you compiled that got his attention. Do you want to call them from here?"

Karl nodded.

Ten minutes later, he walked out with the next four years of his life apparently spoken for. He immediately began to miss Anna but told himself he was being silly. If anyone knew that time passed quickly, it was Karl.

The young lovers spent a lot of time together that summer. It was always hard on high school relationships when one half of the pair went on to college while the other stayed behind. There would be no more library dates, holding hands at lunches, or laughing at stupid jokes in the halls between classes.

They did what they could with their time that summer.

Karl had long since eradicated the cat smell out of the Falcon. That made it easier to suggest taking her to see movies at The Silvery Moon Drive-in. The Pickwick was nice, a little elegant, even, but there was something special about snuggling up together and watching a movie on the big drive-in screen.

They went to The Silvery Moon at least once every week. It didn't matter what was playing. It was their time to feel completely on their own. It was a good year for movies. They saw *E.T. – The Extraterrestrial*, *Blade Runner*, *The Thing*, and *An Officer and a Gentleman*.

The thing that made Karl and Anna unusual among the regulars of the drive-in was that they actually spent a lot of time watching the movies. It wasn't that the attraction—the undeniable heat—wasn't there for them because it undeniably was.

In this life, when they got off on a good footing, they were able to treat the idea of sex in a more level-headed way.

For one, Karl felt slightly uncomfortable having sex with a teenager. For another, they both knew that if an accidental pregnancy arose, it would put the dreams they both had on hold.

So they waited. It wasn't always patiently, and it wasn't always easy, but at least one of them managed to keep a cool head, even if the other did not.

They watched a lot of movies and ate a lot of popcorn that summer. Every time Karl left the Falcon and went to the snack bar, he passed the mural that someone had painted on the white walls. It had obviously been done some years before as it showed mostly the stars of yesteryear—Bogie, Bacall, Glenn Ford, and Jimmy Stewart. It was probably twenty years old by then, but someone had obviously been retouching it from time to time, because the colors were still bright and vibrant.

Karl often paused to look at it, feeling drawn into its scene of old-time glamour. Often, he stopped and let his hand reach out and touch the painting of a small black and white dog in the corner of the mural. It didn't seem to fit with the subject matter, but at the same time, the whole thing would have been incomplete without it.

Karl had once again gotten a job delivering for Pizza! Pizza! Pizza! He remembered reading a Robert Heinlein book called *Job: A Comedy of Justice*. In that book, the protagonist said that the one job any person could get in a new town was as a dishwasher. Karl thought that as long as you had a car, you could add pizza delivery driver to that.

Having the job gave Karl enough money to spend many of his days that summer out on the municipal course with Eric.

It was easy for Eric to see that Karl was not looking forward to being separated from Anna, so he promised that he would keep her company while Karl was away.

In a bad teen movie, they would have developed a crush on each other and had a hard time finding a way to tell Karl about it. In their real life, they became friends and talked about how they missed Karl. Real life was better.

As the end of August arrived, Karl moved into the dorm in Corvallis and Anna started her senior year at Middle Falls High.

College at Oregon State wasn't such an adjustment for Karl this time. He remembered the layout and even some of the freshman-required classes that he had to take a second time.

Being a member of the football team was more strenuous than playing golf, though. When Karl showed up for his first practices, he found himself seventh on the depth chart at halfback. That meant that he wouldn't even make the traveling squad for away games.

High school football players who receive scholarships are almost always the best players on their high school team. So it was with Karl.

It's often a surprise when they get to college and find out that they are surrounded by an entire team of players who were also the best. It was the same for Karl.

He did what he normally did when faced with situations like that. He put his head down and worked. He soon realized that he was probably never going to be a Heisman Trophy candidate—that took almost otherworldly talent, but he wanted to give the best he had.

By the start of the season, he had worked his way up to fifth on the depth chart. His hustle and willingness to throw his body around with no consideration for his own safety landed him a spot on the kickoff teams.

That all meant that he got to be on the traveling squad for the first conference away game, which was at Pullman, Washington, against the Washington State University Cougars.

There was no love lost between the two teams, as both were looked down upon as the junior universities in their own states. The University of Washington Huskies and University of Oregon Ducks had dominated their respective states for years.

That put a chip on both the Beavers' and the Cougars' shoulders.

It was quite a trip from Middle Falls to Pullman, but Karl's parents made the drive with Anna along for the ride. At the last minute, all three Swansons decided they couldn't miss Karl's conference debut and made the trip as well.

Martin Stadium was awash in crimson and gray—the WSU Cougars' colors. There were only small splashes of black and orange rooting on the OSU Beavers.

Karl lined up as the outside gunner on the opening kickoff. He bounced on the balls of his feet and looked up at the nearly forty thousand screaming fans and tried to keep his adrenaline under control. He felt like he could jump out of the stadium.

The OSU kicker sailed the kickoff to the goal line and Karl finally found a place to burn his energy. He flew down the sideline, dodged a blocker and closed in on the ball carrier. He was half a second away from the tackle when he was blindsided by a block that knocked him off his feet.

He landed on his back and tried to pop up but found he couldn't catch his breath.

Teammates gathered around him, full of advice. "Get your bell rung?" "You got the wind knocked out of you." "Here, let me help you up."

Karl finally found his feet but had to go down on one knee. He looked to his right and couldn't believe what he saw. It was a slightly undersized player in a Cougar uniform. Number forty-five.

Karl drew as deep a breath as he could and said, "Freight Train?"

The kid smiled around his mouth guard and said, "That's right. Remember my name," then jogged off to the Cougar sidelines.

The OSU coaching staff gathered around Karl and eventually helped him off the field.

He sat on the visitor's bench while the medical staff looked him over.

"Son," the white-haired team doctor said, "we're going to send you for X-rays, but I think you've got a broken clavicle."

Karl was still having a hard time getting a full breath. He winced and said, "How long will that put me out? Can I come back next week?"

The doctor laughed a little. "That's going to put you out for the year." He stood up and turned to his assistant. "Get him over to the hospital and let's get some X-rays to be sure."

Karl stood up and followed the other doctor to the tunnel, trying not to limp or look too injured. He looked in the stands for Anna, his parents, or the Swansons, but couldn't find them.

He was embarrassed that the medical staff made him get in an ambulance in the tunnel to ride to the hospital. He tried to sit up inside, but they made him stretch out.

Lying on the gurney in the ambulance felt too much like his ride to the hospital in Middle Falls when he'd had his heart attack.

In this case, he was young, in great shape, and only had a broken bone, not a malfunctioning heart.

X-rays revealed that his collarbone was broken. The treatment for that was to put his arm in a sling until the bones had a chance to knit back together. That could typically take two to three months, which meant his football season was over almost before it began.

He was given a painkiller and put in a room until someone picked him up.

Karl assumed that would be someone from the team, but instead, his small rooting section poured into the room. Anna was at the front and ran toward him until she saw the sling and the expression on Karl's face. She stopped in time to offer him a kiss on the cheek.

Everyone had questions he couldn't answer, but Christina made the final decision. "They can have you back next week, maybe, but for now, we're taking you home."

Karl didn't argue, and the light in Anna's eyes when she heard he was coming home made everything feel better.

Chapter Forty-Eight

Karl never returned to OSU. He called Coach Andrews on Monday and they had an honest discussion. Karl knew that he had barely qualified for the scholarship in the first place and missing essentially the entire season would mean he wouldn't have it the next year.

Coach Andrews made sure that Karl knew he could still attend for the rest of the year and sounded apologetic about the turn of events.

Karl did what he could to relieve him of any guilt. The truth was, he had never dreamed of going to school to play football in this life. He had given it everything he had, but he was not devastated not to be going back.

Finley and Christina drove him back to Corvallis to get his belongings from the dorm and he moved back home.

Karl couldn't work for the next few months, but he spent a lot of time planning what he wanted to do next. He knew that Anna had dreams of being a veterinarian and tried to think of what he could do to help her with that goal. Over the winter, he encouraged her to apply at schools that offered Animal Science degrees and had Veterinary Schools. Ironically, in Washington and Oregon, that meant WSU and OSU.

Karl wasn't surprised that WSU offered the necessary degrees and training. When the OSU team was preparing to play the Cougars, they almost always called the school *Moo U*. Partially because Pullman was in the middle of nowhere and partially because they had a reputation for turning out vets and farmers.

In January, Anna sent off applications to both schools. Her grades were excellent, and she was ultimately accepted into both programs.

After she graduated from Middle Falls High, she, Karl, and Candace Masterson took a car trip to visit both schools.

Karl felt almost sure that she would choose OSU, if only to be closer to her mother.

Instead, she fell in love with the WSU campus. The rural feel of it reminded her of home, she said.

This didn't make Candace very happy.

Not long after they got home from their trip, Karl picked Anna up and made the short drive to Middle Falls Falls.

They stood against the fence and looked out at the water that gave the town its name.

"I've got something I want to talk to you about."

Anna leaned against him and said, "So what else is new? We talk every day."

"It's serious."

"Oh," Anna said, and her voice was suddenly small. "What? You're not breaking up with me, are you?"

"I said I was serious."

"That would be serious."

"I want us to get married."

That stopped any chatter.

Anna looked at him with tears forming in her eyes and said, "Aren't you supposed to ask me, instead of tell me?"

"I figured you'd be okay with it, but I want to talk to you about what I have in mind."

"I should have known you can't do anything the conventional way."

"I think we should move to Pullman. Right now. As soon as we can. I'll get a job and see if I can work my way up somewhere. You go to school, get your degree, then get your doctorate so you can be a vet."

"That's super expensive. And, eight years."

"And in eight years, you're going to be twenty-six, no matter whether you go to school or not. I figure it's better to be twenty-six and be *Dr.* Strong, instead of just Mrs. Strong. But of course, as you pointed out, that would depend on you saying yes."

Karl dropped to a knee and pulled out the small blue box. He popped it open to show a wedding set with a modest diamond.

Now, Anna's hands flew to her mouth. She tried to speak, but the words lodged in her throat. She nodded her head vigorously and finally blurted out, "Yes!"

Karl took her in his arms, and she melted into him. He always thought they fit together perfectly.

《 》

THE REST OF THIS LIFE was not tumultuous for Karl and Anna.

Karl found a job within a few days of moving to Pullman. He started out working the front counter at a Godfather's pizza. Within two years, he was the manager, which didn't make them rich, but kept them in pizza and covered their expenses while Anna went to school.

They had a goal that Anna would make it through all eight years of school without having to take out student loans, but they didn't achieve that. Their income was low enough, though, that they were able to get grants and low-interest loans.

Anna graduated with her doctorate in Veterinary Science in the spring of 1990. This time, it was her turn to have her own cheering section, as the Strongs, the Swansons, and of course her mother and uncle drove up from Middle Falls.

Anna went to work for the same veterinarian she had once worked for as a receptionist. She much preferred to be the doctor.

Candace still held out hope for grandchildren, but after ten years of marriage, had figured it wasn't going to happen. When she offered to pay for the fertilization clinic again, Karl made a different suggestion. He knew that they had been down that road before and it hadn't worked out.

Instead, he asked Candace if she would like to become partners. They made an offer to the primary vet, who was ready to retire, and Middle Falls Veterinary had new owners.

Some people might look at Karl's life and think that he did not accomplish very much. He lost his scholarship in the first year, he didn't have any important jobs, and he had to borrow money to buy the vet clinic.

Those people didn't know Karl Strong.

The most important things in this life were not things at all.

It was the people that Karl cared about.

The Swansons. Finley and Christina. Candace. And of course, Anna.

They had already had one good lifetime of marriage, but that one had started off shaky and had to improve. In this life, there was never any doubt for either of them.

They were partners, in every way, and in everything.

No life is perfect, of course. People get old, their bodies break down, they leave this Earth.

Karl knew it wasn't forever, though. He knew now that when he lost someone, he would see them again.

In this life, Finley was the first of his parents to die. He passed away—not at his station at the box factory—but in his backyard as he and Christina sat and watched the sunset. It was a quick death, and they'd had a good, long life together.

Christina did not crawl into a hole after Finley died in 2017. She stayed active and social until her own death in 2019.

Anna lost her mom that same year.

Those losses were horrible, but not heartbreaking. All lives must end. No one knew that better than Karl Strong.

The Swansons lived long lives, long enough to see the grandchildren that Eric gave them grow up to beat Don on the course a few times.

They passed away within a year of each other in 2023.

Karl and Anna's lives shrunk a little at each of those losses.

Karl had never outlived Anna, but in this life, he did. She was diagnosed with breast cancer in 2031 and passed away the next year, just after their fiftieth wedding anniversary.

That loss was hard on Karl. He had loved his life. He hoped and prayed at the end that he would be restarted in exactly the same point. So he could save his mother again, which saved his father. That he could have another fifty years of love with Anna and friendship with the Swansons.

Karl was alone but did not kill himself. He was incapable of that, no matter that he knew he would just open his eyes in another place and time.

Life was too precious to give it away.

Instead, he let himself slowly drift away. In the weeks and months after Anna's death, he seemed to belong more to an ethereal world in his own mind than in the real world.

Three months after Anna passed, Karl sat in his rocker in their lovely house. He was contemplating the people he loved.

And then, he was gone.

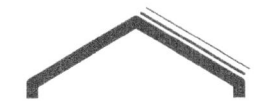

Final Interlude
Universal Life Center

Karl Strong opened his eyes.

He was not anywhere he expected to be. He was in a white room with white benches. It was empty except for two people who stood in front of him, looking down.

"Welcome, Karl," the woman said. She was dressed in a robe so shimmering white, Karl had a difficult time looking straight at it. "My name is Carrie. I know that waking up here can be disorienting. Take a moment to adjust if you'd like. This is my friend Charles."

Karl looked at the man. He wore a robe as well, though his seemed to consist of a pale blue so light as to appear to be the sky. He wore what was not quite a smile, but still was a welcoming expression.

"Where am I?"

Carrie nodded. This was always the first question. It had been the question she had asked.

"This is the Universal Life Center. Think of it as a way station between lives."

"But I've never been here before."

"Well, perhaps you haven't been here in your current memory, but that may change."

"What am I supposed to do here?"

"That's the lovely thing. You can do anything you want. You can explore the universe. There are many different incarnations of heaven that you can go to. You can rest and relax as much as you want."

"Unfortunately," Charles said, "these most recent lives were more challenging than they should have been. Feel free to rest and recharge before you make any decision."

"I already know," Karl said.

"Oh?" That surprised Carrie.

"I want to go back. To start at the same place I started my last life. Can I do that?"

"Definitely," Charles said and pulled an odd, milky-colored cylinder out of the folds of his robe.

Carrie laid a gentle hand on Charles' arm. Charles understood so much of the universe, but he did not always understand human nature.

"Why do you want to go back right now?"

"Everyone I cared about was in that life. Repeating that life over and over would be heaven to me."

"The people you loved," Carrie said.

"Yes. I was so lonely for so long, but this last life, I only knew love."

Carrie nodded and waved her hand.

In an instant, a small group of people were there.

Anna. Finley and Christina. Don and Ellonyia. Candace. Even Jake.

They all were smiling and nodding at him. They all looked so young, so beautiful.

"This is your true family, Karl. You need never be separated from them again unless you choose to do so."

"Eric?" Karl asked, missing his friend.

"He'll be here," Ellonyia said. "We've been waiting for the two of you."

Finley stepped forward. "We help each other learn what we need to learn. I had some things to work on and all of you did this to help me."

Christina and Anna put an arm around Finley and reached out toward Karl. "That's what families do for each other."

Warm tears spilled from Karl's eyes. He leaped up from the bench and was surrounded by the people he loved.

Coming Soon

The Ambitious Lives of Evan Sanderson[1]

Book 19 in The Middle Falls Time Travel Series[2]

---

1. https://www.amazon.com/dp/B0BZ57415K
2. https://www.amazon.com/dp/B0BZ57415K

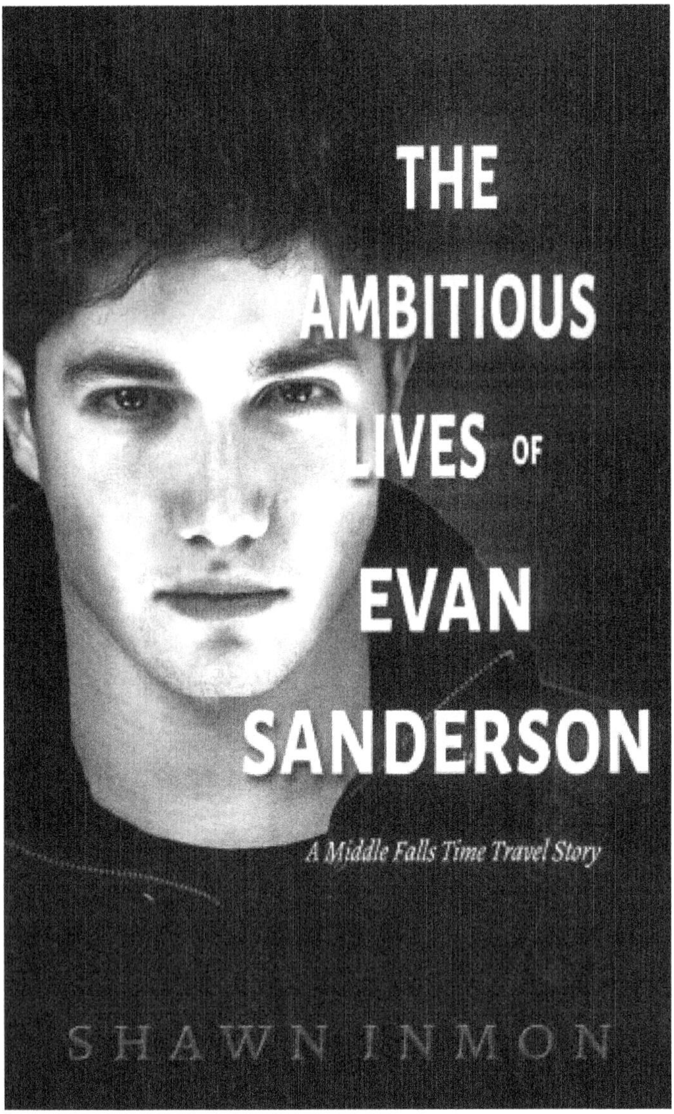
THE
AMBITIOUS
LIVES OF
EVAN
SANDERSON
A Middle Falls Time Travel Story
SHAWN INMON

Author's Note

I wrote this book like I was in a fever dream. Start to finish, it only took me twenty-two days to write. What is a little unusual about that is that I probably knew less about the eventual plot of this book than anything I've ever written.

Karl Strong made an appearance in an earlier Middle Falls book. He was the young golfer who Richard Bell thought he could soundly beat in *The Regretful Life of Richard Bell*. Richard learned a little lesson that Karl shouldn't be underestimated that day. I learned the same lesson in many ways as I wrote this book.

Based on his brief cameo in Richard's story, I only knew a few things about Karl. I knew that at least at some point in his lives, he was going to be an excellent golfer. That's not much to build a book around, but I was confident that Karl would reveal himself to me as I wrote.

That started as soon as I closed my eyes and waited for the opening scene to drop into my head. I didn't have to wait long. As soon as I looked, the scene of Karl walking into an empty kitchen was there. I hadn't known that his mother was dead until that moment.

From there, everything else fell into place.

This is the third time in the Middle Falls series that I've written about a father and son living together after the loss of a wife and mother. Ned Summers and his father were the first, and they responded well to the situation. They were both devastated by the loss, but soldiered on together as a team. The same was true of Bobby Parsale and his father in Effie Edenson's story.

This time around, I saw a different story, with Finley retreating from the world and leaving Karl to figure out things on his own.

This also brought Karl's greatest need to the fore. He was lonely.

In some ways, I found his reaction to loneliness to be not all that different from Finley's. Finley found escape in the bottle and the Do-Si-Do. Karl found it by building a wall around himself.

Others in his life saw it—at one point Lisa Hanson so much as tells him so—but Karl himself was mostly blind to it.

This is the second book where I've mentioned Al-Anon. It's an organization that I respect and, like Karl, I attended my fair share of meetings. However, all my experience was with one particular group, so the description of the meetings that I include in this book may not line up with yours. When it comes to things like this, I can only write what I know.

When I started writing the book, I thought it was possible that maybe Karl was good enough—with the advantage of repeated lives—to actually make it on the PGA tour. As I got to know the story, though, I thought it was more interesting that Karl missed being good enough by just that last little ounce of talent.

Besides, I don't know if becoming a successful, wealthy golfer would have helped him toward his ultimate goal of having a family.

Several of my advance readers asked if I was going to tell more of the story of Margenta, the Watcher who became Marge when she was reborn on Earth. The honest answer is, I don't know, but I'm leaning toward *no*. To effectively write a character, I have to be able to crawl inside their skin, and I admit to having a hard time doing that with Marge.

There were a number of moments that surprised me as I wrote this book, which I love. In the scene where Karl and Anna sit in their little house and he finally tells her that he knew she had set him up, I was sure that was the end for them. Not just in that life, but probably in all future lives for Karl.

And I was wrong. I don't know where it came from, but when Anna stripped herself emotionally bare and said, "Can you forgive me?" I saw that Karl could, and did. She was there, part of his true family, all along and I didn't know it until that moment.

These are the surprises I love to stumble on as I write.

Oh, I need to tell what song I listened to as I wrote this book. It was *A Pillow of Winds*, a semi-obscure but completely lovely song by Pink Floyd. Writing Karl's story actually made me a little anxious. So many parts of his story ran parallel to my own life. I chose this soft, sweet song to calm me while I wrote.

If you'd like to keep up with me, I have a number of ways to do so. The easiest way is to sign up for my New Release Newsletter, which I send out each time I publish a new book. If you sign up for that, I'll send you a free ebook copy of my book *Rock 'n Roll Heaven*. You can sign up for that here[1].

I also have a very active Facebook page here[2]. I post on there every day, as well as asking and answering questions from readers.

There's also a Facebook group dedicated to the Middle Falls series. There are almost a thousand dedicated fans who talk not just all things Middle Falls, but any and all time travel stories. It's a fun group, and I hang out in there nearly every day. You can find that group here[3].

Finally, I have a Patreon page. If you're not familiar with Patreon, it's a site where creators and fans hang out together. On my page, there are a number of different levels that include being able to read each new book as I write it, naming characters, and receiving signed

---

1. http://bit.ly/1cU1iS0
2. https://facebook.com/shawninmonwriter
3. https://www.facebook.com/groups/MFTTS

paperbacks of each new book I publish. If you'd like to check it out, you can find it https://www.patreon.com/shawninmon.

As always, I have a lot of people to thank. Writing a book is a lonely business, but publishing it is more of a group activity.

Linda Boulanger of TreasureLine Books created the cover for me. I love the simplicity of the Middle Falls covers, and Linda does a beautiful job on making each one stand alone.

Melissa Prideaux is my editor. She's patient, kind, and brutal when she needs to be. She is also fast, efficient, and every other quality I could want from my editor. I hope she's with me forever.

I have a wonderful group of proofreaders, including my old guard, which is Mark Sturgill, Kim K. O'Hara, and Marta Rubin. The three of them have been with me for many books over the years and know what I don't know. They each have their areas of specialty, and they help me look much smarter than I am.

My newer proofreaders are really stepping up and helping me create a clean product. Big thanks to Steven D. Smith, Bill Whetstone, Susie Janov, and Skye Fister.

Why so many proofreaders? Because I make a lot of mistakes!

More than anything, I owe a big thanks to you for reading. I only start the story by writing it down. You do the heavy lifting by finishing the story in your mind, and I thank you.

Shawn Inmon
Tumwater WA
March 2023